Friends and Other Enemies

She almost fell into the car. Of course he was teasing. He probably guessed she'd never been kissed. A man like that would see it written in her face. She wished she could say something clever and worldly, as Alix would have done. 'You must let me give you a lift,' she said, retreating behind formality.

'With you driving! No, thanks. I have a motorbike.'

'You could come back for tea . . . or a drink . . . or whatever?' She was torn between not wanting him to leave and fear of what her parents would say to his arrival.

'You live near here?'

She pointed up the drive. 'Dingwall Court.'

'Paul Harding's house?'

'Yes. He's my father.'

He gave a cynical laugh and stepped back. 'Trust Paul Harding to have a dumb bitch daughter who drives around the countryside as if she owns it.'

FRIENDS AND OTHER ENEMIES

Diana Stainforth

ROWAN

A ROWAN BOOK

Published by Arrow Books Limited
20 Vauxhall Bridge Road, London SW1V 2SA

An imprint of Random Century Group

London Melbourne Sydney Auckland Johannesburg
and agencies throughout the world

First published in Great Britain
by Century 1989
Rowan edition 1990
Reprinted 1990

Phototypeset by Input Typesetting Ltd, London
Printed and bound by Firmin-Didot (France),
Group Herissey. No d'impression : 27747.

ISBN 0 09 958650 9

ACKNOWLEDGEMENTS

I had fun researching this book. I flew an aeroplane. I rode a polo pony. I drove across the heartland of America. In London, I visited film sets. In East Anglia, I explored disused airfields. In New York, Chicago, Minneapolis and London I tramped the marble halls of busy, modern airports.

For their help in the field of aviation I should like to thank, alphabetically: Lloyd and Evelyn Alsworth of Fairmont, Minnesota; Bob Barker at Shipdham Airfield, Norfolk; Kathleen Barsh, air traffic controller; Jerry Ducker of the Civil Aviation Authority; Dick Kenny of Boeing; Captain Dayne Markham of Singapore Airlines; Peter Ormrod; Merlyn Suckling of Suckling Airways; and at Virgin Atlantic, Eric Holloway and Fiona Miller.

In the world of property, the law and business, several persons have asked to remain anonymous. I respect their wishes. My thanks to: Ann Barsh; Carolyn Draper of 3D Distribution Systems, Dallas; Peter Ferguson of Veuve Clicquot, Sponsors of the Business Woman of the Year Award; Henry Rose; Michael Stimpson.

For my instruction on the game of polo, I thank: Richard and Susie Graham-Wood, and Celia Medley.

For their advice on the film world, I am grateful to: Carol Allen; Julian Belfrage of Julian Belfrage Associates; Ceci Dempsey; Holly de Jong; Rory MacLean; Sara Randall of Saraband Associates; Robert and Julia Watts.

I thank for their various help: Issy Nicholas; Karen

McLaughlin and Mark Schubin; the officers of Wandsworth and Brixton prisons, and the Central Drugs Squad, New Scotland Yard.

Finally, I thank separately for their continual assistance throughout the writing of this book: Penny Baily for her research, insights and hospitality in East Anglia; Susan Denny for her ever-open addressbook of contacts; and Ray Giles for his insights into international business and the American Mid-West.

I'm not only grateful — but you all made it such fun!

Diana Stainforth

7 August 1989   London

1

Minnesota, October 1970

Of all the old pioneer legends her grandfather told, the one Ryder liked best concerned the White Squaw of Fox Lake. It was about a girl, the daughter of European settlers, who'd loved a man of whom her parents disapproved. On hearing of his death, she prepared to drown herself. But an Indian brave saved her — and took her to live with him on the island in the middle of Fox Lake.

Sitting at the end of the old wooden jetty, her feet dangling in the water, Ryder looked across at the island. It wasn't big, just a strip of land covered with trees and red autumnal prairie grass, but water added a magical dimension. She envied the girl who'd lived there a hundred years earlier. Closing her eyes she pictured herself slender and beautiful in a deerskin. She saw herself wake each morning to the gilded light on the lake and swim in the turquoise water where fallen leaves sailed in golden flotillas. She imagined herself loved by a man. Beautiful for him. Never stupid. Never unwanted. The aspect that didn't fit her picture was how the girl, loving one man, had switched so quickly to loving another.

She wished she knew the girl's name. No one seemed to. Not even her grandfather. She'd have liked to discover all about her. What she looked like. If she'd worn her high-necked, long sleeved Victorian dress till it dropped in rags or if she'd tossed it away and dressed like a Sioux, as Ryder would have done. What her parents had said. Did she care? Ryder was sure her own parents wouldn't give a damn so long as their friends didn't find out.

She screwed up her tawny hair into an unflattering elastic band and tried to picture herself slender and beautiful in a deerskin. She had a mobile face. When she smiled, it lit up and became pretty. Or if not exactly pretty, arresting. Her large pale eyes shone. Her nose wrinkled. Her mouth developed an unconsciously seductive lilt. But that was only when she smiled. Most of the time she was hunched in thought.

The smell of frying steak drifted from one of the small clapboard houses among the trees. The sounds of evening brought back tomorrow. She glanced at her watch, willing it to turn back. Six months. A day. Even an hour. By the time she'd pushed her bicycle free of the trees, the sun was sinking into South Dakota. It lit the sky behind the island whose glorious turning trees stood out against the fire of sunset. The light made the lake look blacker. Flatter. She thought of the white squaw, and wondered how often she'd watched that same sun go down.

It was heavy going on her cousin Frankie's bike. He was a small thirteen, she was nearly nineteen. The bald tyres skidded on the dirt road. Stones shot out from beneath the wheels. The black earth, baked hard from months of summer sun, threw up its stored heat into her face. She stopped to take off her sweater and wiped her grubby hands on her jeans.

The countryside between Fox Lake and Prairieville was flat. The road dead straight. Wherever she looked, mile after mile of ripening corn stretched away to the horizon, interrupted only by white or dark red farm buildings, each with a semi-circle of cottonwoods curled around the northwest side as protection against the Alaskan wind: settlers' trees, the homesteaders named them.

8

People from elsewhere called this part of Minnesota boring. They took Interstate 90, turned up their radios, and counted the miles to Sioux Falls. But Ryder loved it. She loved everything about it. Even the heat and the endless corn.

The first gas station on that side of Prairieville was 'Wise's Wayside'. It had been the best ice cream parlour in town but since his wife had run off with a trucker, Doug Wise had let the place fall apart. As Ryder drew near, she slowed. She should say goodbye. She'd visited everyone else. But she recalled his sweat-stained shirt and beery eyes, and she bent her head and pedalled faster.

The door flew open. 'Hey! Ryder! Weren't you going to say goodbye?'

She skidded to a guilty halt. 'I was coming tomorrow.'

'You leave for England tomorrow. Come on! I'll give you some ice cream.'

Ryder tried not to look at his oily hands as she took the cone from him.

'My daughter says you don't want to go,' he said.

'I don't. I hate England.' The ice cream tasted of gas. But that was her penance. She forced a smile. 'It's delicious. Thank you.'

He cleared a space among the empty cans of beer and leaned on the counter. 'I was stationed in Norfolk during the war. We used to fly Liberators out of Shipdham. *The Flying Eightballs*, they called us. I've always wanted to go back just to visit.' He rubbed his unshaven chin. 'I could have afforded it if they'd brought Interstate 90 through here.'

'Oh, I like Prairieville as it is.'

'I'd have been a rich man. Maybe my wife wouldn't have left me.'

'I'd best be going, Mr Wise.' She hurried out. 'Thanks for the ice cream.'

From the gas station she freewheeled across the car-park of the Norwegian Lutheran Church, the one her grandmother attended. Behind it was a public trash can. She dropped the remains of her oily ice cream into it.

Prairieville was a nice town. Everyone raised there said so. Well, everyone except for her mother and Mrs Wise. It consisted of a wide Main Street, a couple of cross streets, a redbrick Post Office, and half a dozen churches. It was a typical prairie town. People were born, raised, married and died in Prairieville. Some never ventured as far as Minneapolis, which always struck Ryder as strange considering the pioneer spirit of their ancestors.

Scot's Farm was five miles beyond the town. It was dusk by the time she reached their land. Her uncle was driving the combine harvester. She watched as the huge machine lumbered down the near section, its four headlights picking out the corn which trembled at its approach. The greedy reel turned relentlessly. The corn hissed as it was thrashed into submission. The dust and the chaff spewed out of the back. Before the combine reached Ryder, it swung in a large circle. Her uncle waved. In the cab beside him was Frankie, her thirteen-year-old cousin. They were both covered in a layer of dust.

The old farmhouse stood out against the dark blue sky. It was made of wood and painted white, with a pale grey roof. Built on the square to retain heat during the howling winters, it had a long porch to give shade in the fierce summers. Ryder loved Scot's Farm as much as her mother had hated it. She loved the heavy dark wood interior, solid like her grandfather, and the dainty lace tablecloths made by her grandmother. She loved the scruffiness. The ugly but comfortable armchairs, the overpatterned carpet chosen because it didn't show the dirt, the fact that no one shouted at her if she put her feet on the table when watching television.

The Sioux had roamed this land until treaties and the

10

homesteaders had pushed them west. That part of the history Ryder preferred to forget. She couldn't see a western without hoping the Indians would win. Yet, if they had won, there'd have been no Scot's Farm. Her great great grandfather, John Milne, had settled here and built the original log cabin. The second son of a tenant farmer from near Aberdeen, he'd married a sixteen-year-old parlourmaid from Edinburgh, and set sail for the New World. On the stairs in the farmhouse was a photograph of them taken on the day they left Scotland forever. It was in an oval gilded frame with a velvet backing. John Milne was fierce and bearded. His wife, Helen, looked pale and terrified. They both had that faded flat-eyed look of early photography.

Helen had died in childbirth. In Ryder's bedroom there was a trunk which had belonged to her. It contained bundles of letters from Helen's mother — and one, unfinished and unposted, which Helen had been writing at the time she died. The pages were yellowed and musted together, the semi-illiterate writing greatly faded, but the sentiment was clear. Helen hated the log cabin, the Indians, the howling prairie, and the isolation. She longed desperately for her mother whom she never saw again.

Halting beneath the cottonwoods, Ryder savoured the dying moments of her last evening. Above her the leaves rustled. When she was young she used to terrify herself by imagining that Indian braves were creeping through the trees. A breaking twig became a moccasined foot. The moan of the wind turned into a war cry. She smiled at the memory. It was dear to her, as everything was at Scot's Farm.

There was a shriek of laughter from the barn. Susan Wise ran out and leaped on to her bicycle. She was followed by Carl, boyfriend of Debbie, Ryder's cousin, who was waving what looked like a dead snake. He chased Susan down the drive. Debbie followed, laughing. Ryder watched her with envy. Everyone liked Debbie. She was a jolly blonde with big white teeth and an easy manner.

Susan rode away, calling, 'Say goodbye to Ryder for me!' From the cottonwoods Ryder watched her go. Remembering the ice cream melting in the public trash can, she felt remorse. She knew she should step forward and shout out, 'Goodbye, Susan!' But she kept quiet because Carl would terrorise her with the snake. He was a weasel and she couldn't think what Debbie saw in him. But suddenly she was angry. With Carl and with herself. Mainly with herself. Her ancestors had built this farm from nothing and she wasn't going to be frightened off it by a bully from a hardware store. She stepped from the trees.

Carl's pickup was parked beyond the barn but there was no sign of him or Debbie. Only Alfie, the rooster, pecked at the dust near the barn. He turned his curved beak and eyed her bare ankles. 'Go away!' She kicked the dirt in his direction. 'Git!' He squawked and moved off. But she felt robbed, as if David had gone down into the valley with his sling only to find Goliath had turned into a midget.

'I guess you've been saying goodbye to Fox Lake.' She hadn't noticed her grandfather who was sitting in the gloom of the porch. He was a craggy whitehaired old lion with frosted blue eyes and a slow measured speech, as though with each word he weighed out the corn kernels for the spring planting.

'It's not fair that I have to go back to England. I'm as much a Milne as Debbie and Frankie.' Ryder picked at the flaking paint on the porch rail.

'You know we'd keep you if we could.' He rocked his chair and sucked on his pipe. 'But you gave your word you'd go home without fuss at the end of six months, and Milnes don't break their word. They square up to life.'

12

'Mother doesn't want me, not now she has Leo. Nor does father. He never has.' She stepped in front of her grandfather. 'I'm old enough to live where I like. I'll get a job as a waitress and earn the money to come back here.'

He shook his head. 'You can't stay at Scot's Farm against your parents' wishes, whatever I think of your father. Damned slumlord!'

The kitchen door flew open and her grandmother appeared. Her gentle porcelain face was crossed by a frown and her pale silky hair had slipped from a neat bun. 'Dan,' she said quietly. 'He's our daughter's husband and she loves him.'

'Carrie needs her head examined. She should have married Doctor Jeff. He'd have made her the happiest woman in Prairieville.'

'She'd never have been happy here. You know that.'

'I ain't going to pretend I like her husband when every time I shake hands with him I count my fingers to make sure I get 'em all back!'

2

England

Ryder stood by the French windows in her mother's bedroom and looked down on the manicured garden of Dingwall Court which rolled away in velvety lawns to the river Thames. She stood with her back to her mother.

'Oh, don't sulk, Ryder! Please! I can't bear it.' Carrie Harding was resting. She lay against the satin pillows of her four-poster bed whilst Leo ran his model tractor up and down her quilted bedcover. She was dressed in a sensuous peach silk nightdress reminiscent of the nineteen thirties and about her shoulders was a peach satin jacket. The colour matched the bedcover and the draped curtains. It toned in with the deep pile carpet. It enhanced the honey blonde of her hair.

'I'm not sulking.' Ryder fingered the heavy taffeta curtains. 'I just can't understand why I was dragged home if I'm not going to live here.'

'Most girls long to share flats in London. Alix Bassingham is very social. You'll soon meet her friends.'

'But why should she want to live with me if she knows so many people!'

'The flat is for three. She already has one friend there and needs another girl.'

'The odd one out!'

'Oh, do stop pulling that silly face! Your father's gone to a lot of trouble to arrange it.' A frown crossed her

14

mother's delicate features but it changed to a smile when she looked down at Leo. Ryder had been born when she was twenty-one. There had followed five miscarriages and nearly seventeen years, until Leo.

Ryder watched her mother with admiration, and longing for that smile. Leo had been barely walking when she'd left. Now he was a demanding two-year-old, with blond curls and beautiful blue eyes like her mother and all the Milnes. Ryder had Harding eyes. Like her father. Like the pale grey sky in a watercolour. She longed for Milne eyes.

'Please take Leo to nanny,' said her mother. 'I have to dress. We're taking the Bassinghams to the opera.'

'On my first night home?'

'Darling, don't be difficult!'

Ryder picked up Leo. He began to scream.

She lay on her bed till it grew dark without bothering to turn on the light. This room had been hers only since Leo had arrived. Prior to that she'd slept in the east wing, in the room now used as Leo's nursery. She closed her eyes and imagined Leo taken ill when her parents were out. She saw herself touch his fevered brow and rush to call the doctor, pushing aside nanny's protests. She saw the doctors fight to save his life. But they'd fail. He'd die peacefully in her arms — whilst her parents were at the opera.

She pulled the duvet around herself and imagined their guilt. She heard the doctors say that without her intervention Leo would have died in agony. She pictured her mother's tears and felt her father's hand on her shoulder as he said, 'At least we still have you.'

A car crunched along the gravel drive. Ryder crept to the window. She saw Griffiths, the chauffeur, open the back door of the Rolls. Her father stepped out. He was a powerful man with short greying hair but a surprisingly boyish face. This youthful look came from his features,

15

which in many ways were similar to Ryder's. He too had a mobile face, with a generous mouth, and grey eyes set wide.

From her window she watched him bend to speak to Griffiths: he had to bend because the chauffeur, a sandy-haired Welshman, was a foot shorter. Then he raised his hand to smooth his hair, and glanced up sharply at the house, his eyes darting along the windows till they fixed on Ryder's room.

The curtain moved as she jumped back. She knew he would have seen it. He missed nothing. She hurried to her door, then hesitated because he disliked to be crowded the minute he walked in the house. Quickly she brushed her hair, straightened her clothes and tidied her room. His footsteps sounded on the stairs. She heard him call, 'Carrie! Darling! We have to leave in two minutes.' His footsteps reached the landing. She waited. But they moved off, fading towards the west wing. Ryder lay down on her bed and told herself she didn't care.

Carrie Harding seldom rose for breakfast but Ryder was up early. When Mrs Trumpet, the housekeeper, sounded the gong she tucked her jeans into her new cowboy boots and ran down stairs: her father detested unpunctuality. But on the bottom step she caught the toe of one boot in the spur of the other. She tripped and fell against the breakfast room door.

Paul Harding was alone. He was sitting at the head of the table, reading the *Financial Times*. He lowered his newspaper. 'Do you have to make such a noise?'

She flushed and slunk into her place.

He glanced at her feet. 'It's those stupid boots! They may suit Prairieville but they're ridiculous in Henley.'

'Grandpa Milne gave them to me — and I like them!'

He stared at her till she looked away, as an animal from a cobra. 'Don't you think it was rude not to greet me yesterday evening?' he said. 'You've been away for six months!'

'I waited in my room. You've always told me not to rush to you,' she shouted, though she didn't mean to.

'I see Scot's Farm's done nothing to improve your temper.'

She reached for a piece of toast, but her hand was shaking so much that she knocked a white freesia from its cut-glass vase.

Her father groaned.

She dropped the toast and pushed back her chair. 'If you don't want me here, why did you make me come back? Why didn't you let me stay at Scot's Farm where I'm wanted? Where I'm loved!'

'Because you're my daughter and I won't let you turn into a narrow-minded bigot like Dan Milne.'

She ran out of the house and across the dew-laden lawn, her feet leaving a dark trail in the wet grass. She went to the rose arbour near the river, her favourite place. Dingwall Court was a graceful Queen Anne. It had a well-proportioned central body with east and west wings, which gave it the luxury of length as well as width. Her father had bought it when she was a baby, when he'd begun to make serious money. Before that they'd lived in London. In a flat somewhere. That was all Ryder knew, because her mother preferred to forget that they hadn't always lived in style.

Her father had been a pilot in the RAF and, like so many, had come out of the war to face unemployment. With his friend and navigator, George Broughton, he'd pooled his resources and purchased the first of many bomb-damaged properties. That had been the start of Harding-Broughton Enterprises.

Ryder loved the seclusion of the arbour. Over the years her mother had trained glorious-scented rambling roses around its wooden frame. Only there weren't any roses today. Just dripping leaves and a few dead heads. She stared at the black serpent body of the Thames. A large branch was drifting downstream. She thought longingly of Fox Lake and the flotillas of golden leaves, and wondered how long it would take her to drown and if anyone would care.

Ryder had never heard of the Bassinghams before she returned from Prairieville, but that wasn't unusual. Her father was a master of instant friendships. She gleaned details from Mrs Trumpet, who'd learned them from Griffiths. The Bassinghams lived in a large, decaying house full of mouldering heirlooms which they sold off in order to pay the electricity and the telephone. Alix was their only child. She was said to be very beautiful. Her father was a retired major. He hunted twice a week on other people's horses: he couldn't afford his own. Her mother was the younger daughter of a baronet. They had no money and no idea how to earn it. They could hardly have been more different from Paul and Carrie Harding.

On a wet Sunday afternoon Griffiths drove Ryder to the station and put her on the train for London. She had three large suitcases, one containing sheets and blankets. She felt sick with apprehension.

'You'll be all right when you get there.' Griffiths lifted her cases on to the rack. 'It's the going that's the tough bit.'

'Don't tell my father I complained.'

'Course I won't.' He settled her in a corner of the carriage with tenderness, as though she were a child.

Ryder hadn't spoken to Alix yet. Mrs Bassingham had merely passed on the message that the girls would be at the flat in the afternoon to welcome her. Watching the Thames Valley speed past, she wished she'd asked Mrs Trumpet to make a chocolate cake for their tea.

At Paddington there was no porter in sight, so she dragged her cases one by one to the taxi rank. By the time the cab arrived, she was hot and tired. She hardly knew London and she'd never taken a taxi on her own.

18

Visits had been to Harrods or Harvey Nichols with her mother, driven by Griffiths. As they rattled through the backstreets of Notting Hill, past seedy hotels whose once-white façades were blackened by exhaust fumes, she alternated between studying her A-Z and watching the taxi's meter race upwards. She opened her purse and checked her money.

The houses improved. The streets grew cleaner. They crossed the park and cut down past the museums where a street vendor was doing a fast line selling umbrellas to tourists. Ryder clutched the strap as they whizzed round South Kensington station. In the central island disconsolate pigeons sat on a wet park bench.

The flat was just off the Old Brompton Road, in a street of elegant white houses, each with black wrought iron railings and steps up to a smart porch and a black front door. The taxi stopped. The driver lifted out her cases. She fumbled as she paid him.

By the front door was a row of bells. The top was marked: *A. Bassingham & I. Lydden.* There was no space for a third name.

She rang the bell.

The intercom crackled. 'Yes?'

'It's Ryder.'

'Who?'

'Ryder Harding.'

'Come up. Fifth floor. No lift.' There was a buzz and the front door clicked, but before Ryder had time to open it, the catch relocked itself. She pressed the bell again.

'Yes!' The voice sounded irritated.

'Sorry but the door's shut.'

'Prop it open with the doormat.'

Ryder dragged her luggage into the hall. It was stark but clean. The dark blue carpet was new. The walls were freshly painted. A large mirror occupied one. Beneath it was a table littered with circulars, postcards and bills in buff envelopes addressed to tenants. A door higher up opened and footsteps came down. She looked up, smiling, expecting it was Alix to help her. But it was a man. He stepped over her cases and walked out.

By the time Ryder reached the fifth floor she was gasping for air and her hair was sticking to her hot face. She staggered across the landing to a bright blue door and knocked harder than she meant to:

She heard voices inside, then a sharp giggle. The door opened slowly. In the threshold stood a delicately pretty girl in an ice pink mini dress and matching pink lace tights. She had a dainty upturned face, enhanced by a smattering of freckles and a mass of red Renaissance curls tumbling about her shoulders. 'I'm Imogen,' she said. 'Come in.'

'Thanks.' Ryder dragged her bags into the flat.

'And I'm Alix.' A willowy black-haired girl was lounging on the sofa beneath the window, her long legs were draped across one man, her body leaned on another. She had the most beautiful haughty face Ryder had ever seen. Her skin was white and luminous like a camellia. Her eyebrows were arched as though in a mixture of surprise and disdain. Her mouth was deep red. It matched her skintight satin hipster trousers and her little crocheted bolero underneath which she didn't wear a bra.

Ryder could barely look at her. She felt a mess. 'I'll fetch my other cases,' she mumbled.

'You didn't bring a lot of clothes, I hope,' Alix yawned. 'Surely mother told you? We only have two cupboards and they're jammed already.'

'Haven't I space in my room?'

'You're sleeping in here.' Alix waved a languid hand to indicate a bed pushed into an alcove on one side of the cluttered sitting room. 'We only have one bedroom and Immy and I are in it.'

Ryder marched downstairs, the door slamming behind

20

her. She didn't mean to slam it but it slipped. Not that she cared. Alix was a bitch and she, Ryder, wasn't going to stay here to be snubbed. Her father could say what he liked but she was taking the train straight back to Dingwall Court.

'Can I help?' asked a voice from the stairs. It was one of Alix's men. He took a case from her. 'Imogen sent me down. She thought you'd need a hand.'

Alix and Imogen were standing just inside the flat. They looked like a pair of Easter bunnies in their short rabbit fur coats, identical except in colour. Alix's was red. Imogen's was white.

'We've cleared you a space in one of the cupboards,' said Imogen. 'And a drawer in each chest.'

'Thank you,' Ryder answered sullenly, still planning her departure.

'Make yourself at home.'

'Yes.' She wasn't going to be won over so easily.

'We're off now.' Alix picked up her keys. 'Come on, boys! This town needs painting red.'

'Have a nice time,' said Ryder. But she said it only to Imogen.

Silence fell on the flat. Ryder listened to their footsteps. The front door slammed. Laughter echoed up from the street. She crept to the window. Alix was doing the can-can in the middle of the road. A red sportscar drove up. They all piled in. It roared away. Thank God she hadn't brought the chocolate cake. How they would have laughed! Especially Alix.

She explored the flat. Like the hall, it was stark and freshly painted. White walls and a beige cord carpet. But because they were in an attic and the roof sloped to the windows, the place had character where otherwise it would have had none.

The furniture was minimal. In the sitting room there was a pine table with six chairs, an armchair near the fireplace, the dark blue sofa, and the bed — her bed.

The bathroom was minute. The galley kitchen was functional. In the bedroom were two single beds, two cupboards and two chests. The bottom drawer of each had been cleared. The former contents were piled high on one of the beds. On the other bed was a brochure connected with a modelling course at Lucie Clayton's and a series of black and white photographs, all of Alix, all with her body twisted into haughty, angular poses. Ryder stared at them.

By the time she'd unpacked and made up her bed, she was hungry. Picking up her purse, she opened the front door. Then stopped. She had no key. She returned to the kitchen. In the fridge was a pint of milk, half a loaf of bread and some butter. She pictured the well-stocked fridge at Scot's Farm as she poured herself a glass of milk and made a marmalade sandwich. But she was still hungry. She made herself two more sandwiches and drank the rest of the milk, and went to bed.

It was early when Ryder woke with someone shaking her. 'Did you drink *all* our milk?' demanded Alix.

'And eat all our bread,' said Imogen.

'I'm sorry. I was hungry and you didn't leave me a key. I couldn't go out.'

'We did. It's on the table. You've eaten our breakfast!' Imogen threw on her white bunny coat. 'I can't even have a piece of toast and I'm in drama classes all morning. I'll faint with hunger.'

They marched out.

The Sydney Street Secretarial College, or Syd's as it was known, occupied a large house just off Sydney Street. It was an old fashioned establishment permeated by the lingering smell of a taxidermist's. When Ryder arrived she found a queue of girls waiting outside the secretary's office. They all wore knee length pleated skirts in sober colours and had their hair brushed back off their faces.

22

She was in her jeans and boots. They stared at her. She looked away.

A side door opened and a desiccated old maid appeared with a list in one hand. 'Ryder Harding?'

'Yes.'

'Oh, dear.' The fossil adjusted her glasses. 'Didn't you read our brochure? No trousers or boots allowed. What would a prospective employer say!' She turned to the queue of girls who tittered in their twinsets.

'I'm real sorry. I didn't know.'

'Oh, you're an American. Of course you wear jeans all the time. But I'm sure you have one skirt for tomorrow. Come along!'

Ryder followed her down into the basement, to a classroom where rows of girls thumped on manual typewriters whilst a teacher called, 'Q . . . W . . . E . . . R . . . T.' It had been a masterstroke to imitate Debbie's accent.

At four o'clock the girls poured out of Syd's and headed for the King's Road. Ryder took a taxi to Harrods. In the food hall she bought two carrier bags full of groceries. Fresh bread, butter, milk, biscuits, and a pound of smoked salmon. She pictured Alix and Imogen's faces when they opened the fridge. She heard herself say, 'I'm sorry,' and Imogen reply, 'It's our fault too.'

The flat was deserted but Ryder knew Alix had been back because her cigarette ends floated in a saucer in the kitchen. She threw open the windows to rid the place of its left-over-morning stuffiness and wiped the dead flies off the sill, plumped up the cushions on the sofa, tidied the kitchen, and arranged her photos of Prairieville beside her bed. Then she buttered the fresh brown bread and made a large plateful of smoked salmon sandwiches.

The phone rang. She hurried to it.

'Is Alix there?'

'No.'

'Tell her Adam called.'

Ryder wrote '*Adam. Monday. 6.30 p.m.*'

Then she noticed a list pinned above the phone:

> *If Gavin phones tell him I've moved away.*
> *If Adam phones tell him I'm free on Saturday.*
> *If Dominic phones tell him I'm at Sybilla's.*

She ate a sandwich and rearranged the plate so it didn't show, then she opened her shorthand book and practised the symbols, copying a few downward strokes, trying unsuccessfully to recall what they stood for without reference to the textbook.

The phone rang again.

'Alix?' said a male voice.

'She's not back yet.'

'It's Hugo. She was meant to meet me. Tell her I've waited an hour and I'm furious.'

Nine o'clock. Ryder stood by the window listening. High-heeled shoes clattered down the street — but went on to another destination. A taxi drew up. Laughter. But the merriment went next door. Hungry, she started on the remaining sandwiches. At midnight she went to bed.

She woke to hear footsteps creep past her bed and the light switch on in the kitchen. She heard giggles and Alix say, 'I wish my father was rich,' and Imogen reply, 'She's very gauche.' More giggles, and the sound of the fridge door opening. 'Look at all this food!' exclaimed Imogen. 'How delicious!' There was a rustle of paper and the top of the rubbish bin clicked. Then Alix's voice rang out. 'See this wrapper. She's eaten a whole pound of smoked salmon. What a pig! No wonder she's fat!'

Ryder bit her lower lip and stared at the light patterns on the ceiling, and willed them to become the sun dappled waters of Fox Lake.

3

That weekend Ryder went to Dingwall Court because she didn't want to sit in the flat on her own. She mooched around the house. Her mother was having a massage. Leo was with nanny. In the late afternoon she stood in the hall, her nose pressed against the big pane of the sash window as she watched the rain bounce off the terrace. Suddenly she turned.

Her father was sitting at his desk watching her through the open door of his study. 'What is Alix Bassingham like?' he asked.

'She's a bitch.'

He laughed. 'Just like her mother.'

'If you think that, why do you want me to live with her?'

'Because people like the Bassinghams are useful.'

'I don't want to use people. I want to like them. And them to like me.'

'Real friends are a rarity.' Her father glanced at the photograph on his desk. It showed two men in flying jackets standing in front of a Lancaster bomber. One was himself, the other was dark and debonair. Underneath was written:

> *To Paul,*
> *the best friend a man could have,*
> *George Broughton*
> *Bailing, November 1944*

Ryder returned to London. The flat was deserted. Standing in the kitchen, looking out over the rooftops, she listened to laughter from the flats below. She'd never felt so alone.

On Monday she typed at Syd's. Walking home she passed an art gallery. An exhibition was in progress. She stared at the psychedelic swirls and wondered if she had some hidden talent, and if so what it was and why it couldn't instantly reveal itself to save her from shorthand and typing and Alix. In the dark isolation of the flat, she closed her eyes and pictured the warm welcoming kitchen at Scot's Farm. She saw her grandfather sucking his pipe and her grandmother kneading the dough. The image was so vivid she could smell the fresh baked bread. She put on her coat to buy a loaf but at the door she hesitated. Alix was right. She did need to lost weight. She returned to the kitchen and a cold chicken leg, without the skin, and a salad with no dressing. That night she couldn't sleep for hunger.

At the weekend Ryder brought her old bicycle up from the country. Each day she cycled to college. Each evening she forced down another salad. By December she'd lost half a stone. Not that anyone noticed. If Alix came home before midnight it was to rush through the flat in a whirl of clothes, scent and telephone calls, and dash out again. Imogen was seldom back before eleven. Sometimes the only sign Ryder had that she didn't live alone was the dirty plates in the sink and the sound of feet creeping past her bed late at night – and the telephone which always rang for Alix.

One evening she found a newspaper on her bed with a big asterisk next to:

HARDING EVICTS CRIPPLE
Outraged tenants of Harding-Broughton Enterprises are picketing the offices of their landlord, millionaire Paul Harding, in protest over the eviction of 81-year-old Mrs

Mavis Tibbs from the flat which has been her home since 1924. Mrs Tibbs admits she has not paid rent for two years.

Ryder screwed it up and threw it at Alix's bed.

The other girls at Syd's regarded Ryder as odd, initially because of her clothes and American accent, latterly because they felt deceived when they realised she was English. Only Hetty Radipole was friendly. But then Hetty talked to everyone. Blonde and jolly, with a voice like the captain of a hockey team, she reminded Ryder of Debbie.

'Wait for me!' she shouted at Ryder, pedalling up beside her. 'I'm off to dinner with my aunt. She lives in the Boltons.'

They weaved in and out of the rush-hour traffic. It was a cold, dank evening, the cars were bumper to bumper, and the smell of exhaust hung heavy in the air but none of that affected Hetty who kept up a steady stream of loud chatter. 'What's your flat like?' she asked.

'I'm looking for somewhere else.'

'Why?'

'Alix is a viper and Imogen isn't much better.'

'Not Alix Bassingham and Imogen Lydden? I was at school with them. But Immy's sweet. Nervy, but so talented. And Alix is a brick when she isn't looking in the mirror. No one could have been kinder when my parents divorced.'

'Alix is the most unpleasant person I've ever met,' said Ryder, and she cycled away.

After that she avoided Hetty.

Imogen came home early. She looked agitated.

'Is anything wrong?' asked Ryder, who was watching a comedy show on the television.

'Nothing that's not my own fault. Want a cup of tea?'

'Oh, yes. Thanks.' Ryder turned off the set and moved

27

her coat from the armchair. 'It must be fun to be at acting school,' she said eagerly.

'It's hard work but the people are nice.' Imogen leaned against the kitchen door. 'I've always wanted to be an actress. Just as Alix has always wanted to be a model. We were at school together.'

'Bad luck!'

'Alix is my friend.' Imogen handed her a mug of tea. 'Goodnight.'

Ryder turned on the television. But the show didn't seem so funny now.

At Christmas Syd's closed for a month. Ryder spent the time at Dingwall Court. Anything was preferable to the flat. In one of her father's sudden twists of generosity, he allocated Griffiths to teach her to drive. She enjoyed it. She hadn't expected to, but she did. And she had aptitude, so the little Welsh chauffeur told her.

On a dull Monday morning she took her test and passed. That afternoon she drove alone for the first time. Taking the straight road out of Henley along the bottom of the valley, she followed it through the woods to Nettlebed. From there she jinked north, across the Chilterns, further than she'd planned. But the exhilaration swept her along. She was in control.

Driving changed Ryder's life. It gave her confidence. She'd passed her test first time, where many failed. Not even her father's 'I should think so too' could dampen her spirits. She returned to London in a mood of determination. Roaring along the motorway she thought of old John Milne driving his bullock cart across the prairie at all of twenty miles a day. No, she wasn't a Helen. She'd find another flat, look for an evening job, save money, and when she'd finished at Syd's, she'd return to Prairieville. If her grandparents wouldn't let her live at Scot's Farm, she'd find a place in town.

Imogen was sitting at the pine table, sharing a bottle of wine with a man who looked so like her that they had

28

to be related. He had the same auburn attractiveness. The quick smile. Only his complexion differed. He was lightly tanned between the freckles whereas she was white translucent.

'This is my brother, Adam,' she said. 'Would you like a glass of wine with us?'

'No, thanks.' It was too late for them to start being friendly. She opened the back of the newspaper and began to circle possible flats.

'You don't mind if Adam leaves his skiing gear here for a week or two, do you?' Imogen waved at a pile of bags. 'He's given up his flat and mother won't let him keep it at home.'

Adam's face lit with glee like a small boy. 'She's having a maternal fit because I've chucked in boring accountancy and I'm off to work in a ski resort.'

Ryder lowered her paper. 'How exciting!'

'Want to come with me.'

'I don't think Alix would be pleased!'

'Adam's only joking, Ryder.' Imogen topped up his glass.

'How do you know, sis?' He looked across at Ryder. 'Well?'

She met his glance and a flicker seemed to pass between them. Blushing, she hurried to the bedroom to finish her unpacking. Behind her she heard Imogen say, 'Don't tease Ryder. She's very unsophisticated. She might think you mean it.'

Adam flitted in and out of the flat, usually with Alix. They were all over each other, kissing in the kitchen, sprawled on the sofa, sharing a bath. Ryder ignored them. Or she tried to. But Adam made a point of talking to her. 'What are you doing?' He sauntered out of the bedroom where Alix was changing and seized Ryder's newspaper. 'What are all these circles?'

She grabbed it back. 'Mind your own business!'

'Moving out?' he whispered.

She shrugged.

'It's all right. I won't tell anyone.'

One evening when Ryder had planned to telephone several flats advertised, she arrived home to find Alix lying on the floor with a mud pack on her face and Imogen attempting to bleach her freckles with a lemon. She waited for them to go out. But they showed no sign. She contemplated going out herself to use a public phone. Finally, she decided that she didn't care what they thought and she dialled the first number. 'I'm ringing about the vacancy,' she said loudly. 'Yes, I'd like to come and see it now.'

Alix sat up. 'What are you doing, Ryder?'

'Looking for somewhere else to live.' She picked up her coat. 'I'm not going to share with people who don't want me.'

'But you can't go,' said Alix.

'Try to stop me!' Ryder walked out of the flat and slammed the door.

When she returned they were waiting, sitting side by side on the sofa. With her head held high, she said, 'I'm moving out at the end of the month.'

'We'll go,' said Alix.

'Don't be silly! It's your flat.'

'No, it isn't. The lease is in your father's name. He pays the rent. All of our rents. He agreed this with my parents.' Alix lit a cigarette. 'He purchased our friendship for you.'

'Then I'm certainly leaving.' Ryder's voice shook. 'I may not make friends easily but I don't need them bought for me!'

There was an uneasy truce next morning. No one spoke. When Ryder arrived home from college she found a taxi at the door. For a moment she thought they were moving out already. She felt both relief and failure. Then Adam appeared, struggling down the stairs with two pairs of skis and a mountain of bags.

'Could you hold the door,' he said. 'The damned thing keeps slamming.'

She waited as he ferried his baggage to the taxi, then helped him fit in his skis. They protruded from one window. 'Why can't I meet a nice girl like you?' He gave her his most charming boyish grin. 'Alix wouldn't have lifted a finger in case she broke a nail.' He climbed into the taxi. 'If she asks, say I tried to phone her but Lucie Clayton's said she hasn't been in. Only if she asks, mind you!' The taxi pulled away. He waved and shouted, 'See you when I come back!'

Ryder turned into the house. Without Adam, it seemed drabber.

The phone was ringing as she entered the flat.

'Can I speak to Immy?' said a deep male voice, gentle in spite of the rough accent.

'Oh, umm . . . Imogen? Oh, she's not here at the moment.'

'You must be Ryder. Tell her that Tony rang, will you, luv?'

Imogen went pink when she heard the message. 'Adam wasn't here, was he?' she asked quickly.

'No.' Ryder turned on the radio to avoid discussing the flat. Suddenly she realised Imogen was quietly crying in the kitchen. She tried to ignore her, afraid of a further snub, but the sound of unhappiness twisted inside her. 'Can I help?' she asked tentatively.

Imogen lifted her tearstained face. 'You'll be shocked.'

'Try me.'

'I've met this man and he's not . . . he's a lot older than me. Thirty years.' Imogen took the chair opposite Ryder. 'That's not the only problem. You see, he's not . . . our type. He's very ordinary. He lives in a council house in Streatham. Of course I don't care. Money means nothing to me.'

'My relatives in Prairieville are ordinary working people.'

31

'But my mother'd have a fit. She's always saying I must marry well. And Alix would be appalled. All my friends would be.'

'My mother married against her parents' wishes.'

'There's another problem.' Imogen's face crumbled. 'He's married, with three children.'

Ryder didn't know what to say. Eventually she asked, 'How did you meet him?'

'He's a taxi driver. I took a taxi to RADA on my first morning and it was his. I was nervous, and he was so kind to me. Since then he's been giving me a lift most mornings. And sometimes in the evenings.'

'Oh, so he's just a . . . friend?'

'I'm in love with him.' Imogen brushed the tears from her eyes. 'Don't tell anyone. Please! Not Alix. Not Adam. Not anyone.'

Ryder warmed. 'Of course I won't.'

Imogen smiled tentatively. 'Thanks for listening. I'm sorry we haven't been very nice to you. If it hadn't been for your father we'd never have afforded this nice flat,' Imogen went on. 'Alix's parents live on hand-outs and my mother only has a widow's pension.'

'So now you want me for my money!'

'I didn't mean that. I was just trying to explain that Alix and I had planned to share a flat on our own and we were angry at having a stranger forced on us.'

'Well it won't be for much longer.' Ryder stood up. 'So don't insult me by pretending you like me.'

When Ryder told her father she was moving, to her surprise he laughed and said it served the Bassinghams right. She returned to London early to start packing up. In the sitting room she found Imogen, Alix and an elegant, angular woman with a face of ravaged beauty who was dressed in black and smoked foul-smelling Turkish cigarettes through an ebony holder. The whole flat stank.

'So you're Paul Harding's daughter.' She blew a

smoke ring. 'And like father like daughter, you think nothing of evicting others into the street.'

'I'm not evicting anyone.'

'But Alix and Immy will have to leave if you go.'

'Keep out of it, mother!' said Alix.

'Why should I? We were promised a year's rent-free accommodation for you. We were wined and dined and taken to the opera. We were whisked to Villa Harding in Marbella. We went to Ascot and Wimbledon and Henley, where we introduced that profiteer to our friends. Now guess who's going to Barbados? Not Dudley and Sonia Bassingham!'

'If you allow my father to buy you, you shouldn't be surprised if he treats you like a slave,' said Ryder icily.

'Buy me! We were doing him a favour.'

'Shut up, mother!' Alix pulled her to her feet. 'Leave Ryder alone! Go home and don't drink any more.'

'We've been dropped like hot potatoes.' Sonia Bassingham teetered towards the door on very thin legs. 'But that's par for the course with Paul Harding, isn't it?' She gave a brittle laugh. 'I should know, darlings. He was my lover when he met that prissy Carrie Milne from Hicksville taking her silly photographs outside Buckingham Palace – and dropped me to marry her!'

The door closed behind her. Ryder and Alix stared at each other.

'Did you know?' asked Alix.

Ryder shook her head. She felt sick.

'Nor did I. When did your parents meet?'

'1950 – I think.'

'Mine married at the end of the war.' Alix spoke through gritted teeth. 'Not that I care, of course.' She wiped her cheek with the back of her hand. 'But poor Daddy! I bet he has no idea. He's so stupid. He puts up with the most unbelievable crap because he adores her.' She opened the windows. 'God, I loathe the smell of her cigarettes. Let's get out of here.'

Ryder tried not to think of her father and the ravaged Mrs Bassingham. Behind her Imogen and Alix put on their coats.

'Come on, Ryder,' said Alix. 'This affects us both.'

They wandered through empty streets on that freezing Sunday afternoon. The paving stones glistened. Old ladies hurried small dogs into the gutter. Lights came on in cosy flats where people drew curtains on the approaching night. Ryder glanced at Alix, hunched in her red bunny coat, beautiful even with smudges of mascara on her cheeks.

'I wish she hadn't told us.' Alix stopped suddenly in the middle of the pavement.

'So do I,' said Ryder. They turned for home. They didn't talk about it any more. There was nothing else to say.

When they reached the house, they found two men talking outside the second-floor flat. One stood in the doorway. He was fair and chubby. The other leaned against the banisters. He was wiry and laughing-eyed. Alix brightened. Quickly she checked her face in the landing window and rubbed the streaks of mascara from her cheeks with the back of her hand.

'Hello, girls!' said the fair one. 'We're the new tenants. I'm Jonathan and this is my flatmate, Miles. How about a neighbourly drink?'

'Just what I need.' Alix stepped forward.

As Ryder crept on up the stairs she heard Miles say, 'What about the other girl?' and Alix reply, 'Oh, Ryder's very shy.'

The flat seemed even more deserted. From downstairs she could hear laughter. She closed the windows and turned on the television. But the laughter insinuated itself into the attic. She went to bed.

A few minutes later Imogen returned.

'You should have stayed.' She plonked herself down on the end of Ryder's bed.

'They only wanted you and Alix.'

'Silly! They've invited us to a party on Saturday and if you'd been there, they'd have asked you too. That's how you get to know people.'

'You sound like my mother. Where's Alix?'

'Downstairs . . . with Jonathan.' Imogen twisted the bedspread through her small fingers. 'I don't think she'll be back tonight.'

'I thought she was Adam's girlfriend.'

'So did I.' Imogen looked miserable. 'So does he.'

They didn't talk any more about Ryder moving out. There was an unspoken agreement that she'd give it a few more weeks and see what happened. Life in the flat didn't alter visibly, but if Alix or Imogen were home they were friendly. Ryder still spent many lonely evenings. She went back on her diet, or tried to. She started to learn Russian at evening classes but didn't get much beyond *niet*. The highlight of her week was when she and Hetty went to the ABC Cinema in Fulham and walked back via a plate of spaghetti in the Bistro Vino.

'You remember I told you about Tony,' said Imogen one day. 'I'd like you to meet him. How about tomorrow?'

That night Ryder lay in bed watching the light patterns on the ceiling and wondering if she would ever have someone to love.

She met Tony and Imogen in a pub in Bloomsbury. He wasn't at all what she'd expected. She'd pictured him ginger and whippety like Griffiths, whereas he was a tower of a man with a handsome face and iron grey hair. He stood as Ryder joined him. 'So you come from America,' he said. 'I was in the merchant navy. I've been to every port in the world.' He took Imogen's dainty white fingers in his large hands and played with them as he talked of faraway places in the same measured tones Ryder's grandfather used.

When he drove them home, Imogen said, 'Don't you want to come in?'

'No.' He took her in his arms as Ryder busied herself with opening the front door.

'Did you like him?' Imogen asked her on the stairs.

'Yes. I like him a lot.'

'He makes me feel safe. I've never felt so safe since my father died.' Imogen opened the flat door and turned on the light.

There was a scuffle and Alix exclaimed, 'Oh, hell!' She was sprawled across Ryder's bed, and her very white legs were separated by a man who was fully clothed except for his trousers hanging about his knees. For a split second Imogen and Ryder stared, then they rushed into the bedroom and closed the door.

'Thank goodness Adam isn't here,' said Imogen, looking very white.

'One thing's for sure.' Ryder lay down on Alix's bed. 'I'm sleeping in here from now on.'

They heard the flat door shut. Alix came into the bedroom. 'Don't say anything!' She held up her hands. 'I know I shouldn't have used your bed, Ryder, but I didn't expect you two home so early.'

'It's your bed now.'

'But I don't want to sleep in the sitting room.'

'Ryder's right. You come home latest – if at all.' Imogen burst into tears. 'Oh, Alix, how could you! Just think, if Adam knew.'

'Damn Adam!'

'Don't say that about my brother!'

'I suppose you think I'm immoral.' She looked at Ryder.

'Not if you love him.'

'Love! Do you think he's the first? Oh, don't cry, Imogen! I know you two are as pure as the driven snow but I want to have fun. Men won't take a girl out unless they get something in return. I learned that from dear

Adam.' Alix marched into the bathroom and began to scrub the make up from her face with frantic movements. 'But I soon discovered that he had other girls. All he wanted was a good fuck. The same goes for Jonathan. For all of them.'

'But it's so beastly and unromantic,' sobbed Imogen.

'What do you want? Violins and wedding bells? Sex isn't like that. It's disgusting and it hurts – to begin with. But not any more. Now, it's just boring. They slobber all over you and mess up your hair, and if you don't get your dress off in time they ruin that too.'

'Then say no,' said Ryder.

'And sit at home every evening like you? Not bloody likely! Not when I can go to all the most fashionable nightclubs and never have to pay for myself.'

'I'd rather pay.'

'And how often do you get invited to a nightclub?' sneered Alix. 'How often have you been to Tramp or Sybilla's?'

'Never.'

'At least *I'm* not a social failure! Why, I bet no one's even asked you out for a pizza!'

She slammed out of the room. Imogen burst into tears. Ryder turned her face to the wall.

A moment later the door flew open. 'Just in case you want to talk about me behind my back, I won't be here,' Alix shouted. 'I'm going over to Adam.'

'You can't,' Ryder shouted back. 'He left days ago.'

The bedroom door slammed. Then the front door. Then the street door.

4

Ryder was washing up when Alix returned five days later looking white and hollow-cheeked. 'Hello,' she said.

'Hello,' said Ryder, stiffly.

'Immy out?'

'Yes.'

'Look, I'm . . . er . . . sorry I said you were a social failure.'

'You're right.' Ryder threw the dish cloth into the bowl. 'I am.'

'I'm no better.' Alix lit a cigarette. 'I slept with Adam but he didn't even say goodbye to me.'

'He tried to. I should have told you but I was mad.'

'I don't blame you. Oh, bugger life! Let's have some coffee.'

Imogen returned as they were sitting down in front of the fire. She looked from one to the other and smiled. 'Don't start the gossip till I'm there.' She grabbed a glass of milk and joined them. 'How did the fashion show go, Alix?'

'I failed.' Alix stared up at the ceiling as tears welled in her dark eyes. 'They won't take me on their books. Oh, I know I missed the odd day but . . . oh, hell!' She lit another cigarette although the first was only half smoked.

'I don't believe it.' Imogen was stricken with unreasonable fear. 'You're beautiful. Everyone says so.'

'I'm also unreliable and arrogant, according to Lucie Clayton's.'

Imogen started to cry. 'Why does everything go wrong?'

'Oh, stop wailing!' Alix snapped. 'I can't bear it.'

'There must be other agencies.' Ryder reached for the business directory.

Alix gave her a genuine smile. 'I've never failed before. It's a new experience.'

Ryder ran her finger down the index. 'As my grandfather says, life's a bitch and you have to square up to her.'

It took Alix some time to find another agency but finally one took her on their books. They weren't very prestigious: they specialised in underwear catalogues. 'I have to have a photo composite,' she told Ryder. 'I need to look more approachable. Do you think your father would let me owe him on the phone bill till next month so I can pay the photographer?'

'Don't ask him! Please!'

'Okay! I shouldn't have mentioned it. I'm already living rent free.'

When Alix showed Ryder the composite she had to force herself to say, 'It's wonderful.' But she was appalled. Elegant aristocratic Alix had been turned into an upmarket tart.

At Easter, Ryder told her father she was staying in the flat. They were having breakfast: that was the only time she ever saw him. 'Trust you to only befriend Alix Bassingham when we tired of the parents,' he mocked.

'Strange, isn't it!' She met his gaze.

He raised an eyebrow, challenging her to elaborate. She knew then that what Mrs Bassingham had said was true. Embarrassed, she turned to her mother. 'I'll ask Syds to find me a temporary job till I go to Prairieville.'

'You're not going,' her father cut in.

'You can't stop me!' Ryder pushed back her chair. 'Not now. I can earn my own money.'

'That fool Debbie is pregnant.'

'You're making it up.'

'Don't shout, Ryder!' A frown touched her mother's face. 'Your grandmother phoned last night. She said it would be better if you didn't go. Prairieville's a small town and a disgrace like this hits a family hard.'

'What's going to happen to Debbie?'

'She's marrying the father, someone called Carl.'

'But she's split up with him! She said so in her last letter.'

'The baby has to have a proper father.'

'Oh, things *have* to be proper in Prairieville!' Her father gave a derisive snort. He picked up one of the newspapers and scanned the headlines. 'Who is this idiot writing that property's about to crash? Prices are up 30 per cent on last year. I hate pessimists! Cancel this paper. I don't want this rubbish in my house.'

Ryder went out into the garden, where the river mist was slowly giving way to sunshine. She walked over to the rose arbour. A few minutes later the French windows opened and her mother stepped out. She crossed the grass, a woman who walked daintily even when traversing a soft lawn in high heels. 'Ryder, you must learn not to argue,' she said. 'Men don't like it.'

'You mean father doesn't like it.'

'Oh, why are you so difficult!' Her mother sighed. 'And what's happened to the pretty pink skirt I bought you?'

'It doesn't suit me.'

'I suppose baggy shirts and jeans do!' She walked away in frigid disapproval. A moment later she called, 'Leo! Leo, darling, come to Mummy!'

Ryder stayed in the arbour surrounded by the roses and the misery of her mother's rejection.

Eventually she trailed back across the lawn. On the

terrace nanny was pushing Leo on his tricycle. 'Rye-rye! Rye-rye!' he shouted, running to her and grabbing her round the knees. He was such an attractive little boy with a mop of blond hair and those Milne blue eyes.

'Hello, monster, want a swing?' She took him by the arms and swung him round her.

When she put him down, he stamped his foot. 'More! More!'

'Later.'

He kicked out at her. 'You're horrid!'

'And you're a spoilt brat!' It was stupid of her to be jealous of him but she couldn't help it.

To get away from the Court, she went for a long drive. It was dusk when she began the long descent through the tree tunnel of Remenham Hill into Henley. From the radio came 'Sounds of Silence'. She turned it up, humming as she crossed the old stone bridge and headed through the town. At last she reached the glossy-leafed rhododendrons which bunched around the entrance to the Court. She turned in. Then suddenly she saw a man in the middle of the drive. She braked hard. But she was going too fast. Her tyres skidded on the gravel. There was a sickening thud — and the man crashed backwards into the bushes.

Ryder leaped from the car and ran to him, pushing the branches aside. 'I'm sorry,' she cried. 'Are you all right?'

'I'm alive — at least I think I am.' He sat up slowly, moving his shoulder to ascertain if it was injured.

'Shall I call a doctor?'

'No.'

'I'm terribly sorry.' She choked back tears of fright.

'It could be worse.'

'You could be dead.'

'I could be paralysed.' He stood up and dusted the dirt from his jeans. He was tall and athletic, moving with a feline sinewyness.

'Do you live round here?' she asked, wondering why he was hanging about in their drive.

He held the branches for her. 'Just passing through.'

When he stepped into the beam of her headlights, she saw him clearly. He was the most attractive man she'd ever seen. His face was defiantly handsome, with fine classic features. His hair was brown and wavy and beautifully cut. But it wasn't his handsome face which unnerved Ryder, it was his potent sexuality. She found herself staring at him. Then she blushed furiously and hurried to the car, fumbling for her keys. She dropped the keys. He picked them up. She stammered. Their hands touched.

'Shall I check the car for dents?' he asked.

'Oh, yes. Please. Father will be furious.'

He examined the bumper. She watched his face in the headlights. 'Only a scratch. Tell him you hit a fox.'

'What's wrong with a rat?'

'I'd rather be a fox, if you don't mind.'

'You can be a rabbit.'

'Patrick Rabbit.'

'It's Peter Rabbit.'

'My name's Patrick.'

'And do you steal carrots from Mr Macgregor's garden?'

'No.' He laughed, and his whole face lit up. 'But I wouldn't mind stealing avocados from your garden.' He took her by the shoulders and kissed her surprised mouth.

She almost fell into the car. Of course he was teasing. He probably guessed she'd never been kissed. A man like that would see it written in her face. He'd tell by her response. She wished she could say something clever and worldly, as Alix would have done. 'You must let me give you a lift,' she said, retreating behind formality.

'With you driving! No, thanks. I have a motorbike.'

'You could come back for tea . . . or a drink . . . or

whatever?' She was torn between not wanting him to leave and fear of what her parents would say to his arrival.

'You live near here?'

She pointed up the drive. 'Dingwall Court.'

'Paul Harding's house?'

'Yes. He's my father.'

He gave a cynical laugh and stepped back. 'Trust Paul Harding to have a dumb bitch daughter who drives around the countryside as if she owns it.'

Ryder told no one about the man in the drive but that didn't stop her thinking about him. He'd spoken to her as if she were Hitler's daughter, and she raged at the injustice. He'd kissed her, and she couldn't forget it. At night she would close her eyes and recall his mouth on hers, the grip of his hands on her shoulders, and the hard muscles of his thighs as he'd pulled her towards him.

She completed the Syd's basic course. Her typing speed was 50 wpm, her shorthand was 90 wpm, and she could seldom read it back. 'We pride ourselves on placing all our girls,' Mrs Brocklebank, the principal, told her. 'We shall endeavour to find you a position somewhere.' She emphasised the words *endeavour* and *somewhere*.

With a giggle of relief Ryder let the college front door slam behind her. She pedalled home through dusty summer streets. Nannies pushed prams to the park. Tourists stood at traffic lights consulting maps. Clematis and honeysuckle hung over garden walls, caressing those who walked along the pavement. The house slumbered in midday quietness. Sun streamed into the attic. Alix was out, making 'go-see' calls on photographers to show them her composite. Not one had led to a booking. Ryder admired her tenacity. In fact, there were many things about Alix she admired although she was still unsure if she liked her.

Pulling on a pair of shorts and a T-shirt, she went down to the communal gardens to which all the flats had access. Lying on a rug in the sunshine in the middle of a weekday afternoon, listening to the buzz of the city, Ryder felt deliciously guilty. She kicked off her shoes and relished the warmth. She yawned and dozed, remembering the summers at Scot's Farm and the hammock which swung across the end of the porch to catch every hint of breeze.

She woke to her feet being tickled. She kicked out. A hand grabbed her ankle.

'Let me go!'

'What do you expect if you lie around half-dressed in a public place.' Adam stood by her feet, laughing. He was dressed for tennis and his white cotton shorts enhanced the light tan of his muscular legs. In one hand he carried two rackets.

She reached for her baggy sweatshirt.

'Oh, no!' He put his foot on it. 'This is the first time I've seen you out of those tents.'

She stood up. 'I have to go in.'

'To do what? Clear up after the others?'

'No.'

'Don't tell me Alix has become domesticated.'

'Does Immy know you're back?'

'Of course. I had lunch with her today. I've taken Miles' room in Jonathan's flat. Can you play tennis?'

'Yes.'

'Can you serve overarm?'

'Of course I can!'

'Here's your racket. Come on! I booked the court for three o'clock.'

Adam whacked the balls over the net. Ryder missed the first three. Then she hit one and it sailed right out of the court and into the road.

'Sorry.' She ran to fetch it whilst he paced up and down. She hit it again. It went into the net. 'Sorry.'

'For God's sake, stop apologising!' He thumped the ball down the centre line. It hit her on the elbow. Tears pricked her eyes at the sudden pain. Then she took a deep breath, told herself she was just as good as Adam, and she smashed the ball back.

He won the first game. And the second. But by the third Ryder's confidence had increased. To his astonishment, she broke his serve — and went on to win the next game. For a full hour they battled it out. He beat her by two sets to one. The last set went to seven-five before he broke her serve.

'Another game tomorrow?' he asked, as they returned to the house, hot and exhausted. 'I'd no idea you could play so well. A few more times and you might even beat me.'

'A few more times and I'll definitely beat you!'

He studied her as she passed ahead of him into the hall. 'You look better. Not so chubby.'

She blushed. 'I went on a diet. I ate so many lettuce leaves I nearly turned into a rabbit.'

He smiled. 'It's a definite improvement. Alix and Imogen will have to watch out.'

'Oh, I'll never be anything compared to them.'

'You won't be till you stop putting yourself down.'

It rained. Ryder mooned around the flat, polishing the rubber plant's leaves, ironing her tennis dress and cleaning her gym shoes. Every time the street door banged she peeped out. Every time a car drew up, she held her breath. She was being ridiculous. Of course she was. Adam belonged to Alix. Well, he had done once. And even if he didn't belong to Alix, he wouldn't be interested in her.

But logic didn't stop Ryder from thinking about him. Wondering what he was doing. Trying to picture his flat. Imagining him lying on his bed. He wasn't as physical as the man in the drive, nor was he as threatening. She couldn't imagine Adam calling someone a dumb bitch.

The phone rang. 'Fancy seeing *The Graduate*?'

'I'd . . . love to.'

'I'll meet you down in the hall in five minutes.'

'Oh . . . you mean this afternoon.' She swallowed back her vision of a romantic evening and hurried into the bedroom to change. Her pink skirt was too babyish, the red shorts too garish, the yellow dress made her look sick, the white made her look fat. She settled for a blue T-shirt and her tightest jeans. In spite of losing weight, she still had to lie on the floor in order to zip them up.

Adam was pacing the hall. 'Hurry up or we'll miss the beginning.' He ran down the steps to his Mini, ducking his head against the rain. Ryder followed. The car was small and wet and steamed up. Her hair dripped like rats' tails. The rope soles of her espadrilles were sodden. The waistband of her jeans cut into her.

The film had already begun. As they sat down Dustin Hoffman was being seduced by Mrs Robinson. Ryder was acutely aware of Adam next to her and of the scene they were watching. She wondered if he would hold her hand. The prospect made her so nervous that she could barely concentrate on the story. But Adam's attention remained fixed on the screen until the credits rolled. 'That's the third time I've seen it,' he said, eyeing up a girl in a micro skirt. 'The last time was with Alix. In fact, we sat in the very same seats.'

She couldn't think what to say. They drove back to the house in silence. 'Fancy a quick drink?' he asked on the doorstep.

'No thanks. But thanks for taking me to the cinema.'

He went into his flat and closed the door. She went on up the stairs.

The flat was empty. She kicked off her wet shoes, wriggled thankfully from her jeans, and lay down on her bed. The mark of the zip ran up her stomach like the scar of a horrendous operation. Whatever she was meant to do or say on a first date, she obviously hadn't done. But of course Adam didn't think of her like that. If Alix had been home, he'd have taken her. If he'd known the micro skirt, he'd have gone with her.

It rained for the rest of that week and Ryder saw nothing of Adam. She knew that he was around, because Imogen in her innocent guileless way told her, 'I've hardly seen Adam since he's been back. He's out every night. Mind you, it means he's less likely to find out about Tony.'

Alix was booked for a modelling job. 'A lingerie catalogue,' she confessed to Ryder. 'Not what I'd hoped for. But it's a beginning.' She gave an unexpected flicker of vulnerability. 'And at least I can now truthfully say I'm a model. How about you? Aren't you bored of mooching around the flat?'

'Oh, I quite enjoy it.' Now was the moment to tell Alix that she'd been to the cinema with Adam but she couldn't find the words.

Ryder returned to Syd's for her job placement dressed in her most officey clothes, a pleated skirt and a cream blouse. Mrs Brocklebank flicked through a pile of vacancy cards, shaking her head and murmuring. 'Secretary to a solicitor? Speeds too low. Personal assistant? Not a hope. Secretary to an artists' agent?'

'That sounds interesting.' Ryder sat up. 'My flatmate is an actress.' She saw herself helping Imogen, another strength to their blossoming friendship.

'You're not smart enough. Jeremy Heythorp's very fussy. I've sent him twenty girls and he's rejected all of them.'

'Please!'

'Oh, very well.' She made an appointment for the following afternoon.

Passing a hair dressing salon on her way home, Ryder

halted to study her reflection. Mrs Brocklebank was right. Shyly she opened the door and stepped inside.

Three hours later Ryder stared at her new self in the mirror. Subtle blonde streaks had lifted the colour. A layered length gave her cheekbones width. Somehow her hair looked both wild and controlled.

'Pleased?' asked the young man.

'Yes.' She giggled nervously. 'But is it me?'

In the street she felt conspicuous. Out of sight of the salon, she ruffled her hair. Then she wished she hadn't, and flicked it out again.

Suddenly she saw a familiar pair of red and white floral knickerbockers. 'Alix!' she called.

'My God!'

'Don't you like it?'

'I'm speechless.'

'Is it that bad?'

'You look wonderful.'

Ryder blushed. 'Do I really?'

'What do you want? A signed proclamation?'

Adam was on the doorstep. He waved as they approached. 'Just the people I need. I've locked myself out. Hey, Ryder, you're looking very glamorous. Who's the lucky man?'

'She has an interview tomorrow,' said Alix.

'Must be a pretty important job?'

Ryder blushed. 'Just secretarial.'

'Well, if I were your boss I'd let you sit on my knee.'

Alix took his arm. 'And if I were offered a drink I wouldn't say no.'

Adam smiled at Ryder. 'I think we should all have a drink.'

She shook her head. She could not bear to see him with Alix.

5

Jeremy Heythorp lived in an elegant Georgian house near Berkeley Square. In keeping with the rest of the street it was painted white and had a glossy black front door with a highly polished brass door knocker. Ryder knocked. After a few moments a girl's voice called through the intercom, 'Come in and make sure you close the door.'

She was admitted to a ground floor office, where a receptionist was sitting at a huge glass desk, reading a magazine. Behind her was a jungle of exotic plants. 'Ryder Harding? Sit down. He won't be long.' She waved Ryder to a white leather sofa, adding, 'I'm only a temp. I wouldn't work here for all the tea in China. He's impossible. I suppose it's because he's . . . well . . . you know.'

'What?'

'One of them. A lot of actors are. Not that you meet any stars in this job. All you do is book a table for two at Le Caprice. You don't see anyone either except for Edith, the cleaner, and Lady Heythorp upstairs. The old bitch!'

A door opened and a tall, slim man with the featureless face of a lizard appeared. 'Miss Harding. Do come in.' His handshake was surprisingly firm and his book-lined office austerely masculine.

'So you've never worked before?' he said, after reading her curriculum vitae. 'Oh, well, you can't be worse than some of the girls I've seen. Did they explain the job? I don't just want someone to type and answer the phone. I need a right hand. Someone to free me from the trivia of life. Look at these.' He pointed at a pile of letters. 'I receive twenty a day from hopeful, hopeless young actors and actresses. All with no experience. All without Equity cards. All looking for an agent.'

'Do you see them?'

'Hardly ever. I'd have no time for anything else.'

Ryder thought of Imogen. 'They might be talented.'

'If they are I'll see them act at RADA, or wherever. Have you any idea how an artists' agent works? It isn't just taking a cut of their earnings, you know.' He spread his fingers wide on the edge of his desk. 'To be an agent is to be adviser, nanny, agony aunt, dictator and friend. I represent some forty actors of all ages. They take up every day of my life, every evening of every day. They are obsessive, selfish, egotists. I live through their successes and their failures, their marriages, divorces, adulteries and deaths. With few exceptions, they are barking mad. I cannot imagine any other life but this. I adore it.'

'Mr Heythorp.'

'Yes.'

'There's water coming through the ceiling.'

'Oh, God! Janet! Janet!'

The receptionist opened the door. 'Yes, Mr Heythorp?'

'Tell that bloody mother of mine that she's let her basin overflow again.' He turned to Ryder. 'The job's yours. Anyone who can watch the ceiling pour in without interrupting will get on well with actors.'

Ryder wasn't sure she liked the job but she took it because she was so relieved that someone wanted to employ her. When she told Alix and Imogen who she was to work for they gasped, 'Jeremy Heythorp! Brilliant! Why didn't you say so before?' and they rushed out to buy a bottle of champagne.

At nine o'clock in the morning Ryder joined the droves who surfaced from Green Park underground station. Twenty minutes were spent walking very slowly down to Berkeley Square, killing time and overcoming butterflies. At exactly half past nine she lifted the brass knocker on the black shiny door.

Jeremy Heythorp opened it. He was wearing dark glasses and a burgundy silk dressing gown. 'I must give you a key,' he said. 'I never get up till ten.'

'What . . . what would you like me to do, Mr Heythorp?'

'Call me Jeremy, sweetie.'

'What would you like me to do . . . Jeremy?'

'Everything! Everything! There's a mountain of letters to answer. I've scribbled a reply on the bottom of each.' He started up the stairs. 'I suppose you'd better introduce yourself to mother.'

'Shall I do that now?'

'My God, no! She's bad enough in the afternoon. She'll be pure hell if you wake her this early.'

Ryder sat down at the glass desk. Beside the typewriter was a heap of letters. Across the bottom of each was an incomprehensible squiggle. She opened the drawers of the desk. She switched on the typewriter. Nothing happened. She tried again. Still nothing. She tested the plug in the wall. Panic swept over her.

The door opened and a tiny mouse of a woman looked in. 'Hello, dearie, I'm Edith. Want a cup of coffee?'

'Thanks.' Ryder gave her an anxious smile. 'I can't make the typewriter work.'

'Oh, it's been broken since Thursday.'

'How did the temporary secretary answer the mail?'

'She didn't. She stuffed it in the drawers and he's been too busy to notice.'

Ryder slumped in her chair.

51

At midday Jeremy appeared. 'Getting on all right?'

'The typewriter's broken and they can't send an engineer till tomorrow.'

'How careless of you!'

'It happened last week.'

'The temporary managed.'

'She didn't.' Ryder pointed to the drawers full of unanswered letters.

'Oh. Oh. Well, I'm off to lunch. You did book my table?'

'I'm sorry. You didn't ask me to.'

'Didn't you look in my diary? Oh, I can't bear it! Telephone now! My usual table.'

'But where?' she almost cried.

'Le Caprice, of course!'

Edith put her head round the door. 'He's impossible. No one stays.'

Ryder thought of her grandfather. 'I'll be fine once I get the hang of things.'

The phone rang. 'It's Letitia Bellevue. I *have* to speak to Jeremy very urgently.'

'I'm sorry, but he's at lunch.' Ryder added timidly, 'Miss Bellevue, I loved your last film.'

'Find that primping little queen! Now!'

Ryder was shaking as she dialled Le Caprice. Jeremy took five minutes to come to the phone. 'Yes!' he snapped.

'Miss Bellevue says . . .'

'I am lunching with a client.'

'She said it was urgent.'

'I said, I am lunching with a client. Goodbye.'

She awaited his return with dread. When she heard his footsteps she dug her fingernails into the palm of her hand and held her breath.

He threw the door open. 'Don't ever interrupt me again,' he said.

'I'm terribly sorry.'

'Letitia's a bitch and if she didn't earn so much I'd drop her.' He went into the office, tapped out a number. 'Letitia, my sweet . . .'

Ryder waited till Jeremy went out, then she telephoned Syd's. 'Miss Harding,' said Mrs Brocklebank crossly, 'if you walk out of your first job after one day you'll never get another. I was astonished that Mr Heythorp even agreed to interview you.'

Ryder thumped down the receiver.

'Running away already?'

Ryder found herself being watched by an elderly woman in a wheelchair. She had Jeremy's lizard eyes, a beaky aristocratic face, and white hair swept into a roll. 'You must be Lady Heythorp.'

'I was this morning when I got up. Now, before you sneak off would you mind pushing me back to the lift.'

Ryder took Lady Heythorp all the way up to her flat, which after Jeremy's stark tastes looked like the dressing room of the Folies Bergères. Every wall was covered with mirrors, every surface with silver-framed photographs and Dresden figures and dyed feathers in silver salvers.

'Run along!' Lady Heythorp waved her beringed hand towards the door. 'Or he'll be back and you'll have to explain yourself. I'm sure in your previous life you were the kind of maid who never admitted to breaking tea cups.'

'Not liking a job doesn't make me a coward.'

'Running away does.'

To disprove Lady Heythorp, Ryder sat out the rest of the day and returned on the following morning. The typewriter was mended. She deciphered Jeremy's handwriting. She booked his lunch. She answered the telephone.

'So you're still here.' Lady Heythorp appeared in the doorway.

'Yes.' Ryder carried on typing.

'You are contrary. Most of them run away when I'm rude.' She spun the wheels on her wheelchair and returned to the lift.

Jeremy's life was one of continuous business entertaining. Every day he lunched with clients, producers, directors and journalists. Often he had tea with others at the Ritz. Each evening he dined with more useful people. If not at dinner he went to the theatre: he saw all of his clients in every part they played. Ryder saw Edith and Lady Heythorp.

As she walked home along the Old Brompton Road on Friday, Adam tapped her on the shoulder. 'Where are you going with your nose in the pavement?'

'I'm fed up with my new job. All I do is type and book lunches. I don't see a soul, except for the cleaner and my boss's mother, who looks as though she dines on rats' blood.'

He laughed. 'Join the unemployed. I have.'

'I thought you worked for an estate agent.'

'I did. But there's no future in this company, not unless you're qualified, and I'm not that hot on studying. I want to have fun. You don't have to pass exams to succeed. Look at your father!'

Ryder stiffened. 'How did you know about my father?'

'Alix told me. I'd like to meet him. He's the kind of risk-taker I admire.'

'He's a tyrant — and I don't want to talk about him.'

'Okay!' He linked his arm through hers, unaware of her reaction to his touch. But Ryder could feel her heart thudding. The noise was so loud she felt sure he must hear. 'Let's stop for a drink.'

She thought of Alix. 'No thanks.'

But once back at the flat the evening stretched ahead. Hour after hour of solitude, exacerbated by the restless streets of an early summer Friday night.

At nine o'clock there was a knock at the door. It was Adam.

54

'Alix isn't home,' she said.

'Oh, what a shame!' He turned away. Then he spun back, laughing. 'Don't be silly! It's you I came to see. Want to come to a party tomorrow evening?'

'What about . . . Alix?'

'What's she got to do with it?'

'She might not like it.'

'Listen to me.' He pushed her into the flat and shut the door. 'Your friend Alix has had more men than most people have hot dinners. I wasn't the first. I certainly wasn't the last. She's a fun girl — and she has fun with everyone. Me. Jonathan. Even Miles, and he's engaged.'

The door opened and Alix walked in. 'Hi sweeties! Why the serious faces?'

'I've invited Ryder to a party tomorrow night but she won't come because she thinks you might be hurt. Put her straight, Alix.'

'Me! Hurt! Don't be silly! Got a new man myself.' She went into the bathroom and rummaged through the cabinet. 'Oh, hell, what have I done with this month's Pill!' She reappeared, stuffing a pair of red knickers into her bag. 'Must dash. See ya.'

'What did I tell you?' said Adam.

'I still feel awkward.'

'Eight o'clock tomorrow evening.'

That night Ryder could hardly sleep for nerves. She ran the gamut of every conceivable excuse to cancel.

'You look like a condemned man on his last morning,' said Imogen as they ate their cornflakes.

'Adam has invited me to a party.'

'My brother!' Imogen leaned forward. 'Do you like him?'

Ryder blushed. 'Yes, but I'm worried about Alix.'

'She's got hundreds of boyfriends. Come on! We'll go shopping. You need some new clothes. Yours are all so baggy and old-fashioned.'

'I can't go out. I might meet Adam on the stairs.'

'I thought you liked him.'

'I'm scared. I wish I'd said no.' Ryder picked up the newspaper. 'What's on the television tonight?'

Imogen snatched it from her. 'You're not standing up my brother in order to watch television.'

They tried the shops in the King's Road, searching the rails of every boutique from Beaufort Street to Sloane Square. Then they took a taxi to High Street Kensington. In Biba she found a pink suede fringed mini dress. It reminded her of the White Squaw of Fox Lake. In the scrum of the communal changing room, whilst Imogen sat on the floor, Ryder wriggled into the dress. 'Is it too tight? Do I look fat?'

'It's great!' Imogen straightened the fringe. 'Everyone's wearing the ethnic look.'

She bought the dress and some matching suede boots. Then Imogen persuaded her into a pair of very short black culottes teamed with a black and white flowered shirt, knotted beneath her breasts to reveal her bare stomach. In the antique market Ryder fell for a pink and green Indian skirt and a shocking pink T-shirt. In a small boutique she found a black and pink bikini. On the bus going home she counted the money she'd spent and wailed, 'When am I going to wear them all?'

'On your second date!'

She laughed, then shook with nerves.

At five to eight Ryder was ready. Her hair was soft and shiny. Her eyes were large with excitement. The suede dress gave her a wild coltish look, like an Indian bride awaiting her brave.

'I still feel bad about Alix,' she told Imogen.

'Forget her. I have to forget Tony's wife. If I didn't, I'd go crazy.' Imogen hesitated. 'Don't tell Adam about Tony.'

The bell rang. Ryder opened the door. Adam looked her up and down. 'Well, if it isn't Minnehaha!' He kissed her on the cheek. 'You look wonderful. Doesn't she, sis?'

Over Adam's shoulder Ryder caught Imogen's eye and giggled.

The party was in a large dilapidated house in North Kensington. As they arrived the Rolling Stones were thumping out through the open window and a couple were making love beside the dustbins in the front garden, the girl's purple mini dress ruched up above her buttocks. Embarrassed, Ryder looked away. Adam laughed. He took her hand and led her through to the kitchen which was stacked with wine and beer and plastic mugs and people becoming seriously drunk. He found her some wine and himself a beer, then steered her back towards the dancing. Under the stairs three girls were heating a lump of hashish over a candle. On the sitting room floor a man in a kaftan was meditating. In the bay window of the dining room a naked girl was gyrating. Adam squeezed Ryder's hand. She responded tentatively.

A very pretty girl approached. 'Hi, Adam. Thought you were dead.'

'Hi, Janey. Sorry I didn't answer your calls.'

'Bastard!' She walked on.

'Don't look so anxious.' Adam touched Ryder's face. 'She meant nothing to me. Come on! Let's dance!'

She hesitated.

'Don't you want to?'

'I don't really know how.'

'It's easy.' He dragged her into the centre of the floor. The room was packed. The music pumped. It didn't take Ryder long to pick up the beat. Adam fetched more wine. By the time she'd had three glasses, she could dance as well as anyone. The record changed, the music slowed, the lights were dimmed, and through the hot smoky crowd came the haunting beat of 'By the Time I Get to Phoenix'.

'I love this song,' she said. 'It reminds me of a place called Prairieville.'

He took her in his arms. 'Women are so sentimental. They're always thinking about the past. I think about now.' He pulled her close to him. 'About us.' He ran his lips down her neck and kissed her collar bone. She moved against him. Their bodies swayed with the music. She was drunk but she didn't care. Nothing mattered except Adam. He kissed her. At first gently. Then passionately, his mouth hard on hers. She responded, opening up to him. Melting. Pressing her body against him.

'Let's go,' he said.

'Where?'

'Home, of course.' He moved his hand up her thigh, under the fringe of her skirt. 'Don't you want to?' he whispered hoarsely.

She knew she should stop him, but she didn't. She wanted him.

'Are you on the pill?' he asked. 'If you're not, I'll be careful.'

The song. Debbie. Pregnant. She pulled away from him and hurried out of the room, pushing through the crowd by the front door till she reached the safety of the street.

Adam came after her. He seized her by the arm. 'What the hell's the matter?'

She hid her face. 'I don't want to just . . . do it. Not with someone I hardly know. I've never done it before. I want it to be special.'

He cupped her face in his hands, forcing her to look at him. 'Alix said you were a virgin but when I took you in my arms I decided she was lying. You don't kiss like an innocent.'

Ryder blushed. He kissed her. She responded. He stopped. 'Either you want to or you don't.'

'I don't.'

They drove home with the radio blaring Joe Cocker and Adam drumming on the steering wheel. Ryder glanced across at him. He didn't even look at her. She turned her face to the passing houses.

Outside her door, he patted her on the cheek. 'Goodnight.'

She felt utterly deflated.

'I didn't realise he was so sex mad,' said Imogen, next morning when she'd heard Ryder's story. 'I only think of him as my brother.'

Ryder opened the window and looked down on the gardens where a game of tennis was in progress. 'I knew I should have stayed in and watched television.'

'Oh, you'll see him again. Even if he doesn't come up, you're bound to meet him on the stairs.'

'I'll learn to parachute so I don't have to use them.'

'How are you going to get up here?'

'I shall take lessons from a cat burglar.'

The sun shone. The gardens beckoned. But Ryder refused to leave the flat for fear of meeting Adam. At midday the front door banged. She rushed to the window. 'It's him. He's leaving. Quick!' She threw on her new bikini and a pair of shorts whilst Imogen slipped into a sun dress and a floppy hat. Then she picked up a blanket and some suncream, and raced down the stairs, across the road and into the gardens.

'I'm going to buy the *Sunday Express*. I want to see the film reviews,' said Imogen.

'Get me a *News of the World*.' Ryder stretched out in the sunshine. 'If I'm not going to lead a life of sin at least let me read about it.'

Five minutes later Imogen kicked her foot. 'He's back. I met him in the papershop.'

'What did he say.'

'Hello.'

'Just like that.'

'No. Like this.' Imogen deepened her voice. 'Hello, Immy. Have you called mother today?'

'Idiot! Did he ask after me?'

'Oh, I told him you were lying here, ready and waiting, swatting up sexual techniques in the *News of the World*.'

Ryder threw the newspaper at her.

They lay in companionable silence, Imogen in the shade to protect her white skin, Ryder in the sun to enhance her tan. She closed her eyes and pictured Adam. She wriggled her toes and felt his body against hers.

'Hello, Adam,' said Imogen.

Ryder looked around. There was no one. 'Beast!'

An hour later, Ryder was lying on her stomach reading the confessions of a Hollywood starlet. The sun shone on her bare back and her hair hung like a curtain around her face.

'Hello, Adam,' said Imogen.

Ryder chuckled. 'You won't catch me out twice. This is much too interesting.'

'More interesting than me?'

She turned sharply. Adam was standing over her. Under the tree, Imogen was laughing into her floppy hat. 'Ryder's trying to learn about vice from the newspaper.' She was giggling as she gathered up her belongings. 'And I'm going in to learn my lines. They're auditioning for the kind of production where the Jeremy Heythorps of this world notice "fresh flesh" — and I intend to be noticed.'

Ryder was acutely aware of the smallness of her bikini and of Adam as he stretched out beside her. 'Do you really want to know about vice?' he asked in a silky voice.

'Of course not!'

'Liar!' He pushed up her hair and kissed her bare shoulder, running his hand down the length of her back. Her whole body rippled at his touch. Instinctively, she moved against him. He slid his fingers under her hip bone. 'Come back to the flat.' He nibbled at her shoulder. 'I know you want to.'

'Adam, please!'

He slid his hand further under her until his fingers slipped inside her bikini. She gave a little shudder. 'I won't hurt you,' he whispered.

'No!' She rolled away and jumped to her feet.

'You little cocktease!' he snapped. 'If you get raped it'll be your own bloody fault.'

She grabbed up her bag and her suncream, yanked the rug from under him, and marched away. He caught up with her as she reached the street door. 'Here's your fucking newspaper!' He screwed it into a ball and threw it at her. It caught her on the back of the head and bounced over the railings, into the basement.

Somehow Ryder dragged herself to work that week and somehow she avoided meeting Adam on the stairs. On Friday evening she went straight from the office to Dingwall Court. It drizzled all weekend. She lay on her bed and stared at the ceiling. Seven days ago she and Imogen had been giggling through the boutiques. On Monday she caught an early train to London, pushing and jostling with all the other commuters. She went straight to the office. Jeremy had left her a note. He was away till Wednesday. So was his mother. She spent the day with her head in her hands and her elbows on the typewriter.

At half past five, she closed the front door.

'Ryder!' Adam crossed the street. 'Where have you been all weekend?'

'Away.' She started walking.

He caught up with her. 'Still angry?'

'Why should I be?' She kept her face nonchalant.

'I'm sorry I shouted at you.' He took her by the hand. She tried to pull away but he refused to release her.

On Tuesday he met her again. On Wednesday he was

61

waiting at the flat. On Thursday they played tennis. Ryder had to pinch herself to believe that she was being pursued by someone as attractive as Adam. On Friday he didn't appear. Ryder paced the flat. She picked up the phone to see if it was working. She rushed to the window each time she heard footsteps. At eleven, she said to Imogen, 'He's met someone else.'

Immy smiled anxiously. 'Adam isn't very dependable. He never has been. Mother's spoiled him rotten. All his life, he's only had to smile.'

He arrived at midnight, drunk. Whilst Ryder made him a sobering cup of coffee, he said, 'I wish I could spend the weekend with you but I have to take mother to Uncle Algie's birthday party. He's bound to get at me about my lack of career. He always does at family parties.'

'But you have a job.'

'I left. The woman who ran the branch was imposs-ible. So tomorrow it'll be the money-doesn't-grow-on-trees lecture when I ask to borrow fifty quid.'

'I can lend you some money. I have twenty pounds in my purse.'

'You're sweet but no. I couldn't.' He hesitated. 'Well, I suppose if I borrowed a fiver I could buy the old buzzard a present. I'll give it back to you on Monday.'

It was Thursday before Adam repaid her but Ryder didn't mind. Helping him gave her a warm glow. She decided to buy him a present. She spent a lunch hour in Simpsons, choosing a cashmere sweater. It was wildly expensive. She couldn't wait to give it to him.

'A cashmere sweater,' said Lady Heythorp, who was having her weekly snoop around the office. 'For the boyfriend who's been upsetting you! You're sillier than I thought.'

Ryder went scarlet. Later she returned the sweater.

On Saturday evening Adam took Ryder out to dinner. She wore her second-date outfit, the short black linen culottes and the black and white shirt knotted tightly under her breasts.

'You must let me pay for myself,' she said when the bill came.

'Certainly not! Mother slipped me an extra thirty. She wants me to have fun. Let's have a brandy.'

'At least let that be my treat.'

'Oh, well . . . if you insist.' He squeezed her hand. 'Alix would never have offered.'

She swallowed hard.

'It bothers you about Alix, doesn't it?'

'I can't help it.'

'Alix is a fun girl who has fun with a lot of men. It was just sex with her. You and I are different. I've never spent so much time with anyone as I have with you.' He dipped his finger into his glass, then leaned across the table and put it to her mouth. She licked the brandy from it.

'Don't do that unless . . .'

She looked at him uncertainly. She wanted him so much that she could think of nothing else. But she was scared. Of doing it. Of not knowing how. Of getting pregnant. Of everything.

Adam downed his brandy and stood up. 'Let's go.' He led her from the restaurant, down the street, and to his flat. She went to sit down on the sofa but he steered her into the bedroom. 'Darling, you look as if you're going to a funeral.' He ran his hands down her tense body. 'Relax! Relax! Oh, you're so sweet.'

'I might get pregnant.'

'I'll use a French letter.'

She sat down on the end of his bed. 'I'm . . . I'm . . . nervous.'

'You'll enjoy it.' His hand moved up the soft inside of her thigh. 'Sex is fun. You wait and see.'

He pushed her back on the bed and kissed her, very gently, his hand moving higher and higher. She responded, at first tentatively, then with passion, pulling him down to her. He untied her shirt and slipped it from her shoulders. He unclipped her bra, kissing her breasts, rolling her nipples between his lips until she exuded tiny moans of pleasure. She felt him pull her culottes and the wisp of pink lace panties from her hips. He turned away, ripped his clothes off, and opened a drawer in the bedside cabinet.

She sat up. 'What are you doing?'

'Preventing you from getting pregnant.'

'Oh.' She looked at him, this naked semi-stranger. 'Adam, I'm not sure if . . .'

'For God's sake! You can't change your mind now!' He pushed her back.

'Adam! Please! Wait!' She tried to get up but he grabbed her.

'Stop struggling.' He pinned her arms above her head.

'Don't! Don't!'

He forced his knee between her thighs and man-handled her into position. She pleaded. He took no notice. She sobbed. He thrust. She cried out. It was over and he collapsed across her.

'I'm sorry.' He touched her wet face.

She was stunned.

'I'm sorry I hurt you.'

She didn't reply.

'I really didn't mean to. But you can't just stop a man like that, not when you're naked and in bed with him.'

She stared at the far wall. She was hot and sticky, and she longed to go home and lie in a hot bath — and wash Adam away.

'You're the first virgin I've had. I should have been more patient. I realise that now. But I suppose I'm used to girls like Alix. Oh, don't freeze up on me. Please!'

She sat up very slowly.

'Do you want to use the bathroom?' he said. 'I mean, you might be all . . .'

She swung her legs over the side of the bed and walked gingerly across the floor. In the bathroom mirror the left side of her face was red and blotchy.

'If you want to borrow my robe its the blue one behind the door,' shouted Adam.

Washed, hair combed, and in his soft towelling robe she came out.

'I've made you a cup of tea.' He pointed to the bedside table.

She perched on the side of the bed. He was bunched up near the headboard.

'All right?'

Her face crumpled.

'Come on.' He put an arm around her. 'It always hurts the first time. I mean, it's bound to, isn't it? You must have known that. But it won't hurt next time. You'll enjoy it then.'

'I'd like to go home.'

'Please don't. I'll feel terrible. Please! Stay here tonight. I promise not to touch you again.'

'I'm not upset because it hurt. I expected that. It's because you forced me. You unnerved me.' She looked at him through tear-heavy lashes. 'You reminded me of my father.'

He took her hand in his. 'Don't you ever ruin things that you really care about and wish you could put back the clock?'

'Frequently.'

'Then give me another chance. Please!'

'Only if you promise not to touch me.'

'I promise.'

She lay down, with his dressing gown wrapped tightly about her. Adam turned out the light.

'You won't tell Immy, will you?' he said into the darkness.

'No.'

He felt forgiven. Within minutes he was asleep. But

Ryder couldn't sleep. She was unused to the breathing and snuffling of someone else in her bed. Around the unfamiliar room her thoughts whirled. She'd imagined her first night with Adam as loving and romantic. She felt robbed.

In the morning he made breakfast while she had a bath. Then they sat side by side on the balcony and read the Sunday newspapers. Ryder stretched out her legs to the sun and as its warmth crept into her, she looked at Adam. Since he'd come into her life everything, even her job, had gained a fullness. She loved him. He was Imogen's brother. Nothing could be more perfect.

He caught her eye and smiled. 'Have you forgiven me?'

She blushed.

He lifted her chin and looked deep into her eyes. 'We mustn't end this day till things are right between us.' He kissed her very gently on the lips. 'Are they improving?' His fingers circled the soft inside of her thigh. 'Come to bed. I want to make love to you gently, slowly, as I should have done.' He stood up and took her hand.

They lay down on the bed. He caressed and reassured, waiting for her to respond fully. He made love to her tenderly, watching her face for any hint of fear, holding himself back as long as he could, which was not long enough for Ryder. But he was gentle and he made her feel desirable and loved.

6

Adam and Ryder became so inseparable that out of his earshot Imogen called her 'sister-in-law'. Ryder called her Immy, which only family and close friends were permitted to do. The overweight lonely girl of the previous winter who'd plucked up courage to have her hair streaked was a lifetime away from the glossy creature who strode down the King's Road in white hipster trousers and one of Adam's shirts knotted beneath her breasts. And yet, they were the same person. Ryder knew that. There were moments when she looked in the mirror and wondered if she were dreaming.

Alix took the news well. She smiled brightly and kissed them both on the cheek, then she said she too had a new man and disappeared for a week.

'You see, she really doesn't mind,' said Adam.

Ryder sensed that wasn't true but she didn't want to think about Alix, she was too-wrapped in the selfishness of happiness.

Adam had a new job, working for a scruffy little estate agent in the back end of Fulham, an area waiting to be discovered. With his first pay cheque he said, 'Let's go to Paris for the weekend.'

They rushed out to the nearest travel agency and came away with armfuls of brochures, all depicting Paris as the city for lovers. Arriving home they found Alix crying in the bathroom.

'What's wrong?' asked Ryder, hovering in the doorway.

'Just life.'

'You're pregnant?'

Alix shook her head. 'Remember I needed money for photos? Well, I went ahead and had them taken even though I couldn't pay. I knew the photographer fancied me, so I played up to him. He agreed to wait. But I needed the money from my first job to live on. I bought new clothes. I have to look good. When he found out, he started hounding me. He said if I slept with him he'd see things differently.' She pulled a face. 'That was my new man. And that's not all. Now he's found someone else and he says he never let me off my debt and that I was only buying time. If I don't pay up, he's going to put the word about. I'll never be booked again.'

'How much do you owe?'

'Three hundred.'

Ryder took out her cheque book. 'Pay me when you can.'

'But that's our Paris spending money,' protested Adam. 'We're going to buy smart clothes and have dinner at the Moulin Rouge.'

'What's a few rags and a meal.' She filled in the amount.

Adam watched her sullenly. 'Everyone thinks you're so wonderful,' he snapped. 'But you're no better than anyone else. You're only giving Alix the money because you feel guilty over us.'

'That's a lie!' She flushed and turned away, unable to look at Alix. But later, although she didn't admit it, she realised there was a grain of truth in what Adam said.

The first major row she had with Adam was over Imogen — or rather, over Tony. Jonathan, Adam's flatmate, invited a new girlfriend to a candlelit dinner in the flat and Ryder and Adam volunteered to make themselves scarce. They went to the cinema in Notting

Hill, then stopped at an Indian restaurant for a curry. Sitting opposite the door were Imogen and Tony, she with her dainty, petal face pressed into his shoulder.

Adam turned pale. 'Imogen! Who's that man?'

'The name's Tony Daltry.' Tony stood up and held out his hand. 'How do ye do.'

Adam ignored him. 'Imogen, who is he?'

'The man I love.'

'I'm sorry you found out this way,' said Tony. 'I understand how you feel. I'd be the same if she were my sister. But I love Immy. Be assured of that.'

'Are you married?'

'I am.'

'How disgusting! How could you, Imogen! My sister with a middleaged married labourer.' Adam marched out of the restaurant.

Ryder ran after him. 'Adam! Please wait.'

'Did you know about . . . him?'

'Yes.'

'Why didn't you tell me?'

'She asked me not to.'

'I'm your boyfriend. Your first loyalty's to me, not to my sister.'

They had reached the car. They drove home in silence. Ryder stared out of the window. Sometimes Adam was so childish. But that was unfair. He was right to worry about Imogen. She reached for his hand. That night she was particularly tender with Adam. They made love slowly, languorously, touching with fingertips so deft that it was as if they did not touch at all. In the morning, he said, 'What hurts me is that you kept a secret from me. Promise me you'll never exclude me again.'

She lay on top of him, her body stretched on his, her chin just below his chin. 'I promise.'

He ran his hands down her naked back and gripped her buttocks, pulling her to him. 'Make love to me,' he said. 'I don't want to do anything except lie here whilst you make love to me.'

Because Ryder was anxious to include Adam in every aspect of her life she showed him a confidential letter from Debbie in which her cousin talked of leaving Carl. Their baby, Rudy, was two months old but Carl showed little interest. Debbie suspected he was seeing another girl. They lived above the hardware store with his father who seldom spoke. She longed for Scot's Farm but Carl wouldn't allow her to use the car.

Adam read it and tossed it back. 'Another lame dog!'

'Debbie's not a lame dog!' Ryder folded the letter.

'I bet she asks you for money.'

'I've already sent her some.'

'If you're throwing money down the drain why don't you throw some my way and buy a new battery for my car? After all, you ride in it too.'

'I'm sorry I didn't think of it.'

'Forget it!'

'Adam, there's no need to shout. I don't know what's got into you.'

'I need your sympathy too. It's not much fun being between jobs, you know.'

She nearly said, 'You're always between jobs,' but she stopped herself.

They sat in silence. She felt battered by his outburst. Suddenly he took her hand. 'Mother's giving a New Year's Eve party. I'd like her to meet you.'

At four o'clock on New Year's Eve, Ryder paced the drawing room of Dingwall Court, waiting for Adam. She was wearing a silk dress in a brilliant singing blue. The top was cut tight. The skirt was soft and swirling. She had to walk with her arms out so that her nervous, sticky hands didn't mark it.

Her parents and Leo were having tea in front of the

fire. Her mother was busy adding extra cream to a chocolate eclair for Leo. Ryder waited for her to comment on the dress.

'What did you say Adam does?' asked her father from his armchair.

'He's . . . er . . . between jobs.'

'Trust my daughter to find a layabout.'

'He's very nice.' She blushed and turned to her mother. 'Do I look all right?'

'Don't distract me now, Ryder. Oh, Leo! Not chocolate on my lovely sofa.'

Her father frowned. 'Leo! Stop it! Or you'll go to nanny. And don't cry. Even Ryder didn't cry like you do.' He turned to her. 'The dress is fine — it's the boyfriend I'm concerned about.'

The front bell sounded. Ryder jumped with nerves. She tried to look casual as Mrs Trumpet ushered in Adam. He walked straight over to her father, his hand outstretched, his smile its most deferential. 'Good evening, sir. I apologise for intruding. I must say what a magnificent home you have.'

Ryder didn't know whether to be proud of him or to kick him.

Adam's mother lived in an attractive flint cottage on the edge of the Sussex Downs. It had a thatched roof and small windows which looked south across the chalky hills to Glyndebourne. Every summer Mrs Lydden moved to a boarding house in Eastbourne whilst she rented the cottage to opera buffs. It paid for the upkeep. Ryder knew this from Immy, not Adam.

'Hardly what you're used to at Dingwall Court.' Adam opened the front door to the sound of voices and laughter.

'I don't mind.' Ryder wondered nervously if Mrs Lydden would like her.

'Well I do! I'd sell my soul to live in a place like that.'

71

A voice from the sitting room interrupted them. It came from a huge walrus of a man standing at the far end. 'I was a polo man, which someone called — probably that man Kipling — "the sport of kings and the king of sports".'

Adam groaned. 'Oh, God! Uncle Algie's here. Poor mother! I don't know why she asks him. He's never approved of her. None of father's family did.'

'Why not?'

'Because her family didn't own strings of polo ponies.'

'Darling.' Joyce Lydden floated out of the drawing room. She was a brittle redhead with a disappointed mouth. 'And Ryder! Well, you are a change from Adam's usual girlfriends.' She gave a little laugh. 'Imogen's upstairs. You're sharing a room with her. In my house it's separate bedrooms.'

'Mother!' Adam exclaimed, as Ryder turned scarlet with embarrassment.

'Darling, you know my rules. Now, come along. I need you to pour the drinks.' She led him firmly away from Ryder.

'Mother stolen Adam?' Imogen appeared on the landing in a white angora mini dress and no shoes.

'Yes.'

'He reminds her of Daddy. That's why she's so possessive.'

Ryder cleared a space on one of the beds whilst Imogen hunted under the other for a pair of red shoes. She tried to think of something nice to say about Immy's mother but couldn't. 'Adam told me about her problems with your father's family,' she said eventually.

'He must be in love. You're the only person he's told.' Imogen slipped on her high heels. 'He's always made such a secret of it. Just as mother was forced to. Father's family even wanted her to convert.' She smiled at Ryder who was looking puzzled. 'But if my parents loved each

72

other, it's their business if he's Roman Catholic and she's Jewish.'

Ryder didn't admit that Adam hadn't told her.

As they drove back to London the next morning Adam asked, 'Do you think your parents liked me?'

'I'm sure they did.' She waited for him to say his mother approved of her.

'We should spend some weekends at Dingwall Court.'

'I'd rather not.' Obviously Mrs Lydden hadn't liked her.

'But I ought to get to know your parents better,' he reached for Ryder's hand, 'because I am seriously interested in their daughter.'

7

1972

Adam and Ryder spent many weekends at Dingwall Court: many more than she wished.

'Why don't you invite your flatmates and have a house-party,' her mother suggested over dinner. 'You know how I love people to see our home.'

Adam lit up. 'Oh, do let's!'

Ryder hesitated. She looked at her father, expecting him to say no. But he laughed. 'I'd love to see the Bassinghams' faces when they hear their daughter has been here. Did they imagine I'd pay for everything forever?' He smiled at Adam. 'People who can be bought deserve to be dropped.'

'I agree with you, sir.'

Ryder was uneasy about the houseparty. She knew how her father's mood could change. But he was charming that weekend. So much so that afterwards Alix and Immy would frequently pile into cars and drive down from London, to swim and play tennis. Jonathan came with Charlotte. Miles brought his new wife. Hetty brought her brother. Sometimes there were twenty of them, drinking Pimms' on the terrace.

'Now the polo season's underway I'd like to go over to Smith's Lawn,' her father said casually over dinner. 'I've always promised myself I'd take it up, when I had the time and the means.'

'That's easy,' Adam laid down his knife and fork. 'My Uncle Algie's a member of the Guards' Club. He's there every weekend. He used to play for his regiment. He knows everything — and everyone — in polo.'

'But you can't ride, Paul,' protested Carrie.

'I shall learn — as I have learned to do other things.' He smiled down the table at his wife. 'When I was young, I used to muck out the stables of the local squire every morning before school. His son played polo.'

'And he encouraged you?' said Adam.

'I was a stable boy. He never even spoke to me!'

Ryder saw her father's eyes narrow but no one else did. They went on drinking and eating.

On Sunday afternoon they drove over to Windsor, entering the park by way of Blacknest Gate and following the road up through the lush woods and rhododendrons on Breakheart Hill. Smith's Lawn, home of the Guards' Club, was named after Barnard Smith, a stud-groom to the Duke of Cumberland during the eighteenth century. It was Ryder's first visit. As the car turned for the club-house she saw the beautifully manicured polo grounds stretching away to distant trees.

Suddenly, eight ponies thundered into view. Riders leaned forward. Sticks were held aloft. Thigh muscles strained under tight white breeches. Gleaming brown leather boots were pressed into ponies' sides. As they drew level, one player rose in his saddle, turned his body sideways, and brought his stick back before swinging it through to hit the ball with all the momentum of muscle and gallop.

'I like this sport,' murmured Alix, fixing her eyes on the players whose every muscle within their buttocks rippled beneath their breeches.

Major Algie Kelmscott was waiting by the clubhouse. 'Ah, there you are, Adam, my boy. Mr Harding, I've been wanting to thank you for your hospitality towards my nephew. Damned good of you! I've always found him a nuisance but I gather your daughter doesn't think so.'

He ushered them down the side of the clubhouse and on to the lawn where Adam was grouping chairs around a table in the sunshine. The club was packed with the kind of people who made Ryder cringe with shyness. They had an air of exclusivity. Of understated wealth and supreme confidence. The women were casually elegant. Some even scruffily elegant. They mixed Dior silk shirts with jeans, Gucci handbags and tailored suits, and everyone wore dark glasses. Alix put on hers.

The ponies thundered up and down, kicking up the divots and the red sand beneath. They raced after the ball. Rode off each other with their shoulders. Stopped. Turned. Twisted.

'Aren't the horses beautiful!' said her mother, smiling at Major Kelmscott.

'Ponies, my dear Mrs Harding! Ponies! Must get the jargon right.'

'Then perhaps you'd better tell us,' said her father. But before the old major could open his mouth, he added, 'Forget the history. I know polo began in Persia. The word comes from the Tibetan *pulu*. It was introduced to England in 1869. I can see that there are four players to a team, and the object is to hit a white ball through the goal post with a four foot long stick whilst galloping across a field on a pony. What are the rules?'

The Major spoke without drawing breath, probably because he was afraid of being interrupted. 'Teams play against others with the same team handicap — or goal rating — which is an aggregate of all the players' handicaps,' he explained. 'A high goal team is a "22-goal team". A low goal team is an "8-goal". A beginner's handicap is minus two. A brilliant player at his peak might reach ten.'

'Could I ever be a ten?' asked her father.

The major chuckled. 'Not a chance. You'd have to be

born to it. These Argentinians ride the pampas before they can walk. Juan Carlos Harriott's the best player since the war. He's a ten. Eduardo Moore. He's a ten over here but not in his own country. Hector Barrantes. Not a ten, but an excellent player.'

'How high could I get?'

'Depends on how well you ride.'

'I can't ride at all — yet.'

The major choked. 'You can't ride and you ask if you could be a ten! See over there.' He pointed to two young men, one fair, the other dark. 'Howard and Julian Hipwood. Our best players. But even they may not make ten. You have to start young, Mr Harding, and you have to be a professional. A patron of a team, after all, has other things in his life.'

'Like making the money to pay for it all?'

'To put it bluntly . . . yes. There's no prize money. A patron plays for pleasure. It's up to the professionals he hires to play in his team to make sure he enjoys it.'

'If I wanted to take up polo, how would I go about it?'

'As a patron?'

'I'm not a man to play in other people's teams.'

'You'd need a damned good professional. Maybe two. I'd be glad to advise you. I know everyone there is to know.' The major smiled. 'It's my world.'

That was the beginning of Paul Harding's obsession with polo. On her next visit Ryder found the old stables had been cleared to accommodate three horses and the field had been turned into a ring where he had daily lessons.

'You two are coming with me tomorrow,' he told Ryder and Adam at dinner.

'Not me.' Adam threw up his hands in horror. 'I haven't ridden for years.'

'I'd never ridden until a month ago.'

'You're a braver man than I am, sir.'

'So it seems! Well, Ryder, are you afraid too?'

'Of course not! Nor is Adam. He just doesn't like horses.'

In the morning she felt less brave. She hadn't ridden since she was eight and she could barely remember how to mount. As they trotted out of the yard she wondered how soon she'd fall off. A little way up the road they turned into a field. She nearly lost a kneecap on the gatepost. Clutching her horse's mane she bounced in the saddle as they swished through the long dewy grass. At least if she fell off here it wouldn't hurt so much.

Her father slowed when he reached the river and waited for her to draw alongside. 'I wish the squire's son could see me now,' he said. 'I wish my mother could see me now. Do you know she once told me I'd never amount to anything?'

Ryder was so stunned by the suddenness of his confidence that she could only stare at him, too afraid of ruining the moment to speak. He rode on. She followed.

After that morning she rode willingly with him. That moment of intimacy had created a hunger in her. She longed for more, as if sensing an untapped well of potential between them. They would canter through the soft green fields of the Thames Valley, through the long grasses and the buttercups. He rode well. He learned quickly. She tried to match him.

'Are you going to marry Adam?' he asked her one day, halting at the edge of a meadow.

'I don't know. He hasn't asked me yet.'

'If he does, it'll be because he's after my money.'

She was stung. 'Of course you can't believe anyone would want me for myself.'

'Don't be a bloody fool!' He galloped off.

On her next visit she refused to ride. He never asked her again.

Imogen was chosen to play a supporting role in one of

RADA's showcase plays. 'I should have won the lead,' she confided in Ryder. 'Everyone says so. But I'm too nervous.' She slumped into a chair.

Ryder was ironing one of Adam's shirts. She'd done them once as a favour and now he expected it. She pulled the collar tight against the iron, wondering why she was so afraid of losing him that she couldn't bring herself to say, 'No, I won't wash your shirts, pour your drinks, collect your dry cleaning, clean your flat.'

'It's not just the play that scares me.' Immy twisted her hair in and out of her fingers. 'To get an Equity card I need experience with a rep company but they're all out of London. I don't want to leave Tony. I love him. I need him.' She stood up and began to pace the flat. 'When I'm like this, when I'm scared, I just want to marry Tony, have his baby, and stay at home — and never have to think for myself again. But when I'm feeling good, when I'm on the stage, I want to act. Ryder, if you could get Jeremy Heythorp to see me I know everything would be all right.'

'I'll try. But he hates being asked favours.'

It was several days before she could corner Jeremy. 'If she's that good I'll hear about her,' was all he'd say.

Ryder didn't want to join her parents' party at Henley Regatta: she'd barely spoken to her father since that morning in the meadow and she sensed he was tiring of her guests. But her mother refused to listen. She issued independent invitations to Adam, Immy and Alix. 'You must appreciate your friends more or you'll lose them,' she told Ryder as they waited in the hall. 'Remember, for years you had none.'

Ryder adjusted her straw boater. 'How can I forget when you keep reminding me?'

They were cut short by her father. 'I don't like people who help themselves to my malt whisky without asking.'

Ryder flushed. 'I'll pay for it.'

'I suppose it was that sycophantic boyfriend of yours.'

There was a clatter of high heels on the stairs. Doors opened. Alix appeared, followed by Adam. They were chatting and laughing. Ryder could barely speak. They picnicked in the Lion Meadow, from hampers of smoked salmon, caviar, foie de gras, and raspberries, all beautifully prepared by Mrs Trumpet and nestling in heavy white damask napkins. Ryder ate nothing. She felt sick.

That evening as she and Adam drove back to London, she said, 'I don't want to go to Dingwall Court for the next few months. Father was angry about the whisky. I've had to pay for it.'

'But he's rolling in money.'

'That's not the point. We shouldn't have taken it.'

'This is the first time I've heard you defend him.'

'Because he's right.'

'And I'm not! But how would I know what's right and wrong amongst the rich.' His jaw set. That night Ryder slept in her own narrow bed.

Adam didn't telephone her all day. When she arrived home there was no sign of him. His flat door was maliciously silent. The evening dragged past, as did the next day. She heard nothing all week. The loneliness of those first months in London returned. At night she lay in bed confused and unhappy, listening for footsteps on the stairs. In the mornings she tried to catch sight of him leaving for work. But she never did. Something made her think he wasn't sleeping at home. She felt sick with jealousy.

'If we do split up I'll have to leave this house,' she told Imogen. 'I couldn't go on living here, meeting him on the stairs.' She looked across at her flatmate who was mending her leotards. Would losing Adam mean losing Immy and Alix and the life she'd built for herself?

In the excitement of her first love affair, Ryder had daydreamed through months at Jeremy's typewriter but now the tedium of her job struck her as unbearable. 'I want to give in my notice,' she told him.

'But why, sweetie? Why?'

'I need more involvement. I'm not getting anywhere.'

'Where do you want to go?'

'I wish I knew!'

He sighed. 'Mother will be most upset. Just don't leave me in the lurch, will you?' He gave her a thin smile. 'I've discovered a young actress. Ask her to have lunch with me.' He handed Ryder a piece of paper on which was written: *Imogen Lydden.*

She leaned across the desk and kissed him on the cheek. She'd grown fond of him, as much as it was possible to grow fond of someone who wasn't quite human.

Imogen was euphoric about Jeremy Heythorp. 'I can't think why you want to leave him,' she told Ryder.

'I need a change. I'm no genius but there must be more for me than the keyboard of a typewriter. And don't tell me I'm only depressed because of Adam!'

Alix flung open the flat door. 'If you're thinking of throwing yourselves off Chelsea Bridge, wait for me. I've given up modelling. I wanted to be on the cover of *Vogue*, not parading in sleazy underwear. I'm going to become an agent. I'd be much better on the business side. If you're giving up your job, Ryder, I'll take it.'

'Can you type?'

'I'll learn.'

'You'll be bored.'

'Probably — but I shall be learning my trade.'

Ryder looked at Alix with respect. Imogen could only think of Alix's shattered dream.

It was three weeks before Adam telephoned Ryder, by which time she'd given up hope of hearing from him.

'You don't sound as if you're missing me,' he said sharply.

'I am.' She swallowed as the loneliness of the recent days rolled over her.

'Ryder.' He paused. 'Let's get married!'

She was so excited that afterwards she couldn't remember having said yes, but she presumed she must have because Adam was saying, 'I'll speak to your father this weekend.'

'Do you have to?'

'Of course. It's only proper.'

Whilst Adam cornered her father in the study, Ryder steered her mother into the garden. They had barely crossed the terrace before her father called, 'Carrie, Adam wants to marry Ryder.'

'How exciting!' Her mother hurried to Adam and kissed him on both cheeks.

'But I think Ryder's too young,' her father went on. 'We can't stop them, of course.' He turned to Adam. 'But if you two want a big lavish wedding, here at Dingwall Court, and at my expense, then you have to wait a year.'

'We don't need a big wedding,' said Ryder quickly. 'Do we, Adam?'

He took her hand. 'No.'

She turned to her father as if to say, 'You see.'

But her mother gave a cry of dismay. 'I want a huge wedding. I want to show off our lovely home.'

'No!' Ryder cut in. 'I hate that kind of thing. So does Adam.'

'It's my day too.' Turning her back on her daughter, Carrie entwined her arms around her husband's neck. 'I am the bride's Mom. I know you and Ryder are like peas in a pod, but don't I count?'

'I think we should respect your mother's wishes,' Adam squeezed Ryder's hand. 'After all, you are her only daughter. We mustn't be selfish.'

Paul and Carrie Harding gave an engagement party for Ryder and Adam. They invited five hundred people of which four hundred and fifty were their own friends. Or rather, Paul's business contacts. Three days beforehand, a pale pink marquee festooned with ribbons and roses was erected on the lawn at the Court. It was pink because her mother thought it fitting for a bride and Ryder, not wishing to be called selfish, didn't argue.

Alix wore a bright red satin tube. Immy wore green muslin. Ryder had an off-the-shoulders dress in flounces of pale pink silk, the same shade as the marquee. She'd wanted black silk but her mother had protested and been backed up by Adam. As she looked across at Alix she felt a pang of envy for the confidence to wear something exotic, stunning and wonderfully unsuitable.

'You look lovely, Ryder.' Adam's mother offered her a hard white cheek to kiss.

'Thank you, Mrs Lydden.' She wished Adam had a nicer mother.

'Joyce to you now, dear.'

'Are you pleased I'm going to marry your sister?' Adam asked Leo, who was allowed to stay up for an hour.

'Who am I going to marry?'

'You'll find a nice girl when you're older.'

'I don't want one that cries.'

'Quite right, old chap.' His father ruffled his blond curls as everyone smiled. 'Now, off you go to bed.'

Leo's face puckered. 'Mummy said . . .'

'Bed! This is Ryder's party.' He turned to her. 'I claim the first dance with my daughter.' He took her in his arms. They were tight like a band of steel. 'You're making a mistake,' he said quietly. 'Adam's too weak for you.'

She stiffened. 'Mother's amazed anyone wants me.'

'And you're stupid enough to marry him to prove her wrong.'

'Of course not. I love him. He makes me feel good about myself — which is more than you and mother have ever done.'

He gave a mocking laugh. 'I'll pay for your divorce.'

'There won't be one.' She walked away, leaving him in the centre of the dancefloor.

It was nearly dawn when the last guest left. 'Let's go down to the river,' Adam whispered as her parents disappeared. He took her hand and they slipped across the lawn, passed the band who were packing away their equipment, to the privacy of the rose arbour. 'I've wanted to make love to you all evening.' He kissed her neck, pushing her dress down so that it revealed her naked breasts. 'There's something about you, and the night. And this dress.' He rolled her nipple between his lips, sending shivers through her body.

She ran her hands up the inside of his thighs.

He gasped and went to lay her on the ground.

'I can't,' she whispered.

'Why not?' He unzipped his trousers.

'My dress. It'll get dirty. Mother'll have a fit.'

'Then take it off.'

'I'm sewn into it.'

'Lift it up.' He reached for her amid the flounces of crêpe de chine. The material covered her head. She couldn't see him. She could only feel him. He could have been anyone. For a brief moment she imagined he was the man in the drive.

A week later Adam said, 'I had lunch with your father today. He's offered me a job.'

She remembered the conversation on the dancefloor. 'You're not going to take it?'

'You bet I am! He's going to pay me twice what I earn now.'

'Adam, please don't. You know the way I feel about my father. He sucks people into his power.'

'Don't be so dramatic!' He tossed his briefcase on to

the sofa. 'I know your father used to be tough but you were a child then. You've got to grow up. We have to live and I'm sick of scrimping. I want to be rich. I want to move with rich people — people like your father.'

Ryder burst into tears.

Adam slammed out of the flat.

Half an hour later he returned. 'I'll only take it for a couple of years. Just till we're established.' He took her in his arms. 'I promise.'

When Alix took over at Jeremy's, Ryder was left with nothing to do but arrange the wedding. At the same time Adam started at Harding-Broughton where her father made him work long hours.

'He keeps you late to show us you're in his power,' Ryder told Adam.

'He keeps me late because we're busy,' he snapped. 'Property's up 30 per cent and rising.' He banged the *Evening Standard* down in front of her. 'It's time you stopped misjudging your father.'

HARDING, THE CHILDREN'S FRIEND

Paul Harding, not known as a philanthropist, has surprised competitors by buying condemned houses in an area of Victoria rumoured to be set aside for use as a playground. When questioned about his purchase, Harding told reporters, 'I was a poor kid. I know what it's like to have nowhere to play.'

'I don't believe it,' said Ryder.

He groaned and turned on the television. She opened a magazine but the words blurred before her eyes.

When Immy wasn't attending auditions, she and Ryder spent every day together. Sometimes they took the underground to Bond Street, to meet Alix for lunch, but mostly they wandered down to the King's Road for

85

a browse around the shops, and a plate of spaghetti with a glass of wine.

Then Imogen won a replacement role in a film being shot in India: the original actress had fallen ill. In a whirl of excitement, packing and tears at leaving Tony, she flew off at a week's notice. She wouldn't be back till Christmas. Ryder was thrilled for her. At least she tried to be, but her own days now stretched ahead, interminable and lonely.

Shortly afterwards Alix waltzed in, shouting, 'I've been promoted. I'm now Jeremy's assistant.'

That night Ryder lay beside Adam and wondered if there was anything she could do that someone else couldn't immediately do better.

HARDING-BROUGHTON IN PLAYGROUND KILLING

Paul Harding, the entreprenurial developer, who acquired slum land cheaply on rumours it was designated as a playground, has had the pleasant surprise of discovering that the local area plan includes a shopping mall with high rises. Previous owners are kicking themselves — and asking if Paul Harding had inside information.

'See what I mean!' Ryder thrust the paper under Adam's nose.

He pushed it away. 'If your father hadn't bought the land someone else would have. He's only doing what any businessman does. The Harding Centre will provide work for local people. And there'll be some low cost housing. Everyone's going to gain.'

Carrie Harding spent all her time thinking about the wedding. She made lists of relatives who had to be invited. Lists of friends Adam and Ryder wanted to ask. And lists of business acquaintances Paul insisted were invited. Every morning after breakfast she sat at her desk in the yellow drawing room and added yet more names in her round schoolgirlish handwriting.

'Surely we don't have to have the Podmores!' Ryder protested. 'He's such a desiccated old bore.'

'He's Harding-Broughton's solicitor.'

'And the Squareys! He's a toad.'

'He's the loans manager at the bank. They're financing the Harding Centre. He has to come. I know you didn't want a lavish wedding but I do.'

Ryder flopped down on the sofa. 'I feel brain dead.'

'You'll be all right on the day.'

'It's not that day I'm worried about. It's all the other days. The rest of my life. I feel as though I've missed out. Immy's a success. So's Alix. I've never done anything. I've never even tried to do anything.'

Her mother laid down the list of bridesmaids. 'Ryder, you were an awkward child. You didn't make friends. I despaired of you ever having a boyfriend. Then you met Adam! You blossomed. He's popular and he loves you. But don't forget, most of your friends are his. If you lose him, you'll lose them. He doesn't want a career girl for a wife.'

'How do you know?'

'It's obvious.' Her mother returned to her lists. 'If he did, he'd marry Alix.'

8

Nothing her mother could have said would have made Ryder more insecure. She became convinced that Adam would leave her. The odd niggling doubt she'd had about marrying Adam was pushed aside by the sense of inadequacy which her mother had succeeded in arousing in her. She was lucky to have him. She was lucky to have anyone.

Harding-Broughton was news. The Harding Centre was pictured in every stage of construction. But when word leaked out that the low cost housing was to be scrapped in favour of luxury apartments, irate locals picketed Paul's office. In public, he expressed concern for their welfare. 'In reality, he couldn't give a damn,' Adam told Ryder, laughing.

'But those people have nowhere to go,' she protested.

'Who cares?'

'I do.' She too felt as though she had nowhere to go.

The gossip columns had a field day with Paul Harding as he scaled the dizzy social heights of the Guards' Polo club. He was pictured shaking hands with minor royalty. His wife was featured in *Vogue*. He became a patron of a polo team. The previous summer he'd bought Gatehouse Stables, a Georgian house with stabling for forty ponies just off the road which led to Blacknest Gate.

On a crisp spring afternoon, Ryder and Adam went to the stables with her parents and Major Kelmscott to see the new ponies arrive from Argentina after a month-long boat trip. It was Ryder's first visit to Gatehouse and she liked the place immediately. The stables were mellow brick and set around a courtyard. The house nestled against a backdrop of ancient oaks.

Between the two was an arch rampant with honeysuckle whose tendrils swung in the light breeze. Ryder perched on a low wall, sharing it with clumps of crocuses.

Her mother joined her. 'You look pretty in that blue jacket,' she said.

'I do!'

'Can't I say something nice without you jumping down my throat?'

'Perhaps I'm not used to it.'

Her mother bent down to pick a crocus whose yellow complemented so perfectly the colour of her suit.

A man appeared through the arch in the wall. He was dark and swarthy with a hard, compact body. Ryder recognised Rodolfo Martinez, the Argentinian professional polo player hired by her father for the season. There was a second professional, but he had travelled with the ponies. 'I love Gatehouse already.' Rodolfo waved his arms with Latin enthusiasm. 'It has a good atmosphere.' He turned to her father. 'We're going to make a great team.'

They were interrupted by the arrival of the first horsebox. It lumbered into the stableyard, followed by a second. A third. And a fourth. A girl groom jumped down from each cab. Rodolfo introduced them. They were hardy girls with strong handshakes and permanent suntans from working the winter season in Florida.

'I'm afraid we lost a pony,' said one of the girls. 'It panicked in the storms and broke a leg.'

Paul Harding's eyes narrowed. 'Where was Brendan when this happened? I thought he was meant to be in charge.'

'Brendan? Oh, he was on deck with the ponies. We

all were. They were so crazy with fear we couldn't leave them for a minute.'

The last horsebox lumbered into view. It parked on the other side of the courtyard. The door opened and a figure swung down. He said something to the driver. It sounded to Ryder like, 'I may need a lift out of here.' Then he walked round the front of the vehicle.

She stared at him. It was the man in the drive. She'd have known him anywhere. That debonair sensuality. That defiance. She stepped forward, smiling uncertainly. But he walked straight past her. 'Mr Harding,' he said, 'I'm sorry about the pony. At least it wasn't Bruja. She's the best.'

Her father's face was white with anger but he said nothing. Nervously her mother stepped forward. 'I'm Carrie Harding. That's my daughter, Ryder, and her fiancé, Adam Lydden.'

'Haven't . . . haven't we met before?' said Ryder.

He barely glanced at her. 'I doubt it.'

'Yes we have. I was driving and you were . . .'

'Oh, for God's sake, Ryder!' snapped her father. 'Listen, Brendan, you lost one of my ponies. I call that damned careless.'

'I call it damned lucky we didn't lose more. If I hadn't been on board you would have.'

'He's right, Paul.' Major Kelmscott looked embarrassed. 'Most professionals haven't time to travel with the ponies.'

Patrick gave him a brief nod. 'Mr Harding, have you any idea how horses travel on the boat? They stand on deck in covered crates. They can't turn or lie down. They're sick. They're frightened. They don't understand what's happened to their world. For a month the only exercise they have is a walk round the deck. They hate it.' He paused. 'I don't ride for a man who doesn't have confidence in me.'

There was silence. Ryder watched her father hesitate.

90

She sensed that he longed to sack this arrogant young man but at the same time he wanted his team to win. He held out his hand. 'I look forward to seeing you play for me.'

As they drove away from Gatehouse, her father said, 'I don't like Brendan. What's his history, Algie?'

'His mother was English. She was widowed young and went out to be housekeeper to a polo chum of mine who owned one of those huge sheep stations in Northern Australia. Was she a beauty! Jack left his wife for her. But before they could marry, they were killed in a car crash. Jack's son inherited, and he kicked Patrick off the station.'

'How did he come to be in Argentina?'

'Rodolfo had seen Patrick play polo and given him his address. He turned up out of the blue, having worked his passage. I find him arrogant, but he has guts — and he's a hell of a player.'

Ryder stared out of the window. Who was this man who'd said 'trust Paul Harding to have a dumb bitch daughter who drives around the countryside as if she owns it'?

That night Adam suddenly turned on her. 'Why did you say you'd met that man before?'

'I thought I had.'

'I think you fancy him. I saw the way you looked at him.' He took her by the shoulders. 'I bet you'd like to go to bed with him. I bet you'd like to feel him inside you.'

'Of course I wouldn't.'

'How do I know what you get up to when I'm at work? Who do you play tennis with in the afternoons? Who do you bring back to the flat when I'm out?'

'Adam, I love you.'

'Prove it!'

She undressed slowly. Seductively. As he liked her to do. Keeping on her high heels. Adam sat in an armchair and watched. She unbuttoned her silk blouse. It slithered down her arms. She tossed her belt to one side. With a whisper her skirt slipped from her hips. She arched her back to unhook her bra, thrusting forward her breasts, thrusting out her buttocks.

'Keep the shoes on!' he ordered as she bent to remove them.

She stepped towards him. He ran his hands up the back of her thighs. She knelt. He gripped her body with his knees, rubbing himself against her breasts.

'Do it to me, Ryder!' he whispered hoarsely, twisting his fingers in her hair, moaning softly as her mouth traced a path down his chest. Down. Down. Uninhibited in a way she had never been before, because she wanted to do something so intimate with Adam that it put her out of reach of Patrick Brendan.

Ryder's father talked polo. Her mother talked weddings. Adam talked money. Alix talked about the young actors and actresses she'd discovered. It was now she, not Jeremy, who attended showcase plays, looking for 'fresh flesh'. Ryder had no one to talk to. She stayed in bed till noon, then lay in a scented bath for hours, rubbing rough skin off her feet and watching the time tick by. When she mentioned finding a temporary job, Adam said, 'I don't want my wife to work,' and she remembered what her mother had said about Alix.

Imogen had finished her first film. Those who'd seen the rushes talked of her potential. She was rehearsing Cecily in *The Importance of Being Ernest*. Between her career and Tony she had little free time. Sometimes Ryder met her for lunch at a small Italian restaurant in Covent Garden.

One afternoon she joined her mother at the dressmaker to choose her wedding dress. 'I hate fussy things.' She vetoed a sample of white broderie anglaise which her mother had set aside.

'But I want you in white lace,' protested her mother. 'The marquee is draped with lace.'

'I'm not going to spend my wedding day looking like a cross between Miss Havisham and the Sugar Plum Fairy in order to match a marquee.'

'It's my day too.'

'Then wear it yourself!'

They parted acrimoniously outside the dressmaker, where Griffiths was waiting with the Rolls. Her mother was frosty. She always was when she was thwarted. 'I shouldn't tell the Milnes about Adam's mother being Jewish,' she said, watching Ryder's face register distress.

'They're not racist!'

'Aren't they!' Her mother gave a little mocking laugh. 'I was raised in Prairieville. You've only been there for holidays.'

Ryder didn't believe her, because she didn't want to believe her, but that didn't stop her from being especially tender with Adam that night.

'Your father wants us to watch the polo this afternoon,' said Adam one hot August Sunday.

She thought of Patrick Brendan. 'I'd rather not.'

'We've only been once this season. You were mad about it last year.'

Alix looked up from her magazine. 'Who's mad about polo? Oh, do let's go! I love it.'

'It's the players you love,' said Adam.

'Without players there'd be no polo. Immy! Stop counting your freckles. We're off to Windsor.'

Ryder went too. She had to, or she'd have spoiled Adam's day and been accused of being selfish. The park was showing the effects of summer. The trees looked tired. The ground was dry. Too many hooves had kicked up too many divots. In the stand, spectators fanned themselves with their programmes. Beside the score board the umpires waited in the shade. To Ryder's relief there was no sign of Patrick although her father's ponies stood in lines nearby, their manes clipped and tails plaited.

'I'd love to ride one,' Adam told Ryder. 'Just for a few minutes.'

'You'd have to be a very good horseman, and you wouldn't even ride with father.'

'I suppose you think that because we were poor we never learned to do things rich kids did.'

'Oh, for God's sake, Adam!' snapped Alix. 'Stop getting at Ryder. You only want to ride the pony to prove you're not a puppet.'

'Don't shout at me! You're just as envious as I am of her money.'

Ryder turned to Alix. 'You can't be envious of me.'

'Can't I!'

Adam was calling to one of the grooms. She came over, leading a black pony. 'I'm Mr Harding's future son-in-law,' he said, 'and I'd like to ride one of the ponies.'

'They're about to play a chukka. You might upset them.'

'I only want to get up on one.'

'You'd have to have Mr Harding's permission.'

'I have it.'

'You don't!' Ryder cut in.

'How would you know?' He reached for the reins.

'Adam, leave it!'

He grabbed again. The animal reared. She bucked and snorted.

'What the hell do you think you're doing?' Patrick seized the reins.

'You'll regret being rude to me when you lose your job, Brendan,' said Adam.

'And you'll be sorry if you don't keep away from Bruja.' Patrick walked away, the pony following.

94

Adam turned on Ryder. 'You made me look a bloody fool.'

'You are a fool.' She headed for the stand, expecting him to shout at her. But he didn't. He followed in silence.

Seven riders appeared on the ground. They were joined by the two umpires in black and white shirts. Then Bruja burst through the crowd bucking furiously.

'Patrick Brendan, one of the most promising young players we've seen at Smith's Lawn this year, seems to be having a bit of trouble with Bruja,' came over the loudspeaker.

The other players circled as Patrick fought to control his mount, forcing her on with the grip of his knees until he brought her in line with the rest of his team. Then he gave Rodolfo the thumbs up.

The umpire tossed the ball between the teams. No sooner had it left his hand than the ponies surged forward. Rodolfo hit the ball. They raced after it. An opponent rode off him. Back the ball went. Paul hit it. It shot into the crowd. A foul. The umpire bowled it in. Patrick hit a backhand. He raced after it. Hit another. A goal! The crowd cheered.

The teams changed ends. The ball was thrown in. Patrick again. Straight down the field. Another backhand. No one could catch him. The ball lay ahead. He rose in the saddle. Twisted. Swung back his stick. But at that moment Bruja's reins caught on an advancing pony's saddle. She forgot her schooling and remembered only that someone had grabbed at her. In panic, she reared. Her back hooves skidded on the dry turf. She flayed the air and turned — and toppled over backwards on top of Patrick.

9

The umpire blew his whistle. The players skidded to a halt. Bruja staggered to her feet and limped away. But Patrick lay motionless. A doctor raced across the ground. He knelt beside Patrick. A moment later he beckoned for a stretcher.

'*Ladies and gentlemen, as you can see Patrick Brendan has been injured. At present we don't know how seriously . . .*'

A man in front of Ryder said, 'Wouldn't surprise me if he's broken his back,' and his neighbour replied, 'Damned shame when a young man ends up in a wheelchair.'

Ryder pushed her way down the stand. By the time she reached the ambulance, Patrick was being lifted inside. His eyes were closed and his face was grey, though the only sign of injury was a cut across the eyebrow.

'Is he badly hurt?' she asked anxiously, watching a thin trickle of blood roll down the side of his face.

'He'll be X-rayed at the hospital,' replied the ambulance man.

Adam caught up with her as she reversed her car. 'Where the hell are you going now?' he demanded.

'To the hospital.'

'But why?'

'Because I feel responsible. I told you not to touch the pony.'

He grabbed the car door. 'If you weren't so attracted to Patrick Brendan you wouldn't care.'

She drove off, nearly wrenching his arm from its socket.

The Heatherwood Hospital was sprawled across a corner of the roundabout near Ascot racecourse. It was a hotchpotch of buildings, some redbrick Victorian and some one-storey Nissen hut, all stretching back through the pine trees. When Ryder reached Casualty, Patrick was being examined by a doctor.

'Are you a relative?' asked the receptionist, filling in a card.

'My father is his patron — his employer.'

'Does he have any relatives?'

'I don't know.'

Rodolfo joined her. 'I didn't expect to find you here,' he said acidly, stepping in to answer the receptionist's queries.

When he'd finished, Ryder said, 'You've every reason to be angry. Patrick's your protégé. But Adam didn't mean any harm. He didn't think.'

'People like him never do. But at least you had the decency to come here. If you want to help, wait till I return. I have a match at four. I'll be straight back. I want to know everything the doctor says.' He walked away.

Ryder waited for an hour. Doctors came and went. Nurses hurried past. On the other side of the room a group sat in awkward silence. In their midst an old woman was crying into her knitting.

'Come on, Grandma, we'll go home and have a nice cup of tea,' said a young girl. 'And some of those digestive biscuits. Grandpa always liked digestive biscuits.'

Ryder looked away.

The doctor finally appeared as Rodolfo walked through the swing doors. 'Mr Brendan's had a very bad fall,' he told them. 'Apart from the concussion, he has an injury to his back.'

'Will he play polo again?' asked Ryder.

'Before he does anything he has to regain consciousness.'

Rodolfo went to see Patrick. Ryder left. There was nothing else for her to do. Outside she was surprised to find dusk was falling. Her car, previously surrounded by others, stood solitary and cold in the lamplight. She drove back to London, her thoughts detached from the motorway and the other vehicles and the act of driving. Adam was right. She was attracted to Patrick.

When she drew up outside the flat she realised that she had no idea if Adam was here or with her parents. And she didn't care. She took her shoes off so as to make no noise and crept up the stairs. Relief came over her as she turned the corner outside his flat. Suddenly his door was flung open and he stepped out. He raised an arm. She ducked. But he didn't hit her. He half fell, his arms around her neck, smothering her in whisky fumes. 'Ryder, don't leave me! Please!'

How could she be angry when he was so unexpectedly vulnerable?

When Adam left for work, she telephoned the hospital. Patrick was still unconscious. She made a point of phoning every couple of days after that but there was no change.

Arrangements for the wedding progressed. Frequently Ryder had the sensation that the event had nothing to do with her. She avoided another showdown with her mother by agreeing to everything, except for the lacy dress. Often when she was at the dressmaker, being fitted into her plain cream silk, or listening to her mother talk about the guests, she'd think of Patrick, unconscious, perhaps crippled, and she'd blush at the frivolity of her existence.

Immy's film was premiered at the Odeon, Leicester

Square. Jeremy took them all in his party. As they drew up outside the crowd pushed forward. There were cries of 'Imogen Lydden!'

'She looks divine,' Jeremy whispered proudly to Alix. 'You were right to put her in the Great Gatsby style. We must wean her off the ethnic doll look.'

'You make my sister sound like a commodity,' said Adam crossly.

'My dear boy, she is. And it's up to us, her agents, to market her.'

'Well, don't change her too much,' said Ryder, as they took their seats in the auditorium.

When the film began she kept thinking, that's my friend Imogen up there, but as it progressed, she forgot. When the credits rolled the audience buzzed. Even the critics smiled.

'I wish I could have invited Tony but Jeremy wouldn't hear of it,' Imogen confided to Ryder in the cloakroom. 'He said the press would slaughter me, because Tony's older and married.' For a moment Immy looked sad and lost. Then she added, 'When I become really famous I shall ask who I damn well please!'

The first stage of the Harding Centre was completed. Twenty luxury flats with 'panoramic views of Central London' came on the market. At the opening ceremony guests sipped pink champagne and rubbed shoulders with the Minister of Housing whilst the pride of the penthouses was televised for the evening news.

'Have all the flats been sold?' Ryder asked Adam, as they drove home.

'Not yet. But I bet they're all sold tomorrow.'

Ten days later the *Evening Standard* enquired, '*Luxury flats stick; has property reached its ceiling?*'

Adam came home exhausted. 'Your father's going crazy about the article,' he said, collapsing on to the sofa as Ryder poured him a gin and tonic.

'Is it true?'

'Hell, no!' He swilled the ice round the glass, then downed the contents.

'It's just some smart-arse journalist covering his tracks in case there's a slight levelling off.' He held out his glass. 'I'd love another.'

But the newspapers didn't let up.

IS HARDING CENTRE A WHITE ELEPHANT?

Flats dropped by 10 per cent as Harding admits, 'I overpriced.'

Ryder planned to cook a special dinner for Adam and he promised to be home by eight. She spent the morning choosing recipes and the afternoon shopping. They didn't have a liquidiser so she had to sieve the boiled leeks and potatoes to make vichyssoise. When the soup was ready to be chilled she garnished it prettily with parsley. Then she flattened the veal for the Wiener schnitzel, coated it with breadcrumbs and left it in the fridge whilst she laid the table. She used the linen tablenapkins and the last two smart red candles, fitted into old champagne bottles.

The new potatoes were boiling. The water for the broccoli was bubbling. The wine was in the fridge. She lay in a delicious scented bath. By eight o'clock she was ready. She wore a wrap-over black silk dress, her gold charm bracelet, and the subtle make up Adam preferred. The candles were lit. The chilled soup was on the table. The potatoes and broccoli were keeping warm in the oven. The heated butter waited for the veal. As she put the finishing touches to the table, she pictured their married dinner parties. She would sit at one end of a long mahogany table, such as her parents possessed, whilst the guests lifted their glasses to her culinary expertise.

At half past eight, she returned the soup to the fridge. One of the candles began to splutter. She pinched it out. At nine, she rang his office. The night reception said he'd just left. Quickly she relit the candle and returned the soup to the table. Then she reheated the butter and began to fry the schnitzels. She arranged them on the plate. They looked deliciously golden. She decorated them with sliced lemon and put the plate in the oven.

By the time Adam arrived Ryder was nearly in tears. The candles were gutted. The parsley had sunk into the soup, the schnitzels had turned to leather, and the lemon slices had shrivelled. He opened the wine. 'I couldn't eat. I'm dead beat. We've had to sell ten flats at a 20 per cent reduction. Your father's livid but that fat little bastard Squarey's screaming for his money. The loan was made on a forward prediction of property increasing by 25 per cent. Without that figure there'd be no Harding Centre.'

She ate an overdone potato. 'The bank have made a fortune out of Harding-Broughton in the past.'

'True.' He finished the bottle of wine and opened another. 'But Squarey's shitting himself in case your father's overstretched. We've had to agree to pay over all monies instantly. That means a sale's completed at midday and by lunchtime Squarey has the cash.' He reached for Ryder's hand. 'Sorry about dinner.'

Ryder and Adam were to live in the attic flat until they could afford to buy a house. By lucky coincidence Jonathan decided to move in with his girlfriend. Alix and Immy arranged to move downstairs and take over his lease. Ryder began to plan how she would reorganise the flat. She was measuring the bedroom to see which way a double bed would fit when the phone rang. It was the Heatherwood to say Patrick had regained consciousness.

There was a crash at the front door and Alix flew in.

'Left my keys behind. Hey, Ryder, you look guilty. What have you been up to?'

'Nothing.'

'Liar! I heard the phone click.'

'It was only the hospital to say that that polo player has come round.'

'You like him, don't you?' Alix stood in front of her. 'Don't worry. I won't tell Adam — or Imogen. But you should have a serious think about getting married. You don't want to end up like my parents. Powerful but dissatisfied woman with less intelligent, weak man.'

Ryder stood by the window, listening to Alix's footsteps race down the stairs. She looked down on the gardens where she and Adam had first played tennis. Alix was wrong. She didn't understand the glow of suddenly being wanted because Alix had always been wanted. A gust of wind brought down the leaves from the trees. They were golden leaves. When they came again she'd be a married woman. She twisted her engagement ring. She'd be Mrs Adam Lydden. The leaves rolled across the grass. She thought of Fox Lake and its golden flotillas. She hadn't been back there in her mind for a long time.

The telephone interrupted her. 'You are coming to Dingwell Court tonight, aren't you?' said her mother. 'We have to discuss your bouquet.'

'Can't we do it now, on the telephone?'

There was an injured silence. Then her mother said, 'I thought it would be nice for us to talk. Your father's bound to be late. It's completion day on the Harding Centre.'

'Surely you have Leo!'

'Oh, darling, don't be like that!'

She stood at the window again, frowning. Then she hurried into her room, tossed a few clothes into a suitcase and headed downstairs to her car. As she sped along the Cromwell Road, towards the motorway, she flicked on the radio. An announcer was saying, '*And now we bring you the latest on the Middle East crisis. Some 20,000 Egyptian troops are advancing across the Sinai towards Israel.*'

The orthopaedic ward was a one-storey building set back amongst the trees. As she opened the door, an old man grumbled, 'Visiting's not till after lunch.'

'I have permission.'

She ignored his disbelief and walked down the central aisle. The men lay on their beds in their striped pyjamas. Some had their legs strapped to the ceiling. Others were hidden under bandages. Patrick was at the far end, lying on his back, totally motionless, staring at the ceiling.

She stood at the end of his bed. 'I know you don't want to see me.'

'I don't.'

'I came to say I'm sorry for what happened.'

His eyes swivelled to her. 'Listen, Miss Harding! Your father's lawyer has just told me that the gentleman's agreement I had to play for the Harding team is worth nothing in a court of law. Your father stopped paying me on the day of my accident. He intends to give me nothing, other than my return fare to Buenos Aires. I could rot here, courtesy of the National Health, until I die, and he wouldn't give a damn. Now, get out!'

'There's no need to shout.'

'Do you think I want your apology when I've lost my livelihood?' He grimaced with pain as he tried to sit up. 'You Hardings are all the same but one day I'll make you pay. Not just for what you and your idiot boyfriend did to me — but for what your father did to George Broughton.'

'George Broughton was my father's best friend. They started Harding-Broughton.'

'George Brendan Broughton was my father — and your father's dishonesty drove him to suicide!'

10

The sanctity of her father's friendship with George Broughton had been part of Ryder's childhood. She'd envied its closeness, questioned her own difficulty in making friends, and admired the strength of feeling which made a man like her father still care after all these years: it was one of the things about her father which she'd always admired.

She drove straight to Dingwall Court. As she entered the hall, her mother hurried from the drawing room. 'Oh, it's you. I hoped it was Paul. Mr Squarey's been trying to reach him.'

'He's probably in a meeting.'

'The office haven't seen him since early morning. Oh, Ryder, I'm terrified he's been taken ill. He's been so tense lately. I called the police but he's not on any hospital list.'

Ryder set her suitcase down. 'Why the panic? It's barely three o'clock.'

Her mother's eyes filled with tears. 'Because he collected a million pounds from Podmore at noon and he never arrived at the bank.'

The house was silent after her mother went to lie down. Ryder stood on the threshold of her father's study, faced by his desk and empty chair. The room was in semi-darkness. The heavy rust velvet curtains were partially drawn to keep the sunlight off the antique furniture. It was a sanctum to which she had rarely been invited.

The desk phone rang. She answered it. 'Adam! Oh, thank goodness it's you. Where's my father?'

'That's what Squarey wants to know! All hell's let loose. The money's missing. I'll call you later.'

She replaced the receiver and picked up the photograph of her father and George Broughton. Now she could see a similarity between Patrick and his father.

She had just replaced the photograph when she heard the French windows in the drawing room open. She stepped back into the shadows. Light footsteps crossed the floor. They approached the study. Hesitated. Then her father flitted across the room and lifted a painting from the wall. Behind it was a safe. Ryder had no idea of its existence. She watched as he spun the dial. The lock clicked and the door swung open. He reached inside for a bundle of papers, stuffed them into his jacket pocket, and closed the safe, quickly replacing the picture.

Then he turned and saw Ryder. 'What the hell are you doing here?'

'Waiting for you to phone. Mother's frantic. Everyone's been looking for you, including Squarey.'

'That greedy little toad. If he hadn't pushed so hard I might have ridden the storm.' He crossed to the door.

Ryder followed. 'You must see mother. She's convinced you're ill.'

'I can't stop now.' He hurried through the drawing room. 'Did she call the police?'

'And the hospitals.'

'Damn!'

'What did you expect?'

He stopped just inside the French windows and studied Ryder as if weighing up her trustworthiness. 'I'm in trouble. Serious trouble. I'm overstretched at the bank. The Harding Centre won't sell. The bottom's falling out of the market. I have to get away while I can — with what I can. You must look after Carrie. I'm depending on you.'

She raged at the casual way he disposed of their future. 'You can't walk out. She'll fall apart. What about Leo? My wedding?'

'I have to.' His jaw set. 'I'll break anyone who gets in my way.' He stepped out on to the terrace. 'That includes you.'

An upstairs window flew open. Her mother leaned out, clutching a peach peignoir around her shoulders. 'Paul! Darling. Wait!'

He looked up, forcing a smile. 'I'm in a hurry. Go back to your rest.'

'Are you all right?'

'Of course.' He gave her a jolly wave. 'I'll phone you later. I won't be in for dinner.' The window closed. He turned to Ryder, lowering his voice. 'I'm going to Spain. I'll send for your mother and Leo. There's a thousand pounds taped inside the back of my leatherbound Johnson's dictionary. Use it for their fares and keep the rest. If the police come, pretend you know nothing.' He set off across the lawn.

She shouted after him, 'So you're leaving mother to face the music. If you've made mistakes, you should square up to them. Because they're yours. Not hers. Not ours.'

He spun round, his heel cutting into the grass. 'And lose all I've worked for? All I've planned and schemed and risked for? To be poor again! Not bloody likely!'

Ryder sat at the study window watching the evening mist roll up over the lawns. Her mother was asleep. Leo was having his bath. Everything seemed ominously still. Even the drift of white chrysanthemums had a curious painted quality.

She went upstairs. Her mother was sitting up,

propped against the peach satin cushions, looking helpless and feminine.

'I'm sorry I was silly,' she said. 'I don't know why I was so worried. Don't tell your father. He'll think I don't trust him.'

Ryder shrugged. If she'd spoken her anger would have poured out. So she kept silent, and felt even more manipulated by her father.

Her mother smiled in blissful ignorance. She flicked the television remote control and settled back to watch the news.

The newscaster looked suitably grim.

'*The Arab-Israeli conflict continues,*' he said. '*Western economies are being badly shaken.*'

The front door bell resounded through the house. Carrie smiled hopefully. 'Perhaps that's Paul.'

'I don't think so.' Ryder kept her eyes on the television where the picture had cut to a war-torn desert.

There was other news. Then the weather. Ryder yawned.

'*And now we bring you a news flash. The millionaire property developer, Paul Harding, has been arrested at Heathrow Airport. Mr Harding, who is wanted for questioning in connection with the disappearance of a large sum of money, was attempting to board a flight to Malaga.*'

'Paul!' her mother screamed. 'It's not true. You wouldn't leave me.'

'Of course he wouldn't.' Ryder gripped her mother by the shoulders. 'He was going to phone you from Spain this evening.'

'You mean, you knew where he'd gone? He told you but not me?'

There was a knock on the door and Mrs Trumpet came in. 'Madam . . . Miss Ryder, the police are downstairs. They have a warrant to search the house.'

Ryder stood up. 'I'll go down if you could look after mother. She has some sedatives in the bathroom.'

She hurried from the room without looking at her mother because she couldn't bear the hurt in those blue Milne eyes. Below, she could hear the police searching her father's study. She went down to meet them.

A heavy, jowled man in a trenchcoat and scuffed shoes who could have doubled for Walter Matthau was directing a dozen others. 'Check the desk for hidden drawers. Tip everything into black bags. If we can't open the safe, we'll have to blow it.' He looked up. 'Miss Harding. I'm Detective Chief Inspector Cargill. Your father's been arrested. We have a warrant to search the house and to take away any relevant papers. I'd like to talk to your mother.'

'She's too upset. She can't see anyone.'

'Then you can help us. Who else is in the house apart from your mother, the housekeeper, a nanny, a governess, your brother and yourself?'

'No one.'

'When did you last see your father?'

'About two and a half hours ago. He came back, just for a few minutes.'

'Did you speak to him?'

'No. I mean, yes. He just said he was going out and would phone later.'

'Did he take anything away?'

She hesitated.

'Miss Harding, you won't help your father or yourself by not telling the truth.'

'He took some papers.' Why should she lie to protect a man who left them to face his music?

The police departed carrying a dozen plastic sacks full of papers. Outside in the drive journalists and cameramen had gathered. They shouted questions to the officers. 'Is it true Harding only had half the money on him? What do you think he's done with the rest? Will you oppose bail?' They sounded like a pack of wolves.

'Your father will appear at Bow Street Magistrates

Court tomorrow, morning,' the inspector told her. He paused, then added gently, 'This falls hard on a family. Believe me, I appreciate that.'

She looked away. She wasn't going to cry in front of him.

Alix was the first to telephone. She wanted to cancel her dinner date and drive out immediately but Ryder said, 'Don't worry. Adam will come.'

Imogen rang from the theatre between acts. 'What hell for you,' she commiserated.

The phone rang again. It was Jeremy. Then Lady Heythorp. Then the *Daily Mail*, the *Daily Express*, and the *News of the World*. In a moment of calm she dialled Adam.

'When are you coming out?' she asked him.

'I'm sorry, darling, I'm so tired I'd fall asleep at the wheel.'

'Please!' The word choked in her throat. 'I need you.'

'It's been a helluva day at the office. You can't imagine.'

'It's been a helluva day here!'

'Ryder, don't be like that. I know I ought to come but . . . Look, I'll see you in court tomorrow. That's a promise.'

She sat at the desk, her head resting in her hands.

'I've made you some hot soup, dear.' Mrs Trumpet stood in the doorway bearing a tray. 'You're going to need your strength.'

Just before ten-thirty the Harding Rolls drew up outside Bow Street Magistrates Court, a stone building on a corner opposite Covent Garden Opera House. There was a group of reporters near the telephone boxes in the pedestrian walkway. They hurried forward. When she saw them Carrie Harding clung to the back seat, her eyes brimming with tears.

'Stay in the car,' ordered Ryder, searching wildly for Adam. 'Griffiths will drive you around. I'll go in.'

'I can't do that. Paul needs me. He never told me he was going to Spain. He told you. I mustn't fail him again.'

'He didn't want to worry you.' Ryder took her mother's arm and steered her through the curious.

The building smelled of hot radiators and lino. There was a bench by the wall where barristers conferred with their clients. They sat down. Beyond them a young boy smoked defiantly whilst a motherly barrister tried to coach his responses.

'Do I look all right?' Her mother twisted her hands inside her gloves. 'No bags under my eyes?'

'None.' But Ryder was lying.

Mr Podmore, the solicitor, hurried into the building. He was a tall, skeletal man with thin rubbery lips. He was followed by two gowned barristers. 'Mrs Harding,' he said, 'you realise that today the magistrate will merely decide the date for the committal hearing.'

'Will they let Paul come home?'

'We'll apply for bail.'

'He's innocent. I know my husband.'

Podmore didn't reply.

The courtroom was on the ground floor. It was wood panelled and carpeted, with wooden benches at the back and a dock separated by green railings in the centre. Ryder and her mother took their places on a bench. Behind them the press talked loudly. Ryder tried to listen to her mother whilst her eyes raked the courtroom for Adam. At that moment, she hated him for letting her down and she hated her father for subjecting her mother to this ordeal.

The magistrate took his place at the front of the court. A side door opened and her father was led into the dock. He looked tired and dishevelled. Ryder's anger

110

dissolved. Her mother smiled and stood up as if to go to him but Ryder held her back.

The Clerk of the Court asked, 'Are you Paul Harding?'

He swayed between the green railings. 'Yes.'

'Please sit down.'

The Crown prosecutor was a huge man. He towered over everyone as he addressed the magistrate. 'This is an extremely serious case. Not only is the defendant accused of stealing a very large sum of money, but he was arrested when attempting to flee the country. He has been charged with theft. Further charges are likely.' He paused. 'I understand there is an application for bail. The prosecution object strongly. Firstly, a great deal of money is still missing. Secondly, he has worldwide connections and funds abroad. Thirdly, if free he is capable of destroying evidence of which only he knows the location. Finally, he has a villa in Spain — a country with which Great Britain has no extradition treaty at present.'

Her mother was tearing her handkerchief into shreds. She turned to Ryder. 'It's all lies.'

Her father's counsel rose to his feet. 'My client was not running from any crime,' he thundered. 'He had been working very hard and he was merely planning to spend a few days at his villa in Spain. His home is here. His wife and family.' He waved in their direction. 'His daughter is due to be married soon.' Ryder blushed as eyes swivelled her way. 'Mr Harding has no intention of fleeing the country and would be happy to surrender his passport and to report to the authorities as often as they require.'

The magistrate frowned. 'Mr Harding, I've listened to your counsel's plea but I agree with prosecuting counsel. I therefore remand you in custody for one week.'

Her mother cried out and slid sideways. Her father turned white. As he was led from the room, he shouted, 'Look after her, Ryder! Take her home!'

As Ryder steadied her mother on to the bench, a second pair of hands joined hers. She looked up. 'Oh, Adam, thank goodness you've come!'

Her mother went straight to bed, cosseted by Mrs Trumpet. The telephone rang incessantly. Alix. Immy. Hetty. Then endless reporters. Finally Ryder left the receiver off. She and Adam wandered round the house, trailed by Leo until nanny fetched him. They went up to the spare bedroom which had been allocated for wedding presents. There were boxes of cut glass, china, linen and vases, all labelled with the sender's name.

'We'll have to postpone the wedding,' said Ryder.

'Mother'll be furious. She's bought a new hat.'

'I've bought a wedding dress.'

He put his arms around her. 'Oh, why did this have to happen now? Everything was so perfect.'

She buried her face in his shoulder. 'Let's go to bed. I want you to hold me. I couldn't bear to sleep alone tonight.'

They went to her room. Boldly. Not tiptoeing as they used to. Not worrying about creaky floorboards. Undressing quickly, they climbed into her narrow single bed, giggling at the lack of space.

'Do you think missionaries were as cramped as this on those boats that took them to the New World?' she said.

'They couldn't have had less space.' He rolled over on top of her. 'Or they wouldn't even have been able to do the missionary position.'

'It must have been quite exciting.' She moved under him.

He nuzzled her neck. 'Covert fumbling on a leaky ship?'

'Being pinned underneath the man you love.'

'Fighting your way through calico nightdresses.'

'The repressed sexuality.' She bit his ear lobe.

112

'Pretending not to do it.' He arched his back.

'Pretending not to enjoy it.' She reached up to him.

Mr Podmore arrived next morning. Clutching his brief-case, he slipped through the front door like a ghost on the run. 'I saw your father an hour ago,' he told Ryder as she led him into the drawing room. 'He's bearing up. Brixton isn't a cheerful place, but I'm hopeful that our appeal for bail will succeed the next week.'

'Don't raise my mother's hopes. Not unless you're sure.'

He settled into the pale lemon sofa and opened his briefcase. 'Here's a letter for her.'

'She's asleep. I'll take it up later.'

'Oh dear.' His rubbery lips twitched. 'I have to talk to her. She may not understand your father's letter.'

'She's sedated. You'll have to tell me.'

He hesitated.

'Mr Podmore, I'm not asking you to endanger your professional integrity, I merely want to help my mother.'

'Very well.' He sighed. 'The bank have issued civil proceedings against your father to recover the missing funds.'

'Surely he's innocent until proven guilty?'

'The civil charge doesn't depend on the criminal case. The bank lent Harding-Broughton a great deal of money. They want it back, whether or not your father has committed a crime.'

'Why can't he sell the Centre?'

'It's incomplete and with property falling, it doesn't cover the loan.'

'What are you trying to tell me, Mr Podmore?'

'That this house may have to be sold, together with Gatehouse Stables.'

'What about my mother? Where's she going to go? How's she going to live?'

'I'm sorry.' He shrugged. 'Of course, it'll take at least six months for the bank to obtain judgment.'

'But I thought men like my father put assets in their wife's name.'

'Mr Harding found it hard to trust.'

'You mean, he didn't put anything in her name in case she left him?'

'I'm afraid so.' He closed his briefcase.

'What about cash?' asked Ryder.

'He overstretched to build the Harding Centre. Oh, he has some, of course. I'm not at liberty to reveal how much, but it isn't a lot. Not for a man with his commitments.' He closed his briefcase. 'Not for a man in need of top legal advice!'

Her mother was dozing. She sat up as Ryder came into her bedroom. 'Who's downstairs?'

'Podmore. He brought you this.'

Ryder walked over to the window as her mother ripped feverishly at the envelope.

'He doesn't want me to visit him in prison yet,' said her mother.

'He's right. It would upset you.'

'But what's this! He says we may have to sell Dingwall Court. I don't understand.' She looked at Ryder, almost crying with confusion. 'He talks of economising. He says I must dismiss the staff. But I can't run this big house on my own. And who's going to look after Leo? The governess won't bath him and nanny can't teach him.'

'He can go to the local school.'

'Oh, don't start that now!'

'He'll be much better,' said Ryder. 'I would have been much better.'

But her mother wasn't listening. She was crying into the satin cushions. 'I don't understand. How can it all go so quickly? What am I going to do? I don't know how to manage these things. Paul always did it. I can't

114

survive without him. Oh, why did everything go wrong? Oh, God!'

'Mummy, don't cry. I'll help you.'

'But you've got Adam. You're getting married.'

'We've postponed the wedding.'

'You'll be back to London. I'll be all alone.'

'I'll stay till after the weekend. We'll sort things out.' Ryder walked to the door. 'I'll tell Mrs Trumpet about the economies.'

Ryder was drained. She was exhausted. But she couldn't go to bed. She had to wait up for Adam. So she prowled around the house, picking things up, then putting them down again, steeling herself to telephone her grandparents with the bad news.

Her grandfather answered on the first ring. 'Ryder, honey, we was just talking about your wedding.'

'Grandpa, my father's been arrested.'

'Why, that no good slumlord! I knew he'd ruin my little girl's life. Put her on the line. Let me talk with her.'

'She's asleep. I'm calling because I didn't want you to hear the bad news from someone else.'

'You're to come home to Prairieville where you belong. You, Carrie, and little Leo.'

'We can't come now. Father may get bail next week '

'Goddamned scumbag! Hard labour's what he deserves.'

She sat at the desk, picturing the scene at Scot's Farm. Her grandfather would be pacing the old wooden living room floor whilst her grandmother, hands covered in dough, would try to reason with him. Then she opened the top drawer and took the key to the wine cellar. A case of Chateau Latour was the nearest to the steps. She took two bottles.

The wine was deep and red, with a warm, curranty, cedar flavour. She was into the second bottle when the phone rang.

'Ryder,' said Adam, 'you're drunk.'

'So would you be in my position. Adam, you are coming tonight, aren't you?'

'Darling, I'm tired. I've only just got in. I'll see you here tomorrow. We'll have a lovely weekend.'

'I promised mother I'd stay at the Court till Sunday.'

'But that's four days! She doesn't need you for that long, she's got a house full of servants.'

'Not for much longer. Adam, you will come on Friday, won't you?'

'I suppose so. But it's not much fun there, is it?'

'Fun! I don't know what that word means any more.' She drank the rest of the bottle and lay down on the sofa.

'Miss Ryder!' Mrs Trumpet was shaking her. 'Lady Heythorp is here to see you.'

'What?' She was lying on the sofa, fully clothed. Her head was splitting and her mouth felt like the inside of an exhaust pipe.

'I'm taking you out to lunch.' The old lady spun her wheelchair into the centre of the room. 'It'll do you good. I've booked a table at The Compleat Angler.'

'I couldn't eat.' Ryder dragged herself upright. 'And I couldn't face all those people. My father often went there.'

'Why should you be ashamed? You haven't hurt anyone. That's what I told Jeremy, years ago when the newspapers published a letter he'd written to a boyfriend. I made him go out to lunch with me. Face up to your accusers, and they'll leave you alone — especially if you're with a respectable, titled old lady.' She moved her wheelchair near to the sofa and prodded Ryder with her walking stick. 'Hurry up! And don't drink any more.'

Ryder rose unsteadily from the sofa. 'A parent in prison is an extenuating circumstance.' She tottered towards the door. 'Don't take it personally, Lady Heythorp, but I think I'm going to be sick.'

11

Ryder didn't return to London with Adam on Sunday night. She couldn't leave her mother.

'You did promise,' he said, as he tossed his case into the car.

'I know. I'm sorry.'

'So when are you coming back?'

'Father appears before the magistrate again next week. Mother's pinning her hopes on him being released on bail. If he isn't, I'll ask Grandpa and Grandma Milne to come over. They'll be through harvesting by then.'

'That could take weeks!' He sighed.

'I have to come back on Thursday to move flats. Harding-Broughton want ours back. I'll stay up for a couple of days.' She laid her hand on his arm. 'Whatever happens.'

He stepped into his car. 'I need you too, Ryder. Don't forget that.' He roared off before she could answer, his tyres sending gravel leaping into the rhododendrons.

The rhododendrons! How Patrick Brendan must be laughing.

Paul Harding was remanded in custody for a further two weeks. Ryder brought the news to her mother who had remained at Dingwall Court, too upset to attend.

'I must go to him,' said her mother through her tears.

'He doesn't want to see any of us. Not in prison. Not yet.'

Ryder had to steel herself to return to London. Her mother wailed. 'Surely you're not going? Not now Paul hasn't come home?'

'I have to move my things down to Adam's flat today. I told you we're moving out of ours.'

'Can't Imogen and Alix arrange it?'

'They have. But I need to check. Also, I promised Adam I'd stay up for a few days.' She felt so guilty that she couldn't bear to look at her mother's face, so she hurried out, calling, 'I'll phone you this evening.'

The London house was quiet. Ryder climbed the familiar stairs. It seemed a lifetime since she'd hurried down them on her way to the Heatherwood Hospital. Alix and Immy had cleared the attic. The shelves were bare. The coathangers swung free. Already dust was settling and dead flies clustered on the window sill. It was no longer their home.

On the table was a note and two sets of keys.

Dear Ryder,
We've taken everything. Leave your keys with ours. See you downstairs.
Love, Alix and Imogen

Adam's flat stank of cigarettes and stale wine. The sitting room was littered with empty bottles, dirty glasses and overflowing ashtrays. Her clothes were piled on his bed. It looked as though he'd slept on top of them. She started to pack her summer clothes away.

Imogen burst into the flat. 'Hello, stranger! Sorry about the mess. Alix and Adam got legless last night.' She tossed her bag on to a chair. 'They were drowning their sorrows — or rather, Adam was. He's missing your constant attention. Oh, Ryder, I'm so sorry about your father. It's horrid for your mother.' She paused. 'And tough on you. They're all so dependant on you, my brother included. Is there anything I can do to help?'

'Have lunch with me and talk about normal things.'

'I have a matinee. I just popped in to say hello. But we can have breakfast tomorrow. There's a place just opened where they do wonderful croissants. Oh, hell! Look at the time!' Immy grabbed her white leather jacket. 'If I get nominated for an Oscar will you come to the awards with me?'

'If I can.'

'What do you mean?'

'I might not have the fare. And there's this business about my father. In any case, Alix will go. She's your agent.'

'Alix — but she scares me now. She's become so determined. I'm afraid I'll let her down.' Imogen opened the door. 'I've missed you, Ryder. We've all missed you.'

Ryder sorted her possessions and cleaned up the flat as she waited for Adam to telephone. But time ticked by. Finally she dialled Adam's office.

A secretary answered. 'Adam Lydden doesn't work here any more.'

'When did he leave?'

'This morning.'

The phone rang as soon as she replaced the receiver.

'Adam . . . ? Oh, it's you, Mummy. I know I said I'd phone but I meant this evening. How do you know the other children hit Leo? Maybe he fell over. No, I'm not coming back tonight.'

An hour dragged by. Another hour. Alix phoned. Imogen phoned. It grew dark. She turned on the lights. She paced the room. She railed against her fate of permanently waiting for telephone calls. At ten o'clock she wrote:

I waited — but you didn't come.

Her mother was still awake when Ryder arrived at Dingwall Court. 'Adam phoned,' she said. 'Oh, darling, I knew you wouldn't leave me. I knew you wouldn't make me spend the night alone.'

'I'll have to go back tomorrow.'

'But it's Mrs Trumpet's day off.'

'I must see Adam.'

'You saw him today.'

'I didn't.'

She went down to her father's study and dialled the flat. 'Adam . . . Yes, I know I said I'd stay but I waited till ten . . . You could have called me . . . Yes, I know you've left Harding-Broughton. You were sacked? Oh, I'm sorry . . . Because they don't want Paul Harding's future son-in-law? Yes, of course I feel guilty but that was the reason you got the job in the first place. What? I'm not saying you didn't merit it . . . But I can't drive all the way back to London now! I've only just got here . . . Please! I'm exhausted. I'm not being selfish . . . What do you mean by tomorrow's too late? Adam! Adam!'

She went to her mother. 'I'm going back to London.'

'But it's after midnight.'

'If I don't go tonight, Adam doesn't want to see me again.'

Ryder drove hard and fast. It was a clear cold night, the first frost that autumn. The house was quiet when she drew up outside but the light was on in Adam's bedroom. She recognised its soft red glow. Opening her bag, she gave her hair a quick brush and sprayed scent on her wrists and neck.

The hall was in darkness. She didn't bother to switch on the light, she knew the stairs so well. The lock in Adam's flat door turned easily. 'The Sound of Silence' came from his room. A shaft of red light showed under the door. Ryder tiptoed across to it and reached for the door knob.

But when she opened the door, she froze. Adam was

sprawled across the bed, his hair dishevelled and his eyes half-closed. Alix was sitting on top of him. She was riding him slowly. Rhythmically. Her thighs gleaming white against his tanned and hairy legs.

'Ryder!' Adam pushed Alix aside. 'I . . . I didn't know you were coming.'

'So I see.'

'I'm sorry.' He stood up, the light gleaming on his naked body.

'Keep away from me!'

'I can explain.'

'How dare you accuse me of being selfish! How dare you tell me if I don't come tonight we're finished. Then I find this!' She choked. 'With my flatmate!'

'It's my fault,' said Alix, wrapping herself in the duvet. 'We smoked some hash and, well, one thing led to another.'

'You bitch! When you needed money, Alix, I lent it to you. When I need support, you repay me by having sex with my man.'

'Ryder, please!' Adam stepped towards her.

'You weak bastard! Touch me and I'll scratch your eyes out.'

'I love you.'

'I hate you. Both of you. You let me down when I'm at my lowest. I'll never forgive you — and I never want to see either of you again.'

She slammed out of the flat, ran down the stairs, and drove off. As she turned the corner, Adam opened the front door and shouted, 'Ryder! Wait!' But she didn't stop.

It was dawn when Ryder slipped back into Dingwall Court. She'd been driving round and round in circles, too numb to cry, too hurt to think. The house was quiet. She crept up the stairs, longing for sleep and oblivion. As she crossed the landing, she saw Leo outside her mother's door.

'Mummy!' He rattled the handle.

'Sssshhh, Leo! You'll wake her. Go back to bed.'

He rattled it again.

'Shut up!' She pulled him away, itching to slap him. This was all she needed after last night!

'Nanny's gone.' He burst into tears.

Immediately she was racked with guilt. Her world had fallen apart, but so had his and he didn't understand why. 'It's all right, Leo,' she said. 'Just please don't cry. I can't bear it.'

Mrs Trumpet appeared on the landing in a pink candlewick dressing-gown. 'He's been awake most of the night,' she said. 'Poor lad. Everyone keeps disappearing and he's frightened they won't come back. And you, dear. You look all in.'

'I am.' Ryder's eyes filled with tears.

'Go to bed.'

'I'll just check on my mother. She must have woken up by now.' Ryder turned the door handle. 'Funny. It's stuck.' She tried again. 'I think it's locked.'

'It can't be.'

'It is.' She rattled the handle. 'Mummy! Mummy!'

There was no answer. She knelt to peer through the keyhole but it was blocked. 'There's a spare key. It's in father's study.' She sped downstairs. When she returned, Mrs Trumpet was holding Leo away from the door. With the hairs on the backs of her arms standing upright, in dreadful premonition, Ryder turned the key in the lock and opened the door.

Her mother lay back amongst the peach satin pillows. Her eyes were closed, her mouth open, her right hand clasped an empty pill bottle. She could have been sleeping peacefully, except that her skin was a strange parchment colour.

Carrie Harding's suicide was on the television lunchtime news. It added a tragic twist to a story of money and power. In Brixton prison, the Governor informed her husband. At Dingwall Court, Ryder telephoned her grandparents. She felt totally calm until she had to say, 'She killed herself.' The words stuck in her throat. She felt as if someone were preventing her from speaking. At the other end of the line she could hear her grandfather shouting, 'How?' Eventually she managed to squeeze out, 'Suicide.'

Her mother had left three notes propped against the mirror on her dressing table. One was for her husband, one for Ryder, one for Leo when he was old enough to understand. Ryder read hers in the bedroom, in a moment of peace and unreality before the undertaker arrived. She stood at the end of her mother's bed, unable to believe what had happened. Life could never be the same again. It should never be the same again. The face amid the pillows had her mother's features. Her golden hair. Her dainty nose. But it wasn't her mother. It had no life. It was a shell.

'I'm sorry I left you alone,' Ryder whispered, as the words swum before her eyes.

Darling Ryder,
Don't blame yourself. I know you will. But you mustn't. You've got your own life to lead. I realised that tonight — and how selfish I've been. I've no right to ruin your happiness just because mine has been ruined.

I can't cope without Paul. I love him and need him. He's the best husband in the world and I failed him. He couldn't confide in me.

Be happy, darling. I'm happier this way. Look after Leo. Remember me with love.
Mummy.

Ryder covered her face with the letter but she couldn't cry. Her feelings for her mother were locked as deep as those which her mother had had for her. She hurried downstairs and across the lawn to the rose arbour, unable

124

to face pity. In solitude, she reread the letter. A week ago the round, childish handwriting which leaped at her from the page had been happily writing wedding lists. She was reminded suddenly of that other childish writing, in Helen's trunk at Scot's Farm.

On the highest branches of the arbour, the last rose of summer reigned supreme. She reached for it, tearing her hands on the thorns. The stem broke without resistance. She threw it right out into the fast-flowing central current of the river. It glided away, as the golden flotillas of Fox Lake, as her mother.

In the days before the funeral she escaped to the arbour whenever she could free herself from Podmore, Mrs Trumpet, the vicar, and the endless arrangements which choked her with their pettiness. Adam telephoned but she refused to speak to him. Alix wrote, but she returned the letter. Adam sent her flowers. She told the florist to take them back. She wouldn't even talk to Immy. She couldn't bring herself to talk of what had happened at the flat when it was entwined with her mother's death — and her own guilt.

She met her grandparents at Heathrow. It was their first visit to England: her grandfather had refused to stay at the Court. Ryder saw them before they saw her. Her grandfather was pushing their luggage through the arrival gate, looking tired and bewildered but determined not to show it. She hurried to them. They stared at her. Then her grandfather said, 'It's Ryder. How you've changed. Why, you could almost be your mother.' He enveloped her in his embrace. His jacket smelled of tobacco and corn. Of Scot's Farm. The memory brought tears to Ryder's eyes. She wiped them away with the back of her hand. All the times she could have cried alone, and she had to give way now.

When her grandparents saw Griffiths and the Rolls, they were awkward. When they saw Dingwall Court they were speechless. Finally her grandmother said, 'Carrie sent me pictures but I didn't realise it was a palace.'

'Paid for with dishonest money!' Her grandfather stepped from the car, waving away Griffiths' offer of help. 'I ain't dying yet, son.'

Ryder introduced them to Mrs Trumpet, then hurried them up the stairs, talking non-stop so that whatever her grandfather thought of her father he wasn't able to proclaim it. Not whilst her father stared at the blank walls of a cell. 'We've put you in the blue suite,' she said. 'It has a lovely view over the gardens to the Thames.' She opened the door to a spacious bedroom. It had a four-poster bed with pale blue moiré drapes. They matched the curtains. Behind them the balcony was bathed in the pale gold of October sunlight.

'Carrie chose all this?' Her grandmother perched gingerly on the end of the bed and rubbed the moiré silk between her fingers. 'It must have cost a fortune.'

'She had wonderful taste. Look! Here's a copy of *House & Garden*. There's the article about Dingwall Court. Here she is, in this room.'

They stared at the photograph of their daughter sitting on the end of the bed, her slim legs crossed at the knee, her golden hair forming a halo against the blue drapes.

'I'd like to see the room where she died,' her grandmother whispered.

Ryder led them down the corridor and opened the door. Her grandparents remained at the threshold, staring at the peach satin boudoir. It occurred to Ryder that they'd never seen a bedroom like this, except on film. At Scot's Farm bedrooms were places to sleep in.

'Were these hers?' Her grandmother crossed to the dressing table and touched the ivory handled hairbrushes. She lifted one to her head as if to use it, then she lowered it reverently. 'Carrie died in this bed?' she asked.

'Yes.'

She picked up a peach satin cushion and wept silently into it. 'May I keep one of these?'

'You can have them all.'

'No. Just one. To remember her.' She lifted it to her wrinkled tearstained face. 'My daughter grew into a person I never knew and now it's too late.'

The funeral was to be held at the local church, where the kindly old vicar had agreed Carrie Harding could have the full burial service. 'I accept your mother wasn't of sound mind when she took her life,' he assured Ryder.

The church was tiny and Ryder had stipulated 'family and close friends only'. But that didn't stop the swarms of reporters from hoping to catch a glimpse of Paul Harding in handcuffs.

It was drizzling when Ryder and her grandparents arrived. The yewtrees in the graveyard dripped with water. The gravestones stood dark and sullen in the damp grass. They followed the coffin which was adorned with yellow, pink and white roses, mother's favourite colours. Ryder was aware that the church was packed with people but she couldn't identify them. Their faces were a blur. A clawlike hand reached up from a wheelchair. She was choked with gratitude to Lady Heythorp. Then she froze. At the back, behind a pillar were Immy, Adam and Alix.

Her father was sitting at the front, handcuffed to a prison officer. His head was bowed. As Ryder drew level, she stretched out her hand to comfort him but he didn't look round, though he must have known she was there. With the eyes of everyone upon her, she flushed and withdrew her arm. His rejection had been total and public.

They stood to sing the first hymn, 'All Things Bright and Beautiful'. It was Ryder's choice but she sensed her father's disapproval because it was childish. Miserably, she stared at the coffin. Once again she'd let her mother down. Failed, even at the very end. Then suddenly she knew why she'd chosen this hymn. Her mother had been bright and beautiful, and childish in spite of her sophistication.

The service was over quickly. Ryder wanted to say, 'Not yet! Don't take her yet,' but she could only watch in silence as the coffin passed her. A wound of freshly dug earth marred the grass in the graveyard. The drizzle had turned to rain and little rivulets of water were running down the mud into the gaping hole. Her father was led to one side. Ryder and her grandparents stood on the other.

'. . . earth to earth, ashes to ashes, dust to dust . . .'

The vicar paused and nodded to her father. He bent to take a handful of earth. The prison officer was obliged to bend as well. Her father held the wet earth in his hand, letting it run through his fingers, to fall on the coffin with small hollow thuds. He stood for a moment, looking down on his wife's coffin, then he turned to Ryder. 'Why isn't Leo here?'

'He's too young.'

'And who decided that?' he sneered at his father-in-law.

'I did,' said Ryder, cutting between them. 'I make his decisions. I'm all he has left.'

Mr Podmore arrived next morning when they were still at breakfast. As Ryder rose to join him in the drawing room, her grandfather said, 'Sit down! I'll see the lawyer. Your Grandma and I decided that last night.'

'But you don't know how things work in England.'

'Dealing with lawyers ain't no job for a young lady,' he answered tartly.

'I didn't mean to sound ungrateful.' Ryder walked to the door. 'Why don't we all see him?'

Podmore was standing by the window, polishing his

glasses. 'Ah, Miss Harding! And Mr and Mrs Milne. I'm sorry to intrude but I thought you'd want to know exactly where you stand, so I've brought your mother's will.' He sat down on a hardback chair and opened his briefcase on his bony knees. Ryder and her grandparents sat facing him on the sofa.

'Er . . . now . . . where are we?' He frowned. 'To my daughter Ryder, all remaining items of jewellery and apparel and my antique wooden trunk.'

'My Norwegian Grandma's trunk!' exclaimed her grandmother. 'I haven't seen that since Carrie left Prairieville. Oh, I can't believe she's gone.'

Ryder hurried to fill the moment. 'Why does she say *remaining* jewellery?'

'I'm afraid she left the valuable items to your father. The diamond ring. The emeralds. Her engagement ring. The sapphires. The rubies. An antique pearl choker. They'll be sold to pay his debts.'

'What about Leo?'

'The grandfather clock.'

'She bought it with the money we gave her as a wedding present.' Her grandfather shook his head. 'Were we mad at her for not buying something practical. She'd married a man without two cents to rub together and she buys a clock. But that was Carrie all over. So pr . . . pretty, but so impractical.' He gazed at the luxuriant furnishings in the yellow drawing room. 'What about all this? These pictures. The furniture. The silver in the dining room. I'm not thinking of myself, young man, but of my grandchildren.'

Mr Podmore blushed at being called young. 'I regret the house and its contents form part of Mr Harding's assets, unless you can prove otherwise.'

'What about money? The kids are going to need something.'

'She had a thousand pounds in her bank account.'

'But that damned husband of hers was a millionaire!'

'Mr Milne, your daughter used shop accounts and credit cards. She didn't need cash.'

'He was scared to give it to her in case she ran off. Carrie was my favourite child, Mr Lawyer. Part of me died when she married that . . . jailbird.'

Podmore couldn't get out of the house quick enough. He wasn't used to dealing with raw emotion. When Ryder accompanied him to the front door, he said, 'Your father's appointed you as Leo's guardian.'

'Surely my grandfather would be more suitable?'

'Your father'd prefer to see the boy in a children's home.'

'Then I have to agree. What else can I do?' Ryder stood on the top step as the solicitor hurried to his car. 'But I've no idea how I'm going to look after him.'

Podmore didn't reply.

That evening her grandparents said to Ryder, 'We'd like you to come back to Prairieville. So would Debbie and Frankie. You and Leo. To Scot's Farm, where you belong.'

She accepted. It seemed the answer to everything. That night she dreamed of Fox Lake. Only there were no flotillas. The lake was frozen.

In the days that followed Mrs Trumpet and Greta Milne became close. Together they sorted Carrie's clothes. Ryder left them alone. She sensed that her grandmother needed to come to terms with Carrie's death and could only do so by learning every detail of her daughter from someone who had known her as an adult.

Ryder cleared her mother's desk. There were accounts from Harrods marked 'paid', stiff white cards from exclusive boutiques saying, '*Dear Madam, We have a divine little suit which we know you'd love,*' and bundles of old birthday cards. Ryder found one from herself.

mummy
  with love from
    ryder aged 5

She closed her eyes and for a moment she heard her
mother call, 'Ryder!' There was a tap on the French
windows and Imogen walked in. 'I had to come,' she
said. 'I couldn't bear you to leave without us meeting.'

Ryder put her head in her hands and cried. She hadn't
realised how much she'd missed her friends although she
still couldn't bring herself to talk of Adam and Alix.

Immy stayed all day. She enchanted Ryder's grandparents who had once seen her on television. 'Have you
visited your father?' she asked Ryder when they were
alone.

'No. First of all he didn't want to see us. Now I don't
want to see him.' She paused. 'Thanks for not asking
me to forgive Adam and Alix.'

Immy smiled sadly. 'Try to remember the fun we had.
Don't build a Berlin Wall. It'll be so hard to pull it
down.'

Ryder shrugged. It was all very well for Immy. She
hadn't been cut to the quick.

The lower drawers of the desk were full of letters and
photographs, all muddled up. Leo at one month. Ryder
and Leo. Paul, 1951 — the year they'd married. Paul
and George in Capri. Her mother in a fitted brocade
wedding dress with a bridesmaid and a page clutching
at the hem of her skirt. Patrick Broughton, 1951. He
was wearing a sailor suit. His dark hair was tousled and
his dark eyes full of mischief. She felt an urge to send
it to him, saying, 'You haven't changed.'

Something prevented the drawer from closing prop-
erly. She pulled it right out. A piece of paper was
jammed into a corner. It was a half page of Basildon
Bond notepaper, part of a letter in her father's
handwriting.

I'm sorry you found out about Sonia Bassingham but you have nothing to be jealous of. I finished with her when I met you. I promise you, I have never been unfaithful. You are again being suspicious without cause. I love you, Carrie. You're my wife. Please come home.

Ryder stared out of the French windows towards the rose arbour. Was jealousy the key to understanding her mother?

12

Her grandfather was sitting in her father's place at the head of the table when Ryder appeared for breakfast. 'Where are you going, all dressed up?' he asked.

'To visit my father,' she said as casually as possible.

He laid down his cereal spoon. 'You don't have time. We're leaving for Prairieville tomorrow.'

'I have to see him.'

'Ryder, we agreed you'd have no contact.'

'I've changed my mind.' She reached for a piece of toast.

'Why, goddamit?'

'Because he's my father. Mother would want it.' She paused. 'And I want it!'

Driving into London reminded Ryder of Adam. How often they'd crawled back to town through the Sunday evening traffic, his hand stroking the soft inside of her thigh — and all the time he'd wished she were Alix. She switched on the radio to distract herself. A man was saying, 'I'm sixty and my dear old mother is ninety . . .' She turned it off. How dare a man of sixty have a mother when hers was dead?

She followed the South Circular through Clapham to Brixton, passed streets of red brick Victorian houses with dusty privet hedges. The prison was set back, camouflaged by a sprawl of flats, garages and cafés. She parked on the other side of Brixton Hill, in a peaceful suburban street. A man was walking his dog. Two men were gossiping. A girl of her own age came out of a house and called, 'Mum!' Ryder hurried away.

There was a notice saying *H. M. Prison. No Through Road*. It sent a chill down her arms, a feeling which increased as she walked up the long straight road beside the high wall topped by rolling barbed wire. An assortment of people were hanging around near the main gate. Three prison officers with bomber jackets over their uniforms jangled their keys in trouser pockets. A little old lady was crying into a mug of tea from the outdoor canteen. Near the visitors' entrance a heavily made-up girl was smoking nervously, whilst her companion masked a love bite with panstick. Their streetmarket eyes priced Ryder's tan boots and coat. She wished she'd worn something less expensive.

At the visitors' entrance an officer took her name. 'I will see him, won't I?' she asked.

'That's up to him. Not being obliged to see your relatives is one of the few advantages of being locked up.'

Ryder hovered by the booth. Five minutes passed. Ten minutes. A woman arrived, dragging a small boy. As he drew nearer Ryder could see the nits jumping on his scalp. Hurriedly she stepped outside. The lovebite girl was still rubbing her neck. 'Eight years is eight years an' I'm not a bleedin' nun.' She produced her Visitors' Order and went inside. More women arrived. Some with children. Many alone. A sad trail of figures walking briskly up beside the prison wall, tight black skirts riding up thighs, feet forced into new stilettos, cheap scent hanging on the damp morning air.

'Harding! Your ticket.'

Ryder entered through a series of interlocking doors. There was a smell of sweat and hot radiators and the cheap scent of the girl with the lovebite. In an anteroom she was asked if she had brought food or drink. She

134

shook her head. He waved her on, into the visiting room. In the doorway she hesitated, nervously wiping her hands on her coat. There were long tables with seats either side: one side for visitors, the other for detainees. For a moment she couldn't see her father: she was blinded by the barred windows and the prison officers standing guard. Then he raised his hand and beckoned.

He looked pale but composed. 'This is a surprise!' He pointed to a chair. 'I thought your failure to visit me was due to you being on your honeymoon, relieved to be called Harding no longer.'

'I'm not getting married. You know that.' She sat down stiffly. 'I'm taking Leo to Prairieville.'

'Of course!' He gave a dry laugh. 'I don't suppose Adam fancied the idea of threshing corn when he'd planned to marry a rich man's daughter.'

Ryder gripped the handle of her bag so tightly that her knuckles turned white. 'Adam didn't drop me because I had no money. He went off with Alix. So mock all you like!'

He reached for her hand. 'I'm sorry. That was cruel of me. But I've been locked up in here, bored out of my mind, wondering why you didn't come, telling myself that there's no earthly reason why you should.'

She told him about the Court and how they'd sorted and packed her mother's belongings.

'How's Leo?' he asked.

'He doesn't understand what's happened.'

'I'm sure that old bigot, Dan Milne, will put him straight. "Now son, ya know how the good guys always beat the bad guys? Well, ya Dad's in gaol because he's a bad guy." '

His imitation of her grandfather was so clever that she couldn't help but laugh.

The prison officers glanced her way. A woman at a nearby table began to cry. Ryder leaned forward. 'What

135

happened between you and George Broughton?' she asked.

'Why do you say that?'

'Patrick Brendan is his son.'

'The polo player.' He clicked his fingers. 'I knew there was something about him.' He thought for a moment, then looked directly at Ryder. 'George was an idealist. So was I — once! We believed we were fighting to make the world a better place. But life was just as cutthroat afterwards. I persuaded him to buy an option on a war-damaged property with me. We put in our claim for damage. That's the way things worked then. The plan was to repair the building, sell, and buy another. But our claim took a long time to process. The option date approached. We risked losing our deposit. So I took George's disability payment and I bribed our claim to the front. I did it for us. Him and me. Not just for me. It was three years before he found out. He said he'd rather be poor than dishonest and that he never wanted to see me again. An hour later he drove into a bridge. I didn't kill George. Life did.' He paused and frowned. 'When he died I put Bailing Airfield in your name. It's not worth anything but if you come back to England go and see where George and I were stationed.'

They sat in silence till she blurted out, 'What about mother? Did life kill her? You . . . you haven't asked about her. Don't you want to know . . . anything?'

'No! She couldn't trust me to get out of this mess. She couldn't wait.' His voice rose. 'I'd have waited for her.'

'You've no right to be angry. She was desperate.'

'I'm angry at myself.' He stood abruptly. 'I suppose you only came for her sake.'

'No,' she whispered, her words choked by helpless sorrow. 'Not just for her sake.'

13

Minnesota

Debbie met them at Minneapolis/St Paul airport. She came bounding across the terminal, the same jolly girl with blonde hair and a big-toothed smile. When she saw Ryder she stopped dead. 'Is that you?'

'No, I'm a ghost.'

'You're so townie.' Debbie looked her up and down, taking in her tight cream cords tucked into tan boots and casually open trenchcoat. 'I should have tidied myself but I had to drop Rudy at Mom's. It's the first time she's offered to look after him so I didn't want to be late.'

Ryder took her by the shoulders and shook her. 'Tomorrow I'll be in jeans too.'

Scot's Farm was a three-hour drive to the south. Her grandparents and Leo sat in the back of the car, so Debbie and Ryder could chat in the front.

'I'm sorry about your Mom and Dad,' said Debbie. 'It must have been tough.'

'You haven't had an easy time either.'

'The worst part was when I left Carl. Mom wouldn't have me at home and she said our grandparents didn't want a divorcee. A lie! So I moved into a one-room shack on the edge of town. It was all I could afford. I had no phone. No hot water. One day Grandpa turned up. He was that shocked he made me pack up on the spot and return to Scot's Farm. We've converted the small barn into a home for Rudy and me. You'll love it. I love it.'

Ryder pressed her nose against the window, her eyes eagerly raking the beyond for remembered landmarks. It was so flat. So bleak. She had forgotten quite how bleak, or maybe it was because she'd only been here from spring to fall, never in the wintry aftermath of harvest.

Just before Prairieville they abandoned the tarmac road for the dirt track, the one along which Ryder had cycled from Fox Lake. They stopped at the farm belonging to Debbie's parents. Her mother waddled ferociously across the porch, carrying Rudy, who was asleep. Her father followed. He was an amiable man, with Dan Milne's rugged looks but no personality.

'Hi there!' He came to Ryder's side of the car. 'Sorry about your Mom and Dad.'

She smiled. 'Thanks.'

'What a family we are!' Her aunt pursed her lips in disapproval as she handed Rudy to Debbie. 'God knows what shame we'll have to bear next!'

Debbie drove off before Ryder could retaliate. 'It isn't worth it,' she said. 'You can't budge her views.'

Scot's Farm was smaller than Ryder remembered. The barns and the silo seemed closer to the house. The protective semi-circle of cottonwoods didn't have quite the broad sweep. She thought of her mother coming back here each year, seeing it again, comparing it to Dingwall Court, and her throat constricted so she could hardly breathe.

'I know it ain't what you're used to.' Her grandfather stepped out of the car and stretched his legs. 'Hell, it even looks shrunk to me.'

'I've always loved Scot's Farm.' The frost crackled under her feet.

'We'll repaint the outside,' he went on, embarrassed

by the peeling paint on the porch rail. 'It'll look better then.'

The warmth of the old farmhouse enveloped her. The smell of freshbaked bread permeated her nostrils. She stood in the middle of the living room. She hadn't remembered the wood panelling being as dark or the furniture as heavy. Nor did she recall so many lace tablecloths. It seemed so cluttered. Not that she cared. It was merely something she noticed now.

'We've put you in your old room.' Her grandmother smiled anxiously. 'And Leo's next door, in the little room.'

Her bedroom was white and plain, just as it had been, except that a new red quilt lay on the old iron bed and the bedstead, which had been rusty, was painted shiny red.

'Grandma made the quilt last year.' Debbie hauled in the luggage. 'And I painted the bedstead. I copied from a picture of a house in France. It was the first positive thing I did after Carl and I split up.' She went to the window. 'That's my barn. And that's my window.' She turned. 'It's fun to have you back, Ryder. I hope you're going to stay.'

'Of course I will.' Ryder stared out at the bare branches of the cottonwoods. 'All I've ever wanted to do is live here.'

She woke next morning and for a moment she thought she must be dreaming. She lay quite still, her eyes darting round the room, examining the familiar nooks and crannies. She moved. There was a cry from the floor by her bed.

Leo was lying on the mat, wearing just his pyjamas, his bare feet tucked up under his body. He was shivering so much his lips had turned blue.

'You'll freeze.' She pulled him on to the bed, wrapping the quilt around him. 'You'll be ill. Then you won't be able to go to your new school and meet all the nice boys who are going to be your friends.'

He stared at her with her mother's blue accusing eyes. 'I want Trumpet.'

'Mrs Trumpet's in England.'

'I want Mummy.' He began to cry. 'I want to go home.'

'Mummy's in heaven.' She drew him closer. He clung to her, his whole body shaking. 'Don't cry,' she said. 'Please!'

Her grandmother opened the door. At the sight of her, Leo started to scream. 'But Leo, honey, I'm your Grandma. Your Mummy was my little girl.' She stepped closer. He screamed louder.

'Shut up!' shouted Ryder. He stopped. She slid out of bed. He clung to her, whimpering. 'I'm going to have a bath,' she told him, collecting her towel and wash bag. 'If you want to come and talk to me, you have to promise not to cry.'

'But Ryder, he's a boy.' Her grandmother looked appalled. 'You're not going to . . . take your clothes off in front of him!'

'He's my little brother. He's seen me in the bath before. He saw my mother in the bath.'

'Well . . . if that's what he's used to, but . . . this is Prairieville. Folks shock easy.'

Debbie arrived as they were finishing breakfast. She burst in, her cheeks pink from the icy wind, her hair unbrushed, her jeans stretched to tearing. She helped herself to a piece of toast, spreading it thick with butter and jam, chattering non stop. 'Yea, I know, I should be on a diet. But I'm hungry. Ryder, how come you're skinny? You used to be fatter than me. Hey, doesn't Leo look like Aunt Carrie.' She leaned towards him. He hid his face in Ryder's arm. 'Okay. Don't talk to me.' She turned to Ryder. 'I've got a day off. Did I tell you I work at Wise's Wayside? You remember Susan's father? He remarried last summer, to Mrs Macdonald. Her husband owned the airfield. Well, his son Teddy runs the place now. Frankie's out there every weekend. He's still mad to be a pilot.'

'What about Susan?' asked Ryder, when Debbie was obliged to draw breath.

'She teaches in Minneapolis.'

'Are you still friends?'

'We kinda drifted. I stayed with her last fall. She's dating a guy who's an unpublished poet. All their friends are unpublished poets. Seven whole days of unpublished poets! Come on! I'll show you the barn.'

As Ryder stood up Leo grabbed her leg. 'Show him where you're going,' said her grandmother. 'Then make him come back.'

They took Leo to the barn and to the animals. Alfie still terrorised the hen house. Nancy the pony was now in retirement. Two cows provided milk for butter and cheese. Numerous cats prowled the barns, two were little more than kittens. One was marmalade. 'That's Rudy's,' said Debbie, catching a little black one. 'This can be yours.' She handed it to Leo.

He held it in his arms, his face a mixture of fear and excitement. 'Mummy doesn't allow me to have animals because they're dirty.' He dropped the kitten to the ground and hurried into the farmhouse, rubbing his hands together as if they were covered in dust.

'That kid needs to roll in the dirt,' said Debbie, ushering Ryder inside the barn.

It was one big room which served as a living area and kitchen, with stairs where the old ladder used to be leading to two bedrooms in the loft. The furniture was cast-outs from the main house. Beds covered in cushions doubled as sofas. It reminded Ryder of the London flat.

'I sleep down here,' said Debbie. 'Rudy sleeps upstairs. The other room's a mess. I keep meaning to

141

clear it. Hell, the whole place ain't that elegant but it's home.' She glowed with pride.

In the afternoon Debbie drove Ryder into Prairieville. It was bitterly cold and the streets were deserted. She recalled the little town as bustling with people. They stopped at Wise's Wayside. The place was now spruced up and shining. So was Mr Wise. He was serving behind the counter, watched by Mrs Wise, a fierce teetotaller. As they drove away Ryder and Debbie laughed about the oily ice cream left to melt in the public trash can.

They went on to Fox Lake. She was afraid to find it too had shrunk. But the lake and its island still possessed their magical beauty. The wooden jetty still reached out into the water and the clapboard houses on the lakeside looked down through the trees. The difference was that it was winter. The houses were closed. The trees were bare. The island where she pictured herself slender and beautiful in a deerskin was bleak and buffeted by the wind.

That evening Frankie came to supper. He'd been a boy when Ryder had left, now he was in his last year at High School. Neat featured, slight and quick in manner, he reminded Ryder of her mother, so much so that at first she found it hard to look at him.

In the days which followed Ryder settled into life at the farm. She helped her grandmother around the house, taught Leo not to be frightened of the chickens, wrote to Imogen, Mrs Trumpet and her father, and took over the weekly trip to the supermarket with Leo. In London she'd raced from shelf to shelf. In Prairieville it took her all morning because she had nothing else to do.

On the first day of his Christmas vacation Frankie came over to paint the outside of the buildings. 'Let me help,' Ryder offered.

He laughed from the top of his ladder. 'You ever painted a house before?'

'No, but I can learn. And I must do something. I can't sit around the house all day.'

He put up another ladder, saying, 'You have to paint from side to side or you'll miss the overlap.' He watched her climb up, paint tin in one hand. 'That's right. Balance it on the top. Now side to side.'

It was cold outside but exhilarating. Within half an hour she'd stripped off her sweater. By lunchtime she was exhausted.

'Had enough?' Frankie grinned at her over a plate of steaming stew.

She shook her head. But the next morning she was so stiff she could barely get out of bed. Her whole body ached from her shoulders to her pelvis. As she came downstairs her grandfather chortled in his coffee. 'Maybe you should do a little light baking in the kitchen.'

'No thank you!' She eased herself into her chair and attacked her fried eggs and bacon.

As she finished, her grandmother appeared in the kitchen door, shaking her head with disapproval, hands covered in flour. 'You're not gonna catch a husband by knowing how to paint a house,' she said.

'I don't want a husband.' Ryder downed her coffee. 'I've had enough of men.' She dragged herself upright and hobbled out to her painting. Behind her Leo said timidly, 'I'll help you with the baking.'

It took fifteen days to paint the house and the barns. On the sixteenth, she woke to the first heavy snow and wondered what she was going to do next.

She received a letter from her father. He didn't say much, except that his trial was likely to be in May. But that didn't matter to Ryder. What counted was that it was the first time she'd ever received a letter from him.

At supper her grandfather asked her what the letter contained. 'Nothing much,' she replied, passing the potatoes to Debbie.

He laid down his knife and fork. 'Don't you think you should let me read it?'

She stared at him. 'No!'

Ryder was sitting in front of the fire, her legs hooked over the arm of the chair, studying the *Prairieville Gazette* when her grandfather came downstairs. 'What are you looking for?' he asked, peering over her shoulder.

'I'm trying to find a job.'

'What's wrong with helping your Grandma?'

'I mean a proper job. I need an occupation. I can't hang around the house all day. In England I didn't live with my parents. I shared a flat with friends. I worked. I led my own life.'

He sat down heavily. 'You sound just like Carrie. I guess having you for these weeks was better than nothing.'

'I didn't say I'm leaving! Not yet.' Screaming with frustration she went upstairs.

Debbie invited her to the barn for supper. Over coffee she said, 'Why don't we clean up the second bedroom so you can move into the barn with us?'

'Grandpa's spoken to you?'

'They're trying to have the closeness with you that they missed with your mother.'

'I know.' Ryder sighed. 'But they're suffocating me. For the first time in my life I understand why she left.'

When Leo saw Ryder carry the red quilt into the barn, he threw himself on the floor and screamed.

'Stop it!' she told him.

He screamed louder, thumping the wooden boards with his fists and feet. Then he grabbed her suitcase and tipped the contents on to the floor.

'Don't do that!' She slapped his leg. He howled.

144

'Ignore him!' shouted her grandmother. 'It's the only way.'

He was scarlet in the face and kicking at the furniture. Ryder itched to hit him again but she hurried to the barn and closed the door. A moment later there was a scratching noise. 'Rye-rye!'

She opened it. He was standing there, his face wet with tears. 'You can only come in if you don't cry,' she said, giving him a chocolate cookie out of sheer guilt.

'No jobs?' asked Debbie when she came home with Rudy.

'Waitressing at the Seven/Eleven or part-time bottling at the creamery.'

Debbie laughed at Ryder's pained expression. 'This is Prairieville. They don't have vacancies for high-powered executive secretaries here.'

'I don't want to be a secretary.' Ryder watched the wind whip up the snow, blowing it across the yard, piling it up against the farmhouse. 'I want more.'

14

It snowed so hard on Christmas Eve that they were forced to miss the carol service. So they had their own carols, around the Christmas tree at Scot's Farm. The room glowed warm. The candles fluttered. Outside a howling winter gripped the prairie.

Ryder woke before dawn. She lay in bed, watching the snow slide down the window pane, white crystals against a still dark sky. This was the first Christmas without her mother. The first of many Christmases. Sadness weighed heavy on her. She climbed out of bed and opened the window. The snowstorm hit her in the face but she did not close it. She reached her hand out into it as if by reaching high enough and far enough she would touch her mother, who was out there. Somewhere.

Debbie burst in. 'What are you doing? There's snow in the house. It's coming through under the door.'

'I'm sorry.'

'You're crying.'

'I just wish I hadn't gone to see Adam that night.' She hurried to the shower and put her face under the tap.

Debbie and Ryder cooked Christmas dinner in the barn for the whole family, including Debbie's parents. They spent all day preparing the turkey and chopping vegetables. It didn't matter. There was nothing else to do, except dig a channel across the farmyard so that their guests could reach the barn.

The storm abated on New Year's Day. The road was cleared. Debbie returned to work. Ryder lay on the sofa and stared at the ceiling with Imogen's latest gossipy letter on her knees. Immy's career was going brilliantly. She had bought a mews house behind Harrods. Adam was moving in. He often talked of Ryder. Tony was being possessive. Hetty was getting married. The only person she never mentioned was Alix and although Ryder would never have admitted it, she longed to hear of her. She hated her. But she still missed her.

Ryder was waiting by the door when Debbie arrived home from work. 'Can I borrow your car?' she asked. 'Just for an hour.'

'Sure — but why?'

'Look at this!' Ryder waved the newspaper under her nose. ' "Prairieville Airfield requires administrator. Apply in person." '

'That's Teddy Macdonald. It's his Mom who married Mr Wise. Teddy's nice. When I fell pregnant, he was one of the few who'd talk to me. You don't need to apply in person.' She reached for the phone. 'I'll call him.'

'No!' Ryder pulled her hand away. 'I want to do this myself.'

'I'll come along for the ride, then. After all, you've never driven in the US before.'

'If you don't want to lend me the car, I'll walk.' Ryder started up the stairs. Then she turned. Debbie was looking at her with no attempt to conceal her hurt. 'You told me that painting the bedstead was the first positive thing you did after Carl,' said Ryder. 'If I don't do something, on my own, soon, I'll never have the courage to try anything again.'

When she came down, in a tight black skirt, with her lips glossed and her hair flicked back, Debbie handed

147

her the keys. 'I guess I'm jealous,' she said. 'You're going to make other friends and you won't need me.'

'They can be your friends too.'

'That's what Susan said.'

'Don't worry, I'm not into unpublished poets.'

She managed to get the car going, with difficulty. It lumbered across the farmyard, its back tyres skidding on the ice. As she passed the henhouse there was a frightful squawking. She wondered if she'd run over Alfie but didn't dare stop.

The airfield was to the south of Prairieville. It took her an hour to reach it. The snowchains bit into the packed ice. The wind piled the snow on the windscreen, so heavy that the wipers could barely function. She was mad. Crazy! But exhilarated. She parked by the only terminal. It was little more than a prefab, in the shadow of the hangar. A light burned from inside. She hunched her shoulders and battled through the wind to the swing doors.

'Hi, there!' A large fair-haired young man was sitting on a desk, swinging his legs backwards and forwards. 'What can I do for you?' He had a chubby, friendly face and an engaging smile.

'I've come about the job.'

'You have to be Debbie's cousin. I recognise the English accent. Teddy Macdonald.' He stood up and held out his hand. 'But why didn't you call?'

'Ryder Harding.' She shook his hand. 'The paper said apply in person.'

'Well, the job's yours. No one else will apply. Coffee?'

'Thanks.' She followed him into a small back kitchen. The place was in chaos. There were half-empty milk cartons. Dirty coffee mugs. Invoices and bills, piled in no order. 'Why won't anyone else apply?'

'Because I can't pay much. Not yet. I have to build up the airfield first. And I want someone who'll work weekends. That's when we're busiest. I close on Mondays.' He poured boiling water on the coffee granules. 'And girls want to work where there are other girls, so they can talk about boyfriends and homebakes.'

Ryder laughed. 'Not me!'

Two days later she started work. Her grandfather lent her the old pickup truck and she roared up to the terminal doing all of ten miles an hour, black smoke pouring from its exhaust.

Teddy appeared in the doorway. 'I thought someone was about to land on the building.'

Warned by Debbie to dress for warmth, she had on her cream cords and a heavy cream Aran knit sweater. As she passed in front of Teddy he gave her a sideways glance but she pretended not to notice.

'What would you like me to do?' she asked, after he'd shown her to a desk where a small switchboard was swamped by piles of paperwork.

'Answer the phone. Give out the weather forecast if anyone asks. You'll see it on the teleprinter. We're the only airfield round here with a constant update so we get a lot of enquiries.'

'What about all these papers?'

'Tidy 'em if you want to.'

'Fine. Shall I make some coffee first?'

He gave her his big wholesome grin. 'Do whatever you think. I ain't gotta clue about paperwork. I only know about flying.'

Ryder went to the kitchen. It looked as though a whirlwind had struck. Rolling up her sleeves she set to work, scooping all the empty cartons and cans into a plastic sack, scrubbing out the sink, and doing a week's worth of dirty cups. Teddy came to the door as she was cleaning out the fridge. 'You don't need to do all that!' he said. 'Lisa never did.'

'Who's Lisa?'

'Oh . . .' He blushed. 'She worked here till Christmas.'

149

In the top drawer of Ryder's desk were three copies of *True Love* and a half-knitted pink fluffy sweater with little sequins sewn around the neck. She placed them in the bottom drawer.

The phone rang. She answered, 'Prairieville Airfield, good morning.'

'What's the weather like northeast of the Twin Cities?'

'Oh . . . you mean Minneapolis/St Paul?'

'You must be Dan Milne's granddaughter.'

Teddy checked the teleprinter and took over. 'You'd better learn how to read this,' he said afterwards.

The machine spewed out endless meteorological information direct from Minneapolis. He pointed at the various symbols. 'Temperature. Depth of snow. Forecast. Wind speed and direction. Here we have a warmer front. That'll bring more snow. And here we have a continual update on the state of all airfields in the region.'

The phone rang. He nodded to Ryder. She answered it.

'I want to fly a patient to Rochester,' said a man's voice. 'He's checking into the Mayo Clinic. Is their airfield clear?'

She studied the machine. 'The Rochester runway was cleared one hour ago.'

'You must be Carrie's daughter. I'm Doctor Jeff. We met when you were here on vacation. I was sorry to hear about your mother.' There was a depth to his voice. Ryder remembered that he'd once loved her mother.

She spent the day separating Teddy's unpaid bills from the airfield's invoices for landing, refuelling and hangarage; his income.

'It's no wonder you're short of money,' she told him. 'You never charge anyone.'

'How did it go?' asked Debbie, who was cooking supper in the barn for Rudy and Leo when Ryder returned.

'Interesting.' She collapsed on to the sofa. 'But exhausting.'

'Teddy worked you that hard! I don't believe it.'

'It's such chaos. This Lisa who worked there till Christmas must have spent her whole time knitting.'

'She's Teddy's girl. They've been dating since High School.' Debbie stepped closer and lowered her voice so the boys couldn't hear. 'Not my favourite person. But Teddy's kinda cute, don't you think?'

'Too wholesome.'

'Prefer 'em dirty and degenerate?'

Patrick Brendan came into Ryder's mind. 'Dirty, no. But with a hint of sin.'

It stopped snowing at the weekend. The sun shone from a cerulean sky and the biting wind dropped. Teddy cleared the runway with the snowplough, whilst Frankie gritted it. Ryder watched them from the steps of the terminal, a mug of coffee clasped in her gloved hands. The phone rang. Reluctantly she abandoned the brilliant morning for the stuffy interior of the terminal.

'Where's Teddy?' demanded a girl's petulant voice.

'He's out with the snowplough.'

'It's Lisa. I want to speak with him.'

She went outside. Teddy was parking the snowplough. 'It's Lisa,' she shouted.

He jumped down from the cab. 'Women!'

She laughed. 'Men!'

'You sound bitter,' he said, stamping the excess snow from his boots.

'Not bitter — just singed!'

A dozen light aircraft landed at Prairieville that day. Frankie kept the runway swept of snow. Teddy talked flying with the pilots. Ryder logged their landing and refuelling charges. It was fun. She met wizened old farmers and less wizened young ones, touching down to refuel before flying up to Minneapolis for machinery parts or Rochester to visit a friend in hospital or Sioux

Falls for a wedding. For this was flying country, as Teddy told her. Charles Lindbergh came from Little Falls.

Monday was her day off and Leo's first day at school. Silent and whitefaced he sat in the back of the car with Rudy as Debbie drove them to school. Ryder tried to talk to him but he wouldn't answer. At the entrance Rudy ran to join his class but Leo clung to Ryder, his face hidden against her legs.

'Here comes your teacher,' said Debbie, trying to distract him. She introduced Miss Edge to Ryder. A kindly but humourless woman in her late fifties, Miss Edge was the backbone of the junior school.

She took Leo firmly by the hand. 'You're not scared of me, are you? Of course not! You're a big boy.' She led him towards the classroom.

Debbie grabbed Ryder. 'Quick!'

They jumped into the car and headed for the town centre.

'Poor Leo,' Ryder sighed. 'I'm not a very good guardian. When he has those tantrums, I want to thump him.'

'I want to thump him too.' Debbie pulled up outside the shopping mall. 'He's so spoiled.'

'Nothing I ever said was half as interesting to my mother as two burbles from Leo. I resented him then and I resent being lumbered with him now. And yet, my heart goes out to him.' She opened the car door. 'I'll buy him a sweater. A nice thick one.'

'Stop feeling guilty.'

'A blue one. He likes blue.'

That night Leo slept with the blue sweater under his pillow.

Ryder arrived at work to find a small-town bottle-blonde sifting through the contents of her desk.

She looked up. 'Hi. I'm Lisa.'

'I'm Ryder. Can I help you?'

'I'm waiting for Teddy.'

'I meant — in my desk.'

'It was my desk.' She flicked a piece of chewed gum into the waste paper basket and moved away. Ryder sat down. She began to type.

'Teddy and I are gettin' married,' said Lisa. 'Did he tell you?'

'No.' Ryder carried on typing.

'Well, I am — just so you don't go getting ideas.'

'Don't worry.' Ryder rolled an envelope into the typewriter.

'Oh, I ain't worried.' Lisa lit a cigarette. 'I reckon you could start looking for another job.'

Teddy roared up to the terminal, banged out of his car, and flung open the door. 'What's so urgent?' he asked Lisa.

'Nothing.' She slid her arms around his waist. 'I thought we could have lunch. After all, it is my birthday.'

They went out. Teddy didn't come back all day. It was the first time Ryder had been alone at the airfield. The buildings were silent, the airstrip desolate. She stood by the front window and looked out. Much of the snow had melted. Just a thin layer covered the muddy ground. Mile after mile of it. She was glad when it was time to go home.

Teddy called in sick. Again Ryder spent the day alone. In the late afternoon Frankie arrived. Together they logged the landing and refuelling charges.

'You've finally got this place organised,' one wizened old farmer told Ryder as he climbed into the cockpit of his Cessna.

'Why do you say that?'

'I got my bill this morning!'

Teddy returned looking pale and subdued. 'Place looks great.' He forced a smile.

153

'Thanks. But you look terrible. Can I get you anything?'

He slumped down at his desk. 'Lisa and I have split up. That's why she left before Christmas.'

'I'm sorry,' she said, thinking Teddy was well out of it.

'Oh, but I want it to end.' He stood up and walked to the window. 'I just feel bad about hurting her. We've been going together since High School. Our mothers are best friends. Everyone assumed we'd marry. I did, till Dad died and I started to run the airfield. I love it out here. Lisa resented that.' He gave a sad smile. 'It isn't just Lisa I've hurt. Now her Mom won't speak to mine. Her Dad won't buy his gas from Doug Wise. You could cut the atmosphere with a knife. It's as bad as when they found out Susan was living with the poet.'

A plane coming in to land cut Teddy short. He threw on his jacket and headed for the door. Hand on the knob, he stopped and looked at Ryder. 'Lisa accused me of liking you. She's right. I do.'

He opened the door and went out into the wind.

Teddy could barely look Ryder in the eye but she pretended not to notice, busying herself with work. 'Earnings on hangarage and refuelling are up by 30 per cent this month.' She showed him the accounts.

'It's all due to you.' He smiled tentatively.

She returned to her desk. 'You could earn more if you cleaned up the second hangar and rented out the space.'

'There's no demand.'

'Create it! You'd soon fill the hangar — and the more aircraft that use Prairieville, the more fuel sold.'

'I'll think it over.' He sat back in his chair. 'Would you . . . come to the movies with me on Saturday? They're showing *The Graduate*.'

'I've seen it.' Memories of Adam and that wet after-

154

noon in London made her answer more abruptly than she meant to.

He went out and spent the rest of that day in the hangar, servicing his two-seater Piper.

Working at the airfield meant Ryder saw little of Leo. She was seldom home before supper and at the weekend frequently later. Monday and Tuesday were her days off, when she did the school run. But even then she wasn't alone with Leo: Rudy was in the pickup. She sensed that Leo was unhappy and made an appointment with his teacher.

'Miss Edge reckons that he won't speak in class because the other kids tease him about his accent,' she told her grandmother when she returned from the school.

'Then he must learn to talk like us.'

'Or I try to find a more cosmopolitan school to suit him.'

'You're just like Carrie. Prairieville High weren't good enough for her either.'

'I didn't say it wasn't good enough! It just doesn't suit Leo.'

Her father's trial was due to take place in May. As it approached he wrote more frequently. A buyer had been found for Dingwall Court but the sale would not be completed till May. Mrs Trumpet planned to live with her brother, who had a cottage nearby. In reply Ryder described the airfield and sent him photos of herself and Leo. He never asked her to return for his trial, but sometimes she would suddenly stop what she was doing and an image of his cell would come before her eyes.

A reporter from the *Prairieville Gazette* arrived at the airfield when Teddy was out. He was small and stocky like an overfed terrier. 'It's you I want to see,' he told Ryder, drawing up a chair opposite her desk.

'About what?'

'Oh . . . er . . . Prairieville couple give home to daughter's children. That kind of thing.'

She opened the door. 'Get out!'

Three days later an article appeared.

FRAUDSTERS CHILDREN WELCOME IN PRAIRIEVILLE

After the suicide of their mother, the former Carrie Milne, and the imprisonment of their father, Ryder and Leo Harding have found peace and happiness with their grandparents, Dan and Greta Milne.

'It's my fault,' Teddy confessed when Ryder stormed into the terminal. 'The reporter's a friend. I told him you worked here.'

'Why the hell did you do that?'

'I didn't know he'd follow it up.'

'Of course he would! He's a journalist. Don't you think we've been hounded enough? Okay, so I'm Paul Harding's daughter. My father's in prison.' She raised her hands to her face. 'What more do people want from me?'

'Don't cry! Please.'

'It's just so . . . so unfair. I can cope with it but Leo can't. He's being teased enough at school.'

'Ryder.' He put his arms around her. Tentatively. Unsure of her reaction. She was folded into his protective warmth. She pressed her face into his shoulder. His arms held her tight. Protecting her. Caring for her. 'I've wanted to hold you since that first day when you drove here in the snow,' he said. 'No one else would have come. Not on a day like that.'

'Teddy, I . . . I'm very grateful to you but . . .'

'Lisa knew. She knew before I did.'

'I don't think we should . . . I mean, I think we should stay just friends. We're too different.'

'But I've never met anyone as similar to me. You love

156

Prairieville. You love the airfield.' He smoothed back her hair and looked into her eyes. Then he brushed her mouth with his, kissing her gently.

She felt herself respond. She didn't mean to. But she needed to be wonderful to someone. He ran his hands through her tousled hair. Holding her head. Whispering that he loved her against the softness of her mouth. Her lips opened to him, her body pressed into his. She slid her arms around his neck as he ran his hands down her back. Down. Down.

'Let's go through to the back,' he whispered.

'Someone might come.'

'We'll lock up.'

'Teddy, we mustn't. I'm not on the pill.'

'I'll take care of that.' He opened the door of the small back storeroom. 'I'll never let anything bad happen to you again.'

They were in half-light, surrounded by empty cardboard boxes. He tossed an old blanket on the floor and pulled her down on it. The ground was hard. The room was cold. He unzipped her trousers and slipped them from her hips. She responded to him, kissing him. Wanting him to make love to her slowly. To turn her desire for affection into passion.

He unbuttoned her shirt and buried his face in the nape of her neck. The buckle of his belt dug into her stomach. She reached for it. He took her hand. 'Oh, Ryder, this is wonderful!' He pushed her back among the boxes, lowering himself on to her, unable to wait any longer. 'Oh, it's the best.' He gasped. 'The best!'

All afternoon he kissed and fondled her, whispering that she was wonderful: he didn't seem to realise that she had remained unsatisfied. It was dark when they left work. He drew her to him in the shadow of the building. 'Let's get in the car,' he murmured, running his hand up the inside of her leg. 'Come on! It'll be more comfortable.'

She chuckled. 'It could hardly be less so.'

They climbed into the back and fell on each other, shivering with cold and desire. 'I love to see a woman's breasts.' He unbuttoned her shirt. 'I like to hold them.' She gasped as his freezing hands touched her. He tried to cover her and at the same time expose her. The windows steamed up. Their clothes became entangled. Discomfort added excitement. Fear of discovery inflicted urgency. He manoeuvred her, till she sat astride him. 'I want to see your face when I make love to you.' He kissed her tenderly. She arched her back and his mouth moved down between her breasts. She moved rhythmically. Slowly. Till she cried out with pleasure. Only then did he move faster.

Ryder did her best to keep her relationship with Teddy secret because she didn't want it ruined by Prairieville gossip. So when Teddy took her to the cinema, she told Debbie it was because — coincidentally — they wanted to see the same film. When he took her out to dinner, she claimed he felt guilty at making her work late. When they went to Minneapolis, she said it was to study new landing lights for the airfield.

'So how come you're not taking Frankie?' asked Debbie with a knowing wink.

Ryder answered her with a look of wide-eyed innocence. 'Because he's at school during the week.'

Spring arrived suddenly. The sun shone. The prairie turned into a carpet of wild flowers. They grew right up to the edge of the runway. At Scot's Farm, her grandfather replaced the storm windows with fly screens whilst her grandmother springcleaned. In the henhouse chicks were hatching. Beside the barn a new family of kittens played in the dust.

The airfield was busy. A dozen planes landed every day. Sometimes they had to wait in line to take off. With the light evenings, the terminal stayed open later. Pilots hung around, talking flying, unaware that Teddy and Ryder were itching to be alone.

'Thought any more about the unused hangar?' she asked him.

'We don't need it. We're doing just fine.'

'We could rent out the space within a week.'

'Ryder, this ain't a metropolis. This is Prairieville.'

She turned away. He watched her face set and her eyes look towards the horizon. 'Shall we go to Fox Lake?' he said anxiously. 'I know you love that place.'

The lake was bathed in the glow of spring. The trees which had been so stark were bursting into bud, their leaves still fresh green and unhardened. The little clapboard houses had come alive. Washing hung across their back porches. Wisps of smoke rose from their chimneys.

Teddy borrowed a boat. It was tied up by the wooden jetty where Ryder had dangled her feet in the water. She sat in the bows as he rowed her across to the island, watching as the strip of land drew nearer. Flowers grew among the reeds along the shore. The old autumnal prairie grass was being pushed aside by the new. The trees seemed even more beautiful than those on the lakeside as if absence of human contact brought forth some extra dimension to their freshness. Ryder was entranced by its magic.

'I wonder how the White Squaw changed so quickly from loving the soldier to loving the Indian,' she said, dipping her fingers in the icy water.

Teddy turned the boat for home. 'It's only a legend.'

Debbie brought Ryder a cup of coffee early one morning. 'So . . . !' She sat down on the end of the bed. 'I guess I'm talking to the future Mrs Macdonald.'

'Teddy and I are just friends.'

'That's not what he told his Mom.'

Ryder arrived at work angry. 'I wish you'd kept quiet,' she said. 'I can't bear this gossip.'

'But I'm proud of you.' He put his arms around her. 'I'm proud to be with you. And I want everyone to know it.'

She pulled away. 'If you'd been pointed at as much as I have you'd understand.'

He spent the day in hurt silence. She spent the day feeling guilty. That evening she was especially tender. But next morning she was angry with herself though not sure why.

She asked Teddy to teach her to fly, expecting him to be delighted. 'You don't need to learn,' he said. 'I'll take you up whenever you want.'

'Fine — but I still want to learn.'

He fiddled with the papers on his desk. 'Flying's a man's sport.'

'What about Amy Johnson and Amelia Earhart?'

'I ain't teaching you and that's that!'

'Then I'll learn from someone else.' She rolled a page into the typewriter and thumped furiously on the keys whilst Teddy gazed miserably at her.

'We'll go flying tomorrow,' he said eventually. 'I'll take you up to Fort Ridgley. Show you our Minnesota history. We deserve a day's vacation.' He paused. 'You'd like to go, wouldn't you?'

He smiled at her so lovingly that she couldn't refuse.

They set off early in his old two-seater Piper, Teddy at the controls, Ryder behind, her legs on either side of his seat. They taxied to the runway and turned into the wind. He opened the throttle. They ambled forward, gradually picking up speed till they were bouncing along the airstrip, the ground whizzing beneath them. At last they were airborne. Below, the farmland stretched away in square hedgeless fields and dead straight tracks through which the six-lane Interstate 90 stretched like a silver ribbon.

They flew north, over tiny lakes which glistened like dewdrops in the sun and unremarkable towns with evocative names like Sleepy Eye. Then they followed the wooded Minnesota Valley.

'Fort Ridgley!' Teddy pointed down as they swooped over a hill where the stone foundations of several buildings stood out clearly in the short grass. 'Where Little Crow attacked the fort.' They swung round and came in along the twisting Minnesota River. He banked the plane up the hillside, flying so low that the prairie grass was flattened by the slipstream. 'Some of the Sioux attacked through the brush,' he shouted. 'They fired blazing arrows at the fort. The others waited on their ponies. Little Crow rode a black. Eight days later the cavalry arrived and the siege was over.'

'What happened to Little Crow?'

'Wounded.' Teddy swooped the fort once more, then headed back down the valley. 'That was a hundred years ago!' He shouted. 'History.'

She laughed. 'That was yesterday.' And she turned to look back at the fort. The hill was framed against the late afternoon sun. One tree stood out, its uppermost branches like the feathered headdress of a warrior. And for a moment it seemed as though Chief Little Crow had returned.

As Ryder parked the pickup under the settler's trees, her grandmother called to her from the kitchen. 'Mrs Wise has invited us to Sunday lunch.'

'I have to work at the weekends.'

'Not this Sunday.'

Ryder entered the farmhouse, her jacket draped over one shoulder, her bag over the other. Her grandfather was sitting in his armchair reading the *Prairieville Gazette*. He barely glanced up. Frankie was lounging in front of the television. He winked. Leo was eating his supper. He giggled.

'What's going on?' she demanded. 'Have I won the pools or have I got leprosy?'

'Neither, dear.' Her grandmother bustled out of the

kitchen, wiping her hands on her apron. 'It's very kind of Mrs Wise. Teddy'll be there.'

'Grandma!'

'Well it's only natural that she should want to know the girl her son's going to marry.'

'Teddy and I are just . . . friends.'

Her grandfather laid down his paper. 'We may be ancient but we ain't dumb. No one stays out late every night with just a friend.'

'Or comes home looking flushed if they ain't intending to marry.' Her grandmother pursed her lips in disapproval. 'In fact,' she lowered her voice so Leo couldn't hear, 'there shouldn't be any "looking flushed" till you're married.'

'Grandma, I'm an adult and my relationship with Teddy is my own business.'

'Not in Prairieville. We've already had one shotgun wedding in this family and we don't want another.'

Ryder slammed out of the house and into the barn.

'Did they have a go at you?' asked Debbie, who was helping Rudy with his homework.

'Anyone would think I was fourteen.'

'People are talking.'

'You mean I'm a scarlet woman.' Ryder started to laugh. 'My God, they should meet Alix.' She went on laughing with a kind of hysterical desperation. Then suddenly she stopped, dialled Teddy's number, and said, 'Meet me at Fox Lake.'

Two hours later Ryder returned to Scot's Farm. The lights were still on. Their glow poured out across the porch, gleaming on the damp night grass. She parked beneath the cottonwoods. For a moment she sat there, her arms resting on the steering wheel, as she drank in the sounds of the night. The distant barking of a dog. Alfie clucking in the hen house. The rustle of the trees. The breaking of a twig which she had once feared to be a moccasined foot.

162

Her grandparents were watching television. They smiled expectantly as Ryder entered. 'I have something to tell you,' she said.

Their faces lit up. 'You're going to marry Teddy?'

'No — I'm going back to England.'

Her grandparents were watching television. They smiled expectantly as Ryder entered. 'I have something to tell you,' she said.

Their faces lit up. 'Stop it, you're going to marry Teddy?'

'No——' 'I'm going back to England.'

15

England

It was drizzling when they landed at Heathrow. The airport looked grey and greasy. Water dripped from the terminal on to the tarmac. The smell of fuel hung on the damp air. Leo was asleep. Ryder unbuckled his seat belt and helped him out of the plane. She should have left him in Prairieville till her father's trial was over and she could concentrate on finding them somewhere to live. Her grandparents were right. He was five. Too young to drag around the world. But how could she leave him in a place where he was clearly unhappy.

She piled their cases on to a trolley, sat Leo on top, and pushed him through the swing doors, to where the crowds leaned against the barriers waiting for friends and relatives.

'There she is!' A flashlight exploded in her face. Then another. 'Miss Harding, did you know your father's been found guilty?'

'How could I when I've only just landed?' She walked on, determined not to show emotion.

'Will you be in court tomorrow for his sentencing?'

'He is my father.' She pushed the trolley forward. They chased after her, shouting out their questions. One man grabbed at her arm. Leo screamed. Ryder turned. 'Stop hounding me! Is it my fault what my father does? Is it your fault . . . or yours . . . what your father did or didn't do? If Hitler had a daughter would you blame her for what he did? Now leave me alone, you dumb bastards!'

They fell back. She hurried on.

'Ryder, dear.'

'Oh, Mrs Trumpet!' She wanted to cry with relief.

'I couldn't let you arrive with no one to meet you. Not with your father just been found guilty. Oh, my poor dear! And you, Leo.' Mrs Trumpet ruffled his blond hair as he gazed up at her in rapture. 'You're coming with me for a few days.'

'I'm so grateful. I know your brother has a bad heart and I hope Leo won't tire him.' She was now dear and not Miss Ryder, and she preferred it.

Ryder took the underground into London. It was still drizzling when she came out of the station into the squalid rat run of the Earl's Court Road, where lorries raced from north to south, belching exhaust into the already fetid air. She turned off the main road into a sidestreet of tired hotels and entered the nearest. An old man shuffled to the reception desk . . . 'Just one night?' He looked glum. 'Don't like doing one-nighters.'

'I'll pay in advance.'

'All right. But no men in your room.' He showed her a room which was as small and characterless as a shoebox but Ryder was too tired to care. She lay down on the narrow bed. Men! There was barely room for a stick insect. She thought of Teddy standing beside Fox Lake saying bitterly, 'If you didn't see us as permanent, why did you lead me on?' It would be some consolation for him to see her now.

When she woke the rain had stopped and pale shafts of sunlight forced their way through the drab net curtains. She rose, showered, and dressed in red culottes and a white sweat-shirt: clothes she had bought in London last summer. A year ago. A lifetime. *Yesterday*.

The public telephone was in the hall. She dialled the

165

number of Imogen's new house. As it rang she saw Immy. The dainty walk. The mass of curling red hair. The pleasure when she heard Ryder's voice. In her mind she was in the shoebox, repacking her case, hurrying to Immy.

But Adam answered. She slammed down the receiver. Just to hear his voice made her feel sick. She dialled the theatre. A girl replied, 'Miss Lydden left the cast last week. She's in Hollywood.'

Ryder replaced the receiver. Her mother had been right. If she split up with Adam, their friends would take his side. And who more than Imogen, his sister?

The sun was shining. People were laughing: people who had other people. Two women passed, walking arm-in-arm. They were clearly mother and daughter. Ryder watched them. If only she could have had that closeness with her mother. She felt desolate, in this city which had been her home and now didn't want to know her. She longed for a voice to say, 'How nice to hear from you. Let's meet! Where are you? A hotel! Do stay with us.' But there was no one. She couldn't even phone Jeremy in case Alix answered.

Without thinking where she was going, she found herself in the Old Brompton Road, not far from the flat. She hadn't meant to come here but some demon magnet had led her. A headline caught her eyes.

HARDING GUILTY — SENTENCED TOMORROW

She purchased an *Evening Standard*. On the second page was a picture of herself, head thrown back, eyes wild, hair unkempt. ' *"Leave me alone, you dumb bastards!"* *shouts fraudster's daughter*.' With her head bent she hurried back to the hotel, afraid that everyone on the streets of London would recognise her.

Early next morning Ryder left the shoebox and took

the underground to Paddington. There she breakfasted — or rather tried to — but the toast stuck in her throat and the coffee choked her. In the Ladies she stared at her reflection in the mirror. Her face was gaunt. Her hair hung in rats' tails. Her eyes had a haunted, hunted wariness. She rubbed some lipstick into her cheeks to give them colour but it made her look like Frankenstein's sister, so she washed it off. She dampened her hair and dragged it back into a short neat plait. It looked severe but tidy. She swapped her culottes and sweatshirt for a black skirt and jacket. They were far too hot for May but she had nothing else. She wanted to laugh and cry as she pictured herself accosting a Harrods' sales assistant with, *'I'm looking for a suit in which to watch my father go to gaol.'*

The rush hour was at its most execrable when Ryder hit the underground for the second time. No free seats. No spare hanging strap. Someone's garlic in her face. At Notting Hill she changed trains. Again no seats. At St Paul's she exited, gasping for air.

The reporters were grouped around the entrance to the Old Bailey. With each arriving taxi they pushed forward. Ryder hesitated. She was overtaken by two lady barristers, both in black suits. They walked briskly, exuding purpose. The people parted before them. Sticking her nose in the air, Ryder marched along behind them. At every step she expected someone to shout, 'There she is!' But the press hardly glanced her way — till she reached the arched entrance to the spectators' gallery and dashed inside and up the stairs to the safety of the security office.

The gallery was already full. An usher stopped Ryder at the door. 'No more public seats.'

'But I'm Paul Harding's daughter. I've come all the way from America.'

He moved people to make a space in the front row. She'd have preferred the anonymity of the back. The noise caught Podmore's attention. He gave Ryder a look of astonishment. At one minute before ten-thirty a side door opened and her father was led in. He was pale and composed, though his hair was greyer than she remembered. Ryder was glad she'd come. She saw Podmore pass him a note. He read it and looked up. 'Thanks,' he mouthed, giving her the thumbs up.

She blushed as everyone turned to stare.

The court rose as the judge entered. They sat when he sat.

'Defendant, please rise,' said the clerk.

Her father stood. He gripped the bar till his knuckles turned white.

'Paul Harding,' the judge frowned at him. 'Your counsel has put forth many arguments in your defence. I have listened carefully, but I find no mitigating circumstances. You were a public figure and you stole a very large sum. Much has not been recovered. I sentence you to eight years imprisonment.'

'Eight years!' shouted her father. 'When muggers get off with a suspended sentence!'

'Take the prisoner away.'

'Eight years when men who rape old ladies get half of that.'

He was hustled down into the cells, leaving the courtroom in an uproar as journalists rushed to the telephones. Ryder buried her face in her hands. Not crying. Nothing. She felt utterly drained.

'Miss Harding!' Mr Podmore touched her arm. 'We'll appeal, of course.'

She stood up. 'Can I see him?'

'Not now.'

'But he's only downstairs.'

'Miss Harding, this is a court of law!'

'Law or justice?' She stood up. 'Father was right. He should have been a mugger or a rapist.' She marched out of the courtroom with Podmore following. As she

168

headed down the stone stairs, a woman said, 'His daughter! What's she got to be so proud about!' But Ryder took no notice. Nothing could hurt her any more.

Outside the Old Bailey a man from the BBC lunchtime news was summarising the trial to the black face of a camera. He turned as Ryder appeared. The camera zoomed towards her. Podmore took her arm and steered her towards a taxi, with the pack of journalists baying at her heels. She sank thankfully into the back seat. 'Where will he be sent?' she asked as the taxi drew away.

'Wandsworth to start with. You can visit him twice a month. Then he'll go to Ford, I expect. It's an open prison near Arundel. But he won't be sent to Ford till they are sure he won't abscond.' Podmore paused to polish his spectacles. 'He could get parole after he's completed one third. There's no guarantee, of course. Some get it. Some don't. But remission is his due if he behaves, so he'll be out in about five and a half years.'

She stared out of the window at the office workers queueing for sandwiches and polystyrene soup, amazed that such things continued when her father was beginning an eight-year gaol sentence. 'How long can I stay at Dingwall Court?' she asked Podmore.

'Two weeks.'

'I see.' She leaned forward and knocked on the glass partition. 'Stop here please!' She had the door open before the taxi halted. 'I meant to ask you,' she said as she stepped out. 'My father told me I own Bailing airfield.'

He gave a thin smile. 'You own half. I'll send you the deeds. There's a map and various rights.'

'Can I live there?'

'My dear Miss Harding, there's no house. Just a couple of hangars and a control tower. All very rundown.'

'Can I sell?'

169

'Only to your co-owner — Miss Bronwen Brendan Broughton.'

Ryder left Leo with Mrs Trumpet and drove up to Bailing. The journey took several hours in her rattling old mini. She clipped the top of North London and ploughed through the semi-suburbs of Hertfordshire, before turning north on to the motorway, to fight for roadspace against lorries whose slipstreams buffeted her from side to side. Outside Ely she stopped and bought a sandwich. She ate it on the garage forecourt, looking across at the great brooding cathedral. It reminded her of prison. Of her father.

Bailing didn't appear on Ryder's road map but according to Podmore's enclosure it was about six miles east of King's Lynn. She turned off the main road, down a winding lane. The potato fields of the fens had given way to rolling agricultural land, vast fields of ripening corn beneath huge pale skies raked by strange cloud formations.

The lane was so narrow that the grass verges stroked her car and the hedges were so high that she couldn't see the houses, until suddenly she saw a sign, *BAILING*, and a sharp bend landed her in the village. It consisted of a dozen flint cottages grouped around a duckpond, a square-towered Norman church, a shop selling milk, bread and the *Eastern Daily Press*, a butcher closed for the afternoon, and an old dog asleep outside the pub — The Bailing Arms.

She checked Podmore's map and drove on over the stone bridge which spanned the River Bailum. She slowed. Frowned. Then she saw it: a wartime pillbox, half-hidden by earth and trees, beside a five bar gate with:

BAILING AIRFIELD
Private Property
Trespassers Will Be Prosecuted.

170

She opened the gate and crossed a stretch of windswept tarmac. Ahead were two hangars, rusted and open to the elements. She parked her car and walked around. Beyond the hangars was the main runway. To one side was the control tower, a two-storey redbrick block with each window pane blasted by time.

Picking her way through the debris of thirty years of disuse, Ryder explored the tower. The ground floor was just one large room with an arch leading to a small kitchen — or what would once have counted as a kitchen. It had a stone sink, a wooden draining board and a cold tap. She turned it on. Rusty water spluttered out. At the far end of the room was a bathroom, with an ancient claw-footed enamel bath, another cold tap, and more rusty water. On the wall by a cracked mirror was a torn poster of Betty Grable.

Iron stairs, the kind found in country railway stations, led to the first floor. She climbed them gingerly, nervous of what she might find, afraid that the floor might collapse under her. Upstairs was another large open space, with paneless windows looking out in all directions. They rattled ceaselessly in the wind. Next to the window which had the best view of the runway was a blackboard. It was wind-wiped clean, except for one small illegible chalk mark: the last memento of those who flew on the final bombing raid out of Bailing.

The runways were built in the shape of an A, to allow for take-off in all wind directions, with the main runway — the lefthand stroke — running southwest to northeast. Ryder pictured the waiting pilots. Her father pacing up and down, flying jacket on, goggles pushed back on his forehead. Then the phone would ring. The order would come. Scramble! The crews would rush to their aircraft, to take off one by one, heading out across the North Sea.

Then would come the long wait for the men in this control tower. They'd track the bombers' route. Drink coffee. Wait. Wonder. Until, at last, they'd hear the distant hum of a Lancaster. The first would land. The second. The third. Some shot up. Some with wounded. The fourth. The fifth. A long gap. Anxious moments. The sixth, crash-landing. Then nothing. Nothing — except the pale Norfolk skies and the unaccounted names on the blackboard.

A black alsatian was running across the tarmac. It raced into the control tower and up the stairs, barking furiously. Ryder pressed herself into the corner as it bunched its haunches. Eyes yellow. Teeth bared.

'Wolf!' a woman shouted.

It hesitated. Then sank to the ground.

'Heel!'

It slunk down the stairs.

'And you! Whoever you are up there. Show yourself at the window or I'll set the dog on you.'

A leathery, aquiline woman was standing on the tarmac. Her grey hair was stuffed up under a black felt hat and, in spite of it being May, she wore the kind of black serge riding habit in which Edwardian ladies hunted sidesaddle. 'This is private property,' she bellowed, 'and I'm the owner.'

'I'm the other owner.' Ryder smiled politely. 'You must be Miss Brendan Broughton.'

'Harding's daughter! I wondered how soon you'd come snooping around.'

'I was going to telephone you.'

'I don't have a telephone.' The woman walked away.

'Miss Brendan Broughton. Please wait!' Ryder ran down the stairs. 'I want to talk to you about the airfield.'

'I wouldn't sell to your father and I'm not selling to you.'

'I'm not trying to buy you out. I couldn't afford to. Look, I realise that you probably didn't get on with my father but . . .'

'He killed George.'

'That's what Patrick said but it's not strictly true.'

Miss Brendan Broughton hit the tarmac with her shooting stick. 'I haven't spoken to your father for twenty years and I've no intention of having anything to do with you. So go back to London. Bailing doesn't want you.' She walked off, the dog following.

'I've as much right to be here as you have,' Ryder shouted after her. She marched to the runway. Grass encroached on either side. Yellow ragwort poked through the cracked tarmac. She grabbed a handful and pulled. It came away, roots and all. Tossing it to one side, she grabbed some more. And more. Heading for the sun.

16

It was after midnight when Ryder reached Dingwall Court. The house was in darkness. She'd never seen it like that before. The front lights were always left on. But tonight the building loomed up gaunt into the night sky, the only relief being a slight reflection of river mist on the window panes. Ryder sat outside in the car. She was mad to have come. Stupid not to have gone to a cheap hotel. If she'd had a rug, she'd have slept in the back seat of the car but she didn't have one and it was cold. She stepped out, freezing with fear as the gravel crunched beneath her feet. She was reminded of the frost crackling beneath her feet on that first night when she'd arrived at Scot's Farm.

There's nothing to be afraid of. She took another step. *Who's going to be here?* No one. But it was all so silent. So ominous. Perhaps she should drive to Mrs Trumpet's. Dawn Cottage was only a mile away. There'd be room on the floor near Leo, where she'd slept the night before driving up to Norfolk. But she couldn't bang on their door in the middle of the night, not when Mrs Trumpet's brother had a bad heart. They certainly wouldn't keep Leo if she did that. She gripped the backdoor key and marched into the forbidding darkness.

The door opened easily. She felt for the switch. Flicked it. Nothing. She eased her way along the passage towards the kitchens. Another switch. Nothing. The electricity had been switched off. She felt her way into the kitchen and opened the drawers, searching for matches. There were none. She tried to light the stove but the gas had been turned off. Hand on the banister, she crept up the back stairs and along the corridor which led from the servants' quarters to the main house. There was a heavy oak door. It creaked as she opened it. Past more spare rooms, she came to the main stairs and the landing outside her mother's room, where she'd found Leo crying.

She mustn't think about her mother now. Not when she was alone in the house. She'd go through it all one day, when she was stronger. She'd relive it slowly, and come to terms with it. Or try to. But she mustn't think about the past yet — or she'd never escape from it.

The door to her bedroom was open. She hesitated, her scalp prickling. *Come on!* She straightened her shoulders. *Come on!* She crossed the room to the antique trunk where her duvet and blankets were stored, took them out, and lay down on the floor where her bed used to be. It had been sold along with everything, except for the trunk, the grandfather clock, an old pine table with a couple of chairs saved for her by Mrs Trumpet, and Leo's bed and chest decorated with Donald Duck and Mickey Mouse. They could hardly claim that belonged to her father.

Ryder hadn't expected to sleep but she did: she was exhausted. In the early morning she woke, confused by the position of the window. What had been level with her was now above her. For a moment she couldn't think where she was. Then she dragged herself up, limbs aching from the hard floor, hands stiff and sore from pulling up weeds, and tottered into the bathroom. She turned on the bath tap. Water gushed out. Stripping off her dirty clothes, she jumped in and sat down.

She shrieked. The water was cold. The boiler was off. Teeth chattering, she forced herself to stay in the water, as she scrubbed the dirt from her body and her lacerated

175

hands. Finally, she slopped shampoo over her head and turned on the shower. The only pleasure was when she stepped out into a dry towel.

The house had been cleared, apart from a pile of suitcases and boxes belonging to herself and Leo. They were stacked in the hall beside the clock and labelled, *R. Harding — destination to be advised*. She paced the hollow rooms, her hair dripping on the dusty floor. In the study she touched the marks in the floor where her father's desk had stood. In the drawing room she stood by the window where her father had confessed, 'I'm in serious trouble.' In her parents' bedroom she closed her eyes, and for a moment she could recall her mother's scent. Flowery. Dainty. Elegant.

That's where Mrs Trumpet found her in the late morning, fast asleep, slumped against the wall of her mother's bedroom. 'You shouldn't be here alone.' She helped Ryder to her feet. 'You should have come to the cottage, dear.'

'I didn't want to wake you. Your brother must find Leo exhausting.'

'It's his tantrums. He's worse than ever. After what you've both been through it's not surprising he's upset, but you'll have to be firm or you'll have a terrible time. Firm but kind.' She patted Ryder's arm. 'My brother doesn't mind for a few days. Oh, dear! You didn't think we'd keep him longer?'

'Of course not.' Ryder forced a smile. *Damn Leo! Why couldn't he behave.*

She spent the morning dragging suitcases downstairs and piling them up in the hall, whilst Mrs Trumpet packed those items of kitchenware ignored by the auctioneers: a couple of saucepans, a frying pan, some odd plates and glasses. When all was ready, she hooked the horse trailer to the Land-Rover.

Mrs Trumpet shook her head. 'You're not driving that to Norfolk.'

'It's cheaper than a removal van. The garage are buying the Land-Rover so I have to return it. I'll leave my car there.' She heaved the pine table up the ramp of the horsebox. 'At least I don't have to bring this old trailer back too.'

Ryder spent that night on a mattress at the cottage. In the morning she returned alone to Dingwall Court. She wanted to say goodbye to it in solitude. She walked through the rooms for the last time, checking every cupboard, looking out of every window. Remembering. Saying goodbye. Then she marched out of the front door, locked it, dropped her key into the letter box – and drove away.

Ryder had never towed a trailer before but she kept that to herself. Not that there was anyone to tell, except for Leo who sat beside her, silent and anxious. That was one of the worst aspects. Being so alone. There was no one to turn to. No one to whom she could be a child.

The last thing she wanted to do was to revisit Gate-house Stables but Podmore's secretary, a woman who'd previously oozed charm, had sent her a curt note to say she could keep the trailer but not the new saddles.

The ponies had been sold and the stables looked deserted. Doors swung open and odd bits of straw fluttered around the yard.

'Is this our new home?' Leo looked even more anxious.

'No. Stay in the car.'

Honeysuckle swung beneath the arch which led to the main house. She pushed it aside and crossed the drive to the front door. Even before she rang the bell she sensed the house was unoccupied. She scribbled a note: *'Harness from Dingwall returned. R. Harding.'*

The tackroom was unlocked. She lifted the saddles on to their stout wooden pegs. When she stepped backwards, she nearly fell over Leo. 'I told you to stay in the Land-Rover,' she snapped.

177

'There's . . . a . . . man.'

She took him by the hand. 'No need to be frightened.' Then she realised her mistake. She should be teaching him about sweets from strangers, or he'd end up strangled in a ditch and it would be all her fault.

An old gardener was leaning on a rake scratching his head.

'I brought the saddles back,' she told him. 'The solicitor asked me to.'

'Nothin' to do with me.' He took out a tin of tobacco and began to roll a cigarette. 'I'm just waitin' for them to collect the pony.' He pointed to a black pony which was walking stiffly across the paddock towards them.

'But that's Bruja. She's the best of the lot.'

He shrugged. 'She 'ad a fall so they fired 'er legs but it didn't work. Lame as Long John Silver.' He cackled, 'But the hounds'll enjoy 'er.'

'What do you mean?'

'The kennels are payin' twenty quid. It'd be more if she weren't pining.'

'I refuse to allow it.'

'Refuse! Harding's daughter! At least none o' my family's been in prison.'

Ryder longed to slap him but that would have been the end of Bruja. 'I didn't mean to be rude.' She forced herself to sound apologetic. 'It's just . . . Oh, you don't want to see her eaten, do you?'

'I want my twenty quid.'

'I'll give you fifteen.'

'Twenty — or she goes to the dogs.'

Ryder looked at the pony. What was she going to do with her? It was mad even to think of it. But Bruja's big brown liquid eyes were full of accusation. 'All right. Twenty — and I take her bridle and anything else she needs.'

'Take what you please.' He pocketed the money and shuffled off.

178

It took Ryder an hour to repack the horsebox and the Land-Rover, making space for Bruja in one half of the box, whilst Leo searched the stables for hay and oats.

'Do you think she knows we've saved her?' His eyes brightened each time he looked at the pony, squeezed between the pine table and the grandfather clock.

'I don't know — but she'd better be grateful!'

A cold northeast wind was sweeping down the runway at Bailing as Ryder parked beside the control tower. 'Come on, Leo,' she called, leading Bruja towards the river which was some fifty yards away. 'Your job is to look after Bruja. I'm tying her to this tree, so she can get to the water and eat some grass. But you must make sure the rope doesn't hook round her legs.'

Leo's face puckered. 'Where are you going?'

'Just over there. By the tower.'

'Where's our new home?'

'That's it.'

'But it hasn't any windows.' He began to cry.

'I'm going to mend them. Now be quiet or you'll frighten the pony.'

He threw himself on the ground and screamed. Bruja jumped away, her ears flat against her head.

'If you don't shut up I'll send you back to Prairieville.' Ryder started for the tower. He ran after her and kicked at her ankles. She turned, caught him, and slapped his bare leg. He howled. She threw him on to the grass and walked on. He was going back to Prairieville whether he liked it or not.

It wasn't possible to unpack the trailer until the tower was clean, but there was no point in cleaning it until she'd replaced the windows, and once she'd returned the Land-Rover to Henley, she'd have no means to move the trailer. Ignoring Leo's screaming, she counted the windows. There were ten, and each window needed two panes. Inside the tower she measured the walls to be painted and calculated the floor area to be varnished. Then she sat in the jeep and wrote her shopping list. Out of the corner of her eye she could see Leo creeping closer. His face was white. His eyes anxious.

'Leo!' she called. 'If you're hungry wash your hands and face.'

He raced into the bathroom and was back in a second, scrambling up beside her.

'What a mess your hair is.' She raised her hand to smooth it. He flinched. She was filled with guilt.

They drove into King's Lynn. She tried not to look at the ugly mark on his leg but it glared at her accusingly. They parked in Tuesday Market, their muddy Land-Rover gazed on with disapproval by the elegant Georgian houses of the square. She took Leo's hand. He clung on tight.

In a narrow sidestreet she found a café and ordered fish and chips. They sat on uncomfortable chairs at a yellow formica-topped table.

'Don't you want ketchup?' she asked him.

'Mummy doesn't allow me to have it.'

'You ate it in America.'

He looked baffled. She wondered if he were psychologically damaged and what she should do about it.

'I'm sure Mummy wouldn't mind.' She smiled as she squeezed some ketchup on to his plate.

A young mother with two small boys sat down at the next table. They were laughing and shrieking, 'Mummy, I want an ice cream. Mummy I want . . .' Trying not to listen, Ryder pushed her plate to one side and drank her coffee.

Leo was watching the two boys, his knife and fork frozen in mid air. 'Mummy!' he murmured. 'Mummy!'

'Would you like an ice cream?' said Ryder, trying to distract him.

His chin quivered. Tears came to his eyes. Suddenly he was sick. All over himself, the chair and the floor.

Ryder jumped up. The waitress came running. The other boys were shouting, 'That boy's been sick.' Ryder picked up Leo and marched through to the Ladies. He was crying and shaking and covered in vomit. 'Don't hit me! Don't hit me!'

'Of course I won't.' *She was a monster. He was only five and she'd terrified him.* She ran hot water into a basin and cleaned him up with soap and tissues. Then she helped him rinse his mouth out. His face was hot and feverish. Supposing he was seriously ill. Supposing she'd hit him so hard he was permanently scarred, physically as well as mentally . . .

'Are you going to send me away?' he whispered.

'I was just cross.' She hugged him.

'You're not cross now?'

'No.' She kissed his hot face. 'You're my little brother. We're going to stay together. But you mustn't scream every time things go wrong. I don't cry.' She picked him up and carried him back through the café.

As they passed a woman sitting near the door she said loudly, 'Poor lamb! Being taken out when he's ill. These young mothers have no sense of responsibility.'

Ryder found a bench in the High Street where they could sit. The fresh air brought a little colour to Leo's cheeks. She felt his forehead. It was cool. 'Well enough to walk?'

He nodded.

In a hardware shop she bought nails, a hammer, a screwdriver and a door lock. From there they were directed to a discount store selling glass and paint. In a camping shop she bought a gas ring. At least she could feed Leo something hot.

Back at the airfield he seemed happy to sit and watch as she picked the old putty from the window frames. In the afternoon he slept on Bruja's blanket whilst she fitted the first two panes. When he woke, to her relief he seemed fully recovered. That evening they washed in the river, dined on scrambled eggs, and slept wrapped in blankets in the back of the Land-Rover. On the following day she continued with the windows whilst Leo plaited Bruja's tail. From the tower Ryder could hear him talking to the pony.

Miss Brendan Broughton appeared in the late afternoon. She stomped across the tarmac shouting, 'What do you think you're doing?'

'Making the place habitable.' Ryder carried on smoothing putty into the cracks of a window frame.

'You can't live here.'

'Oh, yes, I can.'

'With a child! I'll report you to the social services.'

Ryder laid down the tub of putty. 'I'm going to restore the airfield and rent out hangarage space. I'm going to turn this place round and make it pay — and there's nothing you can do to stop me!'

By the weekend Ryder had mended all the windows and brushed out the tower, choking as decades of dust mushroomed up in her face like a nuclear explosion. Once it had settled she began to paint. As she rolled the white emulsion up the walls she noticed a message carved into the back of the door. *Beware of the Hun in the Sun*! She painted round it. Later, she varnished it. And the blackboard. They were reminders of what Bailing had been.

'Is this my bedroom?' asked Leo, as she dragged his Mickey Mouse bed up the wrought-iron stairs.

'We're going to share it. You're having that end.' She shook out his duvet. 'And I'm having this end.' She pointed to her mattress.

'But I always have my own bedroom.'

'Leo!'

He flinched.

She knelt down beside him. 'When I've painted all the buildings and lots of people are keeping their planes here, and we're making money, we'll have a wall put

182

up. But now I have to spend what little I have on an electrician. We can't go through the winter with no light or hot water. I know you're only five, but you have to be very grown up if you want to live with me.'

That night was the first they slept in the tower. It looked stark but at least it was clean. Ryder was reminded of Debbie's barn. She picked some white lilac from a straggly old bush near the gate and arranged it in a paint tin on the table. Then she laid supper carefully around it. Leo took his place as she fried their sausages and chips. She noticed that for once he'd washed his hands without being told. As she handed him his plate, he said, 'I don't mind you sharing my room.'

After he'd gone to bed Ryder sat at the table with the door open on to an exquisite May evening. The sky was gold. The air smelt of grass and lilac. A woodpigeon was calling from the trees near the gate. The cows in the next field were shuffling through the grass. She walked down to the trailer and checked on Bruja. The pony's water bucket was full. Leo had remembered. Back in the tower she lit the lamp and tried to write to her father. But she felt restless. It was an evening which cried out to be lived. She thought of the pub near the London flat where people spilled out on to the pavement. She remembered the little sidestreet restaurants where she and Adam had dined. She pictured Immy trying to bleach her freckles and Alix juggling one man against another. She was so lonely.

An odd job man named Fred Garratt appeared, recommended by Mrs Dennshurst who ran the village shop. Small and weatherbeaten, he walked bent double with the unblinking eyes of a tortoise. 'Plumbing. Painting. Electrics. You name it. Ten pound a day.'

'It's the electrics. I need lights in the control tower and in the hangars.'

He pushed past her into the tower. 'Bit short o' furniture.' He crossed to the kitchen. 'Cooking on tha' ring?

I'll go up the ole tip. Bound to be a cooker thrown ou'. And a fridge.' He went into the bathroom. 'And a boiler.'

'Mr Garratt, I can't afford to spend much money.'

'The name's Fred. You restoring the ole airfield?'

'I'm trying to.'

'Nine pound a day.' He shuffled off towards the hangar. Ryder followed. 'What you going to do with her?' he asked.

'Rent out hangarage. Refuelling. Servicing.'

'You'll need CAA approval.'

'I know.'

'I was in the RAF. Best days o' my life. Missed it, specially since my ole lady died.' He picked at his teeth with a blade of grass. 'Eight pound a day.'

Fred came to the airfield every day, including Sundays, for forty pounds a week: he wouldn't accept a penny more. As the light broke over the runway he'd come trundling through the gates in his old pickup, always with a lettuce or a marrow from his garden. If he didn't bring vegetables, it was a mackerel caught by a friend or a loaf of bread because he'd bought too many. 'But you can't have grown avocados in Norfolk,' Ryder protested, trying to make him accept payment.

He gave her his obstinate tortoise look. 'I have green fingers.'

The mild weather continued. Ryder and Leo washed in the river. It was stony and not very deep, and the only access was down a muddy bank which Leo called the 'slither-bump'. But at least it wasn't as cold as the rusty tap water and the clawfooted bath. Shivering in her cotton bikini, Ryder rinsed the shampoo from her hair whilst Leo paddled up and down, stark naked like a hairless puppy.

'One day we'll have constant thumping pumping hot water,' she told him, as she beat their dirty clothes on a flat rock, as if she were a Calabrian peasant. 'I shall lie

184

in a scented bath for hours.' She draped the garments on the reeds to dry. 'I shall have a washing machine and an airing cupboard, with piles of thick warm, crunchy towels.' She seized hold of Bruja's trailing rope and shouted at the pony to pull her up the 'slither-bump', the mud oozing between her bare toes. 'And I shall wear beautiful clothes, unscuffed shoes and have bags which match.'

'But where will my home be?' he asked anxiously.

'With me, of course!'

She left him with Fred when she returned the Land-Rover to Henley because she didn't want him upset by memories. It was bad enough for herself: the steep hill with the overhanging trees: the stone bridge over the river: the sun on the roof of the Leander Club. She stopped by the turning which led to Dingwall Court. She hadn't intended to go back, but now she was drawn as though by a magnet.

Even in one week the rhododendrons seemed bushier and the garden beyond had gained a wild, forgotten look. She turned into the driveway and halted, resting her chin on the steering wheel.

A man appeared from the stables. 'This is private property,' he said.

'I know. I used to live here.'

'Well, you don't now.'

'No.' She put the car into reverse. 'I don't.' As she backed away she caught one final glimpse of the rolling lawns and her mother's rose arbour by the river.

It had been a mistake to go there. That man speaking as though she were a trespasser had upset her. She handed the Land-Rover in at the garage and collected her Mini. Thank goodness she'd left Leo with Fred! Leo. Her stomach turned. She'd left her little brother with a strange old man in a place where he knew no one and where there was no telephone.

It took her two hours to reach Bailing. All the way up

185

her mind ran riot as she pictured Leo pinned down by Fred. By the time she swung into the gateway Fred had become a child molester with a long list of convictions.

She roared across the tarmac to the hangars and flung herself out of her car, yelling, 'Leo! Leo!'

There was silence.

'Leo!'

'Rye-rye.' He stumbled out of the hangar, tears rolling down his dirty face.

'Oh, God!' She scooped him up in her arms. 'Are you all right? Are you . . .'

'A man took Bruja.'

'Did he hurt you. Has anyone hurt you?'

'He took the pony. I told you.'

'That's right.' Fred came out of the hangar, a length of wire in his oily hands. 'Miss Bronwen's nephew. Said the beast was his.'

Ryder couldn't look Fred in the eyes.

Bailing Mill was a mile upstream. Built of weatherboard and painted white, it straddled the river, half-house, half-factory, purveyor of a strange and wild industrial beauty. Above it fierce white swans sailed the River Bailum. Beneath it water roared through the sluice gates and into the millpond.

Ryder left her car in the road and crossed the bridge above the gates, the only access to the house. Wind whipped up the spray from the millpond. Gravel crunched under her feet. In the depths of the house, the dog howled.

Bruja was tied up near the back door. She gave a low whinny as Ryder approached. At that moment Patrick sauntered out of the house, looking tanned and fit and attractive. She was suddenly conscious of her grubby jeans and her hair which needed cutting. 'What do you think you're doing?' he demanded.

'Retrieving my property.'

'The pony belongs to me. You stole her from Gatehouse.'

'I paid twenty pounds for her.' Ryder untied the rope. 'If it wasn't for me she'd be dogfood.'

'That's a lie!'

'The kennels promised the old man twenty pounds. You couldn't be bothered with her, just because she's lame.'

He crossed the yard. She noticed a slight stiffness in his walk. 'Here's your twenty pounds,' he said. 'You know what that pony means to me.'

'I know what she means to my little brother. He's lost his mother, his father, his home. Everything! The only person left is me. And I'm too worried and busy and cross and . . .' She stopped herself and straightened her shoulders. 'He loves Bruja.'

They looked at each other in silence. Then she walked away, leading the pony.

17

Ryder didn't tell Fred that her father was in prison. She didn't tell anyone at Bailing. Only Miss Brendan Broughton knew, and luckily she was practically a recluse. When her father sent a Visiting Order, she asked Fred to look after Leo, saying she had business in London.

The journey to Wandsworth took her through the East End and the docks; streets of once-thriving warehouses she'd never visited during her time at the flat. It could have been another city. She parked near the prison, beside a row of pretty cottages which overlooked a common. There was a pub nearby. People lay on the grass outside, drinking beer in the sunshine. It was all very peaceful, except for the brooding presence of the prison with its dirty yellow brick walls and black squared rooftops.

Ryder was early. She had an hour to kill. She wandered into a garden centre which existed incongruously right under the prison wall. Wrapped in their urban garden worlds, shoppers hovered over geraniums in terracotta pots whilst above them barred eyes glared down in envy and frustration.

The visiting room was similar to that at Brixton. Watched by uniformed officers, people were grouped at tables. Her father was sitting in the furthest corner. Ryder noticed that his face had sagged, as if he'd been left outside all winter. 'You didn't bring Leo,' he said.

She tried not to show that she minded. 'I couldn't. He's so unsettled. But I brought some photos.' She opened her bag.

The warder had to check the pictures before she could hand them over. 'He looks like Carrie. The same face. Same hair. Same blue eyes.' Her father swallowed hard, as Ryder did when she was upset. 'But why are you washing in this river?'

'It's Bailing. I told you. We're living there, in the tower. I couldn't afford a flat for Leo and me in London, not on a salary I could earn. So I'm restoring the airfield. I'm going to run it as a business.'

'But there's no electricity.'

'That's why we're washing in the river. But we'll have light soon. And a phone.'

He went through the pictures again. 'What about old Miss B. B.? She can't be pleased.'

'She nearly set her dog on me. But she can't stop me, so long as I give her half my profit — if I make any.'

'You will if you get your figures right.'

She looked at him with surprise. 'You don't think I'm mad, then?'

He smiled and shook his head. 'I should have done it myself.'

'Money's the big problem,' she confided. 'I have to sell my gold charm bracelet and mother's opal ring.' She paused. 'I hope you don't mind. But we need good equipment. There's no point in doing it otherwise.'

He reached across the table and laid his hand on her arm. 'Let me help. I can tell you where some money is.'

She stiffened. 'No, thanks.'

'Money's money.'

'Not that money!'

'Don't be a fool,' he said in his old derisory tone. 'People who wash in rivers don't become successful.'

She stood up. 'I'd rather wash in a river than use your dirty money. One Harding in gaol is enough!'

189

She drove back to Norfolk swearing never to visit him again.

Fred was a treasure. He rewired the control tower and the hangars. He found an old cooker and tinkered with it. A fridge appeared. It was prehistoric, but better than nothing. Now Ryder didn't have to shop every day for food. He produced an immersion heater. She had her first hot bath. After the river it was a luxury. He unblocked the chimney, made shelves, built cupboards, and created a patio from broken bricks. He even made a bench so they could sit outside the tower in the sunshine.

'I'd like to pay you what I owe,' Ryder told him as they sat on his bench, relishing the quiet of the evening.

'You don't want me any more?'

'I don't want to get into debt.'

'An' I don't want you to tell me not to come because you've got no money.'

'I have enough. I just have to be careful.'

She took the opal ring and sold it: she felt like a grave robber but she had to. Driving back to Bailing she thought of her father in his cell, standing on a chair, gazing down at the shoppers in the garden centre. She stopped to buy a pink rambling rose, such as her mother had trained around the rose arbour.

Word was getting around. The airfield was discussed in The Bailing Arms. The postman asked Ryder if she had a summer job for his son. Mrs Dennshurst bought a second freezer for the shop. The milkman said new people would spoil the village. They'd push up house prices. The place would be full of *furriners*.

'I have to get the farmers on my side,' Ryder told Fred. 'We'll be flying over their land.'

'It's not them you have to worry about. It's the new people. Londoners lookin' for peace and quiet — with a herd of cows on one side an' a cockerel on the other.'

'You mean ignorant townies like me!' She opened a tin of green paint and carried it up the ladder which was propped against the side of the hangar. Painstakingly she began to fill in every tiny crack of the huge building. Fred watched her. 'You'll be drawing your pension before you finish that,' he said. 'Things don't have to be over perfect, Ryder. Bailing people like you for what you are.'

She laid down the brush. 'My father is in prison. I know I should have told you.'

'I don't care if he's a monkey. It ain't your fault what he's done — and you don't need to work twice as hard to prove that.'

She felt tears prick her eyes. She rubbed them away with the back of her hand. 'I want Bailing to look good because it's mine — and no one's ever believed I could accomplish anything. Not father. Not my mother. Not even me. But I'm going to prove them wrong.' She carried on painting. 'I'm going to prove myself wrong.'

'You're going to break your back if you fall off that ladder,' said Patrick Brendan.

He was wearing while polo breeches tucked into tan boots and a white shirt, open at the neck. He looked immaculate. Tough. Sexy. Confident.

'What do you want here?' she asked, turning her back on him as she carried on painting.

'You can't keep Bruja tied up under a tree.'

'I take her for walks.'

'She needs a paddock.'

'She'll have one when I have time and money.'

'Talking about money, my aunt has asked me to point out that any profit you make has to be split with her.'

'I know.' If Ryder hadn't been so broke, she'd have emptied the ten-litre tin of paint over Patrick.

'So it's not going to be worth your while,' he went on.

She faced him. 'I have nothing except for my share of Bailing. I have myself to keep. My brother. And *our* pony. Short of prostitution, I have no other asset to

191

develop. If I make forty pounds and have to give your aunt twenty, that leaves me twenty — which is a helluva lot better than nothing!'

He walked away and didn't come back. She carried on painting. She was glad he'd gone. She didn't like him. But there was something which both annoyed and attracted her in him.

The sun was hot. The wind constant. Her arms ached. The smell of paint was in her nose and her eyes. Out on the runway Fred was filling the cracks. Down by the river Leo was talking to Bruja. A Land-Rover entered the airfield. It crossed to the trees. Leo hid behind Bruja. The door opened and Patrick got out. From the back he took an armful of stakes and cross bars. He began to measure out a strip of land running down the edge of the airfield through the trees to the river. She saw Patrick bend down and talk to Leo. She carried on painting.

At midday she arranged lunch on the patio table: French bread, cheese, a salad, and a couple of tins of beer. Then she quickly washed her face, brushed her hair, and dabbed on some scent.

'Lunch!' she called.

Leo came running. Fred shuffled back. Patrick continued hammering.

'Ask him if he'd like to eat with us,' she told Leo, busying herself with the plates so she didn't have to look as Patrick walked towards her.

'Sure you have enough?' he asked.

'It's only bread and cheese.'

'Lucky to get this.' Fred handed Patrick a beer. 'Two weeks back she was bathin' in the river and eatin' out of tins.'

They tucked into the crisp bread, covering it with lashings of creamy butter and chunks of strong-tasting farmhouse cheddar.

'Heard the ghost yet?' asked Patrick, when Leo had wandered off.

Ryder choked. 'What ghost?'

''Sright,' Fred nodded. 'All these ole airfields are haunted. Bailing's ghost was a pilot shot down in the Battle of Britain.'

'Footsteps cross the hangar.' Patrick rolled his eyes. 'Just a few steps. Then he's gone. Forever!'

Ryder giggled. 'Don't tell Leo!'

Fred was sniffing loudly. 'What's that?' He leaned nearer to Ryder. 'You're wearing scent. It smells like a hairdresser's.'

'I can't smell of paint all the time!' she said crossly.

'Didn't worry you before.' His eyes twinkled. He turned to Patrick. 'You still ridin' them polo ponies?'

'Yes. But not professionally. I had an accident.' He looked at Ryder. 'My leg will always be a little stiff. So now I "make" the ponies.' He paused. 'At Gatehouse.'

Ryder dropped her tomato. 'You bought the stables!'

'Rodolfo and I did. In partnership.'

'From my father?'

'From the bank — with a massive loan.'

She recalled the afternoon when she'd first seen Gatehouse. She remembered her mother perched on the wall as they waited for the ponies to arrive. It came back quickly. Vividly. Because it was one of the few occasions when she had not felt her mother was ashamed of her. The memory turned a knife. She rose abruptly and went into the tower. Footsteps followed. It had to be Patrick. Fred never entered her home unless invited.

'You've done a lot to this place,' he said.

'Yes.' She kept her back to him.

'It reminds me of the guest cottages on the sheep station in Australia. The same starkness. The same whiteness.' He drew closer. 'Wild flowers in a paint tin. Bunches of dried thistles. Who'd have thought it of Paul Harding's daughter!'

'Go away!'

'You're crying. Why?'

193

'I'm tired of being mocked and hounded because my father's in gaol. When people talk of the victim they mean the sufferer of a crime, but the real victims are the families of the criminal. They receive no sympathy. They're allowed no grief. They're ostracised.'

'What are you doing tonight?'

She was speechless.

'I'll call for you at eight.'

'No!'

'Seven — if you need to bring Leo?'

He was so determined. So defiant. So attractive. Then she remembered Adam who was so charming but who'd let her down when she'd needed him. 'No, thank you.' She looked him straight in the eyes. 'I'm grateful for the paddock. But I meant what I said. I'd prefer you didn't come here.'

18

Bailing Airfield was nearing completion. At least, it was as complete as Ryder could afford to make it. The hangars were painted. The runway repaired. The fuel on order. The telephone installed. The firefighting equipment checked. The old tool room had become a smart reception with a window overlooking the entrance, and although furniture was still short, a job lot of wicker blinds gave her needed privacy at the tower. She no longer undressed in full view of the hangars.

The rambling rose she'd planted by the doorway produced its first flower. Each time she looked at it, she was anguished by images of her father. The more the airfield took shape, the less she wanted him involved. This was her venture, not to be contaminated. But she was obsessed with the thought of him locked away behind those high brick walls. At night she wrote him long letters. In the morning she threw them away.

Instead she wrote to Debbie, letters full of Bailing, Leo, her doubts and hopes. In return she received the news from Prairieville. Teddy never mentioned her name. Her grandparents were slowly coming to terms with her departure. Poor Susan had come home unexpectedly. Her poet had turned out to be a drug dealer. To Prairieville this was the wages of sin, and Susan was being treated like a prodigal.

'All we need now is some customers,' Ryder told Fred, as she folded away Debbie's letter. They were waiting anxiously for the inspector from the Civil Aviation Authority. 'Pity the ghost doesn't come every day. We could turn him into an attraction.'

'Here he is.'

'The ghost?'

'No,' he chuckled. 'The Inspector.'

The man from the CAA was neat and dapper, with a small moustache and a clipped voice. 'Good morning, Miss Harding.'

'Good morning. This is Mr Garratt.'

There was silence. The inspector frowned. Ryder's heart sank. 'Sergeant Garratt!' The inspector held out his hand. 'You wouldn't remember me. I joined the RAF as the war was ending. Just eighteen and raring to fly. But I'll never forget you. Best mechanic in the force, you were.'

For the first time since Ryder had known him Fred stood straight.

The inspector went meticulously through his list. He checked the hangars and the servicing area. He measured the runway and tested it for soundness. There were a few points he queried. Most he approved.

'Good luck, Miss Harding.' He shook hands. 'Sergeant Garratt.' He snapped to attention and saluted smartly. 'This has made my day!'

As they watched him drive away, Fred said, 'Thanks.'

'For what?'

'Not telling him I'm just the oddjob man.'

They celebrated with a drink at The Bailing Arms sitting outside in the sunshine with the old pub dog at their feet.

'You know, they still remember your father in this pub,' said Fred.

Ryder shrugged.

'They remember him as a young pilot. One of the best. You should think of him that way. Forget all this bitterness.'

196

'I try.' She finished her drink. 'But he rejects me.'

They walked back to the airfield. The sun was shining. The ducks were sailing on the village pond. Leo trailed two children on bicycles.

Fred nodded at him. 'That lad needs company.'

'I should have sent him to school when we arrived.'

'Blaming yourself again! I'll speak to my niece, Denise. She'll be Leo's teacher next term. Her little Tommy's about his age.'

'You mean Mrs Dennshurst's daughter! I didn't realise you had family, Fred.'

'I'm related to half o' Bailing. Hilda Dennshurst was Jenny's sister. She's been very good to me. Others haven't. Oh, it was fine when we first wed. I was in the RAF. But I left ten years ago. Jenny wanted to come back to Bailing. We're both Bailing folk. The trouble was, I couldn't get a proper job. Not at my age. With all this unemployment, things ain't easy. 'Course I should have come out the RAF earlier and got established. Jenny, bless her heart, never complained when all I could find was the odd bit of plumbing and electrics.' He looked at Ryder. 'But you an' your ole airfield've put the spark back into my life.' He sighed. 'If only my Jenny could've lived to see it. She'd have been that proud.'

Ryder smiled sadly. If only her mother could have said, 'I'm proud of you.'

The phone rang in the tower as she was making scrambled egg for Leo's lunch. She grabbed the receiver, still stirring the egg in the saucepan. 'Bailing Airfield, good afternoon.'

'This is the *Eastern Daily Press*,' said a business-like voice. 'We understand you're restoring the airfield and we'd like to do a local interest piece.'

'I'll consult my diary.' Quickly Ryder buried the telephone in a cushion whilst she whisked the solidifying

197

egg on to a piece of toast and handed it to Leo, hissing, 'Don't make a noise. This is meant to be an office.' Then she picked up the receiver and said briskly, 'How about next Tuesday?'

They fixed a day. She ran to the door. 'Fred! That's *EDP*. Our first publicity! Where's the *Daily Express*? If we're worth a photo to East Anglia, why shouldn't we have a few lines in the national press?'

She dressed as well as she could for the interview, choosing her cream safari suit, the one she'd worn when her father had lost his appeal for bail. All her clothes carried memories. There was the prison-visiting trench-coat. The court-sentencing black suit. The hospital-visiting white jeans. And the lonely-afternoon-in-London red culottes.

The mirror was disheartening. Her hair looked a mess. She trimmed the front as best she could, but that revealed her forehead which was dry from the wind and sun. She slapped on some moisturiser. As she raised her hand to her face she saw her nails were cracked and ingrained with paint. She tried to file them but they flaked. In desperation she glossed her lips but they too were dry.

The photographer positioned her in front of the main hangar. She smiled until her face felt like a death mask. Then he went off to photograph the runway, with Leo trailing behind him, whilst she took the journalist through every step of the airfield's development. 'We want to make flying fun,' she explained. 'We'll have a clubhouse. Film shows. Barbecues.'

A red E-type Jaguar turned into the airfield. Ryder tried to appear as though cars like this turned up all the time. She prepared her airfield-owner smile.

'Ryder!' Imogen stepped out looking every inch the star in a white snakeskin mini dress.

'Immy!' She shrieked and jumped up and down, forgetting the journalist and her prepared manner.

But now he really was impressed. 'You're Imogen Lydden. My favourite actress.'

'How sweet of you.' Immy ran her long slim fingers through her cascading red curls. 'I hope you'll write wonderful things about my friend. Ryder, darling, when's the opening party?'

'In three weeks. We're just printing the invitations.' Ryder turned to the reporter. 'You'll come, won't you?'

The photographer took a picture of them both in front of the hangar. They had to stand for five minutes whilst the light improved. Ryder marvelled how Imogen could hold the same position without moving.

When the men left, she said, 'You're brilliant. I hadn't even thought of a party.'

'Who cares — so long as they write about you.'

'Oh, but there will be now.'

'Let's have a drink. I've been dying for one. This is a celebration. It's taken me a week to track you down.' Imogen flopped down on the bench outside the tower and lit a cigarette. 'I spent last night with a new man.'

'What about Tony?' Ryder opened a bottle of white wine.

'That's over.' Immy downed her glass in one. 'He was always criticising. Nagging about my smoking. Rationing my wine. Treating me like a child.'

'Was he upset?'

'He finished with me.' Her face turned bleak. 'He said he couldn't cope and that Alix and Jeremy were turning me against him. It's true, they were. But I need Tony. I'm just not good on my own.' She stretched for the bottle.

'What about your new man?'

'An actor. It's better than being alone.' She paused. 'I saw Alix last week.'

Ryder shrugged.

'Jeremy's made her a partner and she's bought a flat near Regent's Park. Very grand. I've only been there once, for a party. Of course she's out every evening. Agents are. You remember what Jeremy was like.' Immy fiddled with her watch strap. 'She'd love to see you.'

'No.' Ryder stood up. 'Definitely not.' She paced the uneven stones of the patio.

Imogen leaned back against the wall of the tower, her pale freckled arms stretched out to the sun. 'Why didn't you tell me you were back in England? I only knew because Alix saw your picture in the paper. I was very hurt.'

'I phoned but you were in Hollywood.' Ryder sat down again. 'Mother once said if I split from Adam I'd lose my friends.'

'You will if you don't tell us where you are. It was only chance that I went to Smith's Lawn and saw Patrick Brendan. He gave me your address. He said you were doing wonders to Bailing.'

'Patrick said that!' Ryder laughed. 'I don't believe it.'

'He's very attractive, isn't he?' Imogen's nose wrinkled prettily. 'So dangerous and brooding. Anything between you two?'

'Nothing.' Ryder pictured Imogen, so dainty, fluttering across the clubhouse lawn to Patrick. 'I don't even like him.'

Ryder sacrificed the gold charm bracelet to pay for the party. It was that, her mother's Cartier watch, or the drop pearl earrings her parents had given her for her eighteenth birthday. But when she held them up to her ears they glowed so soft and feminine she couldn't bear to lose them yet. As for the watch, it not only looked expensive but kept perfect time.

She ordered the invitations. Two hundred stiff white cards with smart black lettering. On her way home she bought all the flying magazines and a copy of every newspaper, both local and national. The front page of the *Eastern Daily Press* carried a picture of Imogen looking like porcelain and herself as though her hair had been cut with a hedge trimmer.

'Going to send a copy to your father?' asked Fred.

'No.' She folded the newspaper.

'He'd be proud.'

'Keep out of it, Fred. If you want to help me, find a typewriter.'

'So now we're running a secretarial service.' He went off muttering, and returned several hours later carrying an ancient machine. 'Hilda says you can borrow this. An' she told me to ask you without givin' offence if you'd like an' old sofa.'

'I'm not offended, I'm grateful.'

She typed up a list of all the newspapers and magazines, with their addresses and telephone numbers. Then she made a cup of coffee, told herself to be brave, and dialled the first number. 'I'd like to speak to your aviation correspondent,' she said politely.

'We don't have one.'

'Then your . . . umm . . . motoring correspondent.'

'What name?'

'I don't know his name.'

'Your name!'

Ryder gripped the receiver as though it were the telephonist's neck. If and when she could afford staff, manners would be a primary qualification.

A man came on the line. 'What do you want?'

'I'm . . . er . . . Ryder Harding from Bailing Airfield.'

'Never heard of it!'

'You wouldn't have, because we're just . . .'

'Are you trying to sell me something?'

'No, I'm trying to invite you to . . .'

'Then send me an invitation, sweetie, but don't waste my time.' He slammed down the phone.

She gritted her teeth and dialled the next number. It was answered immediately. 'He's out to lunch.'

'Could you ask him to ring me.'

'He won't — unless you're important.'

'How do you know I'm not!'

'If you were, he'd be chasing you.'

Ryder made another cup of coffee and wondered if it were worth running up a phone bill in order to be humiliated. She tried one more publication: *Aviation Argus*.

'It's Michael Ashby you want but he's busy,' said the switchboard.

'Not too busy to talk to me.'

'What name did you say?'

'I didn't. It's Ryder Harding from Bailing Airfield.'

There was a click. Silence. Ryder wondered if she'd been too pushy, then decided she had nothing to lose. Another click.

'Miss Harding, this is a coincidence,' said an amused voice with a hint of grit and late nights. 'I was in Norwich yesterday and saw your picture in the local paper.'

'Then you know I'm restoring the Bailing Airfield. We're having an inaugural party. I'd like you to come.'

'Is Imogen Lydden opening it?'

'I hadn't got as far as deciding that.'

'It would make good copy.'

'She's opening it!'

Ryder rang Imogen. Adam answered. For once that did not throw her: she was too preoccupied with Bailing. 'This is a surprise,' he said. 'I thought you didn't want to speak to me.'

'I don't. I want Imogen.'

Immy listened to Ryder's request. 'I'd love to come but I'm going to a huge launch party for a new dress designer,' she said.

Ryder tried not to panic. 'Immy,' she said as calmly as possible, 'do you remember when you begged me to ask Jeremy to see you, and I didn't want to, but I did?'

'Of course I do. I'm eternally grateful.'

'Immy, you're my celebrity. I need you.'

202

'Friends before clothes! Pearls before swine! I'll be there.'

'I've decided to make it a barbecue,' Ryder informed Fred one morning when he arrived for work.

'It'll rain.'

'We'll have sausages, chicken, baked potatoes and salads, all laid out on trestle tables.' She waved her arms with enthusiasm, encompassing the tarmac area.

'For a hundred?'

'More or less.'

'I understand.' He shuffled off into the hangar. 'You want to go bankrupt sooner rather tha' later!'

She shouted, 'You horrible old pessimist!' but he took no notice.

There had been no sign from Bronwen Brendan Broughton since her early visit. 'I suppose I should invite her personally,' Ryder said to Fred over lunch. 'We don't want her setting Wolf on the guests.'

'Better go in the afternoon.' He gave her his tortoise stare. 'The dog's fed at noon!'

Ryder washed and ironed the wretched linen suit. The hem was down. She mended it. A button was off. She made do with a safety pin.

Leo was ensconced in the back of the Mini when she came down. 'I can't take you,' she said.

His face crumpled. 'I never go anywhere. You promised I'd meet Tommy.'

'He's got measles. Oh, all right. You can come with me. But you must be very good. We're going to visit the lady with the dog and we have to impress her.' She wondered if she'd be better with her own children than she was with Leo.

The mill appeared deserted. Swans drifted by. A peacock walked beside the river. Leaving Leo in the car, she rang the doorbell. No one answered. She rang again.

Nothing happened. 'Miss Brendan Broughton!' she shouted.

A dog barked.

She crossed to a door in the wall and knocked hard. The dog barked louder.

'What do you want?' called a voice.

'It's Ryder Harding. I'd like to talk to you.'

A bolt rasped. The door opened. Miss Brendan Broughton stood before her in a floral kimono and a Chinese straw hat. 'Well?'

'We're having an opening party.'

'I don't like parties.'

'I've brought your invitation.'

'My parents were missionaries in China. They didn't approve of parties. I don't believe in God but I don't like parties either.' She slammed the door in Ryder's face.

The invitations were sent. A week passed. No one replied. Then the postman brought a stiff white envelope. She opened it.

'Fred!' she raced into the hangar. 'The Mayor of Norwich has accepted.'

'So, it's you, me, Leo, the mayor, an' a hundred chicken legs!'

She went to the butcher to order the meat. He promised her a 15 per cent discount. She spoke to the vicar who agreed to lend the church trestle tables, and the vicar's wife who offered a hand with the food. She invited Mrs Dennshurst, her daughter and little Tommy. 'And anyone from Bailing who'd like to come.' A brewery agreed a special deal: publicity for them and cheap barrels of beer for her. She invited the managing director. He offered two of his staff to help pull beer. She approached an off-licence. They let her have eight crates of wine at little more than cost. She invited the manager.

He offered free glasses and ice: his cousin owned a Slingsby Firefly.

'I don't know how you do it,' Fred marvelled.

Ryder laughed. 'Nor do I.'

There were three days to go and she'd only had forty replies: seventeen refusals and twenty-three acceptances.

'People are so rude,' Ryder confided in Mrs Dennshurst. 'I may have to reduce the sausage order. I feel such a failure. But we can't have two hundred rotting sausages.'

'Failure! Don't talk rubbish. What you've done for old Fred's a miracle. And for Bailing.'

Back at the airfield Ryder tuned in to the weather forecast. *'Rain will move eastwards across the country.'* She filled the washing machine and wondered if all else failed she could get a job as a cleaner.

With one day to go she rose at dawn to clean the house. At least they couldn't say she was a slut. Whilst Leo ate his breakfast, she ironed his clothes. He looked so lonely and sad. If he became a misogynist it would be her fault.

'Before you start school we'll go and see the seals on Blakeney Point,' she said. 'It'll be your special treat for being such a good boy.'

'When?'

She was saved by the telephone.

'Michael Ashby here.'

Her heart sank. Another refusal.

'A friend of mine has been restoring a Sopwith Pup and we thought it would be fun if he flew it into Bailing on Saturday.'

'That's a terrific idea!' She nearly cried with relief that he wasn't cancelling. 'Imogen cuts the ribbon at two o'clock. Could he land as she finishes?'

'I'll tell him two-thirty. Celebrities are notoriously unpunctual.'

'And I'll call Anglia Television. It'll make brilliant copy for their regional news programme.'

He laughed. 'Ryder Harding, you're one sparky lady. I can't wait to meet you.'

Anglia said they'd send an outside broadcast unit. The postman brought just ten more acceptances. She told the vicar about the biplane as he put up the trestle tables. The farmer delivered the potatoes. She'd forgotten they'd need washing. Someone left Bruja's paddock open and she ate half the lettuces. The butcher rang to say she hadn't reduced the meat order in time so all two hundred sausages had arrived. The brewery delivered the beer and one barrel escaped and rolled into the river. If Ryder hadn't been so frantic she'd have laughed.

In the late afternoon she went to the hairdresser in King's Lynn. It was the first time she'd had it cut since her mother died. That realisation overwhelmed her as she watched her hair fall to the ground. She longed to tell the hairdresser but she couldn't. He'd be embarrassed and that would cheapen her feelings.

She took a long route back to the car. If only her mother could be there tomorrow. How she would love the fuss, the people, the television and the mayor. She'd be so elegant. Ryder passed a boutique. In the window was a silk jumpsuit in the exact sunshine yellow of the drawing room at Dingwall Court. It was a colour she'd resisted in clothes, perhaps because she'd been made to wear it so much as a child.

She entered the shop just to touch the fabric and couldn't resist trying the flying suit on. It fitted perfectly. A wide belt flattered her slimmed waist. Turned up trousers tucked into yellow canvas boots emphasised her long legs. The tight bodice with a heavy metal zip gave her a cleavage she didn't know she possessed.

'How much?' she asked.

'A hundred – including the boots.'

Regretfully she took it off. A hundred pounds paid

Fred for two weeks. She started back towards the car, then she thought of her mother who'd always loved yellow.

19

Ryder woke at dawn. Rain was hitting the tarmac like steel rods and the northeast wind was whipping down the runway, hurling spray against the vicar's trestle tables.

Leo sat up. 'Is it time for breakfast?'

'If you like. Now, close your eyes! I've bought you a present for being good.' She placed a small fluffy seal in his outstretched hands.

He was transfixed with pleasure. 'What shall I call my seal?' he asked.

'Whatever you like.' She pulled on her jeans.

'You choose.'

She dug around in her chest for a clean sweatshirt. 'How about Rumble? A mixture of rough and tumble. That's how seals play in the water. You'll see them when we go to Blakeney Point.'

By the time they'd finished breakfast the rain had stopped, leaving a fine mist and a minefield of puddles. She crossed to the hangar and checked the wine, the glasses and the plates. In one crate was a pile of scrubbed potatoes. In another, those lettuces saved from Bruja.

Fred had built a brick barbecue well away from the hangar. Its iron grid dripped gloomily. The hole in which they'd planned to bake the potatoes was full of water. She stood looking down at it, wishing that the day was over, wondering what streak of masochism had led her into all this.

Fred arrived as she was shaking water off the tables.

'Don't say anything!' she snapped.

'I ain't tha' stupid.'

The vicar's wife arrived punctually with ten bowls of rice salad. Mrs Dennshurst followed with a huge container of home pickled beetroot and another of egg mayonnaise. Denise, the teacher, came with more salads and freckle-faced Tommy who raced off to join Leo. They all hovered around Ryder, till in a flash of inspiration she said to Mrs Dennshurst, 'You lay out your shop so attractively. Could you organise the table so the food looks nice?'

A bouquet of flowers arrived. The card said, *'With best wishes from Geraldine Heythorp.'* Ryder had never thought of Lady Heythorp as having a first name. Another bouquet arrived. *'Sorry not to be there, Love Hetty.'* The postman delivered a telegram. It said, *'Best Luck from Scot's Farm.'* She wanted to cry. The florist returned with a glorious bouquet of red roses. For a moment she thought they must be from Adam. She opened the card. *'Well done! Heythorp & Bassingham.'* She ripped it up. How dare Alix be so patronising.

The rain stopped. The sun came out. She went inside to change. From the window she saw Mrs Dennshurst directing the other women like a general marshalling his troops. Tablecloths had been laid. Plates were stacked beside cutlery. Glasses were polished. Delegation was the name of the game, she was learning. She ran her bath, adding a few drops of baby oil, followed by one precious measure of scent. One day she'd have an enormous bottle of fiendishly expensive bath oil which she'd shake lavishly into every bath, just as her mother had done.

The sunshine flying suit looked even better than it had in the shop. The silk clung. The zip front emphasised her bosom. She slipped on the boots and strode up and down in front of the mirror, rolling the sleeves up to her elbows and turning up the trouser legs, to give herself a rangy, sporty air.

The phone rang as she was painting her nails. 'Ryder, it's Adam. Imogen can't come.'

'What!'

'She's not up to it.'

Ryder set down the bottle of nail varnish before she dropped it. 'I have the Mayor of Norwich, Anglia Television, the press, guests.'

'She's drunk.'

'I don't care. She can't let me down. Hand me over to her.'

There was a brief silence, then muffled voices and Imogen came on the line. 'Ryder, I'm sorry. I get scared and . . . oh, God! I can't cope on my own.' She started to cry.

Ryder gripped the receiver. 'Immy, you are my star friend. Everyone's so looking forward to meeting you. One journalist's only coming because of you.'

'I'm a mess and it's such a long drive.'

'If I arrange for someone to drive you up here will you come?'

There was silence.

'Immy, please! Without you the day will be a failure.'

There was a pause, then Imogen said, 'I'll be ready in two hours.'

Adam came on the line. 'Harding charm at its best! I don't know how you do it.'

'I hate to ask you this,' she spoke through gritted teeth, 'but I've promised that someone will drive her. I'd collect her myself but I must be here. I wondered if you'd be good enough to . . .'

'So I'm not a weak bastard any more!'

'Adam, I'm desperate.'

'I like to hear you beg, Ryder.' He gave a vicious laugh. 'But you wouldn't forgive my peccadillo with Alix. You threw me out when I came to Dingwall Court.

210

Your father ruined my career. I haven't held a decent job since Harding-Broughton collapsed.'

'You didn't have one before, you dumb schmuck!' She slammed down the receiver.

It was nearly ten. The party started at one. She raked her mind for someone who could help. Someone in London. Alix! She understood business. Ryder dialled directory enquiries. They seemed to take forever. 'What address? Near Regent's Park . . . a new number . . . One moment.'

At last she had it. She steeled herself. The number rang. She pictured Alix walking towards it. The beautiful hand outstretched. The astonishment.

'*This is Alix Bassingham. I'm in L.A. until Tuesday.*'

Ryder locked herself in the bathroom and cried. The party was a failure. She wished she'd stayed in Prairieville. She should have married Teddy and been safe and . . . bored.

The phone at Gatehouse Stables was answered on the second ring. 'May I speak to Patrick Brendan?' she said.

'He's in Norfolk. He'll be back tonight.'

Ryder dropped the receiver and raced to her Mini, shouting, 'Back in a minute.' Puddles splattered as she roared across the tarmac. In the gateway she nearly hit the postman. Skidding into the mill, she sent gravel leaping into the river.

She rang the bell. The dog howled. She hammered on the door. No one came. 'Patrick!' she shouted, forcing the garden door. Beyond lay an old fashioned kitchen herb garden of gravel paths squared to low box hedges, which gave off a peppery tinder smell especially when wet. She raced along a path, jumped a hedge, pushed through some shrubs, and came out beside a summer house.

Patrick was sitting in a wicker chair, a newspaper in one hand, a cup of coffee in the other. He raised a laconic eyebrow. 'Seen the ghost?'

'I'm desperate.' She stood before him in her yellow flying suit, with its tight bodice and thrusting hipline. 'You must help me. Imogen Lydden is meant to be opening the airfield.'

'The launch party to which I have not been invited.'

'Don't joke, please! This is life or death. She won't come unless someone fetches her. I have television, the mayor, journalists. I've worked so hard.' Tears pricked her eyes. 'If Immy doesn't come it'll be a failure.'

'So you're asking me, the neighbour to whom you've been so friendly, to drive to London to collect her?' He put his feet on the table and rocked back in his chair, looking her up and down, speculatively. 'What'll you give me if I do?'

'I haven't any money.'

He picked up his newspaper and carried on reading.

'But I'd do anything if you got her here by two-thirty.'

He looked up. 'Anything?'

'Whatever you want.'

'Sex?'

'What!'

He raised an eyebrow.

'All right.' She squared up. 'If I have to. Sex!'

At noon a small yellow biplane buzzed the airfield. It headed for the hangars, dancing from side to side like a well-schooled dressage pony. Everyone stopped to watch. They waved. It waggled its wings, then circled round till it faced the runway. But it didn't land. It skimmed the tarmac by some fifty feet, gathering speed all the time, till it rose sharply, nose right up, and executed a perfect backward roll.

'Blimey!' exclaimed Fred, craning his neck. 'It's a Curtiss Jennie. One of those ole planes American barnstormers flew. At least we have one person who knows how to handle an aircraft.'

The biplane parked near the hangars. Ryder walked

towards it, her airfield smile on her face. A man swung down from the open cockpit. He wore a leather flying jacket and goggles pushed back, as her father had done. Laughing with exhilaration, he clasped Ryder by the hand. 'I'm Michael Ashby.'

He looked like the kind of man who'd hit you back. He was tough. There was no denying it. Not much taller than Ryder, he exuded such power that she thought him larger. With his shock of black straight hair and fierce, peculiarly straight eyebrows, he reminded her of a picture of a Cossack in one of her old history books. But his smile touched his eyes. They were warm and soft under his long sooty eyelashes, a paradoxically feminine feature in an otherwise very masculine face.

'I've come to give a hand,' he said. 'I thought you might need it.'

'I do.' She couldn't help noticing that he had a wide and very sensuous mouth. She thought of Patrick's mouth. It was finely chiselled.

Fred was struggling to adjust a table next to the barbecue. Michael tossed his jacket to one side, called to the brewer's men to help, and hurried over. Ryder could imagine him dressed in the skin of a black bear, galloping across the snowy steppe at the head of his troop.

The first guests arrived. The sun shone. People shook Ryder by the hand. She smiled in response. A Slingsby Firefly came in to land, followed by a Cessna. They taxied to the hangar and parked in line with Michael's Jennie.

'Seventy already!' hissed Fred, in disbelief, as more cars turned into the gateway. 'The food won't stretch.'

'Order more sausages. Pessimist!'

A black Rolls-Royce growled across the tarmac. The Mayor of Norwich stepped out. 'Miss Harding,' he said, 'I salute your entrepreneurial spirit. My wife's so looking forward to meeting Miss Lydden.'

As Ryder thanked him, a photographer from the *East-*

ern Daily Press took their picture. She wondered what they'd all say if they knew how she was paying for the star's transport.

Delicious smells drifted from the barbecue. By the beer barrels the brewer's men pulled pint after pint. Behind the trestle tables the vicar's wife and her team dished out the salads. Under the trees Leo was showing Tommy how to feed carrots to Bruja. 'You have to keep your fingers flat,' his piping voice came up from the paddock. 'If you don't she'll eat them.'

Ryder felt a surge of hope and pride. Leo had made a friend. He wasn't going to be a friendless misogynist after all.

Michael Ashby stepped quietly beside her. 'Anglia TV are here. Where's our star?'

'Oh, no! She'll be at least half an hour. What shall I do?'

'Stop looking like a trapped rabbit.' He squeezed her arm and his eyes became soft. 'I'll give them a drink. Don't worry. You're doing fine.'

By two-fifteen, people were moving towards the podium. At two-twenty they were saying, 'Have you seen her latest film? She's awfully good.' By two-twenty-five they were looking round expectantly. At two-thirty there were murmurs of, 'I wonder where she is?'

Ryder stood beside the mayor, a smile cemented to her face. At two-thirty-five she thought she was going to be sick. The mayor coughed politely. 'Miss Harding, we have another engagement.'

'I'm terribly sorry.'

'Would you like me to say a few words?'

'Could you wait one more minute? Please!' She turned to Michael and whispered, 'I'm having a nervous breakdown.'

He answered barely, moving his lips, 'Picture them all stark naked with a rosebud in each nostril.'

She started to giggle. At that moment Imogen's red

214

sportscar roared through the gateway and up to the platform. Patrick stepped out. He walked round to the passenger door and opened it with a flourish. As Imogen swung her pretty legs out, Ryder felt a twist of jealousy for the smile which passed between them. For a moment she was a lonely gawky girl arriving in London. Then the crowd cheered. So did Ryder, with relief. Immy teetered up the stairs on fiendishly high heels, her daintiness enhanced by a white broderie anglaise suit. 'Ryder, darling, I'm sorry we're late.' She tossed back her famous red Renaissance curls. 'My Lord Mayor, Lady Mayoress, ladies and gentlemen . . . aeroplanes . . . my apologies.'

Ryder marvelled at Immy's professionalism. No one would believe that four hours earlier she'd been sobbing that she couldn't cope.

'But now I'm here.' Imogen smiled and tipped her head. 'I can only say what a pleasure it is to see my best friend, Ryder Harding, accomplish so much.' She picked up the scissors and held them above the red ribbon. 'Good luck, Bailing Airfield!'

On cue the Sopwith Camel biplane came chugging over the hangar. The crowd cheered. The pilot dipped his wings. They raised their glasses. 'Bailing Airfield!'

Ryder raised her eyes — and met those of Patrick Brendan. She blushed and turned away, hoping that no one would notice. They didn't. Except for Michael Ashby.

20

Ryder stood in the middle of the deserted hangar surrounded by the debris of half-eaten sausages and paper napkins. One minute the airfield had been thronged with people, the next they were gone in a cloud of exhaust fumes and congratulations.

Footsteps sounded on the tarmac. Her stomach tightened. But it was Michael Ashby. 'Forget all this,' he said. 'I'll take you up for a spin in the Jennie.'

'Another day.' She felt flat and tired. Slowly she began to scoop the mess into a black plastic sack. 'Who drove . . . Immy home?'

'Patrick Brendan.'

'Oh.' She turned away. Patrick must be laughing himself to death. She'd agreed to sex and he didn't even want her.

Michael took the sack from her. 'Sit down before you drop.' Quickly he cleared the worst. Ryder leaned against the wall and watched.

'Any customers?' he asked.

'Not one.' She wished he'd go.

As if reading her mind, he picked up his flying jacket and crossed to his plane. 'Bailing won't forget you,' he called, as he swung up into the cockpit.

'But will they visit me when I'm in debtors' gaol?'

'I will.' He took off into the evening sky, crossing once over her head. She waved. He waggled his wings. Then he was gone, heading south. She almost wished he'd stayed. The airfield was desolate. It was Fox Lake in the winter. It was the blank wall of her father's cell. She walked down the runway, her hands in her pockets.

It took till mid-afternoon on Sunday to clear all the mess. Not that it mattered. She had nothing else to do. As she was hosing the cigarette butts from the tarmac the telephone rang.

'Ryder, it's Michael. What are you doing this afternoon?'

'I'm . . . er . . . taking Leo to see the seals. It's his treat before starting school.'

'I understand. Perhaps another time?'

'Perhaps.' She wasn't in the mood for strangers.

'We're going to see the seals today?' Leo jumped up.

'Not today.'

'But you promised!' His face was bright and eager.

'Oh, all right. But we'll have to be quick. Fetch your blue sweater — and bring down my red one.' She wrote a note to Fred. *'Have taken Leo to see seals. Back sevenish. R.'*

They drove up to Morston, to the marsh creeks and mud flats, where birds hovered over unseen prey and glorious red-gold marram grass was pliant to the north-east wind. A dozen people were already in the motor boat beside the quay. The boatman handed Ryder and Leo in. The boat chugged out through the creek, past anchored dinghies whose halliards flapped ceaselessly against their masts making a lonely, poignant sound like the bell of a lost cow. The open sea beckoned. The boat bounced from wave to wave. The wind tossed the spray into their faces. As they approached Blakeney Point the boatman shouted, 'Seal!'

A rounded head with big bright eyes and whiskers came up beside the boat. It was joined by another. They ducked and dived. Leo laughed and clapped his hands.

The sun was setting as they returned to Morston. The wind had dropped and an evening stillness gripped the

217

marsh. The tide had turned. It sucked the fast-flowing current from the creek. Out on the mudflats the lugwormers called to each other. Above them, seagulls screamed as they searched for food. From Blakeney Point came the distant bark of seals. And on the dune near the quay stood Patrick.

She pretended not to see him as she thanked the boatman. She busied herself helping an exhausted Leo so as not to have to look at him. 'How did you know we were here?' she asked.

'The note.'

She stepped into her car. So he'd gone to the airfield seeking his reward.

'I'll follow you,' he said.

'No! I mean . . . there's no need.' She drove off. Only a savage would expect her to keep such a bargain.

The airfield was in darkness. She parked outside the control tower. 'Leo! Come on! Put your arms around my neck.' She carried him inside.

'I'm hungry. I want sausages and milk.'

'If you wash your hands and face you can have one sausage and a glass of milk.'

'Two sausages with bread and butter.'

She left him upstairs to put on his pyjamas and went down to the kitchen. The frying pan heated quickly. The sausages began to sizzle. She poured a glass of milk and began to butter a slice of bread.

The front door opened. Patrick stepped inside. 'Dinner *à deux* over the sausages?'

'It's Leo's supper.'

'Ah . . . mine's later?'

'Listen Patrick!' She came towards him, the frying pan in one hand, the knife in the other. 'Whatever bargain I made with you yesterday, I intend to keep.'

'Then why did you try to outdrive me?'

'Because of Leo.'

'Do you think I'd exact payment in front of him?'

'A man capable of the terms you demanded is capable of anything.'

'Would you mind putting down the knife?'

'Would you mind getting out!'

'Yes.' He took the frying pan from her, tipped the sausages on to a plate and called, 'Supper!'

Leo ran down the stairs. He saw Patrick, and hesitated. 'Are we all having supper?'

'No!'

'Yes.' Patrick sat down. 'I'd like four sausages please and a glass of red wine.'

'I haven't any!'

'How lucky that I came. Such a thoughtful, welcome guest.' He went out to the Land-Rover.

She darted across the room and slammed the door but before she had time to slide the bolts, he was back, forcing it open inch by inch.

'Such a charming, hospitable hostess.' Calmly he searched the kitchen drawers for a bottle opener.

'Will you please leave!'

'I haven't had what I came for.' He handed her a glass of Chateau Lafite. 'My four sausages!'

She seethed and cooked the supper. He sat and talked to Leo till she said, 'It's his bedtime.'

'It's all of our bedtimes!'

She choked. He laughed. She took Leo upstairs. When she came down Patrick was lounging on the sofa.

'I'll keep my side of our contract.' She stood in front of him, hands on her hips. 'But I'll not have it hanging over me. I'll not have you coming here, tormenting me. If you want your pound of flesh, you have to take it now.'

'Take your clothes off!'

She rolled off her sweater.

'All of them!'

Her fingers trembled as she started to unbutton her shirt.

'Look at me!'

Her eyes were hard. Her shirt was half-open. The lace of her brassiere showed white against her suntanned body.

'Smile!'

'You bought my body — not my soul!'

He stepped towards her. She stiffened. He seized her wrists. 'Do you really think I'd have suggested such a bargain if I'd known you'd take it so seriously? Sex is meant to be fun — not human sacrifice.'

'So you humiliated me for your own amusement!' She pulled away. 'Do you know what it cost me to come begging to you — of all people!'

'Do you know what it meant for me to give up an afternoon's polo for you — of all people!' The phone rang. She answered.

'Bailing Airfield?' said a wellbred male voice. 'This is Rupert Atheldene of Atheldene Hall. I need hangarage for a six-seater Piper Cherokee for six months. What are your charges?'

'Forty pounds a month plus servicing and maintenance.' Her voice rose with excitement. 'Until tomorrow then.' She turned to Patrick. 'Rupert Atheldene. My first client.' She started to laugh.

He hugged her and swung her round the room. 'Congratulations. You deserve it. Don't undercharge Rupert. I know him well. He's rolling in money.' He picked up his car keys and walked to the door.

'Where are you going?'

'The mill.' He paused. 'Don't you want me to leave?'

'Yes . . . no . . . I mean . . .'

He dropped the keys back on the table. 'If I stay and you don't button up your shirt, I'm going to make love to you.'

She looked at him but did not move. He was so attractive to her.

He came towards her, his eyes locked into hers.

220

'You're the most unpredictable — ' He took her face in his hands. 'Intriguing — ' He kissed her gently as he slipped the shirt from her shoulders. 'Do you have a bedroom?'

She ran her fingers through his beautiful brown hair. 'I share with Leo!'

'We'll have to do something about that.' He pulled her to him, running his hands down her back. Holding her tighter. Tighter. She moved against him, wanting him as she'd never wanted any man before. He unzipped her jeans. Slowly. Sliding them from her hips. Kissing her stomach and her breasts. Touching her, until she clung to him, moaning. She sank to the sofa as he stood over her, unbuckling his belt. She ached for him. Longed for him. To get under his skin. To be a part of him. To feel him around her. Inside her.

Afterwards they lay on Mrs Dennshurst's uncomfortable sofa, drinking his rich red wine. 'You didn't tell me that idiot boyfriend of yours would be at Imogen's,' he said.

'I'm sorry. I forgot. And he's an ex-boyfriend. Adam and I finished the night my mother . . . killed herself. He begged me to come to London. When I arrived he was in bed with Alix.' Tears sprung into her eyes. 'I drove back to Dingwall and my mother had . . . She did it whilst I was away . . . I left her when she needed me.'

Patrick took her in his arms and held her tight. 'If it's anyone's fault it's your father's. He's a destroyer.'

'He did love her.'

'You must put all that behind you. It's the past.' Patrick's fingers circled her thighs. Gently. Softly. Demanding.

At five o'clock she slipped upstairs. No sooner had she fallen asleep – or so it seemed – than Leo was shaking her arm. 'Patrick and I want breakfast.'

'Oh.' She was exhausted with a wonderful kind of tiredness. Her skin felt polished. Her eyes shined up.

She stretched her legs and smiled a naughty smile. Slipping on her special Chinese silk dressing gown, she started down the stairs. Patrick was making coffee. 'Good morning.' He winked at her over Leo's head.

'Hello.' She stopped, suddenly shy. Her hands twisted awkwardly. She couldn't even look at him.

Without a word he crossed the room, picked her up, and carried her down.

21

Patrick left early. He had a dozen young ponies arriving at Gatehouse. 'I'll phone you later,' he said, ruffling her hair.

She watched him drive away, trying to quell her need for more reassurance. Then she turned back into the tower to dress.

Rupert Atheldene flew into Bailing at midday. Tall, fair and aquiline he sauntered across the tarmac with all the confidence of money and Eton. 'The bank's sending me to Hong Kong for a year.' He handed her an envelope. 'This should cover it. Keep her serviced. I'll be popping back from time to time.' He glanced at the freshly painted hangar. 'I saw your opening on Anglia news. It looked fun.' He beckoned to a girl in a sportscar who'd arrived to pick him up. 'But don't let any riff-raff in!'

'No riff-raff!' muttered Fred, as they watched him drive away. 'More money than sense, not like his ole father. Now he was a gentleman.'

Ryder tore open the envelope. Inside was a cheque. She waved it under Fred's nose. 'Look at that, you old pessimist! Money!' She skipped into the office and opened her brand new cashbook.

The phone rang. 'How's Mrs Dennshurst's sofa?' asked Patrick.

She blushed and giggled. 'How are the new ponies?'

'In their stables reading *Teach Yourself Polo*. I'll see you tonight.'

'Are you sure? I mean, it's miles.'

'Don't you want me to come?'

'Of course I do!'

She banked the precious cheque. She would have framed it only she needed the money. Arriving home she found Fred was bobbing around the hangar with Leo bobbing around after him. 'We have two more,' shouted Fred. 'A farmer from over Fakenham way an' a friend of Mr No-Riff-Raff Atheldene. Both comin' to see you on Thursday. We're going to be rich!'

'Rich!' Leo clapped his hands.

Later, as she was making fish cakes for his supper, he said, 'Tommy says I can sit next to him at school.'

'You'll soon make other friends as well.'

'But I like Tommy best.' He reached for the ketchup. Now he wouldn't eat without it.

For once he went to bed without protest. When Ryder arrived to say goodnight he was already asleep, the seal on the pillow beside him. She stood and watched, and in that instant knew that for all the problems he created she was glad she hadn't left him in Prairieville.

The tower was silent. She relished the peace. She ran a bath and used up another two precious drops of scent, then lay on the sofa in her Chinese dressing gown, wiggling her toes with anticipation. Patrick arrived half an hour late, by which time she was pacing the floor imagining him crushed beneath a lorry or trapped in his blazing car. 'I thought you'd had an accident.' She threw her arms around him.

'You can't get rid of me that quickly.'

'I was so afraid.' She kissed him, pressing her body against his, naked under her dressing-gown, not even giving him time to remove his leather jacket.

He ran his hands down her spine. 'I can feel a gold embroidered dragon fighting over you.' He traced the dragon's tail gently with the tips of his fingers. It looped around her waist then curled back into her thigh.

She moved her hands to his belt. He slipped the silk from her shoulders, kissing her neck and arms, till she was naked, her breasts pressing against the metal zip of his jacket. It was cold. Hard. Even brutal. But she wanted that hardness. She wanted him to take her. Passionately. Tenderly. She wanted him to hurt her exquisitely. To feel total desire in his hardness. To be sure of him.

In the morning he said, 'Will you come to watch polo on Sunday?'

'I have to be here. The weekend's my busiest time.'

'You could leave Fred and come in the late afternoon.'

'Yes . . . but . . .' She turned away. 'I don't want to see all those people who knew my father. I can't bear their sniggering.'

He took her in his arms. 'The sooner you front up to them the better. Polo's my world.'

'I'll come another day.'

Michael Ashby sent her all the press cuttings from the party. There were three lines in the *Daily Mail*, five in the *Daily Express*, a photograph and two columns in the *Eastern Daily Press*, and half a page in the *Lynn News & Advertiser*. 'Listen to this,' she called to Fred, ' "*Attractive, dynamic Ryder Harding*", "*Glamour comes to North Norfolk*".' She photocopied the articles for Scot's Farm, Immy, Lady Heythorp and Mrs Trumpet. As an after thought she sent a set to her father. It was half an olive branch.

When she phoned Michael to thank him, he asked, 'How were the seals?'

'What seals?'

'Weren't you going to see them on Sunday?'

'Oh . . . er . . . yes.' Sunday was pre-Patrick. Another life.

'Can I ask you something?' he said. 'Are you involved with Patrick Brendan?'

'Well . . . umm . . .'

'Just my luck! But I still think you're one very sparky lady, so if you're ever down in London give me a call and we'll have lunch.'

By Sunday the airfield had four customers renting hangarage, two planes booked to be serviced, and half a dozen machines coming in to refuel.

'It'll quieten down during the week,' Ryder told Fred as they counted the takings.

'I'll have time to put up tha' wall. Give you an' Leo a room each.'

'What a good idea.'

'Thought you might say tha'.' He chuckled as she turned bright pink.

Ryder was in love. She was so happy she thought she'd burst. Often she looked in the mirror and hugged herself. At night Patrick drove up to Bailing, arriving at nine and leaving at dawn. In the morning she went out into the bright September sunshine, exhausted from their lovemaking but filled with such energy and optimism.

Patrick was just leaving for Gatehouse when she opened the envelope containing a Visiting Order from her father. 'Ignore it!' he said, stepping into his car. 'He's a destroyer. He'll manipulate you.'

'I have to go.'

'Ryder, you're incomprehensible.' He switched on the engine. 'You'll brave a prison but you won't face the polo crowd to please me.'

'He's my father and this is his half of the olive branch.' She watched Patrick drive away. She was angry with herself for having spoiled their morning — and angry with him in some indefinable way.

The prison was bathed in sunshine. That made it almost

226

worse. She could feel the heat and the restlessness. It made her nervous.

Her father was sitting near the door. He looked up as she entered but said nothing. She sat stiffly opposite him. He laid a letter on the centre of the table, exactly halfway between them. 'I saw the articles in the newspapers,' he said. 'I'd already written to you. As I finished my letter yours arrived. This is mine.'

She glanced down. It contained just two words, *'Well done!'* She felt tears come into her eyes. She brushed them away with the back of her hand.

'Now, I want to hear all about it,' he said, his voice gruff with emotion. 'Every detail. Bailing's the only property I bought for sentimental reasons and it takes my daughter to see its potential.'

When Ryder left an hour later, she promised to bring Leo once he was settled into school.

There was a message from Patrick to say he was busy that night. She telephoned him. 'Is it because I went to see father?' she blurted out.

'Silly! What you do is your own affair.'

'Of course.' But that wasn't the response she'd longed for.

'Rodolfo and I are dining with an Arab sheik,' he explained. 'He wants ponies to play the Florida season. I'm not sure we have time to make any before we arrive.'

'When are you going there?' She tried to keep the anxiety from her voice.

'In December. Polo moves to Florida for the winter.'

'For how long?'

'Till March. But I'll be leaving here a few weeks ahead because I have some business in Argentina.' He paused. 'You're hurt. I'm sorry. I should have warned you but I've been involved in polo for so long that I forget other people don't know my world.'

227

There was now a hollow feeling in her stomach which added urgency to her love.

The end of the polo season meant Patrick had more free time. He hired a builder to give Bruja a proper stable. He taught Leo to ride. And he commiserated with him when he was jealous of Tommy's other friends at school. Often, if Patrick arrived early, Ryder would beg to go up to Morston where the three of them would walk across the salt marshes, listening to the distant bark of seals and watching the birds migrate south. She loved it there. So did Leo. But Patrick didn't. She asked him why.

'It reminds me of the pampas,' he said.

'Don't you like Argentina?'

'I love the country — it's the memories I can do without.' She longed to ask more but his face closed in.

Ryder didn't visit her father in the run up to Patrick's departure. It was selfish but she treasured every day of that shared autumn. Sometimes she dreamed Patrick had already gone and she'd wake suddenly, only to find him sleeping beside her.

He wanted her to visit Gatehouse. She hesitated because of the memories. 'I can't wait to make love to you in a proper double bed,' he said. 'Without Leo next door.'

'But I can't leave him behind.'

'If that's your problem, then bring him.'

'I wouldn't want him to know that we're sleeping together.'

'He won't. He'll have his own room. And we'll be up before he is.' He paused. 'Now you have no excuse.'

She'd like to have worn a pretty clinging dress but she didn't have one, so she wore her yellow silk flying suit. It was dusk when she arrived at Gatehouse. Lights glowed from the stables. Grooms called to each other. Ponies whinnied into the night.

Patrick appeared as she parked the car. Watching him

228

cross the yard she was again struck by how handsome he was. She felt so proud — and so afraid. 'I'll be a few minutes.' He touched her cheek. 'Where's Leo?'

'Asleep on the back seat.'

Patrick carried Leo straight up to bed. Then he disappeared to shower whilst Ryder wandered through the house. It was Georgian, with a wide central staircase, noble Ionic columns, and wonderful plaster moulding on every cornice. Compared to Dingwall Court it wasn't large, but after living in the control tower it seemed to Ryder like a palace. 'I've always loved this house,' she said to Patrick as he came downstairs.

'I didn't know you'd been inside before.'

'I haven't. I just knew I'd like it.' She linked her arms around his neck.

'I'm glad this is the first time.' He kissed her gently, drawing her up to him. She felt herself melting. Wanting. He led her upstairs, slowly. Stopping on every other step to caress her. In his bedroom he undressed her, slipping the yellow silk from her body, kissing her breasts and her stomach. She responded. Moving over him. Her tongue tracing paths across his body. He touched her till she cried out. She touched him till he could no longer hold back. Then he made love to her, with gentle urgency.

The airfield was taking off. There were seven planes permanently hangared and four paying to sit on the tarmac. Fuel sold well and Fred serviced as many machines as he could manage. But Ryder was still short of money. The bunker was being turned into a clubhouse. She bought tables and chairs and old prints of biplanes. Leo needed new clothes. The control tower, bare and bright in summer, was stark and depressing as the days grew shorter. She bought rugs, cushions and a couple of lamps. Nothing extravagant, but it all cost.

When Leo ruined his shoes playing near the river, she had to pawn her mother's watch to buy another pair.

On the first anniversary of her mother's death Ryder drove up to Morston and walked across the mudflats and the creeks, where the sailing dinghies rocked quietly, abandoned to the winter. She needed to be alone. To think. Or not to think. To be totally blank, with the northeast wind and the rustling golden reeds. To stride through the stiff, unscented sea lavender. To sit on a rickety wooden bridge and look up at the pale October sky, and think of her mother.

Michael Ashby was waiting by her car when she returned.

'How did you know I was here?' she asked, angry at the intrusion.

'Fred told me.' He held out his hand. In his palm was her Cartier watch.

She stared at him. 'Where did you get that?'

'My mother has a drink problem. I was retrieving her wedding ring from a Norwich pawnshop. I thought this watch looked similar to the one you wore. I asked to see the inscription.' His voice became more gentle. 'Doesn't the airfield pay?'

'We need another twenty clients but I'm so busy I don't have time to find any.'

'Hire an assistant.'

'I can't afford to.'

'You can't afford not to.' He opened her car door for her. 'Work out a promotion plan and let me see it.'

She hesitated. 'I haven't thanked you for the watch. I'll pay you when I can.' She dug her teeth into her lower lip. 'It was my mother's. She died a year ago today.'

'Were you very close to her?' he asked.

'No. That's what makes it worse. I longed to please her. But I never could. In the end I let her down at the one time she really needed me.'

Choked by sadness Ryder drove away. Michael watched her go. She wished he could have been Patrick. She would have cried in his arms. But Patrick was at the stables. Had he known of the watch, of course he would have retrieved it too.

Time gathered speed, Patrick's departure loomed towards Ryder like the guillotine, ready to sever her from the man she loved. Over their last dinner at Gatehouse with Rodolfo and his wife Antonella, the talk turned constantly to Florida. Ryder tried to smile but inside she was breaking.

Patrick leaned across the table and took her hand. 'Will you fly out for Christmas?'

She couldn't speak.

'Did you think I'd leave you for a whole three months?'

She swallowed hard. Her eyes shone with tears. 'Can I come on to Argentina with you? It always sounds so romantic.'

There was a sharp silence. Ryder sensed it. She looked at Patrick. He walked out of the room. She turned to Rodolfo and Antonella. Their eyes were fixed on their plates.

Then Patrick returned. 'I forgot the wine,' he said.

She laughed with relief. What a fool she was to see impediment where it did not exist.

'Let's drink to Ryder's visit to Florida!' Patrick raised his glass to her and she wondered if she could ever love him more than she did in that moment.

22

As soon as Patrick left for Florida, Ryder took Leo to see her father.

'But why is Daddy in prison?' Leo asked for the umpteenth time as they parked by the cottages.

'Because he borrowed some money and couldn't pay it back. Then he got frightened and tried to run away. Whereas he should have owned up.' She took his hand as they walked towards the prison. When Leo saw the high walls his face took on its white anxious look. She wondered if it were a mistake to bring him.

The visiting room was packed, which somehow made it worse. Tearful mothers tried to hush whining children. Leo clung to Ryder as she led him to her father. 'Here's Daddy,' she said.

Her father held out his arms. 'How's my boy?'

Leo froze. His face became even whiter. His eyes were dark hollows in his face. 'Where's Mummy?'

'She's not here.' Ryder sat down. 'But Daddy is.' She turned to her father. 'He'll get used to you in a minute.'

Her father dropped his hands to the table. 'I thought he'd run in here and throw his arms around me but he doesn't even know who I am.'

'You haven't given him a chance.' She tried to ease her brother forward but he buried his face in her shoulder.

But her father pushed back his chair and stood up. 'Take him away! I don't want him to hate me. I have enough hate in my life.' He looked at Leo who clung to

Ryder, terrified she might leave without him. 'I never thought he'd prefer you to me,' he said bitterly.

'What did you expect, when I'm all he has,' she replied, not meaning to be as cruel as she sounded.

Without Patrick, Ryder channelled her energies into Bailing. A word with Mrs Dennshurst brought forth Violet, a middle-aged childless widow so efficient that Ryder couldn't imagine how the place had survived before her. Leo already knew and liked Violet, who offered to have him when Ryder went away. She lived next door to Tommy and allowed the boys to play in her garden.

'You were right about me needing an assistant,' Ryder told Michael Ashby. 'I'm planning a trip to London. I'd like to pick your brains on promotion.'

'How's the boyfriend?'

'Fine.'

'What a shame!' He gave an exaggerated sigh which reduced her to giggles.

She telephoned Immy, hoping to meet her, but as Adam was away she gladly agreed to spend the night. Immy's new house was in a mews not far from Harrods. Ryder parked outside the bow windows, from which warmth and light glowed richly into the evening. The front door was cobalt blue, with a brass knocker shaped like a fish; Imogen was Pisces. Before Ryder had even lifted it, the door flew open.

'I was near the window,' said Immy. 'I couldn't wait for you to come.' She gabbled on brightly as she led Ryder inside. The whole house was decorated in dainty floral prints. 'Alix thinks it's ghastly,' Immy confided as she whisked her upstairs. 'I know, because she keeps introducing me to interior designers. But I like to choose things myself. It gives me something to think about, now I don't have Tony.'

'Do you still love him?' asked Ryder, perching on the end of a frilly bed.

'He made me feel safe.'

'Do you see him?'

'He won't. He says I drained the reservoir of love he had for me.' She gave Ryder a sad smile. Then she darted downstairs, returning with a bottle of pink champagne. 'Now I want to hear about everything. Everything!' She handed Ryder a glass. 'That includes Patrick Brendan.'

In the morning Ryder agreed to stay for a second night. 'But I must do some shopping before I meet Michael,' she said. 'I have to buy Patrick a Christmas present. Something special. Something wonderful.'

They trailed around the ground floor of Harrods, followed by murmurs of 'Look! Imogen Lydden!' Nothing Ryder could afford caught her eye. 'I suppose I could spend more.' She studied a silver statue of a horse. 'But I want to buy a bicycle for Leo. All the other boys have them. I also need one smart winter outfit in which to promote Bailing.'

'Only one!'

'I only see each person once. They're not to know I don't have a wardrobe crammed with designer originals.'

They took the lift to the fashion floor where Ryder found a belted suit in brilliant rust, a colour which evoked bonfires and autumn and the windswept reeds of Morston. She hovered between that and an elegant dove grey crêpe suit, with a slinky fishtale skirt and a pale pink camisole top.

'What do you think?' she asked Imogen. 'One or the other — and I only have five minutes.'

'What are your winter coats like?'

'Coats! Immy, I'm still wearing my old trenchcoat.'

'Take the rust. The grey needs that black cashmere coat.'

'I'll wear the rust for lunch today.' Ryder headed for

the changing rooms. 'I may as well get my money's worth.'

When she returned, Imogen and the sales assistant were conspiratorially packing the grey suit and the black coat.

'Aren't they a size too big for you?' said Ryder, trying not to sound envious.

Immy picked up the carrier bags. 'Come on!'

'But I haven't paid for the rust suit.'

'I have. They're all for you.' Imogen smiled at the shop assistant. 'I'll have no argument. I can easily afford it.'

'How can I repay you?' said Ryder.

'Let me use Bailing as an escape if I ever need it.'

'Any time. Now please go home. You have a cold and I've been dragging you round the shops.'

'I don't have a cold.' Imogen put away her handkerchief.

Michael looked so smart that Ryder barely recognised him. Gone was the marauding cossack in a leather flying jacket. Instead he wore a perfectly tailored dark grey suit, which enhanced his powerful build. 'You look different,' she said, joining him in the restaurant where he was already ensconced in a corner table.

'So do you.' He stood to shake her hand. 'You look very smart. Things can't be that bad.'

'Oh, this is a present.'

He raised an eyebrow. She realised he thought that Patrick had bought the suit for her but she didn't enlighten him. She relished the small glow of pleasure at the idea of Patrick providing for her. Of being his woman.

'So how can I help?' asked Michael.

'I need more clients.'

'Advertise.'

'I can't afford to.'

'That's what you said about Violet. You can't afford not to. But wait till the spring, when the amateur flyer remembers he has a plane and thinks about using it.' He broke off a piece of French bread and ate it with relish. 'Another idea. Link up with another airfield. One far enough away so as not to be in competition but within a day's return flight.'

'I hadn't thought of that.' She picked up a stick of asparagus and dipped its tender green bud in the melted butter. 'Of course the answer would be to buy a second airfield and profit from both ends.'

'Now you're talking!'

'You mean dreaming!'

'You'll do it.' He took out a note pad and jotted down a couple of names. She noticed he had beautiful hands with long fine fingers which were at odds with his very physical body. 'Here are two airfields,' he said. 'One's managed by an ex-colleague of mine. We were both pilots with Colossus Air before we went our different ways.'

'Why was that?' She was suddenly curious about him.

'We tired of being small cogs in big corporation wheels. Another ex-pilot is the editor of *Aviation Argus*. That's how I got into journalism. But I miss being part of an airline. I love the excitement and the bustle.'

She gave him an unconsciously suggestive smile. 'You mean, you're a doer not an observer?'

He studied her over the rim of his glass. 'Don't play games with me, Miss Biggles.'

236

23

Florida

Ryder arrived to brilliant sunshine and a cerulean sky. Warm air caressed her face as she stepped from the plane. Light bounced up from the runway. Heat shimmered on distant palm trees. Impatient in a queue for immigration, she took out her compact and checked her make up. Quickly she reglossed her lips and topped up her scent. Then she retied her white sweatshirt over her shoulders and smoothed down her red culottes, wishing her legs were tanned and not winter-anaemic.

She retrieved her case and headed for the waiting friends and relatives. At every step she expected to see him. Hear him. Touch him. But there were so many people she couldn't see him. She stepped to one side. The crowd surged. She looked at her watch. Surely he wouldn't be late? Not today.

'Ryder! Sorry to keep you.'

'Rodolfo, where's Patrick?'

'In Argentina. Didn't he tell you? He went last week.'

'But . . . but . . . when is he coming back?'

'About midnight.' Rodolfo beckoned to a porter. 'I'm in a hurry. I have to play polo at four.' He ushered her out into the sunshine.

'Where am I staying?' She followed him anxiously towards the car park.

'The Breaker's Hotel at Palm Beach.' He unlocked

the boot. 'Patrick and I share a house but Antonella's here with the children and her mother, so he thought the Breaker's would be more . . . private.'

'But I don't understand.' She felt faint with disappointment. 'Patrick phoned me two days ago and he didn't mention Argentina.'

Rodolfo gave her a Latin shrug. 'He'll be here tonight. He'll explain everything.'

They left the airport and the concrete sprawl of Miami, and headed north along the coast road. Huge white hotels with palm fringed swimming pools were interspersed with sweeping views of the ocean rolling up the bone-white sand. But Ryder could enjoy none of it. She wished she hadn't come.

'Boca Raton,' said Rodolfo, after they'd been driving for nearly an hour. 'Where we play polo. The ground's good but the club's not like the Guards'. Not yet. They're talking of opening a polo club at Palm Beach. If they do it'll be bigger and better than anything anywhere else. At least, they'll claim it is!'

Ryder forced herself to smile but her mind was on Patrick.

They were approaching Palm Beach. She saw white Italianate villas surrounded by palm trees and Spanish haciendas draped in purple bougainvillaea, and deep blue water reaching up into a deep blue sky. They crossed a golf course and turned down a drive which led them through lush gardens to a stucco Renaissance palace which looked like the fantasy of a homesick Venetian count.

Rodolfo left her in the reception. As he drove away she had to stifle the desire to run after him. Then she told herself not to be pathetic and she allowed the monied timelessness of the hotel to envelop her; its gilded frescoes on vaulted ceilings, the fresh-cut flowers, the other guests who moved with the casual chic of the very rich — that same casual chic which her mother had possessed.

238

Her room was on the fifth floor. It had a balcony which looked out over palm trees, to white sand and never-ending ocean. Was she really on the same planet as foggy, windswept Bailing?

There was a knock on the door. A porter entered bearing an enormous bouquet of red roses nestling amongst pale green ferns, with a card which read:

Sorry to be late. All my love
Patrick

She smiled. She felt better. She'd have a swim and a sunbathe, then a rest and a shower — then Patrick would come.

The pool was delicious. She swam five lengths before succumbing to a sun lounger and a Manhattan cocktail. The sun brought colour to her arms and legs. Lack of sleep — or was it the whisky, the vermouth and the absinthe — made her light headed. As she left the pool several men glanced her way. But she didn't care. Today they saw her alone. Tomorrow she'd be with Patrick.

It was dark when she woke, dopy and confused by her surroundings. The balcony doors were open. Music mingled with the sound of the ocean. She fumbled for the bedside light. Eleven o'clock. One hour and Patrick would be landing. She showered and added a touch of make up and more than a touch of scent. Midnight. She was hungry. He would have eaten on the plane. She ordered a sandwich and tidied the room. The television was showing ten different films. She ate as she flicked from channel to channel.

She woke again, cold and stiff, lying on top of the covers with her head on the sandwich plate and a horror film on the screen. Her watch said two-fifteen. She reached for the phone.

'Yes, ma'am, it's a quarter after two,' replied the switchboard. 'No, ma'am. No calls. No messages.'

'I was expecting a friend on a flight from Buenos Aires due to land at midnight. Could you check it, please?'

She paced the room, her mind racing with visions of Patrick crashed into the Amazon jungle. She saw him drag himself from the burning wreck. The only survivor. Doomed to die, injured and alone, calling out her name.

The switchboard came back to her. 'No direct flights from Buenos Aires tonight.'

'But I know he's coming.' She heard the panic in her voice but she couldn't control it.

'Maybe he connected through Mexico City.'

'Yes. Maybe. Thank you.' She lay down on the bed. She was near to tears.

She was still there, fully clothed, when the telephone woke her in the morning. 'Ryder?'

'Oh, Patrick . . . Where are you? I've been so worried.'

'I'm at Boca Raton, about to play a few chukkas.'

'What happened last night?'

'I didn't land till after midnight and I thought you'd be tired.'

'It wouldn't have mattered. After all,' she added softly, 'I'm only here for four days.'

'I'll pick you up around noon.'

She felt sick with foreboding. Then she told herself not to be ridiculous. His card said *All my love*, but the slightest hitch and she feared she'd lost him. At this rate she would lose him.

The sun was hot. She went down to the pool to oil and toast her body so that it was soft and tanned for Patrick. With an hour to spare she returned to her room. At noon she was ready, hair fluffed around her sunkissed face, nails painted pink, ice blue sundress showing off her honey-coloured shoulders. At twelve-fifteen she reglossed her lips. At twelve-thirty she resprayed herself with scent. At one o'clock she telephoned Patrick's villa.

There was no answer. She lay down on her bed and cried.

She woke to find him standing at the end of her bed. He was watching her with an angry desperation.

'What's wrong?' she whispered. 'Please tell me. If you don't want me here I'll go back today.'

He walked round to her side. She stared up at him, fearing the worst. 'Want you!' He seized her in his arms. 'Of course I want you!' He kissed her face. Her neck. Her eyes. Her hair.

'I was so afraid that . . .'

But he wouldn't let her finish. He kissed her deeply, drawing her to him. Her dress moved up around her thighs and he slid it from her. Gently. Caressing. She unbuttoned his shirt. He unbuckled his belt.

'I was just afraid that . . .'

But again he wouldn't let her finish. He rolled her nipples between his lips until her words turned to cries of pleasure. He touched her intimately. Gently. And she responded. Opening up to him. Wanting him, so that when he made love to her she moved with him. Rhythmically. Such a part of him that every spasm of his body became hers.

Afterwards when she lay in his arms, sprawled across the huge bed, she wanted to ask him again if anything was wrong. But she didn't. She told herself that she was being stupid.

He glanced at his watch. 'Four o'clock. I'm playing polo at five.'

'Can I watch?'

'If you don't I'll sink my teeth into your left bosom.'

'What's wrong with the right one?'

'I'm saving that for Christmas.' He kissed her nipple. 'Bosom à la Petite Marmite.'

She laughed and snuggled up to him. 'What's the Petite Marmite?'

'The most exclusive, expensive, romantic restaurant

241

in Palm Beach — and I'm taking you there tonight. So unless you intend to give the other diners a thrill, you'd better dress because we won't come back here first. You've got ten minutes . . .' he rolled over on top of her, 'once I've finished making love to you again.'

She wore a black and white silk two-piece. It had a wrapover top with little cap sleeves and a straight skirt with a slit up the side. She'd bought it a week before, in a sale at the 'yellow flying suit' boutique. 'Not for Norwich,' the assistant had explained the hefty price reduction.

'Is this all right?' She hovered in the bathroom door.

He eyed her up and down. 'Perfect! Especially the slit up the side.'

He sang in the shower. She laughed to hear him. 'How's Leo?' he asked, as he towel-dried his hair.

'Furious at being left behind.' She paused. 'Father's angry too. He's so bored and frustrated. Parole's a possibility when he's served a third but he doubts he'll get it. I told him I was coming to Florida. I had to. He wanted to know why I couldn't visit him.'

She waited for Patrick to comment but he didn't. He asked, 'How's Bailing?'

'I've employed an assistant. Michael Ashby suggested it and he was right. He's also given me tips about promotion.' She slipped on her gold high-heeled sandals. 'But this oil price hike could hit us badly.'

'Will you make enough to get through the winter?'

'I want to make more than *enough*.' She looked at him in the mirror. 'I want to buy another airfield and run it as a two-base operation.'

Patrick kissed the back of her neck. 'Is this Michael Ashby's suggestion too?'

'Of course not!'

He pulled her towards him. 'I don't like that man hanging around you. Not whilst I'm away.'

'He's just a friend.' She leaned against him. His chest

was warm and bare. His breeches stretched over his muscle-hard thighs. He held her tighter. She moved. Teasing. Their eyes met in the mirror. He ran his hand down the back of her leg. She raked her fingernails up the inside of his thigh. He unbuckled his belt and hitched up her tight silk skirt.

The Royal Palm Polo Sports Club at Boca Raton was small, friendly and relaxed. As Rodolfo had said, the ground was good. But the clubhouse consisted mainly of a stand, with a restaurant behind and a bar on the second level. Antonella Martinez was sitting with her mother and two very glamorous women.

'There you are. At last!' Antonella called to them. 'Patrick, you mustn't keep Ryder hidden in the hotel. It isn't nice. Mama wants to meet her.' She patted a chair. 'Ryder, join us. My mother. My friends Octavia and Darlene. Octavia's husband, Howard, is our patron.'

'I'm buying you champagne,' said Octavia, a tough-looking, tousled blonde with a face like a gangster's moll made good. 'Beat it, Patrick! This is girls' talk.'

He left — amidst their laughter.

With a flash of diamond rings, Octavia beckoned to the waiter. 'Krug! And caviar!' She turned to Ryder. 'You deserve a medal for taming that guy. He hasn't looked at another woman all season.'

The ponies thundered up and down. Champagne corks popped in front of the clubhouse. Ice tinkled in glasses. Patrick rose in the saddle, twisted, and hit a perfect nearside backhand. Ryder pictured her father in his cell, and the champagne turned to acid in her mouth.

Howard Irving was a distinguished white-haired man well into his sixties, which made him some thirty years older than his wife. His fourth wife, so Ryder gathered. 'We'll be seeing you two lovebirds tomorrow evening,' he told Ryder. 'Our Christmas party. I know it's

Christmas because my wife's been bankrupting me at Martha's.'

'That's the most divinely expensive dress shop in Palm Beach,' added Octavia. 'Patrick's a wise guy not to take you there. Wise but tight.' She looked at her husband with affection.

Patrick and Ryder escaped, and returned to Palm Beach, to the house he shared with Rodolfo. It was a modern Spanish hacienda well hidden behind a wall of palm trees.

'I want to see your room,' she said. 'I want to be able to picture you there.' He led her to a room overlooking the pool. She lay down on his bed and stared at the ceiling. 'I want to know what light patterns you see at night.'

He reached for her foot and stroked her ankle. His fingers gently circling. 'I made love to you all afternoon — and I still want you.'

'I want you too. I kept thinking about you — us — whilst you were playing.' She untied her top, slowly, and tossed it to one side.

He took off his shirt. He was hard and bronzed and muscular. He smelled of sweat and horses, but she didn't mind. She liked it. She ran her big toes up the inside of his thigh. He grabbed her ankles and twisted her over on to her stomach. 'You have naughty feet.' He nibbled on one toe.

'I have delicious feet.'

He ran his hand down her naked back and over her buttocks. 'If you were a polo pony your tail would be plaited.'

'If I were a polo pony I'd only be ridden for seven and a half minutes at a time.'

'But ridden hard.' He knelt to kiss her shoulder blade.

'Very hard?'

'Extremely hard.'

244

She sat by the window as he showered and changed, listening to the rustle of the palm trees and feeling the warm wind caress her back as she memorised every detail of the house.

'When I'm back at Bailing I'll think of you, lying here, listening to the palm trees.'

He smiled. 'They're said to be the result of a ship of drunken sailors which ran aground.'

'I'd love to have come here, when there was no one.'

'I'd love to have come here with you, when there was no one.' He held out his hand. She took it.

Patrick gave her a guided tour of Palm Beach. He showed her Worth Avenue, the main shopping street. It reminded Ryder of old Marbella, with its Spanish alleys leading to fountains, bougainvillaea, Gucci and Yves St Laurent. They stopped for a drink at the Taboo, where the piano player welcomed all with his blue-eyed smile. Then they moved on to the *Petite Marmite*, Patrick's arm around her waist as they passed between the gates of delicate Florentine grillwork.

'I chose the Patio Room because I like the frescoes,' said Patrick, as they were ushered to their table. Above them, banana trees reached into the night sky. Beside them, the walls depicted the isle of Capri.

He reached for her hand. 'One day I'll take you to Capri.'

'Did you know our parents went there? I found some photos and letters. There's even a picture of you, as a page at my parents' wedding!'

'How strange.' He toyed with her fingers. 'And here we are, you and I.'

Her heart missed a beat. 'Yes.'

He picked up the menu. 'The first time I ever came to the *Petite Marmite* was at the beginning of my first Florida season, which was my first season as a professional. Rodolfo brought me here. I was impressed — but I tried not to let it show.' He laughed. 'Since then

I've been here many times but I've never ordered exactly the same menu as I ate on that first occasion. I've done it on purpose, to make that occasion special.' He raised her hand to his lips and gently kissed her fingers. 'Shall we have my special menu? Coquilles St Jacques and Chablis. Duck Bigarade and Mouton-Rothschild. Strawberry Romanoff and Krug champagne.'

The scallops were rich, creamy and browned in their shells. She scooped up the soft flesh and lifted it to her mouth. Patrick watched her lips part to take the spoon. She tasted the ice cold Chablis. Their eyes met over the rim of her glass.

'Four days is far too short,' he said.

'I'm trying not to count the hours.'

'When I come here with Rodolfo, I'll picture you.'

'In windswept Bailing I'll look at my suntanned arms and I'll think of you and the sun and the palm trees.'

'If I see someone sitting here, at our table, I'll have to stop myself from telling them it's private property.'

She smiled. He looked at her intensely. She held her breath. She was sure he was going to ask her to marry him.

The waiter took their plates. He returned with the duck. It was anointed with a delicious hot sauce of orange, grapefruit and Grand Marnier. Ryder waited for Patrick to return to their conversation but he talked of polo. They finished their duck. The waiter brought a bottle of Krug, chilled in a silver bucket.

Patrick raised his glass. 'To us.'

'To us!' She waited for him to say more.

They were interrupted by the strawberries. They were mixed with cream, sherbert, brandy and more Grand Marnier. As Ryder laid down her spoon, Patrick reached for her hand. 'I love to walk along the beach at night. Shall we?'

'Yes.' She linked her fingers through his. Surely now! The moon glittered on the ocean. The surf pounded on the sand. They took off their shoes and walked through the edge of the water, their moon shadows reaching up the beach to the palm trees.

'Look!' Patrick stopped to pick up a shell. 'For you. A souvenir of Palm Beach.' He shook out the water. 'You can listen to the waves when you're back at Bailing.'

'And you're an ocean of miles away.'

He cupped her chin in his hand. 'I love you, Ryder.' He kissed her with a strange ferocity. 'Remember that — when you listen to your shell.'

Patrick loved her. If he chose to wait before asking her to be his wife, she understood.

Early next morning she slipped out of bed and opened her suitcase. 'Happy Christmas!' She woke him by laying her present on his chest. It was flat and oblong, like a very large book, and wrapped in gold paper with a huge gold and black bow.

He opened one eye. 'What is it?'

'Look and see.'

He removed the ribbon and laid it on her bare stomach. She watched his face, waiting for his reaction. He detached the gold tape and slid the paper from its contents. 'A portrait of Bruja!' He held the watercolour at arm's length. Bruja was depicted in full polo tack. 'Her dark eyes have the right gleam of obstinacy,' he said, smiling. 'I remember it well. She looked like that before a game.'

'She looked like that when she ate my lettuces.'

He laughed and kissed her. 'She'll always be my favourite. Darling Ryder, it's the best present I've ever had.'

She waited for him to say, 'Now I have something for you.' But he didn't. He reached for the phone and dialled Rodolfo's number.

She sank back against the pillows, telling herself she didn't mind. Something small and hard dug into her back. She wriggled. It was still there, inside the pillow. She reached for it. A tiny red velvet box — a box big enough for a ring. She nudged Patrick, who was still on the phone. He gave an exaggerated shrug as though it were nothing to do with him.

The moment of anticipation was so delicious that she could hardly bring herself to open it. But she did. And she swallowed hard. Inside were a pair of drop pearl earrings, exactly like the ones she'd had to sell. She lifted them out. They were beautiful. But they weren't a ring. Not that she minded. Not really. There was plenty of time — and he did love her.

She hooked them into her ears and knelt in front of Patrick, lifting up her hair so that he could see the full benefit of his present. He replaced the receiver and smiled. She kissed his neck and his chest, tracing a path down his muscular body as he talked polo and ponies. She buried her face in him. She took him in her mouth, gently, softly.

Ryder spent the morning by the pool. She lay stretched out in the sun, her whole body tingling with Patrick. She ought to call Scot's Farm. Her grandparents would be mortified if they knew she'd been in the States and not done so. But every time she reached for the receiver, she stopped. She couldn't bear to break the magic of Patrick.

For the party, Ryder wore a plain black silk shift. It was her only long dress. Well, it wasn't a dress, but Immy's Christmas present. A thirties-style crêpe de chine nightgown from Harrods, and if Patrick had controlled his ardour long enough for her to deck herself out in it, she'd have worn it already — in bed.

Howard and Octavia lived in a mini-Versailles. It was built around a magnificent courtyard containing floodlit fountains and marble sculpture. There was even a semblance of the *Galerie des Glaces* in the hundred foot long terrace overlooking the pool and ocean beyond. The party was well underway when Patrick and Ryder arrived. People were dancing on the terrace. A band played by the pool. Waiters circulated with pink champagne and caviar.

'Darlings!' Octavia slithered across the terrace with enough emeralds around her neck to clear the national debt. 'Ryder, you look so . . . chic! How clever to wear black.' She introduced them to endless glamorous people, all of whose names Ryder instantly forgot.

The band was playing 'I'm Not In Love'. Patrick took her in his arms. 'This is the first time we've danced.'

'I know.' She moved closer.

'If we'd just met I'd be asking you, "What do you do? Where do you live?" '

'Not "Are you alone"?'

'Not yet!' He held her tighter. 'I'd flatter you first with, "What beautiful earrings you're wearing." '

'I'd reply enigmatically, "They were a present." '

'Then I'd try to figure out which of these men had given them to you.'

'And I'd wonder if some girl were about to tap you on the shoulder and say, "Darling, did you remember to put the cat out?" '

He laughed. 'I love you.' He said it so suddenly that for a moment she thought she'd misheard. Then he touched her cheek. 'It's true.' He looked almost sad.

'I love you too,' she whispered in his ear. Again she waited but he said no more.

Supper was a magnificent buffet. Lobster caught that morning in Florida. Smoked salmon flown out from Harrods. Caviar from Russia. They ate in a secluded alcove, hidden from the other guests by a curtain of bougainvillaea. As they returned to the dancefloor, his arm around her waist, Octavia descended on them. 'Patrick, I'm going to introduce your girlfriend to some single men.'

Ryder laughed. 'Thanks — but I'm happy as I am.'

'Every woman needs a rich husband.'

'I'd only marry for love.'

'Honey, one never knows what's around the corner.' Octavia beckoned to the waiter for another glass of champagne.

'As a matter of fact,' Patrick drew Ryder closer, 'we were thinking of leaving. Ryder only has another two days.'

'Bastard!'

Ryder was speechless. Patrick stiffened. She felt his fingers dig into her arm. Then suddenly Octavia kissed her on both cheeks. 'Don't worry,' she said. 'I've had too much champagne.'

They left immediately. In the car Ryder said, 'Octavia didn't mean it. She was drunk. Perhaps she and Howard had a row.' Her voice trailed off, frozen by his silence.

They drove through the night, beneath palms whose leaves arched up into the inky sky. In the hotel lift he barely looked at her. When she unlocked her door, he pushed past and marched straight out on to the balcony. She dropped her bag on her bed and followed.

'Is anything wrong?' she asked.

He had his back to her, his hands spread out on the top railing. 'I shouldn't have brought you out here.'

'What!' She felt as though she'd been punched.

'It was wrong of me.'

'Why?'

'It was a mistake.'

'I don't believe it.' She reached out her hand to him. 'We've been so happy. We love each other. Look at me!'

He turned, and his face held that same angry desperation that she'd seen when she woke to find him standing at the bottom of her bed.

'Are you in love with someone else?' She had to force the words out.

He shook his head.

250

'Then what's wrong? I deserve to know. Yesterday you loved me. Now you say you don't.'

'Go back to England.' His voice was hoarse. He pushed past her and marched out of the room.

'Wait!' she shouted.

He walked on.

She ran down the corridor. 'Patrick!'

He stepped into the lift.

She thumped the *Door Open* button. 'You can't run out on me for no reason,' she cried. 'You can't bring me out here, make love to me every hour, then tell me to be gone. I'm a person. I have feelings. I love you. You owe me an explanation.'

He looked at her with a deep sadness, intensified by the nostalgia of the Christmas decorations. 'Do you really want to know?'

'Yes.'

'I have a wife and child in Argentina.'

24

England

Fred didn't ask Ryder what had happened in Palm Beach. Nor did Violet. They didn't need to. Unhappiness was etched into every feature of her face during those dark winter days, when the northeasterly whipped down the runway and no one could be sure if it were the wind — or something else — which brought tears to Ryder's eyes.

The only person she told was Imogen, in many late night phone calls. 'I'll never love anyone again,' she said. 'I'll never trust anyone. All the way home I kept remembering incidents. There was an evening at Gatehouse. Then what Octavia said at the party. Everyone knew — except me! I believed he loved me. I thought he was going to marry me.' Her voice broke. 'What happened with Adam was bad, but Patrick has cut me into pieces.'

'You have to stop going for men where you're doing all the loving and giving,' said Imogen.

'Patrick did love me!'

'So long as you didn't mention your father. Don't scream! I know I'm a fine one to talk. But we all see each other's mistakes. Come to London. You need people. We'll go to a party.'

'Immy, I barely have the confidence to buy a pint of milk.'

The shell which Patrick had given Ryder on the beach remained in her suitcase. Sometimes late at night she would take it out and lift it to her ear. Only it wasn't the words of love he'd spoken on the white sand she heard, but 'I have a wife and child in Argentina'.

She visited her father as soon as she could pull herself together to face him. 'You didn't tell me you were going to visit Patrick Brendan,' he accused before she'd even sat down.

She flushed. 'How do you know?'

'I have my sources.' He watched her closely. 'I don't like the idea of my daughter carrying on with a married man.'

'Your source needs updating. Patrick and I are finished.' She lifted her chin. 'And I'd prefer not to talk about it.'

Of course she couldn't stop Leo from talking about Patrick. 'Where is he? When's he coming to see us?' he kept asking.

'He's gone away,' Ryder told him for the umpteenth time.

It was evening and they were sitting at the pine table in the control tower. She was drafting a brochure. He was colouring a book given to him by Mrs Dennshurst.

'Why?' he persisted.

'I don't know! I've told you that before.' She stood up. 'I'll make your supper. Baked beans?'

'I don't want silly old baked beans.'

'There's no need to be rude. What would you like?'

'Scrambled egg.'

'Say please!'

'Please.'

She whipped up an egg and browned some toast. 'Here you are.' She put the plate in front of him.

He took one look. 'I don't want silly old scrambled egg.'

253

'Then go to bed hungry.' She continued writing. Anything to occupy her hand so she didn't hit him.

'I hate you!'

'I hate you too,' she said calmly.

'I want to show my bicycle to Patrick.'

'I can't make him come back. Now eat your supper and then I'll read you a story.'

'I hate egg.' He picked up his plate and threw it on the floor.

Ryder pulled him off his chair and slapped him. He screamed and kicked her. She dragged him upstairs, nearly pulling his arm from its socket, and shut him in his room. He kicked at the door, screaming. She opened it. Slapped him. And threw him on his bed. 'Shut up!'

He lay there, screaming and kicking.

She went out of the room and closed the door. She was shaking. Downstairs, the plate was in three pieces and egg was congealing on the floorboards. She cleared it up and poured herself a tumbler of coarse red wine. It tasted like paint stripper, but it helped her ignore the noise from upstairs. As she poured a second tumbler, the phone rang. She hesitated to answer. If it were Immy, she'd be called a hypocrite for the times Ryder had berated her about drinking. If it were Lady Heythorp, the old crone would give her an earful. On the eighth ring she could resist no longer.

'Ryder?'

'Oh . . . hello, Michael.'

'You don't sound very pleased to hear from me.'

'It's Leo. He's having a tantrum.'

'You have to ignore it. My sister's children were like that when they were two.'

'Leo's seven.'

'Maybe he's backward.'

'He is not backward!'

'Okay! I'm sorry.' He paused. 'Ryder, are you all right?'

254

She tried to speak.

'What's wrong?' he persisted.

'Everything.' She started to cry. 'Everything!'

Michael arrived in the late morning. Patrick would have rushed to comfort her last night. He marched into the tower as Ryder was letrasetting *FLYING'S FUN — AT BAILING* on to her dummy brochure. 'I'm taking you to lunch. You need it.'

'I have to collect Leo today. Violet has flu.'

'You don't look so good yourself.' He cupped her face in his hands and turned it to the light. 'You've either been crying or drinking or both.'

She pulled away. 'Both — if you really want to know.'

He picked up her brochure. 'I like this headline but it needs to be bigger.'

'I'm increasing hangarage prices from Easter.'

'Go for 1 March. It sounds more businesslike.'

She leaned over his shoulder and altered the date. 'Come and see the clubhouse. We open in May.'

They crossed to the old bunker. It had been cleared of debris and the walls had been whitewashed. Across the back was a long wooden bar constructed by Fred over Christmas. Down one side were the cane chairs for the patio, down the other were stacks of framed photos of old biplanes for the walls.

'Looks good.' Michael nodded. 'I like the patio. I can see myself sitting out here in the sun, watching the planes take off.'

'Not just you! But the other fifty members, I hope!'

They walked back to the tower. He stopped when they reached his car. 'You look as if you need a friend,' he said very gently. 'You know my number if you do.'

She turned away to hide her feelings. 'I have to go out. I forgot I have to do some shopping before school finishes.'

255

'Let me take you and Leo to the cinema.' He paused. 'As a friend.'

'Not today.' She scrabbled in her pocket for her car keys. 'Thanks.' She made herself look at him. 'You see, one of the reasons why Leo was upset was that he became very fond of Patrick Brendan.'

'And you?' he asked.

'And me.' She jumped into her car and drove away.

When she returned, half an hour later, there was a note on the table.

I thought you were brave when you started Bailing. But I didn't know then about your father, your mother and Leo. You're one gutsy lady, Miss Biggles — and Patrick Brendan is a fool.

She screwed it up and threw it away. She wanted Patrick – and no one else. Leo was feeding Bruja. 'You must have a bath tonight,' she called to him.

'All right.' Usually he made a fuss.

'What do you want for supper?'

'Baked beans.' He came running up the path. 'I like baked beans.'

She muttered a silent prayer to the saint in charge of patience. 'What did you do at school today?' she asked him, taking time off from her work to sit with him whilst he ate.

'Painting.'

'Do you like it?'

'Yes.'

'What do you do with your pictures?'

'I leave mine at school.' He gulped down his milk. 'But the children who have mummies and daddies take them home.'

'You could bring yours home to me,' she said. 'I'm sure Daddy would like one too. I could take it to him.'

Leo's face closed in. 'No.'

He brought one back next day, rushing from Violet's car to Ryder's desk, waving a piece of paper.

'There!' He laid it in front of her. 'It's a train. Are we going to put it up?'

'Of course.' She stood up. 'Violet, hold all calls for half an hour. I'm having tea with Leo.'

'Tea with just me!' He raced ahead of her.

She followed, bearing his masterpiece. 'Where shall we put it?'

'Tommy's mummy hangs his paintings next to the fridge.'

'Then we'll put yours there too.'

Spring came to north Norfolk. With it came the knowledge that Patrick must certainly be back in England for the polo season. She pictured him at Gatehouse, directing the grooms. She saw him walk beneath the arch where the honeysuckle swung in the breeze. She imagined him in that bed where they had been lovers. She tortured herself with visions of him naked, making love to his wife, a luscious darkhaired Latin, the chosen mother of his child.

The air grew warmer. The river bank turned to a mass of primroses. The woods were carpeted with bluebells. Overhead the birds returned to Morston. But not Ryder. She could not bring herself to go back there.

One wet evening she thought she saw Patrick driving away from the mill. Afraid to see him yet desperate to do so, that night she dialled Gatehouse Stables. No one answered. She tried again, every night for a fortnight. There was still no answer. She had to force herself to stop.

With the spring, the airfield became a hub of activity. Pilots brought friends. Friends brought other friends. They sat on rugs in the sunshine and ate picnics. At weekends up to forty planes a day took off and landed. Demand for fuel escalated as did demand for maintenance: each plane had to be checked after every flight and serviced every fifty flying hours. Ryder hired two mechanics to help Fred, an oddjob man to look after Bruja and mow the grass, and a typist to help Violet.

'Does Miss Brendan Broughton ever acknowledge our monthly accounts?' Ryder asked her one morning.

'Never. But she banks the cheques.'

Michael came up to Bailing most weekends. He was a superb pilot and, when in the mood, would demonstrate his skill in the old Curtiss Jennie. Often in the evenings they would light the barbecue and sit out on the patio, discussing life.

'Have you got over Patrick Brendan yet?' he asked one night.

She stared into the darkness. 'Do you ever get over the people you lose?'

He touched her cheek but said nothing.

In May the clubhouse opened. It was a glorious early summer day, hazy with promise of soft warm afternoons and light evenings. Over a hundred people came. Michael had put the word around among his journalist friends. Radio Norfolk did an on-the-spot interview. The *Eastern Daily Press* took her photograph.

'Another success.' Michael joined her on the patio as the last person drove off into the dusk.

'Thanks.' She leaned back in her cane chair and sipped her ice cold spritzer.

'I'll be off.' Michael walked towards his car. It was the first time he hadn't stayed to chat.

'Goodnight.' Suddenly she felt acutely lonely. The evening stretched interminably. Leo would go to bed. She would sit downstairs, on her own, listening to the stillness of the airfield.

Michael waved and stepped into his car. As he turned she saw he had a front passenger. It was a girl with geometric blonde hair who often hung around the pilots.

She was laughing and lighting a cigarette. Ryder felt an unreasonable twist of jealousy. Michael was hers. She poured herself another glass of wine, without the soda. How could he go off with that little scrubber? She paced the uneven flagstones of the patio. But she didn't care. Of course she didn't! If Patrick returned, she wouldn't give a damn what Michael did.

Her photograph appeared in *The Times* under the heading *Flying Start For Harding's Daughter*. She imagined Patrick glancing through the paper. Stopping. Looking. Remembering. All day she was on tenterhooks, convinced he would call, jumping each time the telephone sounded. That evening she burned Leo's toast and let the bath overflow. As she was mopping up the flood, the phone rang.

She waited till the fourth ring, then picked it up and answered in her silkiest voice.

'Ryder, it's Immy. What's wrong? You sound peculiar.'

'I'm waiting for a call from my cousin Debbie.'

'Then why the satin underwear voice?'

'I have a sore throat, that's all. I'll ring you back.'

Ryder stared at the telephone. It stared back. She picked up the receiver to check it was working. It was. The hours passed. She waited. By midnight the dial had contorted into a mocking grin which mouthed the word 'fool'. She went upstairs to lay on her bed, allowing tears to roll unchecked down her cheeks. To fill her mouth with bitterness and salt.

In the morning she woke angry. She'd loved Patrick but she wasn't going to love him any more. Love pulled you down. Turned you inside out. Cut you up in little pieces. She took the shell, drove up to Morston, and hurled it out to sea.

25

In the four years since Bailing had opened, Ryder had made a healthy profit in summer and covered her costs in winter. Now came a hard winter. Although the price of fuel was frozen in December, fear of an increase caused four clients to sell their aircraft and several more talked of it. Added to this, the weather was harsh. Blizzards lashed the hangars, snow blocked the runway, and the clubhouse was closed. Not that anyone wished to use it. To pay her staff, she ate into her precious savings.

Her father had so far failed to get parole. He lived in hope but he was resigned. At the height of the bad weather he was moved to Ford Prison in Sussex. This meant a longer journey for Ryder but more freedom for him. The benefit was instantly noticeable. He regaled her with stories about the other inmates: dishonest solicitors, embezzling accountants and light-fingered tax inspectors. 'I half expected to find old Podmore in here,' he said with a chuckle.

She told him about her problems at Bailing. 'I have such a good team I don't want to let them go,' she said, not intending to confide in him but needing to talk to someone. 'Anyhow, it's not fair to push them out in winter.'

'You're not running a charity.'

'Oh, I can pay them. But I want to buy a second airfield.'

'Get a bank loan. Use Bailing as collateral. You'll have no problem.'

'Miss B. B. wouldn't hear of it. You know what she's like.'

'Then you must increase the value of your share. I have an idea.' He took a piece of paper from his pocket and jotted down a few figures. 'Open a flying school. It would bump up your turnover and increase your eventual clientele. I'll work it out and write to tell you what to do.'

'Thanks — but I'll think of something.' She stood up. 'I have to go now. I'm meeting Lady Heythorp.'

'Don't worry!' He screwed up the paper and thumped his fist on the table. 'I won't contaminate your precious airfield. Just don't forget that if it wasn't for me you wouldn't own it.'

She drove away from the sprawling prison complex, swearing yet again not to discuss Bailing with him.

With the airfield snowbound, Ryder had time to catch up on jobs around the house. During the previous summer the coalshed had been annexed and extended, its roof raised to create another bedroom: Mrs Trumpet had been their first guest. The kitchen was now large enough to be a dining room. An archway led into a cosy sitting room with French windows overlooking a private walled garden. She sat at her desk near the windows, answering a long letter from Debbie. Frankie was now at college and still set on being a pilot. Teddy had a new girlfriend. Susan had moved to New York: she was having a hard time finding work. Debbie wrote as she spoke, and as Ryder read the words she heard them in Debbie's Mid-West twang.

The bad weather continued. Ryder took out her sewing machine and turned her attention to the cushion covers she'd started to make in the autumn.

'I'm bored,' said Leo, fiddling with the cotton reels. 'When can we have a colour television?'

'You've just had a brand new racing bike.'

'Everyone else has colour.'

She carried on machining.

'I wish Tommy still lived in Bailing,' he said woefully.

'So do I! But his father has a new job in Norwich.'

'He was my best friend. I wish I went to boarding school, then I'd have *lots* of friends. I don't like the boys here. They're always hitting me.'

'Hit back. Then they won't do it. No one used to hit Tommy.' She stopped machining. 'I know it's hard. When I first lived in a flat in London people didn't like me.'

'What happened?'

'I persevered and eventually I made two very good friends. Immy and . . . Alix.'

'I've never seen Alix,' he said. 'She can't have been much of a friend.'

On the first day of the big thaw Michael drove up from London. 'Put your coat on,' he told her. 'I have a brilliant idea. It needs discussing over lunch.'

They went to The Bailing Arms for a hot shepherd's pie. The pub was cheerful and noisy. A fire roared in the grate. The old dog slept before it. Ryder and Michael settled themselves into a corner table. 'I haven't been out for weeks.' She smiled at her surroundings. 'I don't realise how much I miss people until I see them again.'

'All that could change.' He raised his glass to her. 'I have an idea which would raise your turnover and increase club membership.'

'A flying school?'

'How did you guess?'

'Oh . . . someone suggested it.'

'I want to run it with you,' Michael carried on enthusiastically. 'My Commercial Pilot's Licence lapsed after I

262

left Colossus but I still have a Private Pilot's Licence and a full Instructor's Rating, and I enjoy teaching.'

'What about your job?'

'I'll become freelance. They'd pay me well. I'd sell my London flat, buy a place up here, and still have enough for a Cessna with dual controls.'

'You've worked it all out.'

'It's my dream. I've always loved Norfolk. I told you, my mother frequented Norwich pawn shops. Poor old thing, drink finally killed her.'

'I'm sorry.'

'It was such a waste.' He paused and shook his head as if driving the memory to the back of his mind. 'Well? What's your answer?'

She ate her shepherd's pie in silence. 'You're a good friend and I appreciate your advice,' she said eventually. 'But Bailing is mine.'

'And you don't want anyone muscling in on you?'

'Yes.'

'Especially a man you suspect finds you attractive?'

She flushed. Michael made her sound juvenile. 'If you send me a written proposal,' she said, 'I'll consider it.'

She was fed up. Sick of the Arctic wind and the mud and the smell of aviation fuel. She rang Imogen. 'What are you up to?'

'Lying on my chaise longue, eating Bendicks mint chocolates and watching *Casablanca* on the television.'

'Decadent, tasteless debauchery!'

'Am I speaking to a lady who's had enough of wind-swept Norfolk?'

'You most certainly are!'

'Come down to sin city. Instantly! Adam is in Paris, and you and I are going to three parties tonight. Don't make the excuse that you haven't a thing to wear!'

'Immy, I'm that desperate for fun I'd go naked.'

Imogen was pacing up and down the drawing room,

dressed in a white silk shift and armlengths of gold bangles. She looked like an extremely expensive Circassian captive awaiting her turn in a Turkish slave market. 'You're early!' she hugged Ryder. 'I didn't expect you for half an hour. Come on! Quick! I'll run you a bath.'

'Can't I have a cup of coffee first?'

'I'll bring one up.' As she hurried Ryder up the stairs to the spare bedroom, the doorbell rang. Imogen jumped guiltily, or so it seemed to Ryder. 'I'll be back in a minute,' she said, and she dashed down, closing the door behind her.

She returned in a minute, saying, 'Just my agency delivering a script.'

'An interesting one?'

'Oh . . . I've . . . er . . . no idea.'

'I thought Alix always read scripts for you.'

'I'm not with Heythorp & Bassingham any more. I changed at Christmas.' Imogen picked up a comb and ran it through her silky red hair. 'I was fed up with being ordered around. I've made six films. I've been nominated for an Oscar. I've had brilliant reviews. And I'm not going to be treated like a child!' She stopped brushing. 'Look, I don't really want to talk about it.'

'I'm sorry.'

'Let's have some champagne. We're going to have fun.' Immy danced down the stairs, singing, 'Fun! Fun! Fun!'

The first party was at an art gallery. It was the opening of an exhibition of what looked to Ryder like last night's spaghetti bolognese heaped on a dustbin lid. As they stepped inside the door, the gallery owner pounced on Imogen and thrust her towards the diminutive bespectacled artist. Ryder was left to hover in the doorway wishing she hadn't come. She knew no one — and no one bothered to speak to her. They huddled in groups, shrieking about people she didn't know and parties to which she hadn't been invited.

264

A tray of wine was offered. She took a glass. Sipped. Grimaced. It tasted like paint stripper. She reached for some crisps. As she did so, she became aware that the black and gold brocade jacket Immy had lent her was so tight it showed the outline of her nipples. Suddenly she caught sight of a man with dark hair. He had his back to her but she recognised the thick blackness of his hair and the very squareness of his shoulders. With relief she pushed her way through the crowd. 'Michael!' She squeezed his arm.

He turned. It wasn't Michael.

'I'm so sorry.' She backed away, feeling foolish.

'There you are!' Imogen joined her. She lowered her voice. 'Let's leave.'

They bolted for the door. Out in the street, they burst into giggles.

'Hideous pictures,' said Immy, waving at a taxi.

'Horrible people.' Ryder was relieved to know that Immy felt as she did. It made her less of an outsider.

The next party was in Covent Garden. 'You'll enjoy this one,' said Immy as they climbed up four flights of stairs to an attic flat from which loud music was blasting out over the piazza. As they reached the front door a girl came out crying. She was followed by a man. They were both drunk. He started to be sick.

Ryder turned her back on him. 'This is better!'

'I thought it would be.' Imogen opened her bag and took out a smart white invitation. 'Oh, no! We're in the wrong house.'

They scuttled down the stairs, past the vomiting man and the crying girl, and dashed across the other side of the piazza, laughing as their high heels slipped on the cobbled ground. Imogen lifted the brass knocker on a smart black door. It was opened at the first knock, by a middle-aged man in a purple chiffon kaftan. 'Imogen! Darling! Come in!' He led them upstairs to a room of glittering, gossiping people.

The first person Ryder saw was Jeremy. He enfolded her in a delicate embrace. 'What a lovely surprise.' He caught sight of Imogen and stiffened. 'Hello.'

Immy was looking white and anxious. 'Hello, Jeremy. I didn't know you'd be here. Is Alix?'

'No.'

'That's a relief.' She picked up a glass of champagne and disappeared into the crowd.

'I'm so grateful you've kept in touch with mother,' Jeremy told Ryder. 'She does enjoy your teas at the Ritz.'

'So do I,' Ryder smiled, 'although she gives me advice I prefer not to hear.'

'Oh, that's mother! You're her favourite.' He drew nearer and lowered his voice. 'Have you seen Alix?'

'No — and I don't wish to.'

'You know Imogen's not with us any more?'

'She told me.'

'What could Alix do? She didn't want to get rid of her, but . . .'

'Had enough gossip yet?' Imogen linked her arm through Ryder's.

'Almost.' Ryder was looking at Jeremy.

'Well, I'm afraid we have to move on,' said Imogen. 'We have another party. Come on, Ryder!' As they started down the stairs, she said, 'I suppose he told you about Alix?'

'He began to.'

She stopped. 'I didn't mean to lie to you but . . . I was so upset. She was meant to be my friend.'

The front door opened. The noise caught their attention. They looked down as Alix walked in. Imogen gave a small cry. Ryder gripped the banisters. But Alix showed no emotion. She dropped her honey mink onto a chair and stood in the hall, staring up at them, the light from the chandelier enhancing her red silk suit which in turn set off her black hair and camellia skin.

She had been a beautiful girl. She was an even more beautiful woman. 'Are you two coming down or are we staying here all night?' she demanded.

Imogen ran to her. 'Alix, I have to see you.'

'Ring my office.'

'You never call me back.'

'I wonder why!'

Ryder took Immy firmly by the arm. 'Come on! Let's go.'

'Ryder!' Alix stepped towards her. 'I'd like to talk.'

'I have nothing to say.' Ryder pushed Imogen out into the piazza. 'I don't want to talk to you, Alix, any more than you want to talk to Immy.'

'You don't understand.'

'I do. You're a bitch. You always were a bitch, and you haven't changed.'

Alix's eyes glittered. 'I doubt if Patrick Brendan's wife considers you an angel.'

26

They didn't go on to the third party, a buffet supper in a grand house overlooking Eaton Square. Seeing Alix had unnerved them. They went home.

'How dare she link my love for Patrick with her sordid affairs!' Ryder thumped her bag down on the kitchen table. 'How dare she call me a hypocrite.'

'I told you what she was like,' said Imogen a little smugly, opening a bottle of wine and pouring two glasses. 'Come on! Have a drink. Forget Alix. Patrick loved you. What you had with him was beautiful.'

'I thought so.' Ryder stared bleakly into space.

'Alix has never been in love. She has no soul,' Immy went on. 'That's why I walked out.' She caught Ryder's flicker of surprise and added, 'I mean, we had a row and she told me to go. I would have left anyhow. She wanted me to take a part with frontal nudity. I said no. She was furious. There was big money involved.'

'And she fired you because of that?' Ryder toyed with the stem of her glass.

'You saw her mink. Coats like that cost.' Immy sniffed and stood up. 'I must fetch a handkerchief.'

'Use the kitchen roll.'

'It's too rough.'

She came down five minutes later, wiping her nose and sniffing.

'You are getting a cold!' said Ryder. 'Go to bed. I'll make you a hot toddy.'

'I'll be all right in the morning.' Imogen flicked a switch on her music centre. 'If You Leave Me Now' blasted out. 'Oh, yes.' She shook her long red hair. 'I'll be fine.'

The incident with Alix upset Ryder even more than she admitted. Was that how people saw the great passion of her life, as something sordid and underhand?

When she met Lady Heythorp for tea at their usual table at the Ritz she was still preoccupied. 'You've got that hurt look in your eyes,' said Lady Heythorp, waving Ryder to her seat. 'I suppose you're having trouble with one of those weak men you favour.'

'Patrick wasn't weak! He was afraid of losing me.'

'A man who doesn't tell a woman that he's married is weak or dishonest — or both.' Lady Heythorp reached for another cucumber sandwich. 'A woman who fails to see that is deluding herself!'

It was a relief to return to Bailing. Michael was having coffee with Violet and Fred when Ryder arrived. They pulled up a chair for her. She was enveloped by their affection. By the details of Bailing life, the smell of aviation fuel and the soft burr of Fred's voice.

When she went to the tower, Michael followed. 'You look glad to be back,' he said.

'I like cities but there are too many people.' She wasn't going to discuss her problems with him. 'I have some news for you.' She turned to face him, smiling over-brightly. 'I agree to our partnership in the flying school.'

He took her by the shoulders and kissed her on each cheek. 'Now that's news worth waiting for.'

'Our initial agreement will be for five years.'

'Whatever you say.'

'Ownership of all buildings, new and old, and overall control remains mine.'

'Fair — but tough.'

'The extension to the runway, fire fighting equipment,

ground-to-air radio, and anything required by the CAA will be paid jointly even though they enhance my asset.'

'Where have you been this morning? Breakfasting with the Mafia?'

'No — I went to see my father!'

As Ryder crossed to the hangar to inform Fred, she recalled her father's pleasure when she'd said, 'What do you advise?'

She took Fred to one side and told him about the school. 'Student pilots!' he grumbled. 'I suppose this is Michael's idea.'

'No, it's mine.' Ryder hesitated. 'Don't you like Michael?'

'He's better than most.' Fred scratched his head. 'And ole Violet thinks the world of him. But there was a time when I was the man about the place.'

Ryder linked her arm through his. 'You're still the most important man. This place would fall apart without you.'

Michael went into overdrive to start the flying school. He let his London flat and moved up to Norfolk, renting a house whilst he looked for somewhere to buy. Meanwhile, Ryder contacted Oliver Offbach of Jones, Offbach & Littlejohn, Jeremy's London solicitor, and asked him to draw up a deed. Michael's only stipulation was that her father had no involvement in the airfield.

Offbach agreed. 'It'll protect you from your father too,' he told Ryder.

They applied for planning permission to build the school. It was to be a one-storey classroom, with space for administration and ground-to-air radio. Then they pooled their resources and bought a Cessna 152, a high-wing two-seater with dual controls.

'There's one other condition I forgot to mention,' Ryder told Michael as they stood on the tarmac, admiring their new possession.

'Oh, God! What now?'

'You teach me to fly.'

'Now that I don't mind doing. But on condition that when I'm instructor, I'm boss!'

Ryder missed Michael when he went away on his instructor's course. She hadn't expected to, but she'd grown used to sharing every decision. Each evening he rang for a progress report. She tried to have plenty to convey. Every day she chivvied the builder, who worked like lightning for Michael but didn't seem to move quite as fast for her. She hounded the telephone company to release their new numbers. She bullied the oddjob man to lay the extra turf.

It was dusk when Michael returned. Ryder was in the kitchen making Leo's tea. She heard the crunch of his tyres and flung open the door. 'Stay there!' she shouted. 'You have to see the school first.' She seized a torch and ran across the tarmac. 'Look!'

The walls were up, the roof had still to be added. Rafters reached into the sky. A path was marked out and partially laid with paving stones. The turf for the new lawn was piled to one side. He smiled. 'You've done well, partner!'

They returned to the office. 'I've not been slacking either,' he said. 'I've finalised charges. The enrolment fee will include logbook, insurance, all ground tuition, and the first six hours of flying. After that they pay per hour.'

'And I've decided we need a school secretary,' said Ryder. 'Violet and the girls are up to their ears.'

'I agree. We need a mini-skirted, glamorous, subservient blonde.'

'We do not! There are enough flying groupies around.' She started back towards the tower. 'Must finish giving Leo his tea.'

'Am I invited?' he called after her.

She stopped. 'It's my one time alone with him.'

'So I'm not as family as Patrick Brendan yet?'

'Come to supper this evening. Violet's given me some fresh trout.'

'You haven't answered my question.'

'I'll see you later.' She walked away.

To her relief Michael didn't mention Patrick. He told her amusing stories about his time as a pilot with Colossus, whilst she stuffed the trout with sliced lemon and onions and wrapped them in silver foil.

'I've decided what to do about the club membership,' she said as they sat down to eat. 'Students will become honorary members, then they can use the facilities.'

'But no alcohol before lessons. It's "eight hours bottle to throttle".'

'What about medical certificates?' She tried to bone her trout without flicking it all over the kitchen. 'Do we insist they have one when they sign on?'

'We don't have to, but they can't solo without it.' Michael took her plate and boned her fish with the skill of a surgeon. 'Messy!' he said, returning it to her.

She pulled a face. 'Irritating!'

'To me, it's fairer to insist on a medical at the beginning,' he went on. 'We don't want some poor bugger spending a fortune on lessons only to find he can't get a licence.'

'He or she.' Ryder reached for another bottle of wine.

'Yes, Madam President!' He took it from her. 'And the "eight hours" rule applies to you too.'

'I'm not flying tomorrow.'

'No.' He put the bottle back on the shelf. 'But you've had enough. You forget, I saw how my mother started. She drank when she was upset. And you don't need to tell me that something in London upset you.'

Ryder didn't tell Michael about Alix, she was too annoyed by his accusation over drink. She asked Immy, 'Do I drink too much?' But the reply, 'Of course not!'

272

was unsatisfactory. Immy would say that. She drank too much herself.

She was still rankled when she had her first flying lesson, but the stillness of that quiet April Monday and the excitement of flying drove it from her mind. She watched as Michael checked the weather and entered the flight on the record sheet. She couldn't help remembering her last flight with Teddy, who'd refused to contemplate teaching her.

'You always give your aircraft a pre-flight inspection,' he told her as they approached the Cessna. 'Check for leaks. Make sure all control surfaces are free of debris. Check tyres for embedded nails. You don't want a blowout. Flying is safe if you're sensible,' he went on, as she took the right-hand seat. 'We always carry out a procedure of checks.' He slipped in beside her. 'Hatches and harness secure?' He tightened the strap of her harness and tried the doors. 'Most errors are human. As they say, "There are bold pilots and old pilots, but there are no old, bold pilots." '

They taxied to the end of the runway. There he halted. 'The pressure of air on the ground is greater than that at, say, twenty thousand feet,' he shouted. 'Do you know why?'

'Because of the weight of air above it?'

'At sea level, pressure is fifteen pounds per square inch. At twenty thousand feet, it's seven pounds.' He turned into the wind. 'To get off the ground we need lift and thrust. It's obtained by the forward speed and the wings. Look at the wings. The curve of the upper surface is greater than that of the lower. As we move forward, the air is separated by the leading edge. The pressure above the wing decreases. And up we go!'

He opened the throttle. They started down the runway. The runway markers flashed past. They went faster. Ryder held her breath as they raced on. And on. And up into the sky, until they reached a cruising height from which she saw Norfolk stretch out like an agricultural patchwork dotted by church spires.

'This is a trial lesson,' he shouted over the noise of the engine. 'Just to give you the feel. Next time we'll go into detail. You'll have picked up much from the airfield — good and bad habits, I'm sure.'

She studied the panel of dials in front of her. 'What's the difference between the airspeed and the groundspeed?'

'If it takes us an hour to fly a hundred miles, our groundspeed is a hundred miles an hour. But if the wind is blowing towards us at ten miles an hour and we fly that same hundred miles, the speed of the air passing the plane is . . . ?'

'A hundred and ten.'

'Clever girl! That's our airspeed. We take off into the wind to get added lift. The other dials are an altimeter — one thousand and climbing. And those little wings are the attitude indicator. They tell you if you're flying level. Essential in bad visibility. Watch them dip as I bank.'

As they turned Ryder could see almost as far as Morston. Suddenly she had an overwhelming desire to return there. To follow the paths across the mudflats where she had walked with Patrick.

'One thing you must remember,' Michael was saying, 'is that to climb you don't just jerk the nose up or you'll stall. You must increase power.' He grinned at her. 'Want to fly her?'

'I might crash.'

'I won't let you. This aircraft's cost far too much.'

Gingerly she reached for the control column.

'The procedure is challenge and response,' he said. 'I say, "You have control." You reply, "I have control." '

She held the column firmly. 'I have control.'

'Feel all right?'

'Like riding a dragonfly.'

He smiled. 'Move the column back. Gently!'

She did. The nose went up. Their speed decreased.

'Now move it forward. A little!'

She did. The aircraft levelled off. The speed increased.

'Now turn the column to the right. Look at the wings of the altitude indicator. They're tipping. To turn you have to bank. Slowly!'

'Oh, God!' Her hands were wet with nerves.

'He's not going to help you. Slowly! Now centre the controls and the aircraft will remain in the banked position.'

She turned the plane to the left. The outer wing came up a little too steeply, but Michael said it wasn't bad for a beginner.

When they landed she said, 'I'll have my medical tomorrow.'

'I thought you were scared?'

'Terrified.'

'But you still want to learn?'

'I own an airfield. Do you think I'll inspire confidence if I'm too chicken to go up?'

'You don't have to.'

'Have to!' She threw back her head and laughed with exhilaration. 'I can't wait to fly again.'

With six weeks before the school officially opened, Ryder had Michael's undivided attention. She learned quickly. He taught enthusiastically. Weather and wind strength permitting they flew every day. In the crisp of morning. In the lull of a damp afternoon. In that moment of velvet calm before sunset. That was Ryder's favourite time.

Once she'd mastered how to fly the aircraft, she had to learn to make it go where she wanted. Every day they worked the four-legged circuit. Take off. Climb. Level out. Keep her steady. Downward leg. Base leg. Cross-wind. On each turn she hit a different wind — and every day the wind differed. Sometimes she flew the first leg correctly only to bank too steeply. Other times a crosswind carried her off course. Once when she'd completed the circuit perfectly and was coming in to land, flushed with confidence, she forgot to hold the nose up. Only Michael's dual controls prevented her from bouncing the Cessna down the runway.

As they parked, Fred appeared in the entrance to the hangar. 'Would you like your funeral at Bailing church or would you prefer Norwich crematorium?' he asked her.

She swung down from the cockpit. 'Pessimist!'

'It's your fault for encouraging her.' He gave Michael his tortoise stare. 'Women ain't meant to fly planes.'

Ryder walked towards the office calling over her shoulder, 'What about Amy Johnson and Amelia Earhart?'

'That's what I mean. They both disappeared into the sea!'

In the completed classroom Michael taught Ryder her flight procedures, navigation, meteorology and aviation law. She learned how to read a chart and recognise restricted space, military zones and commercial traffic. How to check the windsock for speed and direction. To read a map and plot a course. To use a compass. She learned how much extra fuel was needed in a strong wind and what to do in an emergency.

'The engine fails after takeoff,' he said. 'What do you do?'

'Turn back.'

'No. You have no power. You wouldn't make it. You trim for the best glide speed. Select a field. Place a Mayday call. Turn off fuel and electrics. Check your harness is tight. Stay strapped in till she stops. Then get out. And run!'

He took her up one damp morning. 'Every aeroplane has a minimum flying speed — a stalling speed,' he explained. 'If you pull the nose up too high, the angle of attack of the wings becomes so steep that the airflow

276

over them is no longer smooth. You lose lift. Lose speed. And if you don't rectify, you'll drop or spin. Or both. Understood?'

'Yes.'

'You have to recognise if you're heading for a stall. So, pull her nose up. A little more.'

The Cessna reared up. Ryder felt the lift beneath the wings go.

'More!' he insisted.

The plane lurched. The nose dropped suddenly. Ryder turned grey with fear. But Michael didn't flinch. 'Release pressure on the column and apply power,' he said calmly.

Their speed increased. Ryder felt weak with relief.

'Don't you trust me?' he asked.

'Of course.'

'Good. We'll do it again.'

They advertised the school in the *Aviation Argus*. When the magazine arrived they pored over their advertisement. It looked so professional. 'We're going to be so popular you won't have time to teach me,' she said.

'Oh, I'll squeeze you in if you're nice to me.'

As Ryder followed him across the tarmac to the Cessna she wondered how she'd managed before Michael.

Her lessons continued. She took off and stalled. Banked and stalled. Navigated and stalled. Map read and stalled.

'When am I going to solo?' she asked Michael.

'When you're more confident about stalling. As soon as the plane starts to buffet, you look terrified.'

She pulled a glum face. 'I did want to be the first in our school to get a licence.'

'If you went into a funk, by the time you came out of it you'd be halfway to Australia — by the terrestrial route!'

Her lessons kept their minds off one crucial matter:

although they'd had several enquiries about flying lessons, they had no confirmed bookings.

'Ten days till we open and still no one,' she said, as they stood in the empty classroom.

'No secretary either.' Michael looked at the empty office. 'There must be someone in Bailing.'

'We can't take any old bod. If we sacked a friend of Mrs Dennshurst we'd be banned from the shop. Then we'd have to drive to King's Lynn to buy our newspapers!' Ryder sighed. 'Anyhow, if we have no students what do we want staff for?'

He took her by the shoulders and turned her to face him. 'Don't lose your fight now, Miss Biggles,' he whispered in his late night voice, lifting her chin and looking deep into her eyes. 'You've come a long way.' His mouth brushed hers. His powerful arms enveloped her. She felt herself drawn into him. 'We'll crack a bottle of champagne at lunchtime,' he said. 'We deserve it.'

She pulled away. 'And have you call me an alcoholic! Not bloody likely!'

27

Grandma Milne died on the day Ryder was due to solo. She and Michael were in the classroom, running through her procedures, when Debbie telephoned. 'It was her heart,' she said. 'By the time Doctor Jeff could get here, she'd passed on.'

Ryder dropped on to a chair. 'How's Grandpa taking it?'

'He hasn't spoken since. He's in shock. We all are.'

'Oh, Debbie, I . . .' Ryder buried her face in her hands.

Michael took the receiver from her. 'Go and lie down.' He laid a hand on her shoulder, the first time they'd been more than business partners since the morning when he'd kissed her. 'I'll get you a glass of brandy.'

'No!' She stood up. 'I don't need that! Nothing makes death better. Grandma's dead. Mother's dead. They can't come back. No one does. How can things be better when everyone I care about leaves me and nothing I do ever lasts?' She pushed past him and ran to her car.

'Ryder,' he shouted.

'Leave me alone.'

'You'll kill yourself.' He made a grab for her steering wheel.

'Who cares?' She reversed away.

'I do.'

But she didn't hear him. His words were lost in the

roar of her engine as she crossed the tarmac, heading for Morston.

Ryder didn't fly for a week. She didn't want to. Every day she drove up to the coast and walked across the salt flats, with the marram grass whipping at her legs and the spilled oil from a tanker creating kaleidoscope patterns on the water in the creeks. At the rickety wooden bridge she would stop and sit, chin in hands, grieving for her grandmother.

She spoke to Debbie on the night after the funeral. 'How's Grandpa?' she asked.

'Still hasn't said a word. But the funeral was beautiful. Everyone in Prairieville came. Grandma'd have been so proud. And your flowers were lovely. I laid them on her coffin beside mine.'

'What will you do about Scot's Farm?' asked Ryder, thinking of Frankie who wanted to be a pilot not a farmer.

'Grandpa taught me farming these past years. The land's in my blood and I love it.'

Ryder soloed on the day the flying school opened. She took off in the morning, before the first students arrived. With Michael watching, she went through her checks. Then she climbed into the cockpit and strapped on her harness. It seemed strange not to have Michael beside her.

'Nervous?' he asked, rechecking her harness.

She tried to swallow. 'What do you think?'

'Just keep your head up.' He gave her the thumbs up. 'Good luck!'

She held her breath as she turned on the engine. It sprung to life. She looked around. All clear. Gingerly she taxied to the head of the runway. The wheels bounced on the tarmac. She felt slightly sick.

The wind was 10 mph. The plane lifted as she turned into it. The movement made her heart start to thud. She checked the runway and the sky. Empty. She opened the throttle. Her speed increased. Her hands gripped the control column. Her heart was thudding in her ears. The Cessna raced along the runway. Its tyres bounced on the tarmac. It lifted. Fell back. Went up again. And Up. Up! Thrusting against the air whilst she held it steady.

At eight hundred feet she levelled off and flew straight down the first leg of the circuit. It wasn't difficult. Not now she was up. After two miles she banked to the left. Halfway round she realised she hadn't checked for other aircraft. In panic, and with visions of a head on collision, she raked the sky — and forgot the crosswind. Suddenly she was over the hangars, drifting southwest. Cold sweat poured down her face as she battled to regain the circuit. On the next corner she turned parallel to the runway. The wind was behind her. She held the plane steady. Below, the fields of Norfolk stretched away in varying shades of green. Above them, Ryder Harding rode her dragonfly.

The school opened with twenty pupils. As an introduction to flying, Michael showed them a film on the history of aviation. There was an engraving of the Mongolfier balloon drifting over Paris in 1783. The Wright brothers, a hundred and twenty years later, bouncing off the sand of North Carolina: the first powered flight. Santos-Dumont, the Brazilian, whose airship skimmed the trees of the Bois de Boulogne. A. V. Roe in a plane whose wings were covered with brown paper. Louis Blériot, the first to fly the Channel: he won a thousand pounds! Alcock and Brown, the first non-stop Atlantic crossing: they landed in Ireland. Charles Lindberg, the first non-stop Atlantic solo: he landed in France. Charles Kingsford Smith, the Australian, who conquered the Pacific — and broke everyone else's records. Amy Johnson who raced from London to Brisbane. Amelia Earhart, the first woman to solo the Atlantic. Beryl Markham, the first to fly east to west: she landed in Nova Scotia. And Sheila Scott, the first to cross the icy wastes of the North Pole.

By the time the film ended, everyone at the airfield had sneaked into the classroom. Even Fred. They clapped wildly as the credits rolled. Over their heads, Michael winked at Ryder. She smiled back. Grandma was dead. Her mother was dead. But the living had to go on. It wasn't fair on Michael if she was sad, when they'd worked so hard to start the school. It wasn't fair on Leo. He was so vulnerable to her moods. Clapping her hands she cried, 'Barbecue next Saturday. Two pounds a head. Everyone's welcome.'

As she went out she heard someone say, 'This place is going to be fun!'

On her next visit, she showed the school prospectus to her father. He read it avidly from cover to cover. 'But you still haven't bought that second airfield,' he said.

'Oh, we will,' She was purposefully noncommital.

'So it's "we" now?' His eyes narrowed. 'You allow this Michael Ashby to be involved with Bailing but you won't include me. Didn't I advise you right about him? Didn't I tell you to go ahead with the school?'

'Yes. And I'm grateful.'

'I'll be out in the spring,' he said. 'They may have withheld parole but they can't stop my remission. What's this Michael going to do then? There won't be room for the two of us.'

'Michael's my partner.' She had to make herself look him in the eye so he knew she meant it. 'I couldn't have you involved with my business. I admire your acumen but I don't trust your methods.'

'So you'd push me out for the sake of your latest boyfriend.' He stood up. 'You always were a fool over men, Ryder. No wonder none of them marry you.'

She stormed out of the visiting room and drove back to Bailing at ninety miles an hour, cursing every vehicle which got in her way. She was still angry when she collected Leo from school, although she did her best to hide her feelings. 'I don't want to go to boarding school after all,' he told her in the car.

'Oh . . . good.' She wondered how her father could switch from being so charming to being so vicious.

'I have two new friends.'

'How nice.' She remembered her own treatment of Teddy and the way she'd told him bluntly she was returning to England.

'But I'd still like the colour television,' Leo prattled on.

'You would, would you!' He was so like her mother that sometimes she felt physical pain when she looked at him. She ruffled his blond curls. He no longer flinched when she raised her hand, as he'd once done.

Her cousin Frankie and Susan Wise arrived on bicycles in the middle of the barbecue. Ryder couldn't believe her eyes when she saw them whooping across the tarmac, legs outstretched as if they were riding bucking broncos. 'What . . . what are you doing here?' she stammered.

'We've come to run the school for you. Debbie told us you need help — so here we are.' Frankie dumped his bike, and within a minute was introducing himself round, beer in one hand, hamburger in the other.

'You don't mind?' Susan looked at Ryder.

'Of course not.' She still wasn't sure if they were 'together'.

'We'll be no trouble.' Frankie answered her question by slipping an arm around Susan. 'We have a tent.'

Ryder told herself a seven-year age gap was nothing. 'How's Grandpa?' she said.

'He still doesn't speak. But Debbie's managing brilliantly.'

'And what does Prairieville say about you two?'

'Except for Debbie, Prairieville doesn't know about us two.'

Susan became secretary to the flying school. Frankie helped out where needed. They pitched their tent in a grassy dip beyond the trees, out of sight and out of earshot, but ate their meals with Ryder and Leo — and frequently with Michael.

'Have you got over that polo player?' Susan asked Ryder one evening as they chopped radishes for the salad.

'I think of him.' Ryder looked out of the window to where Michael and Frankie were lighting the barbecue. 'I still can't believe what he did to me.'

Susan's face warmed in sympathy. 'I know what it's like to be kicked. Remember the poet who turned out to be a drug dealer? I thought he loved me but he was using me as a front.'

Ryder sliced a tomato. 'I'm not the greatest picker of men. Maybe I should stick to aeroplanes.'

'Michael's fond of you.'

She thought of that morning when he'd kissed her. 'Oh, we're just friends.'

When Ryder got her Private Pilot's Licence, she'd flown forty-six hours, of which twelve were solo and five were cross country. That evening Susan cooked a celebration dinner. All Bailing employees were invited. Fred. Violet. The typist. The receptionist. The waiter from the clubhouse. The oddjob man. The mechanics. They arranged a long trestle table on the patio and covered it with a heavy damask tablecloth Mrs Trumpet had salvaged from Dingwall Court.

The phone rang as they sat down to eat. Ryder hurried to it. Something made her think it would be Patrick. She couldn't explain what or why, but she suddenly felt him close. She was nervous, excited, apprehensive. She picked up the receiver. 'Hello?'

'Ryder, I'm at King's Lynn Station.'

'Oh . . . umm . . . hello, Immy.' She felt a wave of disappointment followed by a wave of relief.

'I'm sorry to arrive without warning but . . . everything's gone wrong and I was desperate to get away. Can I come?'

'Grab a taxi! We're celebrating. I've got my Pilot's Licence.'

'I haven't any money.'

'Don't worry!' She leaned out of the window. 'Frankie, could you collect Imogen?'

'Imogen Lydden! My favourite lady.' He dashed to Ryder's car. 'Tell her to wait for me. Tell her I'm tall, dark, handsome and devastatingly rich.'

'You'll be devastatingly without-your-dinner if you play around with other women!' Susan shouted after him.

Immy looked pale and drawn but she sparkled when she saw the party, just as she had on the day she'd opened Bailing. Watching her, Ryder envied that inner well of social glamour which Imogen drew on, even when she was at her lowest. 'When I'm depressed, I look like thunder and sound like a death announcement,' she confided in Susan. 'Immy's different. That's why she's such a good actress.'

It was too late to talk that night and at breakfast Immy merely said, 'All actresses have lean times. This is mine. My last two films bombed. One more disaster and I won't even get a one-line part where the words are cut.'

Ryder glanced at her watch. She had work to do. 'You're welcome to stay as long as you like. You know you are.' She stood up. 'We're flying up to Lincolnshire to look for another airfield. It'll be fun.'

Imogen fiddled with her teaspoon. 'Actually, I was going to ask if I could borrow your car. I want to go to the bank in King's Lynn.'

'Then you could draw the wages.'

'I'd rather not.'

'Please! It would save Violet's time — and King's Lynn is perfectly safe.'

Ryder and Michael looked at four airfields before they saw Fortune's Fen. It had been built during the Second World War on land requisitioned from a local farmer. The runway was a reasonable length. The hangars were in good shape, having been used for grain storage. At the back of one was a rusting de Havilland Tiger Moth. It lay on its belly like a fly whose legs had been pulled off by a cruel little boy.

'It would be the most expensive,' said Ryder, as they discussed the purchase over lunch in the garden of an old timbered pub. 'I'll have to tell old Miss B.B. I'm using my entire share of Bailing as security. Even then I'll hardly have enough.' She scuffed her trainers on the ground. 'Father keeps working out complicated ways for me to raise more money but I don't trust his methods.'

His eyes softened. 'It must be tough having a father in prison.'

'It is. We're scarcely on speaking terms at the moment.' She realised that she'd talked naturally about her father: she'd neither disparaged him nor excused him.

They looked over Fortune's Fen once more. 'Why don't I buy it with you,' he said. 'If I sell my London flat, we might even afford two new airfields.'

'A three-legged operation?'

'Or four?'

'Why not start an airline. Bailing Air. Daily flights to London and Manchester.' She laughed. 'Can you imagine what Fred would say!'

'It's just what the area needs,' he said in total seriousness. 'I was brought up in Norfolk. I love it. The last thing I want to see is it swamped by people and industry. But towns need communications to survive. They need jobs or the young people move away.'

They flew home in the still beauty of the early evening, heading out across the Wash with the dying sun behind them. Without her asking, Michael followed the Norfolk coastline until they reached Morston, where he turned and came in so low that she could see the seals, but not so low that the Cessna upset the birds. She smiled at him. He smiled back. Then she turned away, to look down at the mudflats. It wasn't necessary to say thank you.

As they came in to land at Bailing, Ryder noticed a police car parked outside Violet's office. Fred was in the hangar, waiting.

'Have they come to arrest you?' she asked gaily, stepping down from the aircraft.

'Your friend's gone.'

'What do you mean?'

'She went into town but she didn't come back. We thought she'd had an accident.' He paused, then added gently, 'The police found your car in the station car-park.' He handed her a scrap of paper. On it was written, *It's not King's Lynn I was afraid of, it's myself.*

Ryder tried to pretend she wasn't upset. 'I expect she was called to an urgent audition,' she said.

'You don't understand.' Fred gave her his tortoise stare. 'She stole our wages.'

Ryder drove straight to London, to Imogen. She was angry. Hurt. Bitter. Four hundred pounds might be peanuts to a film star but it was hard earned cash to her, and she was going to get it back.

The mews house was in darkness. She rang the bell. A light came on. She steeled herself. The door opened slowly. Adam stood before her, stripped to the waist in just a pair of jeans whose belt was unbuckled as though he were in the middle of undressing.

'What a pleasant surprise!' He ran his hand through his unruly hair.

'Where's Imogen?'

'Upstairs.'

Trying to ignore his bare torso, Ryder stepped forward. But he barred her way. 'I shouldn't go up if I were you.'

'You're not me.' She pushed past him and ran upstairs. Immy's door was shut. Ryder flung it open. 'Where's my money?'

Imogen was sitting on the bed, crosslegged and stark naked, snorting a line of white powder through a rolled five pound note. In front of the mirror, languidly folding twenty pound notes into his wallet, was a swarthy man with dark Andean eyes.

Ryder turned on him. 'That's my money. Give it to me.'

He gave a mocking laugh. 'You're mistaken. This is mine.' He walked out of the room.

Ryder grabbed Imogen by the wrists and shook her, sending the powder flying. 'Where is it?'

'You don't understand. He was threatening us.'

So angry she didn't think of the danger, Ryder ran down the stairs and out into the street. But the mews was deserted. The man with Andean eyes had disappeared.

Immy was crying as she scrabbled for cocaine in the folds of her duvet.

'How could you steal the wages?' Ryder shouted at her. 'How could you take from Fred and Violet — and everyone who's befriended you? Why didn't you ask me?'

'Because you'd have refused.'

'I wouldn't.'

Immy rocked backwards and forwards, tears rolling down her cheeks. 'It was for Adam. That man was going to break his legs. You'd never have given it to me to save Adam.'

'You're right about that!' Ryder marched down the stairs. But when she reached the bottom step, she remembered the evening Michael had accused her of drinking. Who was around to tell Immy to stop? Not Adam. She ran back. 'You're coming with me.' She chucked clothes into a suitcase. 'You'll live at Bailing with us. We're going to help you.' She grabbed Imogen's arm and pulled her to her feet. 'Come on! Get dressed!'

It was after midnight by the time they reached Bailing but Frankie, Susan and Michael were still sitting around the pine table, deep in discussion. Their jaws fell open when they saw Imogen.

'Immy's coming to stay,' Ryder told them. 'She's had a few problems but we're going to help her get better.'

'Yes.' Imogen stepped forward timidly. 'I'm sorry I let you all down. So . . . so very sorry.' She started to cry. 'But . . . but I'm going to pay Ryder back. I promise.'

'Of course you will.' Frankie jumped up and offered her his chair.

'We'll all help you.' Susan lit her a cigarette.

Only Michael remained silent.

The next morning Ryder attacked him as he parked his car. 'All Immy needs is support and encouragement but you resent her being here.'

'She's an addict and she needs professional counselling.'

'She isn't an addict. She just needs to pull herself together. But in your eyes anyone who drinks half a bottle of wine is in the gutter.'

'This is an airfield. We can't afford to have a hint of drugs here. You have to get that across to her.' He marched down the path and into the school building, shouting, 'Unless you're prepared to see our dream sacrificed.'

Ryder ran after him. 'I'm going to help Immy whether you like it or not. She opened Bailing and got me all that publicity. When I had no money, she bought me clothes so I could impress clients. She even bought me the suit I wore to our first lunch.'

He seized her by the elbows, almost lifting her from the ground. 'I thought that was a present from Patrick Brendan.'

'No. That was from Immy. The friend you want me to abandon!'

There was a new dimension to Ryder's relationship with Michael. It had developed slowly without her being aware of it, until she found herself acutely conscious of his presence — and of his absences. She started to dress more carefully, not noticeably enough to attract Fred's teasing, but for the first time since Patrick she didn't just throw on the first thing that came to hand.

When Michael bought the Butterfly House, Ryder was his first visitor. It was a rambling wood-panelled building of great character, situated down a narrow lane between the church and the lavender farm. He particularly liked its history: it had been built by a nineteenth-century lepidopterist who spent his days sitting on the wooden verandah, watching butterflies feast in his wild flower garden.

'When I'm old I shall sit here too,' said Michael. 'And my grandchildren will be told not to disturb me by running on the boards.'

She smiled. 'Would you like children?'

He raised an eyebrow. 'Is that an offer, Miss Biggles?'

'Of course not!'

On the pretext of choosing clothes for Leo, Ryder went into King's Lynn, to the flying-suit boutique, and came away with a smart black linen dress, a virulent yellow silk suit and a selection of underwear, not just everyday cotton knickers but a dainty cream silk bra with exquisite lace-trimmed French knickers. Back at Bailing she showed the clothes to Immy, who giggled with delight. It was as if they were back in the flat, except that Alix was missing.

Immy seemed subdued but not restless. She helped in

the office. She answered the telephone, made tea and coffee, weighed and franked the post, and entertained Leo when he was bored. She never left the airfield and she didn't ask to use the car — not that Ryder would have lent it to her.

Michael hadn't commented further on Immy, but several times Ryder caught him watching her. 'Do you fancy her?' she asked, very casually, one evening when the school was empty.

'Do you mind?'

'It has nothing to do with me.'

'Well, I don't.' He picked up his car keys and walked out. The doors clicked after him. Ryder stood in the office, watching him go. She wanted to call after him. But she didn't. And he drove away.

In September Frankie and Susan had to return to the States. Ryder and Leo drove them to London. On the way home she planned to visit Mrs Trumpet. She wore the yellow silk suit. As she confided to Immy, this might be its only outing.

'We'll be back next year,' Frankie waved as they headed for passport control.

'Bring Debbie too!'

'We'll try.' They disappeared.

Ryder thought of Scot's Farm. Of her grandfather. Of Fox Lake. A wave of nostalgia rolled over her for those few safe threads of her past. That acute feeling took her through Windsor Great Park to the winding road which led to Blacknest Gate. She remembered each tree. Each corner. Each widening or narrowing of the road. Every feature of that drive brought back memories.

'I thought we were going to Mrs Trumpet,' said Leo.

'In a minute.' She slowed the car as they approached Gatehouse Stables. The polo season had finished. The yard was deserted. A few ponies remained stabled but most were out to grass. Ryder halted in the gateway.

Resting her chin on the steering wheel, she stared at the stables and the house beyond the archway where tendrils of honeysuckle still swung in the breeze. Nothing had changed. But somehow it looked smaller. She reversed.

'There's Patrick!' said Leo. 'Look!'

'Don't be silly!' She crashed into first gear. 'The season's over.'

'I'm not silly!' He opened his door. 'Patrick!'

In the wing mirror she watched as he strode across the yard in his tight breeches and polished boots. She saw Leo dash to him and jump up and down excitedly. She saw every detail of the darkly handsome face which had haunted her. She remembered the hurt, and wished she could run away — but she couldn't.

'I knew you'd come,' he said softly, laying his arm along the car roof above her head.

She couldn't look at him or she'd weaken further. 'It was a mistake. Come on, Leo!'

'You can't go. Not yet.' Patrick opened her car door. 'You came because we were meant to meet again.' He took her by the hand. She stepped out. She couldn't resist him. 'Come into the house,' he said. 'We must talk.'

'About what?' She snatched her hand away. 'Your wife?'

'Ryder! Ryder! I want to explain.'

She backed away from him. She mustn't let him touch her again. 'You're three years too late.'

'This is the first time I've been back to England. I arrived two weeks ago. I leave tomorrow. Don't tell me your coming today isn't fate.'

'We're expected at Mrs Trumpet's,' she protested feebly.

'Phone her. Say you're held up. Ryder, this is important. We're important.'

She hesitated.

He ushered her to the stable phone and sent Leo to look at the ponies, saying, 'I want to talk to your sister.'

She wouldn't go into the house because she was afraid of weakening further, so they sat on the wall where she and her mother had once perched among the crocuses. Only it wasn't the season of crocuses now.

'I don't blame you for hating me,' he said. 'I don't expect you to forgive. I wouldn't either. But you have to know the truth. When you arrived in Palm Beach I was in Argentina to tell my wife I wanted a divorce. Of course I should have told you about Maria Luisa but our marriage only lasted six weeks and I hadn't seen her for two years.' He paused. 'And I didn't know I had a son till I went back. When she told me about Tancredi, I didn't believe he was mine. But when I saw him, I knew. She says that if I remarry I'll never see him again. Under Argentinian law there's no divorce yet, just separation. I could obtain one elsewhere. She can't.'

'But you don't live together.'

'Oh, she doesn't care about that so long as there's no scandal.'

Ryder walked across the yard to the paddock and leaned on the railings, watching the ponies in the field without really seeing them. Patrick followed her. 'I did what I thought best at the time,' he said.

'The truth would have hurt me less.'

'I could have strung you along in order not to lose you.'

'So you'll never . . . divorce her?'

'I thought not. Now I'm not sure.'

The silence hung between them. She wanted to ask more but didn't want to break the moment.

'There is something else,' he said. 'Tancredi is a haemophiliac. How could I abandon my son? My sick son!'

'I'd never have asked you to do that. Never!' Tears pricked her eyes. She bit her lower lip to hold them

293

back. 'But if only you'd told me. Have you any idea what you did to me that night in Palm Beach? Did you ever stop to think of what it was like when I came back to Bailing? To sit by the phone. Night after night. Waiting. Hoping. If you wanted to explain to me, that was the time. If I hadn't come today, you'd never have told me.' She walked back to the car, shouting for Leo.

He caught up with her as she settled into her seat, reaching inside to cup her face in his hands and force her to look at him. 'But you did come — because you were more of a wife to me than Maria Luisa ever was!'

They were too late to visit Mrs Trumpet. 'I'll take you another day,' Ryder told Leo, attempting to fix on the present and to stop thinking of Patrick. She hesitated, then added, 'I told her I wasn't well. Don't mention Patrick. She'd be offended.'

Leo stared out of the car window. 'Will he come to see us?'

'I don't know.'

'I hope not.'

'I thought you liked him.'

'I did.' He pursed his lips. 'But he went away.'

Ryder glanced at Leo. He had his worried white look. She felt guilty, then thoughts of Patrick overtook everything and she was barely conscious of driving or of anything, till she reached King's Lynn, where she stopped at an electrical store. 'Going to help me choose our colour television?' she asked, less guilty as his face came alive with excitement.

It was dusk when they finally reached Bailing. Light shone from the office and the school. Ryder couldn't wait to be alone with Immy to tell her about Patrick. 'Yes, I've finally succumbed,' she told Violet as she carried the television into the tower. She glanced around. 'Where's Immy?'

'I'm sorry, dear.' Violet handed her a note and walked slowly back to the office.

Dear Ryder,

No one could have done more for me than you but I don't have your willpower. There've been times when I've looked at your bag and nearly taken your wallet. I have to leave before I do.

Please forgive me.

Love
Immy

She dialled the mews. Imogen answered. 'I suppose you're angry,' she said.

'I'm going to book you into a clinic. I'll take you there myself.'

'I'm not going.'

'Immy, listen!'

'I'm sick of listening. Aeroplanes! Bailing. *Ryder's so wonderful.* More aeroplanes. All those people watching to see if I'd take their money. Watching and sniggering.'

'They just want to help.'

'There's nothing the matter with me. You're as bad as Alix. Nagging. Belittling. I'm sick of it. Leave me alone!' Imogen slammed down the receiver.

Ryder waited for Immy to ring back. She paced up and down the kitchen, rehearsing her response: 'I understand. No, I'm not offended.' But the telephone remained silent.

She reached for her address book, and scanned the pages. Then she dialled another number. It rang once. She took a deep breath. It rang again. Her lips were white with tension. Again. She swallowed hard. 'Alix. It's Ryder. Imogen needs help.'

'So you've realised at last!' The voice was low and mocking, as it had been that Sunday afternoon when they had first met.

'I'm not going to argue. You're in London. You could do something.'

'How?'

'Take her back on your books. Get her work.'

'Out of the question.'

'Alix, you made a fortune out of Immy. If she's in trouble it's because she's weak. But she's our friend.'

'Then you help her.'

'I've tried!' shouted Ryder.

'So have I,' screamed Alix. 'And I nearly lost my home through her dishonesty.'

Ryder dialled Gatehouse. Patrick was right. Fate had drawn them together. She needed him. She longed for his voice. His touch. The phone rang and rang. No one answered. Why should he? She hadn't said she'd ring. She'd driven off without a word, too choked to talk.

She sat at the table with her head in her hands. She wasn't crying. She was just numb. The door opened and Michael came in. He put his arm around her and held her so tight that she felt as if his strength were transferred to her. 'You did your best, Miss Biggles,' he said.

Then he left her, sensing she wanted to be alone. Outside she heard him say, 'Come on, Leo! Let's have a boys' night out at the fish and chip shop.'

'Do you mean me?' asked Leo.

'Aren't you Leo?'

'Yes, but you never used to want me with you.'

'Oh, that's because you were too young before.'

By the time they returned Ryder was in bed. That night she dreamed she married Michael.

She was in her special Chinese dressing-gown making toast when he arrived. Her hair was soft and smelled of shampoo. Her eyes were bright and polished. He walked towards her, across the kitchen. She smiled uncertainly. He took her by the shoulders and looked deep into her eyes. 'If you're planning to meet Patrick Brendan, don't lie about visiting the housekeeper,' he said angrily.

'It wasn't planned.'

'So why were you wearing your smart silk dress?' He twisted her closer, so close that the metal zip of his flying jacket cut into her breasts. 'Don't play games with me, Ryder,' he said. 'I'm not a forgiving man.'

28

Patrick sent Ryder an enormous bouquet of red roses,
with an open airticket to Miami and a note saying, 'Give
me time.' The florist arrived in the middle of a down-
pour, three days after Ryder had seen Patrick, by which
time she'd given up hope of hearing from him. She
arranged the roses in a vase on the kitchen table, savour-
ing the heady scent of each velvet bloom. Then she
reread the note, again and again. She couldn't wait to
go. To see him.

Fred interrupted her reverie. He opened the door,
letting in a gust of wind and rain. 'The ole river's breaking her banks but the flood channel's half empty. Violet
says Miss B.B.'s away. You going to open the sluice
gates or will you stay here an' tie down our planes while
I do it?'

She stepped in front of the table with the vase of roses.
'Where's Michael?'

'That ought to be your concern.'

'Oh, Fred, keep out of it! You're as bad as my grandmother.' She grabbed a jacket. 'Anyhow, you never used
to like him.'

'I do now.'

She pushed past him, and bent her head against the
rain which was thudding down onto the tarmac like stair-
rods, just as it had on the morning of the launch party
when she'd raced to the mill — to Patrick. When he'd
said, sex, and she'd said, yes. 'I'll do the gates,' she

called. 'The aircraft are the most important. Can you ask Violet to keep Leo?'

'Know what to do?' he shouted as she dashed for her car.

She shook her head, and raindrops flew from the ends of her hair.

'Turn the handle on the wheel. But keep your hands out of it or you'll lose 'em. Patrick Brendan won't send you red roses then!'

She drove away without answering.

The fields around Bailing were flooding. The road was under water. But the mill pond was no higher than usual and the bridge to mill island was its normal twelve feet above the channel — that section which went through the sluice gates, along the tunnel under the house, and out into the pond. She parked in the gravel courtyard. It was already under seige from water, which was seeping up the lawn, drowning an army of wild daffodils. Even as she watched it seemed to edge its way higher, lapping now at the garden wall.

Hesitating to enter someone's home, especially a woman who disliked her, Ryder chose the garden access. But when she opened the door in the wall, she found the water lapping at the steps. The vegetables were submerged. Only the yellowish green tops of the box hedges were visible, their peppery smell hanging heavy on the damp air.

She hurried to the house and banged on the front door, even though she knew it was deserted. No one answered. She turned the handle. The door wasn't locked. It creaked open to reveal a flagstoned hall. It was spartan but surprisingly orderly considering the state of the exterior. At the threshold she hesitated. The mill was groaning as though being pushed by some giant unseen hand. She had visions of it collapsing. Of being trapped beneath rubble as the river rose around her, cutting off her unheard cries for help. She wished she'd stayed with the aircraft. But she couldn't chicken out. Not only did the mill's survival depend on the water level but also Bruja in her stable near the river, the airfield, and even the village.

She forced herself across the flagstones and through an arch into a beamed living area from which a wooden spiral staircase wound up to a gallery. The sound of rushing water was deafening. In the floorboards was a square of heavy glass. It looked straight down on the tunnel which carried the river from the sluice gates to the pond. Beyond it were rusting iron steps leading down into the gloom of the basement. She felt her way down, gingerly reaching out with each foot, until she came to the sluice gates.

They were some ten feet across, with a big iron cog wheel at one end and a crank handle attached to it. This she had to turn to drive the shaft through the central wheels to raise the gates below. Tossing off her jacket, she rolled up her sleeves and seized the handle. It wouldn't move. She pushed her shoulder into it. Nothing happened. Water was rising fast behind her. It was splashing in through a broken pane in the window. Her hands slipped on the handle. It was covered in wet oil. Water was now pouring in behind her. It swilled about her feet. In a moment she'd be trapped.

'Ryder!'

She turned. Michael stood on the steps. His shirt was drenched and torn. It clung to his body. His jeans were soaked and oily. His dark hair stuck to his forehead.

'Help me!' She had to shout to make herself heard.

'There's a branch jammed underneath.' He pointed downwards. 'I have to pull it out from the bottom. Leave the gates or you'll be trapped.'

She was glad to get out of there. At least if she was going to die, let it happen in the open. Not trapped underground. On the bank of the millpond, Michael had secured a rope around his waist. He'd tied the other end to a tree.

'You can't go up the tunnel,' she protested.

'Someone has to.'

Holding a torch and hatchet above his head, he waded into the pond, keeping near the millhouse wall, as far back as possible from the raging water in the middle. For a moment Ryder stood and watched him, then she slithered down the muddy bank and waded after him.

'Go back!' he shouted.

She carried on, her trainers squelching in the mud. 'I'll steady the rope.' She looped the slack around her waist. 'If the gates blow, you'll be knocked unconscious.'

'You won't be able to hold me.'

'I can try.'

He looked at her. She was shivering. Her hair hung in rats' tails. Her blouse was stuck to her breasts. 'Keep back behind the buttress,' he said. 'If the water bursts, grab that iron foothold before it throws you out.' He reached for the rope at her waist and loosened the knot. 'And let me go if you have to.'

He waded up the tunnel. The river barely covered his knees. The roof was only six feet above his head. If the gates broke whilst he was in the tunnel the whole force of the upper river would crash down on him. The torchlight stopped moving. He'd reached the end. He bent to pull at something. Ryder held her breath and watched the gates. They didn't move. He straightened and raised his right arm. There was a crack as the hatchet bit the branch. The noise echoed down the tunnel like a bullet. Ryder jumped with fright. Again he bent to pull the branch. This time it came clear. He turned and saw her watching. He gave the thumbs up. It was too dark for her to see his thumb but she understood. She felt sick with relief.

Michael started back towards her, torch in one hand,

301

hatchet in the other. He passed beneath the square glass hole in the living room floor. 'The rope!' he shouted.

'What?'

There was an explosion like a cannon ball. Ryder screamed. The gate had broken. A great wall of angry water roared down the tunnel. Michael fought to reach the entrance. She held out her hand to him. He stretched for it. But the water caught him. It lifted him up, throwing him out, tightening the slack rope so fast that it burned the skin off her stomach.

Water knocked Ryder back behind the buttress. It filled her mouth. Her eyes. Her lungs. She coughed and spluttered, gasping for air. Her elbow cracked on something hard. She cried out. It was an iron foothold. She grabbed at it, holding tight, her arm aching, as the water buffeted her from side to side.

Suddenly a hand covered hers and Michael's arm gripped her round the waist. He held her steady on the wall. 'We'll be all right,' he shouted in her ear, but she couldn't reply because her teeth were chattering.

One moment they were below the bridge, the next they were floating on to it. 'Come on.' He pulled her to her feet. 'It may collapse. The hall's the safest. It's on firm ground.'

In the courtyard the water had reached the bottom of her car's doors. Ryder hesitated. But Michael hurried her on. In the hall they stood and dripped on the stone floor. Ryder was freezing. The noise of the water passing through the gates was deafening. The building shuddered under pressure. She wanted to cry out every time it creaked but she bit her lip to control herself.

'I'll find some blankets,' said Michael.

He was gone for hours, or so it seemed. She leaned against the wall, her eyes closed. Her stomach burned. She felt it now, whereas in the millpond fear had dulled the pain. She lifted her shirt. The skin was red and scraped.

Michael returned with one blanket. He draped it around her shoulders, lifting her hair gently to squeeze out the worst of the water.

'I'm sorry I didn't pull in the slack,' she said. 'I don't know how I could have forgotten. I was just so relieved to see you safe.'

He gripped her shoulders. 'I don't know many people who'd have braved the water with me.'

There was a crash from the basement and the sound of breaking glass as another window gave under the strain. Ryder tried not to show her fright but she couldn't help it. He drew her closer. She leaned against him, half wrapping her blanket around him as her body sought his warmth.

He took her by the chin, lifting it to look into her eyes. 'Is this another game?'

Tears choked her though she didn't know why. She had nothing to cry about, except the sheer relief of not being dead.

His mouth brushed hers. 'It had better not be.'

She didn't answer. She didn't have to. In any case, she would not have known how. The world beyond the storm had no bearing. Life was here, amid the danger, which made everything so acute: her fear and her desire. He kissed her hard. She responded, clinging to him, her arms entwined around his neck, revelling in his strength. His wet hair in her face. Their wet clothes steamed and slippery. The smell of the millpond on both of them.

Another window crashed in the basement. She closed her ears to it, reaching for his belt as he ripped her shirt from her shoulders and kissed her neck, her breasts, digging his fingers into her shoulder blades, rolling her nipples between his teeth until she moaned in pleasure.

He broke the sodden laces of her trainers, then pulled the clinging jeans from her hips. 'What's that?' He saw the red weal across her stomach.

'Nothing.' She pulled him to her. 'It doesn't matter.' She unzipped his jeans. 'Nothing matters.'

He pushed her up against the stone wall. It dug into the small of her back but she barely felt the pain. If anything it heightened her desire. The roughness. The stark cold hall. The storm. This man whom she could not stop even if she'd wanted to. He lifted her onto him. Entering. Leaving. Teasing. Manipulating. She felt the orgasm roll over her and out of her. Down her limbs. Through her veins. Weakening her muscles. Travelling beneath her skin. Making the hairs on her arms stand rigid. She felt it smooth over her face and down the soft inside of her elbows, till even the backs of her fingers were so highly sensitive that they almost hurt.

Only then did she remember that she was in Patrick's house.

As soon as the rain stopped and the road had drained, Michael drove Ryder back to the airfield. She was silent and guilty in her blanket. Of course, nothing would have happened between them had it not been for the storm. But it had happened. And in Patrick's house. She shivered involuntarily. The intensity of her orgasm was with her still. She couldn't even delude herself that she hadn't enjoyed it.

'You need a hot bath.' Michael turned on the taps, humming as the water gushed out. She watched him, hoping he didn't expect to stay the night. She didn't want to hurt his feelings but in a week she'd be in Palm Beach with Patrick, and tonight would be the forgotten past.

He unwrapped the blanket from her. 'Get in. I'll shampoo your hair.'

'I can manage.' She felt extremely naked.

'Don't argue!' He turned the shower on her head. She closed her eyes behind the dripping curtain of her hair as the residue of the millpond ran down her back, her shoulders and her breasts. How could she have been unfaithful to Patrick? How could she have allowed another man to enter her? To reach up inside her where only Patrick should be.

'That's enough.' She wrapped the towel firmly around herself.

With the duvet covering her, she sat up in bed whilst Michael dried her hair. His fingers were strong against her scalp. When he leaned towards her she could smell the warmth of his body and the millpond on his clothes, and she was reminded of the moment when he'd thrust into her.

'My hair's dry.' She pulled away. Supposing Patrick found out.

'I'll make us a hot toddy.' Michael disappeared downstairs.

She nearly called, 'Don't bother. Just drop the key back through the letter box.' But she didn't.

The warmth of the duvet lulled her. She snuggled down, closing her eyes to call up Patrick's image. His darkly handsome face. His debonair smile. But when she imagined his touch, it wasn't his touch — it was Michael's.

Suddenly she was aware that the shower was running. Michael was planning to stay. His presumption angered her. She prepared a little speech. 'As business partners our relationship should be platonic.' She decided not to mention Patrick unless she had to.

He left the bathroom and crossed to the kitchen. There was silence. She wondered what he was doing. Then the front door opened and he went out. She heard his car door, and paradoxically she felt robbed. She hadn't expected him to take her so casually.

A few minutes later he returned. She heard his footsteps on the stairs. He came in, dressed in the flying suit he kept at the school. He stood beside the bed, looking down at her. She smiled tentatively, trying to recall what she'd planned to say but everything about him reminded her of the mill.

'You forgot to inform me.' In his hand he held her airticket to Miami.

'Why should I?' She flared, with the anger of the guilty.

'I said, no games.' Slowly he tore her ticket in half and dropped the pieces on to her bed. Then he walked back downstairs and drove away.

Ryder lay in bed, seething rage. How dare Michael bully her. He knew how she loved Patrick. The memory of the afternoon made her blush with shame. It was Patrick she'd been unfaithful to, not Michael.

The sooner she left for Florida the better. There was no need to tell Patrick about the torn ticket. That would involve her in explanations. The airline would replace it. She dialled Patrick's number. He didn't answer till the tenth ring. 'Surely you're not asleep,' she said brightly. 'It's only eight o'clock with you.'

'I'm having a siesta.'

She chuckled. 'That sounds inviting.'

'Yes.' The sheets rustled as he turned over.

'Thanks for the flowers — and the ticket.'

'Look,' he paused. 'Can I call you back?'

'Yes. Of course.' She tried to sound as if she didn't mind. 'I've only rung to say I'll fly out next week.'

'We'll speak later.'

She heard a door being carefully shut. 'Is . . . someone there?'

'I'll phone you tomorrow.'

'Patrick!'

'Don't be silly!'

She lay on her back, staring up at the ceiling. Patrick still had an infinite capacity to hurt her. There had been someone with him. She'd sensed it from the moment he'd answered. She knew from the way he'd spoken, which was as he used to speak when he was in bed with her.

Ryder decided to be calm and icy with Patrick. She wasn't going to let him see how hurt she was: not this time.

'You were screwing some woman, you bastard, and don't tell me you weren't!' she screamed down the line at him.

'It's you I want. She means nothing. You must have had other men.'

She was stunned to silence by her own guilt.

He chuckled. 'We'll talk when you arrive.'

'No, Patrick,' she said. 'If you want to talk to me, you come here. I'm not going to trail you round the world like a parcel of goods on approval.'

'I'd come, darling, but I can't. Not in the middle of the season.'

She stood up, so that her voice sounded positive. 'If you can't interrupt a polo season, I can't risk a lifetime.'

29

Some winters at Bailing were harder than others. This was a hard one. Patrick had telephoned every day for a week, but Ryder wouldn't speak to him. If he'd arrived, she'd have thrown herself into his arms. But he didn't come. Much as she longed for him, she couldn't back down. She had to be sure he really loved her before she allowed herself to be vulnerable to him again. When a month had passed and he still hadn't arrived, in a final dramatic gesture she posted him the two halves of her airticket.

Michael had barely spoken to her since the night at the mill but he was aware of Patrick's telephone calls. When she didn't leave for Florida, she was sure he'd assume it was because of what happened between them. Indignantly, she waited for his approach, rehearsing the words she'd use to turn him down.

She returned from the cinema with Leo to find the lights in the school still on. Michael's car was parked outside, his dark head was bent over his desk. She hovered in the kitchen whilst Leo ate his supper. She tried to watch television, but kept listening for Michael's firm tread on the patio. Finally, she decided to confront him. She threw on her coat and opened the door. But his car had gone. She went to bed, feeling like the Sabine woman whom no one wished to rape.

The days grew shorter. By early evening the airfield was deserted. Michael's attitude did not soften. At first

Ryder pretended not to care, but she missed his company and their banter so much that as the weeks passed she would have done almost anything to regain it. One day she said with studied casualness, 'How about a drink at The Bailing Arms?'

'I'm busy.' He walked towards his car.

A fortnight later he went to St Lucia on holiday. Violet let slip that he'd taken the girl with the short blonde hair. That night when Leo had gone to bed Ryder sat alone at the kitchen table, as she did most evenings now. She began a letter to Immy. Then gave up and opened a bottle of wine. She started another letter, but got no further than the first paragraph. What did Imogen care about her problems? What did anyone care? She had no friends, except for Debbie and Susan and Frankie, whom she hardly saw. Everyone else had gone from her life, driven away by her because they'd hurt her or she'd hurt them. Patrick. Alix. Adam. Immy. And now Michael.

She opened a second bottle of wine. It was cheap and red and tasted like paint stripper. Her head began to spin. She dragged herself up to her bedroom and lay down, trying to focus on the central light fitting. She must have passed out because she came to sometime after midnight, feeling so nauseous she thought she was going to die. She staggered down to the bathroom, stuck her fingers down her throat, and vomited down the lavatory. The taste was vile. Cold sweat rolled down her face. She leaned against the wall and cried. She really was her father's daughter. The only friendship he'd maintained was with George Brendan Broughton, and he was dead.

When Michael returned, looking suntanned and fit, Ryder refrained from asking him if he'd enjoyed himself and he didn't tell her. They discussed the school. That was all. Then he drove away, with his tapedeck turned up loud, sending a Caribbean love song pulsating over the airfield.

The cold weather brought a succession of troubles. Three customers decided to sell their aircraft. Snow blocked the runway. The pipes at Fortune's Fen burst. The bank rate rose. So did the interest on their loan. Leo caught measles. Ryder spent days nursing him. The price of fuel escalated. There were strikes. Repossessions. Recession workers on *The Times* came out on strike. Violet caught flu. Imogen ignored her letters.

On an impulse Ryder drove down to London. Whatever had gone wrong between Immy and herself didn't merit the death of a friendship. She arrived at the mews to find music blasting out from Imogen's house. The noise bounced down the street and hit Ryder as she stepped from her car. As the brass fish knocker hit the door, the volume fell. Footsteps approached the door. She prepared her speech. A man opened the door, the same swarthy man with dark, Andean eyes. 'Yes?' he said.

'I want to speak to Imogen.'

'She's in the States.'

'When's she due back?'

'How should I know!' He made a move to close the door.

Ryder blocked it with her foot. 'A week? A month? You must know, if you're staying in her house.'

'I'm not.' He dislodged her foot. 'It's my house now.'

She hadn't planned to spend the night in London but she was so concerned about Immy that she couldn't bear to leave. She checked into a hotel in Pimlico. Next morning she telephoned Jeremy. 'Alix is in LA,' he said. 'Come to the office at twelve. It's one of my "in" days. We'll drink pink champagne.'

'Jeremy, please! I'm worried.'

'Ryder, sweetie, I'm not going to discuss Imogen's drug dependancy at half-past eight in the morning.'

At noon she rang Jeremy's bell, remembering that first time she'd come here, when his mother had let the basin overflow. He opened the door immediately. 'Mother's upstairs. She wants to take us both out to lunch. Dash up and say hello while I open the champagne. But for God's sake tell her to save her chatter till later.'

She started up the white stair carpet.

'Your wet shoes! My white carpets!' he wailed.

'Sorry.' She kicked off her shoes. 'We don't have white carpets at Bailing.'

'No white carpets! Sweetie, you're a savage. But that black wool dress is divine. Karl Lagerfield?'

'King's Lynn market.' She ran up to Lady Heythorp in her stockinged feet.

When she came down, Jeremy was sitting behind his huge masculine desk sipping pink champagne from a fluted glass. 'We didn't throw Imogen out without reason,' he said. 'She borrowed Alix's mink and pretended she'd lost it. After Alix claimed on her insurance, she discovered that Imogen had sold it. There was the most awful scene. But Imogen promised to repay every penny.'

'You mean, Alix gave her a second chance!'

'Two months later Imogen stole her credit cards. She bought thirty thousand pounds' worth of jewellery spread over twenty different shops. By the time we found out, she'd sold the goods and given the money to that Colombian drug dealer. Of course Alix had a card insurance but couldn't claim without pointing the finger at Imogen. So she remortgaged her house to clear the debt. But that was the end of Imogen at Heythorp & Bassingham.'

Ryder watched the bubbles rise in her champagne. 'Why didn't Alix tell me?'

'Did you give her a chance?'

She gave a wry smile. 'Probably not.'

'Alix never forgives.' He lit a small cheroot. 'Any more than you do.'

She stood as Lady Heythorp came into the room. 'I used to think of myself as everybody's pushover,' she said. 'Now I find that others see me as unforgiving and manipulative — which is exactly how I view my father.'

The news from Scot's Farm was gloomy. Her grandfather was deteriorating. With Bailing unusable in bad weather, Ryder took Leo to Prairieville for Christmas. Debbie met them at the airport. It was five years since they'd seen each other but they picked up the threads as though it were yesterday.

'Mom's found out about Frankie and Susan,' Debbie told Ryder.

'What did she say?'

'She didn't say — she screamed. And she hasn't stopped. She calls Susan a Jezebel and says the poet was "one of her many men". She said you jilted poor Teddy a week before the wedding. She's even started to say "poor Carl" as if I were the one who played around. What makes me mad is we three have had our affections recycled into chicken feed by men we trusted.'

'I'm better off with aeroplanes,' said Ryder. 'At least they can't be married or unfaithful.' She watched the moonlight glitter on the frozen countryside and wondered with whom Patrick was walking on the white sand of Palm Beach.

Scot's Farm was tidier. More functional. More Debbie. Less Greta. Her grandmother's absence showed in the lack of lace napkins. Ryder went up to her grandfather's room. The door was shut. She knocked. There was no answer. She opened it tentatively. Her grandfather was sitting in an armchair by the window, a quilt across his knees, staring out at the snow.

'Grandpa!' She touched his arm. 'It's me. Ryder.'

'Greta!'

She twisted with physical hurt as she looked at the empty coffin of his mind and knew loss as though he were already dead.

Christmas wasn't easy but they tried to make it fun for Leo and Rudy. They sang carols around the tree, skated on the lake, and tobogganed up and down the drive. In the evenings, when the boys had gone to bed, Ryder and Debbie would draw the old squashy sofas up to the fire and gossip late into the night, the only sound being the crackling of the burning wood and the dull thud as snow slid off the roof on to the frozen ground.

When Ryder said goodbye to her grandfather she could hardly speak, she was convinced she'd never see him again. She touched his arm and bent to kiss his cheek. He half-turned. She held her breath. In fourteen days he had never reacted to her presence. Then he cried out, 'Greta!' and Ryder turned away.

Her father was due to leave prison in the spring. Ryder dreaded his release. She was sure he hadn't given up on Bailing and she knew his presence would be a disaster — especially if she and Michael were still at loggerheads. In Minneapolis she bought a large bottle of Southern Comfort, gift wrapped in red and gold Christmas paper.

Bailing was sparkling in winter sunshine. The snow had cleared. The buildings looked spruce. Ryder was glad to be home. 'Where's Michael?' she asked Violet.

'He's gone skiing. He left this morning.' Violet looked puzzled. 'Didn't he tell you?'

'I expect he forgot.' Ryder gave a bright smile. 'Did he go in a chalet party or with . . . what's-her-name?'

'With a new what's-her-name, I believe.'

'How nice!' Ryder marched into the tower, opened her suitcase, took out the Southern Comfort, and ripped the gift wrapping from it.

They had gathered quotations for adapting Bailing to

313

night flying. She'd held back because of cost. Now she went ahead, in Michael's absence, and ordered the work to proceed. Simultaneously she decided that the school needed a facelift. She ordered it to be repainted.

When Michael returned, she was sitting at the kitchen table, reading the newspaper. He barged into the tower without knocking. 'Don't you think you should have consulted me?' he demanded.

She glanced up. 'If you wish to speak to me, please do so in the office. This is my home.'

'Oh, for God's sake, Ryder!'

She laid down her paper. 'We are partners in business. Not in Bailing. That is mine.'

He spun on his heel and headed for the door. On the table in the hall was the litre bottle of Southern Comfort. 'Been at the drink again?' he sneered, and he left, slamming the door behind him.

A cold war began. Ryder pretended she didn't care. But she did. 'Michael's impossible,' she complained to Fred, who was tinkering with the engine of Rupert Atheldene's Cherokee.

'That makes two of you.'

'If you don't like it here . . .'

'I can leave.' He gave her his tortoise stare. 'But I won't, because you can't run the ole airfield on your own.'

She sank to her haunches, her head in her hands. 'I'm sorry. I shouldn't take it out on you.'

If only she had Patrick by her side, things would be different. She'd have had his love. His support. He'd fight her battles.

To cover the increased interest on the bank loan, every aspect of Bailing had to be fully utilised. They trebled the intake of pupils and took on three more instructors, one at Bailing and two at Fortune's Fen. She added a restaurant to the clubhouse. Membership doubled. She obtained her Night Rating. Often she flew home from

Fortune's Fen to find Bailing a blaze of lights, with people dancing on the club patio. Gradually she began to make back the capital drained during the winter. But her heart wasn't in it. Not as it had been. She had no one with whom to laugh through the ups and downs.

Michael was conspicuous with his girlfriends. There was Wendy, the geometric blonde, and a redhead with a butterfly tattoed on one shoulder. Ryder ignored them.

Frankie and Susan could only stay for a few weeks that summer. Ryder tried not to show how upset she was, but they knew. 'I have to do some crop-dusting to get my flying hours up for the Commercial Pilot's Licence,' Frankie explained.

'You'll be too grand for Bailing when you're flying a 747.'

He slipped an arm through Ryder's. 'I'll never be grand. I'm a Prairieville farmboy at heart.'

On their first evening, Susan laid a place for Michael at the table.

'He doesn't eat with us,' said Ryder, slicing viciously into an avocado. 'We've had a . . . disagreement. I'm amazed you hadn't noticed.'

'Over that polo player?'

'Sort of.'

'So you're seeing him again?'

'No.' She licked her fingers. 'But I still think about him, though I'm not sure if now I want love or revenge.'

'And Michael?'

'If he doesn't want to speak to me, I don't care.'

Ryder heard of two more airfields for sale: Holdenbury and Nickford. One was near Cambridge, the other north of Bedford. Both owners had gone bankrupt. She used her share of Fortune's Fen as collateral. That stretched her to the limit, but she was determined to exclude Michael.

'Borrowing so much money terrifies me,' she confided to her solicitor, Oliver Offbach, when he took her to lunch at the Waldorf after they'd concluded the Nickford deal. 'When I bought Fortune's Fen the bank rate was 10 per cent. Now it's 12 per cent.'

'And rising! But you'd be mad not to buy Nickford. Recession destroys the weak and allows the strong to capitalise.'

'You're making me sound like a vulture.' She crossed her legs and smoothed down the skirt of her new black jersey wool dress in a movement made more sensuous because she was unaware of it being so.

He gave her a tight, meticulous smile. She wondered if he ever let go in wild passion and decided not. 'The bank like your security,' he said. 'When property booms again — as it will — Nickford with its building permission is going to be very valuable.'

At a nearby table a man like her father was arguing profit and margins. 'I'm not interested in property development,' she said firmly.

'Be that as it may, it's my job to bring these points to your notice.' He rested his elbows on the table, drawing the tips of his fingers together as if praying to some god of commerce. 'As you know, I'd have been happier had you shared the liability of Nickford with Mr Ashby.'

'As a matter of fact,' she replied, 'I want to talk to you about dissolving our partnership.'

316

30

Ryder was grooming Bruja and thinking about Oliver Offbach's advice when Rupert Atheldene roared up in his red Bugatti. 'Hello, there!' he called. 'How's my Cherokee?'

'Awaiting her lord and master. Fred's in the hangar if you want to take her up.'

'I'll wait.' He sauntered towards her. Ryder felt sure he came from a long line of blond ancestors, all dressed like Little Lord Fauntleroy.

He watched her divide Bruja's tail and brush it strand by strand. 'I thought I'd settle up,' he said.

She calculated the financial loss. 'When do you want to remove the Cherokee?'

'Oh, I don't. Not yet.'

He accompanied her to the tower, gliding effortlessly over the rough ground, his thumbs hooked into the pockets of his pale grey flannel trousers. She noticed Michael watching, and turned on her brightest smile, so much so that Rupert said, 'How about having dinner with me one evening?'

'Well, I . . .'

'You're involved with someone?'

'No. I'd love to come. Thank you.' Patrick had kicked her confidence into the gutter, but she wasn't going to get it back by sitting at home watching television.

She wore her yellow silk suit, the one Michael had accused her of wearing for Patrick. Rupert arrived at eight. In his dark suit he looked every inch the escort her mother would have loved. Ryder offered him a gin and tonic, then realised she didn't have any lemon. He said it didn't matter. She was sure it did. He'd barely touched his drink before he said, 'Shall we go? I've booked at The Tollbridge at Guist.'

He drove like a bullet, cornering so fast that he nearly jumped a hedge. Ryder gritted her teeth.

The restaurant was a converted toll cottage by the River Wensum. It was cosy, with wooden beams and intimate tables. The location reminded Ryder of Bailing Mill. Even the gravel seemed to have the same crunch. Their table was by the window. She watched a pair of swans sail past, the last rays of the sunset reflecting on their arched necks.

'Like a drink?' asked Rupert.

'Oh . . . er . . .'

He tapped his fingers.

'Sherry. Thank you.' She didn't want one but she couldn't think what to say. She was out of practice at going out with men.

The waiter handed her a menu. She began to read through the starters.

'I'll have my usual. Salmon mousse, then steak.' Rupert closed his menu. 'I like plenty of pepper. No, I'll add that myself. Ryder?'

She had barely read half the menu but his impatience unnerved her. 'I'll have . . . umm . . . the salmon mousse too and . . . er . . . pigeon with chestnuts.'

This was a nightmare. Rupert was bored. The waiter thought her an idiot. The swans had disappeared into the darkness of the night, lucky devils! She cemented a smile to her face and raked her brain for a subject of conversation. She needn't have bothered. Rupert talked about himself.

It was after midnight when he drove her back to Bailing. She decided not to invite him in for coffee. On the doorstep, she held out her hand. 'Thank you for a lovely evening.'

He waited as she opened her front door. She hoped he didn't expect to kiss her. 'Goodnight,' he said, hurrying back to his car.

He hadn't asked to see her again. Not that she'd have agreed. But it would have been nice to know he wanted to.

A month before his release, she visited her father for the last time. 'You'll fetch me on D-Day?' he said eagerly. 'They'll let me go straight after breakfast.'

'I'll be here.'

'Book a morning appointment with my tailor. I've lost weight. My old clothes won't fit. Then we'll lunch at Simpson's. Make sure we have my favourite table. And book me a suite at the Savoy. I want a river view.'

'Would you rather do something quieter?' she asked, visualising the curious whispers.

'And hide away? Why should I? I've been locked up for nearly six years for a crime I didn't commit.'

'If you didn't commit it, how will you afford to pay for this jamboree?'

'An advance on my salary at Bailing.'

She drove straight to London, to Oliver Offbach's office, cursing the traffic which snarled along Fleet Street and round the law courts. 'Mr Offbach can't possibly see you without an appointment,' protested his secretary when summoned from her sanctum by a panel of receptionists.

'I'll wait.' Ryder selected a magazine from the rack and sank on to a large hessian sofa in the opulent reception.

'But he's tied up for days, Miss Harding.'

'I'll still wait.'

It was eight that evening before Offbach could see her. 'It must be urgent,' he said.

'It is.' She told him what her father had said.

He listened with concentrated attention, his elbows on his desk and his fingertips drawn together as they had been in the restaurant. 'You're under no legal obligation to him.'

She walked to the window and looked down on the lonely figure of an aged tramp stumbling past the golden lions outside the Law Society, his head bent against the evening glare, whilst from a wine bar opposite a dozen young barristers burst out on to the pavement, laughing and shouting. They didn't see the old man. They were blinded by the carelessness of youth. 'I can't abandon him,' she said.

'Don't forget a term of your partnership is that your father has no involvement with the airfields. If Ashby turns nasty, he'll claim you're getting rid of him to bring in your father, in direct contradiction to your agreement.'

'Michael knows that I don't want father at Bailing.'

'I said "if he turns nasty".'

She sat down heavily. 'He's already turned.'

'Then he'll try for his share — and more. As I explained at our last meeting, he's entitled to half the value of the business. That includes improvements to Bailing.'

'The airfield's excluded from the partnership.'

'His contribution enhanced its value. As you're financially stretched, you may have to offer him, say, 5 per cent of your half.'

'And have him join up with Miss Brendan Broughton to oust me? Mr Offbach, Bailing is my home.'

'I warned you this could turn unpleasant.'

'Then I won't dissolve the partnership. Not yet. Not so long as Bailing's at risk. Hold back the letter.'

He stared at her in surprise. 'It was posted last night. I thought you'd received your copy and that's why you were here.'

She was sitting at her desk when Michael burst into her office, waving Offbach's letter. 'What the hell is this?' he demanded.

'Speak to my lawyer.'

He seized her by the chin, twisting her face so she was forced to look into his eyes. 'You devious bitch!'

'What do you expect?' she snapped, forgetting Offbach's advice to say nothing. 'I can't have a partner who only speaks to me through memos.'

'And whose fault is that?' He slammed out of the room.

She sat there, trembling. The phone rang. She knew it would be Michael. 'Yes!' she yelled into the receiver.

'Ryder? It's Rupert Atheldene. Is something wrong?'

'No . . . yes . . . I mean, sorry I shouted.'

'Can you come to dinner at the Hall on Saturday night?' he asked. 'Some old friends are staying. Hadn't seen them in years, till we bumped into each other at polo.' He paused. 'I gather you know him.'

She swallowed hard. 'What's his name?'

'That's a surprise.'

'I hate surprises.'

He laughed. 'Oh, you'll like this one. Shall we say eight for eight-thirty?'

She felt as if she were at sea in a rowing boat without oars. A storm was gathering but she had no control. Her father. Michael. Now this. It had to be Patrick. The prospect of meeting his wife made her feel physically sick. Several times she reached for the telephone to cancel, only to stop. Why should she stay at home like a discarded Victorian mistress twitching curtains in a discreet flat in Maida Vale?

Atheldene Hall was ten miles from Bailing. It was reached by way of a dark wooded tunnel of dripping trees. Ryder was so nervous that she nearly drove into the undergrowth. The Hall was gloriously romantic. It was a fifteenth-century stone manor house surrounded by a moat on which exotic species of duck sailed among clusters of pink water lillies. A drawbridge was the only access. It led under a turreted gatehouse to a floodlit courtyard.

An elderly butler opened the great carved front door and Rupert stepped out, looking laconic and suave in a burgundy smoking jacket.

'Sorry I'm late.' She too was wearing a smoking jacket. A red one over black crêpe trousers. She should have worn a dress. That was obvious now.

He ushered her inside, across a vast baronial hall to an elegant drawing room where exquisite Persian rugs were scattered over uneven flagstones and uncomfortable directoire chairs faced an open fire. 'I know it's summer but I thought you ladies might be cold,' he said.

Of course Patrick's wife would be used to warmer climates.

'They'll be down in a minute. Have a sherry?'

'Thanks.' She imagined them upstairs, making love before dinner.

'Ah, here they come,' said Rupert.

Ryder dug her nails into the palms of her hand and turned to face the door.

A fairish balding man in his thirties was crossing the room, hand outstretched. With him was a dull young matron whose hair was swept into the Alice band hairstyle of the home counties. They looked prosperous, overfed, and vaguely familiar.

'Hello, Ryder,' said the man. 'This is a surprise.'

She scanned her memory as waves of relief and disappointment rolled over her.

'Don't you recognise us? I know I've lost some hair and gained a few pounds.'

'Two stone,' said his wife acidly.

'Jonathan! From the flat. And Charlotte.'

Jonathan kissed her on the cheek. 'I must admit it took me a minute. You look marvellous.'

They were interrupted by the arrival of another couple, who'd known Rupert in Hong Kong. Jonathan drew Ryder to a seat near the window. 'I was sorry to hear about you and Adam,' he said. 'And about your father. I tried to tell Rupert that you might not appreciate a surprise. But . . . er . . . I wasn't sure how much he knew.'

'I've no idea. We've only met a few times.'

'Oh, I thought . . .'

Charlotte sighed, 'Johnnie, I keep telling you not to jump to conclusions. Now, tell me, Ryder, what happened to Alix?'

'We . . . don't see much of each other.'

'I don't blame you. She was a bitch. The way she stole Adam from you was monstrous. But I liked Imogen.' Charlotte gave a pleased smile. 'People are always fascinated that we knew her before she was famous.'

Ryder said nothing. She couldn't bear to talk to Charlotte of her lost friendships.

On the Sunday afternoon Rupert drove Jonathan and Charlotte and their two sons over to Bailing to see the airfield. The boys were dressed in tweed jackets and grey flannel shorts. They looked like marionettes compared to Leo in his rolled up jeans and Chicago Bears sweatshirt. Ryder showed them the aircraft and the hangars, avoiding the school. But as they left the office, they came face to face with Michael. His eyes locked with Ryder's. She blushed and stopped, intending to introduce him. He nodded curtly and walked on.

'What a rude man!' exclaimed Charlotte in her shrillest voice. 'If he were my employee, I'd sack him.'

Without thinking, Ryder jumped to his defence. 'He's my partner and he's highly regarded in flying circles.'

They returned to Atheldene Hall for tea. Leo was entranced by the drawbridge over the moat. He begged to be given a conducted tour.

'Let's all go,' said Ryder. 'I'd love to see the house.'

Many of the bedrooms had been unused for decades but they were still beautiful. Deep-set arched windows and window seats looked down on the moat. Dust particles danced up and down in the rays of sunshine which reached across threadbare carpets. Heavy velvet drapes adorned four-poster beds.

'My father refused to have the place renovated,' said Rupert. 'But I intend to.'

'Will you live here?' asked Ryder, fingering the midnight blue curtains looped back from a half-tester. The colour was fading. The gold brocade had come unstitched.

'One day.' He stepped closer. 'The others seem to have abandoned us.'

'Yes.' She could feel his breath on the back of her neck.

He slid his arms around her, drawing her nearer. She leaned against him, enjoying the physical closeness. 'Have you ever made love in a four-poster?' he murmured.

She shook her head.

'It's very erotic.' He kissed the side of her neck. She stiffened. 'What's wrong?' he asked.

'Leo might come.'

'We'll hear him.' He slid his hands inside the bodice of her jumpsuit, moving the zip slowly downwards.

She seized his wrist to stop him. 'You've forgotten Jonathan and Charlotte?'

'Oh, they'll be fighting.' He bit her ear lobe. 'She's just found out he's been a naughty boy with his secretary, that's why she's so acerbic.'

'I don't blame her. Will they divorce?'

'Of course not!' His fingers played with the lace of her brassiere. 'Lots of men play around but they don't leave their wives.'

She zipped up her jumpsuit. 'Rupert, I'm sorry but . . . maybe I am involved after all.'

She waited for Michael in his office at the school. He was late. She fiddled nervously with his paperclips. Finally, she heard his car. Then his footsteps. He flung open the door. 'What are you doing here?'

'I have to talk to you.'

He tossed his briefcase on to a chair. 'At first I thought you were trying to get rid of me to make way for your father.'

'You know I don't want him here.'

'Now it appears you prefer that degenerate borzoi, Rupert Atheldene.' He gave a derisive snort. 'Not that it matters. Neither has the money to buy me out. Nor do you.' He opened the door for her to leave. 'If you want to talk, contact my lawyer. If you want to save Bailing, start thinking fast!'

The days ticked on towards her father's release. Occasionally Ryder would meet Michael in the hangars or the doorway to the office, and they'd pass without speaking whilst Violet and Fred shook their heads and sighed.

'We're still waiting to hear from Ashby's solicitor,' Offbach told her. 'I gather they're waiting for his final instructions.'

'We must reach agreement within ten days.' Ryder paced the room, the telephone in one hand, the receiver in the other. 'My father comes out of gaol in a fortnight. He'll manipulate the situation. Then I'll have all of them against me.'

She couldn't sleep. She couldn't concentrate. She couldn't work. There was no point in doing anything if she were to lose Bailing. She tried to keep her anxiety from Leo and believed she had succeeded, until one night when she prowled the house in the grip of nervous insomnia she saw a thin ribbon of light under his door.

He was sitting up in bed, reading. 'You should be asleep,' she said. 'It's nearly three.'

325

He gave her the white look of his early years. 'If we lose Bailing where will we live?'

She took the book from him and laid it on the table. 'Michael and I have had a slight disagreement. Nothing serious.'

'That's not what you told Mr Backoff.'

'Offbach! And you shouldn't eavesdrop.' She sat down on the end of his bed. 'Don't worry.' She made her voice sound confident. 'Whatever happens, your home is with me.'

He pulled the bedclothes over his head and said in a muffled voice, which she knew meant he was crying, 'Bailing's my home.'

In the early morning drizzle Ryder paced the runway. Bailing was hers. She had painted the hangars stroke by stroke, her hands rough and sore from the spirit-based paint. She had dug ancient putty from the window frames in the control tower, then painstakingly fitted each sheet of glass. She and Leo had slept in the Land-Rover, cooked on a gas ring, and bathed in the river. She, not Michael Ashby, had weeded the runway, pulling at the stubborn ragwort with her bare hands.

She drove to Michael's house. She didn't want to go, but for Leo's sake she had to confront him. It was raining hard as she dashed from her car to the porch and thumped the old brass bell. The sound echoed through the house. She waited, stamping her wet feet, irritated to note that he'd found time to buy a new doormat.

There was no answer, so she tried the door. It wasn't locked. Not that that was strange. Michael treated possessions generously, believing that they were only lent, and that the pool of worldly treasures should be shared because you couldn't take them with you, even if the pharaohs thought you could.

She stood in the oak-panelled hall and shouted, 'Michael!'

The only reply was the water dripping off the roof on to the wooden porch from which the old lepidopterist had watched his precious butterflies. She crossed to the desk in the study, took a piece of paper from the top drawer, and prepared to write a note. Then her eyes fell on the letter lying on top of the typewriter. It was signed by Michael and addressed to his solicitor. *'With regard to Bailing airfield, I shall pursue everything to which I am entitled, even if it means dispossessing Miss Harding.'*

Beside it lay an envelope, stamped and ready to be posted.

Cold sweat rolled down Ryder's face as she stared at the words. She wanted to cry. She wanted to kill him. With the letter in her hands, she hurried to the front door. Then she stopped. He'd find it gone and write another. She reread the lines. The phrases blurred. Then they reformed. She crossed to the typewriter.

Michael caught up with her in the narrow twisting lane by the bridge. Ryder saw him approach in her driving mirror and accelerated. But his Land-Rover was faster than the airfield pickup. He roared up behind her, so close that she could see the dark pools of his eyes. Then suddenly he clipped her back bumper. Not so hard as to push her off the road but enough to shake her. She swore and gripped the steering wheel. He did it again. This time she missed the corner and skidded sideways into a gateway, her back wheels spinning impotently in the mud.

'You could have killed me!' she yelled at him.

'You deserve it.' He opened her door and dragged her out, his fingers digging into her upper arm. He forced her against the pickup and held up the letter ' *"I shall NOT pursue everything to which I am entitled if that means dispossessing Miss Harding."* How dare you sneak into my house and alter my words!'

327

'I didn't. I came to see you. I wanted to make peace. But what do you expect, when you try to take Bailing?'

'You forged my letter.'

'You tried to steal my home. My livelihood. I renovated that place with my bare hands. It's mine. You want half of everything else. You can have it. But not Bailing.' Tears of rage and desperation filled her eyes. She pulled away. He let her go.

'I never intended to take your precious airfield,' he shouted. 'I couldn't. Surely your solicitor told you that.'

'But you told me I had to think quick to save Bailing.'

'I was angry.'

They stared at each other in silence. Then she stepped into the pickup and laid her arms on the steering wheel, burying her face in them. 'I despised my father for being dishonest,' she said. 'But I'm no better than he is.'

Michael reached out his hand to stroke her tangled hair. 'What happened is as much my fault. I was trying to teach you a lesson — because I love you.'

31

On an overcast morning Ryder and Michael waited in
the car outside Ford Prison.

'I hope he's not going to be upset Leo isn't here,' she
said anxiously.

'You couldn't force him to come.' He squeezed her
hand. 'Everything's going to be all right.'

She scanned the drab sprawl of prison buildings. They
looked like an army encampment erected in a hurry by
someone who didn't have to live there. Suddenly a door
opened. Her father appeared. He walked towards the
gate. Ryder stepped from the car. He waved casually,
calling out, 'Good of you to come,' as if he were a
businessman being met at Heathrow by his family, not
a man who'd been in gaol for over five years.

But Ryder knew him better now. She too faced situ-
ations by pretending not to care. She kissed him on each
cheek. 'This is Michael Ashby,' she said.

Her father's eyes flicked over Michael. 'Thanks for
driving her down. You won't mind if we sit in the back
and talk privately.'

He barely drew breath all the way to London. He
talked of the people he would contact, the places he
would visit, and the magnificent party he would give to
celebrate his release. 'You'll be my hostess.' He patted
Ryder on the shoulder. 'I'll give you a list of guests to
invite.'

She opened her mouth to respond that there were no

friends left, then caught Michael's eye in the driving mirror and said nothing.

As her father had requested, she'd arranged an appointment with his tailor and booked a suite at the Savoy. It looked out over the gardens to the river. 'I asked them to serve lunch here.' She indicated the laid table near the window.

'But I wanted Simpson's. I want to see people.'

'We want to talk to you,' said Michael firmly, ringing for a bottle of champagne.

Her father's jawline hardened. 'Look, son, I appreciate all you've done for my daughter but from now on it'll be her and me making the decisions. I gave her Bailing. I plan to live there. So I suggest you start looking for a job.'

'I'm afraid you're wrong,' said Ryder as gently as she could. 'Michael and I run Bailing. You see, we were married yesterday.'

32

Frankie and Susan got married in the church beside the lake in Pioneer Park. Shimmering in white silk, Susan walked up the aisle on her father's arm. Her eyes sparkled. Her brown curls gleamed beneath the lace of her veil. Ryder remembered her own hurried wedding in King's Lynn Registry Office with two unknown witnesses grabbed from the street, and she felt robbed.

'Everyone thinks your husband's great,' Debbie whispered in her ear. 'He's very attractive.'

'Is he?'

'Surely you think so.' Debbie gave her a puzzled frown.

She looked at Michael. Sometimes she found it hard to believe that she'd married him. It had happened so quickly. That was her fault, not his. She had been obsessed with Bailing, her father, Leo's anxiety, and the dishonest depths to which her desperation had driven her. When Michael said he loved her, she'd seen him as her only saviour. But she'd missed out on the yearning and the heartbreak which she regarded as an essential part of love.

Her grandfather was sitting between Debbie and her mother. It choked Ryder to see him, gnarled hands clasped, mind like an empty coffin. On the other side of the aisle were Susan's family. Teddy had pretended not to see her. She studied him out of the corner of her eye. Compared to Michael, he looked like a pink overweight puppy. She wondered how she could have been attracted to him.

The service ended. Frankie and Susan started back down the aisle. As they drew level her grandfather reached for Susan's veil. 'Greta!' he whispered.

Gently Michael took him by the shoulders and held him in his place whilst the bridal pair moved on. The disturbance had happened so quickly that most people were unaware of it.

'Thanks,' said Frankie, later at Scot's Farm, shaking Michael by the hand. 'We shouldn't have taken him but he's family and we wanted him present.' He grinned at Ryder. 'Susan and I were sure you and Michael would get together one day.'

'I can't think how!' She walked away.

Michael followed her. He gripped her wrist and hissed, 'I put up with your moods at home but don't ever put me down in public again.'

That night he made love to her angrily — and she responded with equal anger.

Michael liked Scot's Farm and Prairieville. He sat on the porch with her grandfather, keeping him silent company. He helped Debbie clear out the barn. He went fishing with Doctor Jeff.

'You're very lucky,' said Debbie one morning when they were alone in the kitchen.

'I know.'

'I don't think you do.'

To avoid being questioned further, Ryder borrowed a bicycle and pedalled over to Fox Lake. The dirt track was full of puddles. Muddy water splashed her legs. The trees were coming into bud. Their spring leaves were fresh and soft. She sat on the end of the old wooden jetty and looked across at the island. Had the White Squaw felt trapped?

For the first time she was sorry to return to Bailing. It seemed so small, so constricting.

'We thought you and Michael'd be gone at least three weeks,' said Fred, shaking his head in disapproval. 'You could have had a late honeymoon.'

'We don't need one.'

'No wedding party. No honeymoon. Next you'll say you don't want youngsters.'

'We don't!'

She went to the tower and began to sort through her clothes. She still hadn't moved all of her possessions to the Butterfly House, as if by keeping them at the tower she did not completely live with Michael. Violet came to the door. 'Miss Brendan Broughton died,' she said. 'Her funeral was last week.' She fiddled with the door handle. 'Patrick came looking for you.'

'What did he say?'

'He didn't know you were married.'

'Is he . . . still at the mill?'

'He went back to America the day after the funeral.' Violet buttoned up her pink cardigan. 'And a good thing too, if you ask me!'

Ryder drove up to Morston. A sharp wind was whipping up the water in the creeks. It rattled the halliards on the dinghies and lashed at the marram grass. As she followed the path to the rickety bridge, she wondered what Patrick thought of her marriage.

It was late when she returned, not to the control tower which she still regarded as her home but to the Butterfly House. Michael came in shortly afterwards. 'I'm starving,' he said. 'What's for supper?'

She was lying on the sofa staring into space. 'Nothing. I'm bored with cooking.'

'I've told you to ask Mrs Dennshurst to find us someone to clean and cook.' He reached for her hand. 'All right. We'll eat out.'

She rolled over and closed her eyes. 'Take Leo. I'm

not hungry.' She was being a bitch and she hated it, but she couldn't stop.

She decided to take Leo to visit her father in Marbella. Michael came home to find her packing. 'This is very sudden,' he said.

'It's time Leo got to know his father.'

'Don't you think we should have discussed it?'

She thumped down the lid of her suitcase. 'Am I allowed no private life!'

'Are you sure it has nothing to do with your new co-owner — or did you think I wasn't aware that you now share your precious Bailing with Patrick Brendan?'

She picked up her bag. 'If I were planning to commit adultery, I'd hardly take Leo.'

'Be unfaithful to me once,' he said, 'and I'll break your bloody neck!'

Her father met them at Malaga, looking every inch the wealthy expatriate businessman. It was Ryder's second visit to him in Spain. After his release, he'd spent less than a month in London, discovering that former friends were all away on holiday or mysteriously failed to receive his messages. Without telling Ryder, he flew out to Spain. He telephoned one day and casually informed her that he'd bought a villa not far from their previous one, on the seaward side of the coast road between Marbella and Puerto Banus. It was in a prime location, set amid pine trees with views out to sea. How he'd paid for it, Ryder didn't know. She didn't want to know. But it infuriated her to see him now, suave and suntanned, chatting about golf and tennis, whilst she had trapped herself into marriage with Michael in order to keep her father from Bailing.

'I've invited a couple of people to join us for dinner,' he told Ryder a little too casually when they reached the villa. 'Jack and Sue who lived next door and Christina, a German friend. The four of us play tennis every morning.' He leaned on the terrace rail, a whisky sour in one

334

hand, and waved to Leo who was swimming. 'I must teach him to play. We'll have a father and son match. Perhaps you could leave him out here for a few days. Christina has a son a year older. He can fly home with Jack on Friday.'

Ryder hesitated.

Her father turned to face her. 'I wouldn't try to keep him if that's what you're afraid of.'

Before she had time to answer a voice called from the garden. Her father smiled and waved. 'Ah, here comes Christina.'

A tall, sinewy woman with her mother's exact honey colouring and blue eyes came up the terrace steps. 'How nice to meet you at last,' she said in a guttural voice, smiling at Ryder and holding out a well-manicured hand. 'Paul is always talking about his children, aren't you, darling?'

Ryder pictured her mother's grave among the dripping yew trees.

She flew home a day early. Of course it was childish to expect her father never to look at another woman but she couldn't help being upset.

Michael was at the airfield when Ryder arrived at the Butterfly House but she didn't telephone him. She sat in the rocking chair on the verandah, watching the drizzle and imagining her father and Christina, arms linked, laughing on the tennis court. The French windows opened. She didn't turn round. She recognised his tread. He stepped in front of her and leaned against the wooden column of the verandah roof. 'Do you want a divorce?' he asked coldly.

The wild garden blurred before her eyes. She swallowed hard and tried to answer. Then she rocked forward, burying her face in her knees to hide her tears.

He lifted her from the chair and carried her inside, his powerful arms holding her as if she were a baby. He carried her upstairs and into their bedroom, laying her

335

gently on the bed. He kissed her wet face, holding her head tightly in his hands so that she was forced to look at him. 'I was a fool to marry you,' he said. 'I knew why you were doing it. I should have remembered that no one, especially someone like you, likes to feel beholden. But I loved you. I still do. Only I'm not prepared to carry on this way.'

'I wish we'd waited,' she said miserably.

'Why didn't you say so at the time?'

'I was scared of losing Bailing.'

'At least that's honest.'

'And ashamed of tampering with your letter.'

He released her and stood up. 'Shall I instruct my solicitor in the morning?'

He was her friend. They'd shared a bed, Bailing, their hopes. They'd laughed and fought together. Her face crumpled at the thought of losing him. 'Don't go,' she said.

He gathered her in his arms and kissed her gently, drawing her to him. She clung to him, wanting his strength to blot out the woman who was trying to take her mother's place. He traced a pattern with his mouth, down between her breasts and across the flat of her stomach. She remembered Adam, who'd judged her on their intimacy. She thought of Alix and Immy, and pulled Michael to her because she was scared of losing him as well.

They made love in the pale light of a wet summer evening. He held her thighs and looked into her face as he entered her. He pulled her on to him and steadied her at the waist as she rode him, her hair tangled and sticky with perspiration. He rolled her on to her stomach and mounted her from behind, grinding her into the bed, thrusting and animal. Then he turned her to face him, and made love to her tenderly. To her body, her mouth, her eyes, kissing her when she cried with the first pulse, holding back until she was ready, until she could not stop.

Afterwards they went out into the soft rain and stood, stark naked and laughing, with their faces upturned and their arms outstretched. The mud squelched up between their toes. The smell of wet earth permeated their nostrils. In the dripping undergrowth at the bottom of the garden a small animal squealed in fright.

'We've forgotten about Leo,' said Michael suddenly.

'He stayed on with father for a few days.' She dropped her arms and turned towards the house, her shoulders hunched dejectedly. 'Father has a girlfriend. A German divorcee with a son whom Leo thinks is marvellous. I never thought father'd replace my mother. It's as if she never existed.'

'Is that why you came home early?'

'Yes.' She crossed the verandah, her wet feet leaving their mark on the wooden boards.

Michael kicked her rocking chair as he passed it: he'd thought she'd come home early to see him.

Their relationship returned to the banter of before their marriage, the difference being they now shared a bed. Constantly. As if the sex between them were a drug which they were each afraid of losing. Once, she cried out to him, as he drew her through a barrier of exquisite pain, 'You're the best.' But he said nothing, and she was left to believe that for him there were others better than her.

The airfields did reasonably well in spite of the continued recession. After a fuel price hike of 15 per cent the previous year, when they had lost a number of clients, costs remained fairly stable. At $2.44, the pound was at its strongest against the dollar. As soon as Leo was settled into the senior school, Michael took Ryder to New York for a belated five-day honeymoon. That was all the time they could spare. He'd flown there frequently when working for Colossus, she'd only passed through. For weeks beforehand she talked excitedly of the shops, the theatres, the opera. Everything which did not exist at Bailing.

They flew on Concorde, and as the cabin mach meter topped 750 miles and they passed through the sound barrier, Ryder reached for his hand. 'We have fun, don't we?'

'That's what life's about,' he answered lightly, as if he'd never wanted to kick her rocking chair.

They stayed at the Plaza, on the corner of Fifth Avenue and Central Park. It had the timeless elegance of the French renaissance, with wide corridors lit by crystal chandeliers and white marble fireplaces. Their suite looked down on the tree tops of Central Park, turning to gold in the approach of winter. They reminded Ryder of Fox Lake.

She pressed her nose against the window pane. 'I've stayed here before,' she said in a small voice. 'With my mother, when I was four or five. I'd forgotten the name but I recognised the front steps. We were on our way to Prairieville. She wanted to do some shopping. I remember we had tea downstairs in the Palm Court dining room. She was wearing a pale gold suit. It matched her hair. She looked beautiful. I was so proud to be with her. Then I knocked the milk jug over and she sent me to my room.'

He put his arms around her. 'Would you prefer another hotel?'

'No.' She leaned against him. 'I just wish she could see I'm not so clumsy now.'

They went out to explore the jingle jangle streets of brightly lit shops, metal-edged pavements and potholes. Elegant women stepped from stretch limousines, ageing intellectuals searched the open air bookstalls of Fifth Avenue for obscure biographies, and fierce joggers pounded through Central Park, their rubber-soled trainers slipping on the damp fallen leaves. They sat in a glass fronted bar and wrote their duty postcards: to Leo, Fred, Violet.

'I'm not mentioning Christina on father's,' said Ryder, pursing her lips.

'Good. Another family row.'

She bristled. 'So you think it's funny?'

'No.' He took her hand and held it tight even though she tried to snatch it away. 'But your father's sixty. He's going to have girlfriends. The sooner you accept it, the less unhappy you'll be.'

'I can't bear the way she paws him and darlings him.'

He touched her cheek. 'I'm on your side.'

She softened. 'I should hope so! This is our honeymoon.'

They watched purposeful people walking fast, and felt deliciously unpurposeful. Then they went back to their hotel and made love, whilst out in the night streets a police siren howled, adding danger and piquancy.

Next morning as they wandered down Fifth Avenue, they passed a travel agency advertising cut fares to Europe. 'Laker seems to be succeeding,' said Ryder.

Michael chuckled. 'I thought we weren't going to talk business.'

'At £59 a single fare, even Violet's planning to visit a cousin in New Jersey, and she's never been abroad before.'

'If I started an airline I wouldn't go for the bottom of the market, like Laker,' said Michael. 'I'd make mine a little more expensive but give a full service. You can't book a seat on Skytrain. Business travellers and people with a fortnight's holiday can't risk hanging around airports for days on end.'

'You've thought it all out, haven't you.' She slid her hand under his jacket and tickled him. 'And where would we fly from? Not Bailing.'

'It would have to be Gatwick. Heathrow's a closed

shop. This end, I'd choose Kennedy. The name has more kudos than Newark, and LaGuardia doesn't have a long enough runway. JFK also has the connecting flights. Gatwick and Heathrow are 75 per cent "O & D" — originate and destinate — but here the Eastern Seaboard airports are gateways.' He paused and laughed at his own intensity. 'Of course it's just a dream. We'd have to do a lot of ground research and even then it might not be feasible.'

She raised her hand to halt a passing cab, and told the driver, 'Kennedy Airport, please!'

John F. Kennedy Airport was opened in July 1948 on the site of the Idlewild Golf Course: it was later renamed after President Kennedy. There were nine terminals: eight belonging to specific airlines, and the International Arrivals Building for some forty other international carriers. 'This is the one we'd have to use,' said Michael as they watched an aircraft taxi through the complex of runways.

She pulled a face. 'It looks like a main drain leaning against a coffee table. What's wrong with the spaceship next door?'

He ruffled her hair. 'I don't think even you could persuade Pan Am to relinquish their building.'

From the Port Authority they obtained fact sheets and brochures. Apart from the nine terminals feeding passengers to over a hundred gate positions, there were cargo-handling buildings, aircraft servicing hangars, customs, immigration, security, not to mention the nine miles of runway, twenty-two miles of taxiway, and fifty miles of underground pipe carrying thirty-two million gallons of aviation fuel.

'No one would believe how we've spent our five days,' said Ryder as they staggered back to the hotel on their last evening, having walked all day. 'Did I wear my smart clothes, go to the theatre, eat in top restaurants?

No, I wore jeans and trainers and I ate in the airport cafeteria.' She flopped on to their bed.

He lay down beside her. 'And are you exhausted by my continual and passionate lovemaking?'

'No.' She snuggled into his shoulder. 'My feet hurt.'

33

Ryder and Michael had been home barely a week when they went to see Oliver Offbach — or Backoff as Leo called him. 'If you don't like him, we won't use him,' Ryder told Michael as the lift whisked them up to the lawyer's luxury office. 'We'll just ask him to register the company.'

He checked his tie in the mirror. It was navy with a thin, burgundy stripe. Ryder had bought it in a boutique at the Plaza. It looked very smart with his charcoal grey suit and crisp white shirt. She smiled. She was proud to be with him. 'If I mention cattle, it means I approve,' he said.

'Cattle!' she laughed. 'He'll think we're mad.'

'We are.' He kissed her fiercely.

Offbach gave them his contained smile. 'Another airfield?' he asked, waving them to the chairs before his desk.

'An airline.' Michael opened his briefcase and took out their calculations. 'We'd like you to register the company.'

Offbach picked up a pen. 'Name?'

'Anglo Atlantic Airways,' said Ryder.

'It has a nice ring.'

'Doesn't it!' Ryder was pink with excitement.

Offbach's thin lips twitched. 'You know you'll have to obtain a licence from our Civil Aviation Authority and the US Federal Aviation Administration, and that is not easy.'

Michael relaxed into his chair. He was speaking to a man who knew his world. 'The other airlines will all file objections, as they did with Skytrain. But if we can prove we're competent, safe, financially secure, and that there's a demand for seats, there's no reason why we should fail.'

'A second Colossus?' asked Offbach.

'Not at all. We'll treat our passengers like guests.' Michael winked at Ryder. 'They treat theirs like cattle.'

Whilst Offbach registered the name of Anglo Atlantic at Companies House, Michael and Ryder wrote to the CAA for an application form. They kept their idea secret, working on it only at the Butterfly House whilst Leo slumped in front of the television or wrote long letters to Christina's son, Stefan.

'When this project is underway, we'll do something nice with you,' Ryder told him, wishing she knew more people with boys of his age.

He gave her a sullen look. 'When?' And walked out of the room.

The application form arrived and they drafted their reply, spreading their papers over every surface in Michael's study.

'To run an airline,' he explained, 'we need an Airport Transport Licence because we're offering carriage for payment and an Air Operator's Certificate to prove we're safe and competent. That's the tough one. We have to satisfy the CAA that our planes aren't going to crash or our passengers be stuck halfway round the world because we've gone bankrupt.'

She nodded and tried not to feel guilty about Leo.

'They'll want proof of finance, data showing demand for seats, costings to show fares justify outgoings, details of aircraft, and service and maintenance arrangements here and in the US.' He paused. 'And the minute the CAA publish our application, every airline that flies that route will file an objection. Especially Colossus.'

'You sound less convinced than you did at Backoff's,' she said.

'I just want to be sure you realise that starting an airline is a catch 22. We have to be ready to fly before the CAA will consider us. To prepare our application will cost us a lot of time and money. And they could still turn us down for our AOC — Air Operator's Certificate.'

She rolled the draft application into the typewriter and next to *applicant* she typed *ANGLO ATLANTIC AIRWAYS LIMITED*.

He leaned across the table and said, 'I love you.'

They spent all evening on the first question. Michael opted to be Managing Director. He was also to be Financial Director. 'I want to run the company, I don't mind whether I'm its figurehead,' he said. 'You're Chairman. You have public flair. Look how you put Bailing on the map.'

She opened a packet of cashew nuts and together they ate them. 'What about other directors?' she said.

'We'll need a Sales & Commercial Director to sell seats, a Marketing Director to reach the public, and a Cabin Services Manager in charge of crew, food, drink and duty free, and many, many others. But not now. Later!'

As they collapsed exhausted into bed, she said, 'I've decided on the company colour.'

'Bright purple and shocking pink?'

'No, idiot!' She rolled into his warmth. 'Black and red.'

They continued working on their application whenever they could, arguing over each word. Finance. Routes. Aircraft.

'A 747,' said Michael. 'Has to be. They carry five hundred passengers and twenty tons of freight.'

'Laker uses a DC10.'

'We need the freight space off-peak.'

She typed BOEING 747. 'How much will this jumbo cost?'

'A new one, seventy-five million dollars. But Boeing should have a good second hand one for twenty-seven to thirty mill. With the dollar down to 2.44, that's about twelve million pounds.'

'Supposing the pound weakens?'

'We'll try to build a safeguard into our loan.'

She remembered the days when she'd washed in the river. 'Twelve million! Can we raise so much?'

'The aircraft is its own collateral. The seats, so long as we sell them, will repay the loan. Starting up is our big cost. We'll use our joint airfields as collateral. Hopefully they're worth enough.'

She hesitated, then said, 'As a last resort, include Bailing.'

'Are you sure?'

She linked her fingers through his. 'If I'm not prepared to take a risk to catch a dream I may as well be dead!'

Now that Ryder no longer lived on the airfield, they'd employed a security guard who lived in the converted ammunition hut near the clubhouse. The tower had been turned into offices for herself and Michael, whilst the bedrooms were used by staff who worked the summer season. Gradually the Butterfly House had become her home. She no longer hankered for the tower. In fact, it was a relief to have some privacy.

Bruja was moving too. Her stable had become unsafe after the big flood. One morning, Ryder, Fred and Leo gave her a special carrot and apple breakfast, and walked her down the lane to the farm where she was to share retirement with two elderly carthorses.

'I'll miss her,' said Ryder, leading her into the field and removing the halter.

'She'll be happier with other horses.' Fred slapped the old pony on the rump, and she ambled off without a backward glance.

'So much for gratitude!' said Ryder. Bruja wasn't just a part of Bailing, she was a reminder of the early days and of her desperate, consuming love for Patrick.

She and Michael consulted Offbach frequently and grew to appreciate his cold, incisive mind. They invited him to lunch at the Waldorf and said, 'We'd very much like you to be a non-executive director.'

He looked from one to the other. 'I'm flattered.'

'We won't be offended if you don't want to,' said Ryder hurriedly.

'No. I'd like it.' He came as close to a smile as he was able.

Afterwards, Ryder said, 'I wonder if there's a Mrs Backoff?'

'Her name's Felicity and they have one son of Leo's age.' Michael pinched her knee. 'So there! Miss Nosy!'

Anglo Atlantic needed a London office: they could hardly run an international airline from Bailing. Whilst Michael worked on the data, Ryder spent days looking over premises, all of which were too expensive.

'I'm going to ask Jonathan's advice,' she told Michael over supper.

'The friend of your ex-fiancé and the degenerate borzoi?'

She flicked a raw mushroom at him. 'If we're going to tell other people, we should tell Fred and Violet — and Leo. They'll be so hurt otherwise.'

He frowned. 'I'm against it. Jonathan'll be bound by professional ethics. They won't be. If they talk, they could blow the whole thing.'

'They've never let me down.' She opened the dining room door, and before he could stop her, called, 'Leo! Come and hear about our airline.'

Jonathan suggested they try to buy a warehouse in Battersea or Vauxhall, but even those were too expensive. As they crossed Tower Bridge on their way home, Ryder sat up. 'Let's try the docks.'

Michael turned down into Wapping, along a potholed road past drab blocks of council flats and dreary patches of litter-strewn grass, till they came to Wapping High Street. It was cobbled and Dickensian. From those few warehouses in use, pale light reached out to touch the damp street. The others, once busy with grain and dried fruit, had broken windows, filthy internal stone steps, and missing iron banisters. A bicycle from which both wheels had been stolen was chained to a railing. Two rats were fighting over a fish-head. A used prophylactic hung in the lower branches of a small bush.

'I wonder how much they cost,' said Ryder.

'With or without the rats?'

'Don't joke! They're spacious. Central. With six storeys, we could turn the top into a penthouse for ourselves. We need a London base.'

'You'd be mugged and raped from the moment you arrived. So would every girl who worked for us — if we could get them to come.'

'We'll employ the people who live here. There must be plenty of unemployed in an area like this.' She took his face in her hands and made him look at her. 'I have an instinct about it. Woman's intuition.'

'Very well.' He kissed the soft palm of her hand. 'Find one you like, get a quote to refurbish, and the Financial Director will consider it.'

She rested her head against the back of the seat and prepared for the long journey home.

'I'm only playing the devil's advocate,' he said, some time later. 'I don't want to see you hurt.' He smiled at her, but Ryder wasn't listening. She was wondering where Immy was tonight.

They sent in their application to the CAA. Taking it

347

in turns to hold the envelope, they delivered it to Bailing Post Office. Then they went home and made love.

In the period before their application was published, they discussed their approaches to the Departments of Transport in Britain and the US, and held preliminary meetings with the British Airports Authority at Gatwick. When Michael flew to New York to talk to the Port Authority, Ryder reluctantly stayed behind because they were busy. She longed to go, particularly as Frankie and Susan were now living in Manhattan: he'd just started his first flying job, with a small freight company. She was in her office at the control tower when the telephone rang and a woman's voice said, 'Mrs Ashby, this is Miss Criffelbrook . . . Leo's headmistress. Could you come and see me this afternoon?'

'Is Leo all right?' asked Ryder anxiously.

'Yes, but I'd like to talk to you.'

Miss Criffelbrook was a large, stern woman in her late fifties. She'd been the headmistress of Bailing Senior School for many years. It had a rural catchment area stretching far beyond the little village. Grown men with children of their own still reached to pull their socks up when Miss Criffelbrook passed in her elderly Morris Minor.

She was at her desk when Ryder arrived. 'We're having problems with Leo,' she said. 'He's a bright artistic boy but he doesn't mix and you're not helping.' She frowned at Ryder, who was glad she'd changed into a sensible skirt. 'You're giving him far too much pocket money.'

'Three pounds a week!'

'Mrs Ashby, when he returned to school after his half term in Spain he had two hundred cigarettes, a gold Dupont lighter, and a hundred pounds. He's been buying friends.'

Ryder waited for Leo to come out of school. She noticed that he walked apart from the other boys. He

348

looked suspicious when he saw her but asked nothing. Once they were clear of the school, she said, 'I suppose father gave you the money.'

'Why shouldn't I have it?' he snapped. 'I'm the son of a millionaire.'

'You're the son of an ex-convict and if father has money, it's dishonestly come by.'

'You're jealous because he didn't give you any.'

She gripped the steering wheel to stop herself from slapping him. 'I don't need to buy friends.'

Tears filled his eyes. 'I hate you. I hate my school. But you don't care.'

'What have I been doing all these years?'

'You don't want me. All you do is criticise. Christina never does. I want to go to school with Stefan. I want to live with father.'

'And grow up to believe that money buys everything!'

'At least they have time for me!' He slammed out of the car and ran into the house.

She sat in the car, her head bowed.

Michael returned, full of Anglo Atlantic. She met him at Heathrow. When she saw him again, she realised how much she'd missed him.

'I spoke to Boeing,' he told her, when they reached the car. 'Just a preliminary chat. They're happy to see us in London, New York or Seattle.'

'Oh . . . good.'

'You don't sound very enthusiastic.'

'I'm sorry.' She paused to pay the car park. 'I've had a row with Leo. I didn't mean to tell you till we reached home.' She recounted her visit to the headmistress and the drive home, ending with, 'He says I don't have time for him and all I do is criticise. He could have been me accusing my father.'

'He has a point.'

'Thanks for the support! I thought you at least would back me up.'

'So you want me to tell you that you're right when you're wrong?'

'I should have known you'd agree I'm like father. I expect you still check your letters to make sure I don't tamper with them.' She braked hard to avoid hitting the car in front and clipped a bollard.

'Pull over!' he shouted. 'I may be tired but I don't want to be dead.'

'I'm all right!' She wished she hadn't bothered to meet him. Without saying another word, she put her foot down hard and drove non-stop to Norfolk.

In Michael's absence she'd had the driveway raked, the lawn mown, the rough grass in the orchard scythed, and a quote to turn the small paddock into a tennis court: things they'd planned to do but never had time to organise. He made no comment and went to bed. She prowled the house, angry and disappointed. Finally, she lay down on one of the spareroom beds.

She was woken by Michael shouting, 'Why the hell did you tell your father about Anglo Atlantic?'

She sat up. 'I didn't.'

'He just telephoned to ask for more details.'

'I did not tell him!' She got off the bed.

'So he's telepathic!' Michael marched downstairs.

'I told him.' Leo was standing in the doorway in his dressing gown. He looked frightened.

'But I asked you not to!' She stopped when he flinched, took a deep breath, and said, 'I'm going to have a shower. Get dressed. We'll talk about it at breakfast.'

Michael was drinking coffee and reading the newspapers in the breakfast room, which looked out over the old herb garden. There was a bowl of wild daffodils in the centre of the table. She'd picked them yesterday, knowing how he liked their herald to approaching spring. Now she wished she hadn't bothered.

'Leo told father,' she said, sitting down. 'And before you say anything, I know that's my fault too. I trusted him.' She rested her elbows on the table and glared at the daffodils.

He laid down his newspaper. 'I'm against Leo living with your father but I think he should be offered the alternative of a better school. Somewhere his drawing will be encouraged. Then, if he likes, he can spend part of each holidays with your father. That's my advice. Do you want it? Or do you want me to tell you you're always right?'

She frowned. He laughed. She plucked a daffodil from the bowl and threw it at him. He caught it in mid-air and kissed its yellow trumpet, and said, 'I did notice.'

34

The CAA published their weekly list of Scheduled Service Applications. Sitting side by side in his study, Michael and Ryder read their entry: *From ANGLO ATLANTIC AIRWAYS LIMITED, for the carriage of passengers, cargo and mail on the LONDON (GATWICK) — NEW YORK (KENNEDY) sector.*

He kissed her nose. 'Now we wait for Colossus to object. They have twenty-one days. Then it's on to the CAA financial hearing, our first of many hurdles. I suggest we use the time to check out Boeing.'

She went to the door and called, 'Leo! Come and see our airline's name in print.'

He came in, hands stuffed in his pockets, still nervous, his face with its white look. 'They've started on the tennis court,' he said.

'Then we'd better go into King's Lynn to buy you a racket,' said Michael. 'That is, if you'd like me to teach you.'

On the day before their departure for Seattle, Ryder heard of two warehouses, one at fifty thousand and the other at sixty-five. Leaving Violet to meet Mrs Trumpet at the station, she abandoned her packing and raced down to London. The first warehouse, the more expensive, was in a reasonable condition but it had no river frontage. The second was on the river but it was in a disgusting state. Every window was broken. Every stair cracked. Each floor was merely one huge concrete space with walls dripping with damp. But the view was magnificent. From its windows the turrets of Tower Bridge could be seen rising into the western sky.

She called Jonathan at his office. 'I'm consulting you professionally. I've found a warehouse. I need to know if it's sound and how much to refurbish.'

'Ryder, you demanding woman, I'm very busy for the next . . .'

'I'll see you on site in an hour.'

He met her in the dank entrance to the building. 'I don't know why I came,' he grumbled as she showed him the second warehouse. 'You're mad. Absolutely barking.'

'Is it sound?'

'It appears so but I'd have to do a full structural survey.'

'What price to turn it into smart open plan offices with a penthouse on the top?'

'Half a million. Maybe a little less. You'd need plumbing, electrics, heating, new roof, fire safety, lifts, internal walls, new stairs. Then there's the decor.'

'How long, if your firm were to do it?'

'Absolute minimum, men working overtime, six months — once we have planning permission.'

'Four months.' She jumped into her car and rolled down the window. 'Call with the results of the survey. I want to sign on this within a fortnight.'

Boeing's 747 factory was at Everett, some twenty-five miles up the coast from Seattle. It had been built in the late sixties especially for the 747 programme. Seven hundred and eighty acres of forest had been cleared to create the giant of the skies. Ryder slipped her hand into Michael's as the limousine carried them northwards, swishing up the coastal highway, the Puget Sound on one side, forest-covered mountains on the other.

They turned off the highway and into the 747 complex, skirting offices, hangars, test areas, and acres of concrete where the huge jets stood in lines looking like deceptively benign sharks. They were met in reception by two senior salesmen who ushered them into a spacious office. The men from Boeing talked new aircraft and new designs. Michael talked old favourites.

'I love the 727,' he mused, 'but she seats less than two hundred.'

'So you're talking 747?' said Boeing.

'Thinking along those lines.'

'There may — I say may — be an aircraft soon to be returned,' said the older salesman. 'Twenty-one thousand flying hours on the clock. One careful owner.'

'Who?'

'Mr Ashby, sir, I don't believe there's a rivet made at Boeing which you wouldn't recognise but that information is confidential — for the time being.'

'Then it must be Colossus. They over ordered and they're in trouble. That's why they want to increase the Gatwick-Kennedy run — and keep us out.'

The salesmen smiled but said nothing.

Michael glanced at his watch as though they had another, more important, meeting. 'What money are we looking at?'

'Twenty-eight million dollars.'

'For a Colossus hand-me-down!'

'For a bargain from an anonymous careful owner.'

They all laughed.

In the car Ryder said, 'Well done! I had no idea you were so expert.'

'Oh, I have my uses.' He slid his hand under her coat and stroked the soft insides of her thighs.

She ran the tip of her tongue along the sharp edge of her teeth. 'I wish we could buy that aircraft today.'

He moved his hand a little higher. 'We can't till we're licensed.'

She moved nearer to him, casually so that the driver

354

did not suspect. 'My nightmare is a jumbo jet but no passengers to pay for it.'

He slid one finger inside the lace of her silk panties. 'How about five hundred angry passengers and no aircraft?'

She chuckled, deep inside her.

'Boeing know our dilemma,' he said. 'Everyone who starts an airline is faced with the same problems. They're not just looking at this one sale. They hope Anglo Atlantic will be fantastically successful and we'll order a whole fleet of 747s.'

He went on talking as if nothing were happening and all the time his fingers circled, and she could think only of that moment when they would be alone.

That evening they were entertained by Boeing. No one mentioned the aircraft. The talk was general aviation gossip. It was midnight when Michael and Ryder reached their room. Ryder kicked off her shoes and turned on the television news as they hacked over the evening, wandering to and fro from the bathroom to make a point or to listen. Whilst Michael was in the bathroom, she flicked through the channels, a habit which drove him mad. Then suddenly Imogen's dainty, freckled face looked straight at her as a voice said, *'Passions. A story of love and revenge set in the humid heat of North Carolina. With Imogen Lydden in a cameo role.'*

When Michael came out of the bathroom he found her crying.

Colossus filed their objection to Anglo Atlantic on the grounds that there were barely enough transatlantic passengers for those airlines already operating. The CAA set the date for the financial hearing; 26 March. Ryder ringed it in her diary. From that moment onwards it became their Mount Everest, the peak to which all paths led, the heights to which they hoped to climb.

The build up was frenetic. They needed a London

base but the warehouse wasn't ready, so they rented temporary office space from Jonathan's firm. They took on a highly experienced aviation accountant called Bernard Trevor, whom Michael had known at Colossus. It was an expense, but they couldn't afford to miss him. They scoured Gatwick for an on-spot base, found a vacant building, then had to stall on the contract till after the hearing.

'If we get gazumped I'll scream,' said Ryder, as they drove back to London.

They hired a cabin services manager named Craig Witherspoon. He worked out a cabin crew training programme and started to interview staff, but again was held back from taking them on till they were past the first hearing.

During this period Leo stayed with Violet when Mrs Trumpet was unable to be at the Butterfly House. Ryder felt guilty at seeing so little of him. They made a point of spending every weekend at the Butterfly House, even if they had to work. On Sundays, Mrs Trumpet would cook an enormous roast lunch. They ate at the long table, with Fred and Violet and anyone else from Bailing who was on their own. Michael and Ryder had only one rule: everyone had to mix, with no formality. They did not invite the Offbachs. Andrew, Michael's friend and editor at *Aviation Argus*, was a frequent visitor. Tall and very thin, he ate so many potatoes that Ryder made him arrive early to help peel them. Hetty Radipole from Syd's came with her horsey husband. It was years since Ryder had seen her but she hadn't changed. Jonathan brought Charlotte, who was so surprised to find herself sitting next to Fred that she forgot to nag. These were cosy Sundays of eating too much, laughing with friends, dozing over the newspapers, and playing tennis in the crisp afternoons. It was always a wrench for Ryder to return to London.

'We have to be airborne by 22 July,' she said at one

of their meetings with Offbach. 'We need press coverage. The royal wedding's a week later and that will fill every page of every newspaper.'

'And we need those American tourists who'll flock to London,' said Michael.

As the meeting concluded, Ryder turned to Offbach. 'Why don't you and your wife come up to Bailing one Sunday? And do bring your son. My brother Leo is the same age.'

Driving home Michael said, 'You'd even sacrifice our Sundays to save Leo from Christina.'

On 26 March, Ryder and Michael arrived at the large circular CAA building on the corner of Kemble Street just off Kingsway. Offbach and his two assistants were waiting in the reception. They took the lift to the eighth floor. As they went up, Ryder felt her heart thud in her ears.

'Of course this is only K2.' Michael sounded calm and confident. 'Mount Everest's the public hearing.'

They were shown into a large conference room. It was functional beige and brown, with four long tables arranged in a square and big windows through which the hum of Covent Garden was occasionally punctuated by the howl of a police siren. The wood-panelled court-room at Bow Street was only down the street.

A door opened and four gentlemen from the CAA processed solemnly to their table. They were followed by two stenographers, one of whom set in motion a huge tape recorder.

'Good morning, ladies and gentlemen,' said the chairman of the panel, adjusting the microphone in front of him. 'Under section 65 of the Civil Aviation Act it is our job to satisfy ourselves that you are financially viable and fit to run an airline. That is the purpose of this first hearing.' He opened a huge file on his table. 'We've studied your application and there are a number of points which need clarifying. Your intended return fare to New York is £199. Why?'

They'd agreed that Michael would answer all financial queries. 'Well, sir,' he said, 'a scheduled fare is around £400. Skytrain started at £118. We want Anglo Atlantic to be competitive.'

'Undercutting Colossus by £20?'

'Offering a better service at a more reasonable price.'

The chairman smiled. 'That point of view is for the public hearing.'

Ryder began to relax. At least they weren't to be dismissed out of hand.

The cross-examining went on for hours. Michael was asked about forward predictions, security, cash flow, insurance, safety, maintenance agreements. In the late afternoon, the chairman suddenly turned to Ryder. 'We have one other question. I think Mrs Ashby should answer this.'

She sat up straight.

'It concerns Bailing. Among your assets to be used as collateral you include the flying school but not the land or the buildings.'

She was acutely aware of Michael beside her. 'That is correct. We decided I would only include Bailing if necessary. I have a joint-owner.' Her voice became hoarse. 'A Mr Brendan. We can only sell to each other.'

'Would he release you from that obligation?'

'I . . . don't know.'

The Chairman closed the file on his table. 'It is the duty of the CAA to protect the public. The world is in a period of recession. We have to be extra vigilant. The panel would be happier to see the value of Bailing added to that of the other airfields. Without it, Anglo Atlantic's financial position is not strong enough.'

Michael and Ryder drove north in silence. When they stopped for petrol, Ryder said, 'There's no point in being angry. The conditions of my ownership of Bailing weren't my idea.'

'I'm not angry.' He handed his keys to the garage attendant. 'I'm just tired of realising that after all this time of living with me you're still in love with Patrick Brendan.'

'That's ridiculous! I haven't seen him in years.'

'Oh yes you have!' He took her head in his hands. 'In here. In your mind. Every time something goes wrong, I can see you thinking, *"If only . . ."* '

She wrote to Patrick at Gatehouse. Michael didn't ask to see the letter and she didn't offer to show it to him. In the days after she posted it, she jumped every time the phone rang and hurried to the front door when she heard the postman's bicycle crunch over the gravel — unless Michael was present. Then she kept perfectly still, only she knew that he knew.

In the end it was a typed letter, from Palm Beach.

Dear Ryder
I release you from the sale restriction on Bailing so long as I have first option at market value should you have to sell.
I'll be at Gatehouse from July.
Good luck with the airline.
Patrick

Folded inside the letter were two guest badges to an international polo match at Windsor in July. Tucked in the bottom of the envelope, handwritten on a separate piece of paper because he realised she must show the typed letter to Michael was, *'Please come!'*

35

On 29 April Anglo Atlantic were called for their public hearing. Colossus were their main objector.

Ryder and Michael spent the previous night at the Waldorf: it was a two-minute walk from the CAA. In the morning Ryder had a long luxurious bath, full of herbs and scents, in an effort to relax herself. Then she dressed carefully in her smartest 'impressing clients' black suit and a cream silk shirt. It wasn't new — she'd been too busy for shopping — but it was a friend. The straight skirt never wriggled or creased or sagged and the fitted matador jacket always made her feel elegant and desirable, even in the days before her period when she felt leaden.

Michael wore the tie she'd bought him in New York. 'It's my lucky tie,' he said, adjusting it in the mirror.

She smiled and flicked a hair from his shoulder. They were still stiff with each other. His accusation that she loved Patrick and her guilt concerning the hidden tickets hung between them, emotionally. But not physically. In their best moments, their most tense moments, and even in the bad times, they found solace in their wonderful sex. Last night they had made love in the shower, with the water pounding on their bodies. This morning she had woken to him enjoying her, so gently that she thought she was dreaming.

Of course she should have thrown the polo badges away, but she hadn't. When she thought of them, tucked down the side of her underwear drawer, they gave her a naughty frisson, especially when Michael was being pigheaded.

Offbach and their barrister, Hanson Dagworthy, were waiting in the reception of the CAA building. Dagworthy was very expensive but he had a terrific reputation. As Offbach had said, 'We need someone to combat Colossus' inhouse man, Ralph Benn.'

They went up in the lift, to the same eighth floor conference room with its functional beige and brown. Anglo Atlantic were the first to arrive. As they took their seats opposite the panel, Michael whispered to Ryder, 'This is Everest.'

She nodded towards the door as the Colossus team entered. 'And here come the abominable snowmen.'

They stood when the panel entered. It consisted of the chairman, a board member, an adviser, the secretary, and a stenographer.

'Good morning everyone.' The chairman nodded to both sides. He waited whilst the tape recorder was set in motion before introducing the members of his panel. There was a lot of nodding and polite smiling. Ryder tried not to look anxious.

The chairman adjusted his spectacles. 'This is a particularly contentious case. The Gatwick-Kennedy route is highly competitive. Whilst it is the policy of this Authority to encourage fair competition, our primary responsibility is to the public. We would be remiss if we permitted more carriers on a route than the market can sustain. This would bring financial difficulties to existing airlines. That would not benefit the public.'

The Colossus team smirked. Ryder felt slightly sick. She turned to Michael. He looked grim.

As the applicant, Anglo Atlantic spoke first. Hanson Dagworthy rose ponderously. 'It is fair competition which we seek, gentlemen. No more. No less. Laker has shown that there is a pool of potential transatlantic travellers. Those who accept the minimum in exchange for bargain fares are served by Skytrain. Others — our potential market — choose to pay slightly more in order to have inflight service and a confirmed booking.'

'The same service as Colossus?' enquired the chairman.

'I said a quality service, sir.'

'Be that as it may, Mr Dagworthy, but you're talking of the same passengers.'

'Potential passengers, yes. But our market research reveals that thousands more would like to cross the Atlantic. We're convinced that Anglo Atlantic can attract them and generate a whole new market of transatlantic travellers.'

'And not attract any existing Colossus passengers, Mr Dagworthy?'

'Some. And why not, sir?' He looked straight at the chairman. 'Because if the policy of the Authority is truly for fair competition, then the only result of this hearing can be to give Anglo Atlantic the routing — and let the market decide!'

The chairman smiled. 'Thank you, Mr Dagworthy. When I visit the theatre I often wish the actors would take lessons in oration from you. We will now break for coffee.'

After the adjournment, Ryder, as the chairman of Anglo Atlantic, was called to give evidence.

'Your name?' said the chairman, adding, 'That's for the record.'

She took a deep breath to quell her nerves. 'Ryder Ashby.'

'Occupation?'

'Chairman of Anglo Atlantic.'

'Mrs Ashby, you've never run an airline before?'

'That is correct. But my husband has many years aviation experience and we have five provincial airfields. All successful businesses which we have built up.'

tal glasses as they tackled their mail. There were notes of congratulation from Mrs Trumpet and Griffiths. A letter from Hetty Radipole. An invitation to lunch from Lady Heythorp and Jeremy. A dry few lines from Mr Podmore. There were lists of telephone messages from Michael's former colleagues at Colossus and *Aviation Argus*. Piles of letters from oil companies, insurance companies, employment agencies, pension schemes, stationers, and window cleaners, all offering their services. And underneath them all, a card in Alix's spiky italic writing: *'Could we celebrate?'*

'Will you see her?' asked Michael.

'When Anglo Atlantic's up and flying and there's nothing she can make me vulnerable about.' She gave a sad smile. 'Except Immy!'

To Ryder's relief, Leo had enjoyed his stay with the Offbachs. 'I wouldn't mind going to Nicholas' school,' he told her.

'It's a boarding school.'

'I know.'

'Then I'll talk to the headmaster.' She made a mental note. If Leo liked boarding school, it would be an answer to the problem of his evenings whilst she and Michael were in London.

In the build up to 22 July, Michael spent most of his time at Gatwick, negotiating his way through the labyrinth of fuel prices, haggling over maintenance and service charges, taking on Gatwick staff, and overseeing crew training. Often he was so tired when he came home that he could barely speak. In London, Ryder employed four key people: a personnel manager, an office manager, a sales manager, and top secretary for herself. She interviewed twelve and chose Judith, a Jewish divorcee with soft brown eyes and an unflappable toughness.

'Trust you to employ a single parent,' said Michael.

'I like people who've seen life bite.'

He drew her closer. 'Perhaps we should start a crèche. We could use it ourselves.'

'Not yet! I've looked after Leo since I was twenty-two and now I want some freedom.'

His eyes flickered. 'Of course.' He stepped away.

It was late. Nearly midnight. They were having their weekly progress meeting. Ryder leaned across the board-room table. 'I've had some ideas on the launch party. We'll have it here, on the river terrace, on the Tuesday evening and fly off to New York on the Wednesday.'

'My dear Ryder,' said Offbach — they now called him Oliver — 'journalists won't come to Wapping.'

'They will — if we make it exciting.'

Leaving Judith to track down a caterer who could produce food in shapes of aircraft and a pianist to play every tune along the lines of 'Fly Me To The Moon', Ryder flew to New York to check on Susan's progress. This time Michael stayed behind. She missed him, even before she took off. Travelling wasn't the same. There was no one with whom to share jokes about the other passengers.

Ryder hadn't mentioned Frankie on the telephone, nor had Susan, but when she arrived at the TriBeCa office, Susan said, 'You're only here for a night. Why not use our spare room?'

'I'd love to.' Ryder felt weak with gratitude. Frankie didn't hate her after all.

They ate a salad lunch in an ice cool restaurant and discussed the New York launch party. 'I want everyone from Prairieville to come.' Ryder listed them. 'Debbie, Rudy, your Mom and Dad, Doctor Jeff.' She paused. 'And Frankie. Most of all Frankie.'

Susan said nothing.

'But I can tell him myself this evening,' Ryder went on.

'He's away.'

'Is that why you can offer me a bed?'

'He's often away for the night when he's flying. You know that.'

'Of course.' Ryder ordered a glass of white wine. She didn't usually drink alcohol during the day, especially in the fierce heat of New York, but she wanted to feel lousy for reasons other than because of what she'd done to Frankie.

37

Ten days to lift-off. The invitations to the party had been sent. The inaugural flight was filling up. At Gatwick, Michael and Ryder gave a party for the crew and ground staff. When she saw them parade in their new black suits with smart red piping, she turned pink with pride.

'At least the uniform looks good,' said Michael.

'You'll never let me forget the penthouse, will you?'

'Not likely!' He laughed and parried her fists.

Nine days to go: Ryder tried on all her clothes, decided none were suitable for the London launch, left them all piled on the bed, and raced up to Harvey Nichols. For New York she'd bought a wildly expensive suit by Calvin Klein. For London, because she was on the spot, she'd left it till the last minute. She hurried from section to section, wishing Immy were there to advise her. Eventually she decided on a cream suit with a fitted jacket which made her look like a page from the Winter Palace, and a simple black dress reminiscent of Holly Golightly. Both made her look slim and elegant. As she started down the escalator, she caught sight of a jacket in that same kicking yellow which her mother had loved and which had brought her luck at Bailing. She turned and ran back, up the down escalator.

Two days to go: Violet brought Leo to Wapping. He arrived as Ryder and Judith were checking final details for the party. 'Tommy's not coming on the inaugural

374

flight,' he told her, standing awkwardly in front of her desk. 'I didn't invite him.'

'Oh, what a pity! Still, Rudy will be in New York and Debbie has promised to take you on the boat trip round Manhattan.'

'I've . . . I've invited someone else.'

'Oh?'

He looked away from her, twisting his hands. 'Stefan.'

She dropped her pen. 'I am not having that boy on my aircraft. You'll have to put him off.'

'I can't!' he cried. 'He arrives tomorrow. He's travelling with Jack.'

'I don't care! You know how I feel about Christina. How could you!'

'Father made me do it.' His voice shook. 'He said if I didn't do it as a favour to Christina, he wouldn't have me to stay this summer.' He ran into his bedroom and slammed the door.

She sank back into her chair. 'I'm sorry to argue in front of you,' she told Judith, who was calmly adding a list of figures.

'My husband remarried. I hate it when my son goes to that woman's house. I hate to hear what delicious meals she cooks.' Judith paused. 'But I try not to show it.'

Ryder took a deep breath and went into Leo's room. He was lying on the bed, staring at the ceiling as she had done so many times at Dingwall Court. 'Listen,' she said, 'we can't take Stefan. All mother's side of the family are coming from Prairieville. But I'll ring father and invite Stefan to Bailing.'

He sat up. 'When?'

She wanted to shout, 'Never,' but she answered, 'This summer.'

She waited until Judith left, by which time all her anger had transferred from Leo to her father. She dialled his number. He answered, 'Hello, Ryder darling.'

'How could you bully Leo into inviting Stefan!' she shouted at him. 'And on my airline!'

'I only said it would repay Christina for the trouble she takes when Leo's here.'

'Hasn't it occurred to you mother's family will be in New York? Have you no respect for her memory.'

There was silence. Then he said, 'I'm sorry. I'll explain to Christina. I didn't think.'

'You never do — except about yourself!' She slammed down the receiver.

Monday, the day their 747 was to arrive. Michael and Ryder left London at five. It was a perfect July morning. The countryside was swathed in hints of summer mist, the terminal buildings glittered in the pale light. They met Oliver for breakfast in the airport. As they sat down, Felicity Offbach arrived with Nicholas and Leo. The men ate with gusto but Ryder could barely swallow. She fiddled nervously with the buttons on her Tsarist suit until Michael leaned across and covered her hand with his.

Accompanied by officials from the British Airports Authority, they all went down on to the tarmac, whilst on the observation roof their employees gathered to watch the arrival of the aircraft.

'Can you see her?' Ryder scanned the western skies.

Michael adjusted his binoculars. 'Not yet.'

'I hope she's all right.' Ryder jigged in her high heels.

'I expect she's crashed,' said Leo. 'They do, you know.'

'Stop it!' She pretended to box his ears.

'Here she comes!' called Michael. 'Over there! Look!'

She seized the binoculars from him. 'Are you sure she's ours?'

'I know she is.' He touched her cheek in a gesture of pride and intimacy.

The aircraft approached the runway. Her undercarriage was down. The sunlight bathed her rounded body. The morning haze shimmered on her wings.

Then she was down. Her brakes locked on. Her tyres screamed. She roared past, huge and white, with wide bands of red and black running along her sides and, most glorious of all, in large red letters: ANGLO ATLANTIC AIRWAYS.

By the time Michael and Ryder reached the evening of the launch party, they were living on such a high that it seemed as if nothing could touch them. They barely slept. Their minds raced. When they went to bed they made love, talked, and made love again, pumping with adrenalin.

Ryder wore the black dress. Michael liked it. When they stepped from the lift to the river terrace, before any guest arrived, the black jazz pianist winked and stroked his long slim fingers over the keys, and played 'Moon River' as Michael swung Ryder into his arms and waltzed her along beside the river Thames.

An hour later the terrace was thronged with guests. Their voices rose into the night sky. Their laughter broke. Waiters squeezed through bearing trays of champagne and caviar. The pianist was playing 'Fly me to the Moon'. He gave it an exotic, honky tonk rhythm. Ryder was giving an interview to London Weekend Television. She smiled at the camera and hoped she didn't sound as hoarse as she felt.

'It's nearly eight o'clock,' Judith reminded her. 'The Fortune's Fen Tiger Moth will fly over in five minutes.'

'Thanks.' She slipped downstairs to check with the security guards. As she walked back towards the party, she heard one of the guards say, 'I'm sorry, sir. Admission is by invitation only.'

'Oh, I'm sure Mrs Ashby will let me in. I'm an old friend.'

That voice made the hairs on her arms stand upright. She turned. 'The guards are correct, Adam.'

'Well, aren't we smart!' He was drunk or drugged. She could tell from his voice.

'Please leave!' she said. 'You're not welcome.'

'My dear Ryder, for an ex-con's daughter you do give yourself airs.'

'Get out or I'll have you thrown out!' Michael boomed from the top of the stairs. He took Ryder's hand, squeezing it hard. 'Come back to the party. Forget him!'

'How can I?'

'You have to — just as you did with the article.'

She let him lead her back to the terrace where the approaching hum of the old Tiger Moth had captured everyone's attention. She took a deep breath and she tried to smile, remembering how Grandpa Milne had told her to square up. But her face was white and her hands still shook.

The inaugural flight departed at eleven o'clock on the following morning. By six, Ryder and Michael were pacing the grey marble floors of Gatwick airport, running through every last detail. The check-in area was already milling with passengers on early flights to the Eastern Mediterranean. They leaned against their luggage trolleys and discussed how many drachmas to the pound. There were English girls heading for Lindos, families wondering if they'd left the iron on, large Scandinavians in Jesus sandals, and obscure American religious groups wearing badges and eating ice cream. The halls echoed to the burble of languages and the constant call of the tannoy. 'Will Mrs Rhosllanerchrug meeting Mr Philippopolis please contact airport information.' Ryder wondered why people called Smith never seemed to be met.

Without saying where she was going, she left Michael at Anglo Atlantic's check-in desk and clicked off across the hall in her black court shoes and her black dress with the sunflower jacket draped over her shoulders. By the entrance to the jetway, she showed the guard her pass. 'Just going aboard again.'

He grinned. 'No one's stolen her yet.'

'They'd better not!'

Freight was being loaded in igloos, curved to fit the Boeing fuselage. Food and drink were being stored in the kitchen areas. The fuel had already been topped up: 56,000 gallons for one round trip. She went up the steps and paused to admire the aircraft's interior. It was all so clean and new. The red carpet was untrod. The black and red seats were stiff and fresh. She wished it could stay this way.

She stepped into the cockpit. A panel of dials and switches, screens and levers faced her. She smiled as she compared it to the tiny Cessna. Quickly and carefully, she slid herself into the pilot's seat. And there she sat, hands clasped in her lap, relishing that moment of solitude with their giant possession.

By the time she returned to the departure lounge, Anglo Atlantic was up on the screen:

Destination	Flight no.	time boarding/delay
New York	AAA 1	wait in lounge

'I bet I know where you've been,' said Michael, slipping an arm around her.

She laughed and blushed.

'I did the same,' he whispered. 'Just after we arrived.'

Slowly their passengers began to arrive. As they checked-in, Ryder stood by the desk to greet them. Half were guests: journalists, heads of travel companies, heads of car rental companies, and television travel personalities. They were all invited to the New York party. 'It'll be worth it,' Ryder had kept telling Oliver to whom it seemed an unnecessary freebie.

At ten-fifteen Ryder walked through into the departure lounge, where three senior ground staff were manning a special Anglo Atlantic desk. As she approached, the white letters on the departure board clattered round to read: *Boarding Gate 10*. Simultaneously the tannoy announced '*The Anglo Atlantic inaugural flight to New York is now boarding from . . .*' The rest was drowned by cheers.

She was too busy seating their guests to notice the time pass, until the doors shut and Michael tapped her on the arm. She went through to the flight deck where the captain, first officer and flight engineer were already seated.

'Are they rolling in the aisles yet?' asked the captain.

'No, but they will be once we open the champagne.' She switched on the tannoy. 'This is Ryder Ashby. Welcome aboard our inaugural flight. This is a special day for us and we're glad you could share it.'

She took the seat behind the pilot. This was her treat. She listened as he ran through his check list. 'Engine One.'

'Green light.'

There was a roar.

'Engine Two.'

'Green light.'

Another roar. The dials were lit. The screens flickered. The check went on: 'Stabiliser trim . . . Stand by horizon . . .'

The captain waited for ground movement control. A man's voice came over the radio. 'Triple Alpha One. Taxi to holding point. Runway 26.'

'Okay.' The captain gave the thumbs up. 'Brakes off. Let's roll.'

They moved forward. The terminal slipped behind. From the side window Ryder could see other passengers disembarking, so far away that they looked like stick men in a Lowry painting.

At the holding point on Runway 26, they halted. A DC10 raced down the runway and up into the sky. Two minutes later it was followed by a 727. Then their radio crackled. Now it was a woman's voice. 'Triple Alpha One. You're cleared for take off.'

Susan had organised the New York party to perfection. The street was lit like a runway. The warehouse was tented like a hangar. The waiters were dressed as pilots. A lump of frozen caviar was fashioned in the shape of an aircraft. And there were people. Hundreds of them. From newspapers, television, travel agencies and car hire firms. They shook Ryder by the hand, pushed cameras and microphones into her face, and asked her endless questions.

'Do you mind?' she said to Michael, in a moment of quiet.

'I like to see you wear our crown.'

She leaned against him, warmed by the power of her love for him, as she had never been before. It made her feel both weak and strong. It made her want to be alone with him. To make love to him. At the same time she was content to share him with all these people, because she was proud of him and because she knew that what he gave them detracted nothing from what he gave her.

'When this is over . . .' she began.

But they were interrupted by the arrival of Debbie and Rudy, and Ryder realised sadly that Frankie had not forgiven her. She didn't say anything to Michael. She didn't have to.

Over breakfast she sparkled to the English press. At lunch, Michael impressed the president of a major travel company. In the afternoon they gave a joint interview. That evening Michael flew home whilst Ryder remained to fulfil a further six interviews.

When she finally staggered on to the flight home, her throat was sore and her eyelids felt as if they'd been caressed by sandpaper. She sank into her seat and stretched out her legs. As she closed her eyes she recalled what she'd intended to tell Michael when they'd been interrupted, and she smiled.

38

Michael didn't meet her at the airport. He hadn't said he would. But it had never occurred to her he wouldn't be there. They had so much to tell each other. He wasn't at the Gatwick office either. He hadn't been there all day. Craig Witherspoon, the Cabin Services Manager, offered her a lift to Wapping. He talked non-stop about the permitted thickness of batter around a shrimp in a first class meal and how many diced carrots constituted one economy portion. She nodded and smiled, and grew increasingly annoyed with the Saturday lunchtime traffic — and with Michael.

The warehouse was deserted except for the porters and the booking clerks. Ryder took the lift to Michael's office. It was empty. She opened the door of the penthouse. It too was deserted. The sun streamed in through the locked terrace windows and the air had a hot, closed-in smell.

Suddenly she was afraid he was ill and that everyone knew, except for her. They hadn't phoned her in New York because he didn't want her worried. Frantically, she dialled the Butterfly House. There was no reply. She rang Bailing. Fred answered. 'Michael? Oh, he's taken the ole Cessna up for a spin.'

She felt silly with relief. She laughed out loud. Michael was never ill. He was invincible. She drove up to Norfolk, through the beauty of the summer afternoon, the radio turned up high, singing happily.

He was in his study when she reached the house, sitting at his desk, the tips of his fingers drawn together in front of his face. Ryder bounced in, dropped her bags, and hugged him. 'I have missed you,' she said. 'I couldn't wait to get back.'

He opened the drawer of his desk and took out the two guest polo badges dated for the following Sunday. 'How lucky you're in time.'

She straightened up. 'Patrick sent those months ago. I'd forgotten about them. Now, let me tell you about New York.'

'Which is why you hid them?' he cut across her, his dark eyes watching her face.

'Oh, I know I should have told you but I knew you'd be angry — and you are!'

'You could have sent them back.'

She perched on his desk. 'You're blowing the whole thing out of proportion. They were merely tucked into the letter of release. And he didn't invite me on my own. After all, he sent two badges.'

'With this?' He held up Patrick's *Please come!*

She flushed.

'Well, we mustn't disappoint him, must we?' Michael stood up.

'But we don't want to go.' She seized his arm. 'I wasn't planning to use them. I admit I was flattered. That's all it was. Let's stay here. Just us. I have something to tell you.'

He shook her off. 'Of course we're going. Do you think I'm going to spend the rest of my days wondering if I'm going to find my wife's lover's billet-doux?'

There was a large, smart crowd at the Guards' Club. The car park behind the clubhouse was lined with Rolls-Royces. The sound of laughter and champagne corks popping mingled with the thud of ponies' hooves from the nearest ground. Ryder straightened her shoulders and pretended to be unconcerned. Beside her, Michael

384

was silent and unforgiving. The only times he'd spoken to her since her return were to discuss Anglo Atlantic. She stepped out of the car and smoothed down her dress. She'd toyed with refusing to come, but decided that would make matters worse.

'Let's watch from the other side.' She pointed to the far stands. 'We'll have a much better view.'

'Oh, no!' He took her by the elbow and steered her down the path and on to the lawn in front of the clubhouse where groups of people sat at tables drinking Pimms' in the sunshine, as her parents had so often done.

She stopped. 'Michael, let's go somewhere and talk. You're being ridiculous.'

'Shut up!' He looked at her with something near dislike. 'Ah,' he lifted his hand and waved. 'Here's our kind host. Patrick! How good of you to send us the tickets. Ryder was thrilled. Women like to be remembered by their past lovers.'

She couldn't look at Patrick, she was too embarrassed. She was aware of him standing there, debonair and disdainful, and of her husband, who looked as if he were about to punch someone. 'Michael, please!' she said. 'Let's go home.'

He pinched the soft flesh on the inside of her arm so hard that she gave a yelp. 'Oh, no, darling. You enjoy yourself. So sorry I can't stay. Look after her, Brendan.' He spun on his heel and walked away.

Ryder was so surprised it took her a moment to react. Then she hurried after him, pushing against a crowd of giggling polo groupies who surged up the path, dark glasses pushed back on their heads, high heels catching in the grass, one too many gold chains around their necks. Ryder screamed at them to get out of her way. As she ran into the car park, Michael stepped into the car.

'Wait!' she shouted.

But he didn't. He drove away.

She returned to Patrick, because she had no alternative. 'Take me to the station,' she said. 'Please! I must go home.'

'I'm in the next game. I'll take you later.' He touched her arm. 'You need a drink. I'll find old Algie Kelmscott. He'll look after you.'

She sank wearily on to a chair and rested her elbows on the round white table, waiting whilst he fetched her a glass of Pimms'. She felt totally detached from her surroundings. From Patrick. These people. Everything which had once meant so much to her because it was a part of Patrick.

She wondered where Michael had gone. She pictured him driving along the motorway, in the fast lane as usual. 'You shouldn't have invited me,' she told Patrick when he came back.

'I didn't know he'd react like that. Poor you!' He laid his hand on hers. 'What a brute.'

'He's not a brute!'

They were interrupted by Major Kelmscott who gave Ryder a whiskery peck on the cheek. 'You and your husband are doing well,' he said. 'Not thinking of starting a polo team, by any chance?'

She gave an ironic smile. 'Polo is the last game my husband would support.'

It was early evening before Patrick could get away and far too late for her to reach Bailing. She was hot and tired, and had spent the past hour half-expecting Michael to return for her. Patrick was subdued as he drove her in to London. From time to time he glanced at her as if she were someone he'd heard about but had only just met. 'How about dinner?' he asked as they skirted Knightsbridge.

'No, thanks.'

'You have to eat.'

They drove on. She thought of the way Michael had

abandoned her and her eyes narrowed. 'May I change my mind?'

He stopped at a small French restaurant. She went to the ladies cloakroom to wash the dust from her face and hands. Then she retouched her make up and combed her hair. For all Michael cared she could be still stuck in Windsor.

Patrick was seated in an intimate bower near the window. 'I have missed you,' he said as she took her place. 'When I read your name in the papers I think of what could have been.' He lowered his voice. 'I'm getting a divorce. Maria Luisa's finally agreed. I shall have Tancredi every summer. How's Leo? I often think of him and old Fred and Violet — and you.' He paused. 'I couldn't believe it when Violet told me you were married. And to Michael!'

'What do you mean?'

'He's so dominant and you're so gentle. The newspapers call him tough. But they always say wonderful things about you.'

'Don't be stupid! They call me the fraudster's daughter. And I'm not gentle.'

He reached for her hand. 'You were with me. He's changed you. He's made you hard and outspoken.'

She withdrew her hand. 'I was malleable because I was in love with you and afraid I'd lose you. I've never been afraid with Michael, so I don't need to play games. I can be the real me — not some me I think would be more pleasing.'

She was convinced Michael would be waiting for her in the penthouse. As the lift carried her up, she pictured his glowering face — and that moment when they would make it up. But the penthouse was empty. The terrace doors were closed. The air even staler. She threw open the window and she lay down on their bed. At midnight the phone rang. She ignored it. Let him think she'd been murdered. At one it rang again. And at two. She let it.

Michael marched in as Ryder was in the shower. She hurried out, wrapped in a towel, still cross but pleased to see him. 'I don't know what game you're playing,' she said.

He walked to his desk and picked up a handful of letters. 'I'm not a game player, Ryder. I told you that before.'

'Oh, for God's sake don't start lecturing me! It's bad enough that you abandoned me at Windsor all day. Anyone would think I'd been unfaithful to you.'

'Haven't you?'

'You know I haven't. But it would bloody well serve you right if I was.'

'If I hadn't found the badges and the note I'd still be living in blissful ignorance. So it makes me wonder what else I'm blissfully ignorant of.'

'I might wonder what you were doing in my underwear drawer?'

'I bought you a necklace. I chose it at Tiffany's whilst you were giving an interview. I decided to hide it. I thought how excited you'd be when you found it. Instead of which, I found your lover's note.'

'He isn't my lover.' She sank on to the sofa and buried her face in her knees. 'I don't care if I never see him again.'

'What a shame you didn't think that when you married me.' He picked up his briefcase. 'Where were you at two o'clock in the morning?' he asked, as he walked out.

She ran to the door, and yelled at him as he stepped into the lift. 'I was here. Alone! You bastard!'

That night he stayed in a hotel near Gatwick. It wasn't the first time. He'd used that hotel in the build up to Anglo Atlantic, when he was too tired to drive back to London. But now it was different. He didn't want to come home.

They should have been so happy. A week ago they were. Even now photographs were appearing of them in women's magazines as 'Aviation's Golden Couple'. But the atmosphere between them continued to be strained. Ryder decided to ignore it. She tried to be cheerful. She told herself she had nothing to feel guilty about. But she missed Michael. She missed their laughter. Their lovemaking. His voice in the night. They continued to share a bed but it was as if there were an invisible barrier down the centre. He didn't touch her, and she was afraid to reach out her hand to him in case he pushed it away.

Work was the only subject on which he would speak to her — and for work they kept up a front.

'Two thousand seven hundred passengers outbound and two thousand four hundred inbound in one week.' She keyed into their computer at the Wapping penthouse. 'That's well over our breakeven point.' She looked across the desk at Michael and smiled. It was the first evening he'd returned before midnight.

'We need to get the inbound up. I'll talk to Susan.'

'The pound's down to $1.90.'

'That should make Britain more attractive.'

She tapped the keyboard and watched the figures on the screen. 'Advance bookings look healthy, especially the first week in October.'

'That's when Gatwick come off peak charges and we can drop our fares.'

'Of course. How could I forget!'

'Overwork.' He said it gently.

She swallowed hard. 'No more than you.'

He was silent.

She braced herself. 'Would you . . . like to eat here or shall we go out?'

'I'm dining out.' He walked to the door, then hesitated.

She held her breath, praying for him to come back.

389

But he went. She listened as the lift doors closed, then she laid her head on her desk and cried.

When she stopped crying, she was angry. Concealing two badges didn't warrant this treatment. Michael was a bully. Just like her father. She dialled Patrick's number. 'Will you take me out tonight?' she asked him.

He picked her up an hour later. They went to Annabel's. He seemed to know everyone on the dance floor. She spent the evening trying not to wonder what Michael was doing.

The spare room door was closed when she returned. She lay on their bed, listening to the sounds of the river, with tears seeping out from under her eyelids, wondering yet again how things had gone wrong so quickly. In the morning she rose early and made him a mug of coffee. Dark and strong, as he liked it. She knocked on the door. There was no answer. She opened it. The room was empty.

That evening he came back not quite so late. She was watching the television news. He sat down beside her. Not close, but at least he wasn't on the other side of the room. She was so tense she could barely concentrate. When the credits rolled, he stood up, 'Goodnight.'

'She looked up at him, her face crumpling. 'Michael, please . . .'

He reached out to touch her face, then withdrew his hand sharply. 'We'll talk at the weekend.'

He slept in the spare room but she didn't mind because she felt there was hope. In the morning she lay in their double bed, hugging his pillow, and planning her responses.

She was in a good mood. She spoke to Fred and Violet for the first time in weeks. She telephoned her father. She gave Judith the afternoon off. In the early afternoon the porters called to say there was a special delivery from Gatwick for her. She recognised Michael's writing on the envelope. Eagerly she ripped it open. Inside was a page from the *Daily Mail*. There was a picture of a famous actress leaving Annabel's. Behind was Patrick and beside him, was her own profile sharply edged.

In desperation, Ryder turned to Lady Heythorp. 'I don't know what to do,' she told the older woman, over brandy and black coffee in the cluttered first floor flat. 'Every step I take ends in disaster.'

'If you're trying to save your marriage, you don't go to night clubs with past lovers. Do you want Patrick?'

'No. But I did. Michael's right about that. Only I don't want him now.' She bit her lower lip, determined not to cry.

'Maybe you've run Michael's reservoir dry.'

'What do you mean?'

'That we can each take so much hurt from any one person. The polo badges and the newspapers may have been the final nails in your coffin.'

Ryder picked up her bag. 'I thought you were going to help me, not make me feel worse.'

'I'm trying to make you realistic. You have to win his love. It won't be easy. It may be impossible. But don't go begging. That won't get you anywhere.'

Ryder buried herself in her work, travelling between Wapping and New York. Michael took a flat near Gatwick. He stayed there during the week. She said nothing. They spoke on the phone ten times a day but it was all work. At the weekends they still met at the Butterfly House. They kept up a pretence for Leo. When Stefan came to stay, Ryder spent the week in Norfolk taking the boys to tennis coaching, sailing lessons, and up in the Cherokee. Her reluctance to have Stefan was obliterated by her problems with Michael.

In the autumn, Leo started at boarding school. Once, she'd looked forward to being alone with Michael at the Butterfly House. Now she dreaded Leo's departure. For Leo's sake, Michael went too when they took him to school, his trunk in the boot of the car. They met the headmaster and the form master, like any other parents. Then they waved Leo goodbye, and drove home in silence. Ryder had never felt so lonely, not even in the worst days at Bailing.

By the end of that year, Anglo Atlantic had carried ninety thousand passengers.

'We're on target,' said Michael, at the next directors' meeting. 'Of course we've had a few teething problems. Bookings are flat for January, but that's to be expected. We may have to change caterers. Witherspoon's warned them about the amount of batter on the prawns in the first class. Or rather, the lack of shrimp inside the batter.'

'What about the security guard?' asked Ryder. 'Do you think he'll take us to the tribunal if we fire him?'

Oliver looked surprised. 'But they're all ex-police or ex-SAS. Surely they're ideal.'

Michael gave a thin smile. 'For the SAS, perhaps. But there's a way of looking in a suspect lady's handbag.'

'Meaning?'

'That if he has to check packets of tampax he should do so politely,' said Ryder. 'And not wave them around shouting, "What have we here?" '

The meeting went on late. 'What are you two up to for Christmas?' asked Oliver conversationally, as he put on his coat.

'Having a rest, I expect,' Ryder smiled brightly. Michael said nothing.

She returned to the penthouse whilst Michael accompanied Oliver down in the lift. Outside it was raining hard. The sound reminded her of the rain thudding on the tarmac at Bailing. She looked down at her hands and started to cry.

39

Michael went skiing at Christmas. Leo went to Spain. Ryder went to Bailing. She shut herself up in the Butterfly House and lay on their bed, listening for the telephone which did not ring. On Christmas Day, she drove to the airfield and took the Cessna up. There was no one around. Everyone was with family and friends. She flew over Morston, and on out over the sea. It was grey and cold like the sky. She wouldn't have cared if she'd never returned, but she couldn't bring herself to point the nose downwards.

As she taxiied back to the hangar Fred appeared. He watched her climb down. 'You shouldn't be here,' he said.

'Why not?'

'A wife's place is with her husband.'

'Michael doesn't want me. Not that it's any of your business.'

'I wouldn't want my wife either if she went to night clubs with other men.'

'Oh, shut up, Fred!' She marched into the office and slammed the door.

Unperturbed, he followed her. 'I was going to write to you, seeing that you don't come to Bailing any more . . .'

'Leave me alone!'

'That's what I'm talking about.' He walked out.

She nearly ran after him but couldn't bear his questioning. She'd talk to him from London.

Ryder waited all day at the penthouse for Michael to arrive back from his holiday. She paced up and down, planning their opening conversation. It was evening before she heard his key in the door. He stepped inside looking tanned and relaxed. Her spirits rose.

She waited till he'd had a shower and something to eat, and was reading his mail at his desk. Then she pulled up a chair in front of him. 'I think we should talk about us,' she said, her voice quavering with nerves.

'So do I.'

'I've done a lot of thinking and . . . and . . . I can't go on like this. I don't know what I've done that's so wrong but I can't live with someone who shuts me out.'

'You don't know!'

She looked up at him, her eyes glistening with tears. 'You were angry about the badges and the article.'

He walked to the window and stared out at the night. 'What's wrong is quite simple. I've had to face the fact that throughout my marriage I've been making love to a woman who wished I was another man. Now I realise why you didn't want children.'

'But I do. I did. I was going to tell you in New York.'

'Don't lie, Ryder. I'll give you your divorce.'

She pushed back her chair. 'I don't want one.'

'I do.'

She was stunned. 'Have you met someone else?' she asked in a small voice.

'No — and I don't want to!'

He went to bed. She lay on the sofa, feeling sick, her teeth clamped against tears, as she listened to the familiar sound of his bedtime movements. When she heard him turn out the main light, she went into the bathroom and ran the water in the basin, crying into her towel so he couldn't hear. Then she stopped. Suddenly. Forcing her head up. In the mirror her face was hideously puffy and her eyelids were red. She bathed them in cold water, brushed her hair, and dabbed scent behind her ears and between her breasts.

Michael was awake. He was lying in bed, staring at the ceiling. He sat up as she opened the door. She walked boldly to his bed and sat down next to him. 'Don't send me away,' she said. 'Please!'

He looked into her eyes. 'It won't make any difference.'

'How can you be so sure?' She leaned towards him, her towelling wrap falling open to reveal her naked body.

'Because . . .' He seized her by the wrist to push her away, but instead pulled her to him, twisting her under him. He kissed her hard. She responded, crying with relief. The bedclothes came between them. She kicked them aside. He pressed her down into the pillows, framing her face with his arms, grinding his pelvis against hers as if he wanted to believe she were just some unknown body he'd brought home. She sank her teeth into his shoulder, then kissed the mark she'd made. He rolled her nipples between his teeth, biting them until she cried out, wanting him to be gentle. Then suddenly he became tender. He caressed her, his lips moving down her throat, between her breasts and across the flat of her stomach, so softly that she could barely feel him. She ran her fingers through his hair, murmuring that she loved him. He changed again. He gripped her thighs in his powerful hands as if he wanted to pull her apart, and thrust into her, trying to make himself abuse her. He tried to have her quickly, to deny her pleasure. Then he tried to hold himself back, to deny her the satisfaction of giving him pleasure. But she met him, savage when he was savage, gentle when he was tender, until he forgot that he was angry with her. They made love rhythmically. Erotically. Sensuously. The moonlight touching their bodies. They made love as they had so often at the Butterfly House, only more so because it had been so long and they were full of anguish. She revelled in his strength. In his arms. In the knowledge that they were joined. When she felt him pulsate inside her, she cried out, and did not know if it were her or him. Then the orgasm rolled up her and over her and out of her, till again the backs of her fingers were sensitive.

Afterwards she lay in his arms, her face buried in his neck, crying with gratitude. 'I knew we were still a couple,' she whispered. 'I knew it.'

'Ssssh!' He covered her lips with his finger.

'I love you — and you love me.' She took his finger in her mouth, gently massaging its soft pad with the tip of her tongue. He moved to pull his hand away but she wouldn't let him. She went on, massaging, till he surrendered to her mouth.

'I never told you that you were the best lover, because then I'd have given you everything,' he said when they finally drifted into sleep.

She woke in the grey dawn to find him fully clothed, watching her from the end of the bed. She smiled tentatively, then she saw his eyes and her smile faded, and the hurt rolled over her, more intense than ever until she felt as if she were about to suffocate. She wanted to scream and beg and plead. But she stood up, his duvet wrapped around her. 'I'm going back to Bailing. You can keep Anglo Atlantic. Everything. All I want is Bailing.'

40

That first week was the worst. The first Monday. The
first Tuesday. Each day was a desert through which she
dragged herself, trying not to cry, longing only for that
time when she could sink into bed and pull Michael's
duvet, the one from London, over her head, burying her
face in the smell of him which lingered in its folds.

On a wet Monday, when he was in America, she
moved out of the Butterfly House and back to the control
tower. It took her just three trips in the Land-Rover.
She removed only her clothes and those things which
had been hers when she married. The tower had the
closed silence of an unused house. No one had slept
there since the students the previous summer. The clock
on the wall had stopped. The magazines in the bathroom
were six months out of date. Ignoring the rain, she
opened the French windows on to the walled garden. It
had become almost as wild as the Butterfly House.

That night she lay in bed, listening to the rain fall on
the runway. She remembered how hard it had been for
her to leave the tower. Now she'd have gladly given it
all up. She rose and went downstairs to pour herself a
glass of brandy. Then she remembered Michael, and
threw it down the sink. She wasn't going to give him
that satisfaction. When she finally went to sleep, it was
with tears sliding down her cheeks. When she woke in
the morning, her eyelashes were still wet. For a moment,
her mind was blank. She stretched out her hand to the

other side of the bed, but an empty space and a smooth pillow mocked her. And the truth rolled over her, pressing down into her.

It was impossible to avoid the curiosity of the village but she couldn't bring herself to say that she and Michael were to be divorced. To talk of it would make it fact, and drive away hope. She went to see Violet in her office. 'Michael and I have decided to live more separate lives,' she said, aware that emotion made her voice sound abrasive. 'He will stay in London. I shall be at Bailing.'

Violet pursed her lips. 'That's not right, dear.'

'I can't help it.' With trembling hands, she picked up the letters and began to rip them open. 'Where's Fred?'

'He left.'

'Why?'

'I thought you knew.' Violet adjusted her spectacles and began to type, loudly, thumping the keyboard as hard as she could.

Ryder drove straight to Fred's house. It was an old redbrick cottage on the edge of the village. He was out the back, weeding his vegetable garden. When he heard the gate click, he picked up his barrow and wheeled it away.

'Fred!' She hurried after him, slithering on the muddy path. 'Wait! Please! Look, I'm sorry I was rude to you but I was very unhappy . . .'

'And Michael isn't?'

'That's right! Take his side.'

'You ride roughshod over people's feelings an' you forget how you were hurt when others rode over yours.'

'Anyone would think Michael had been up here bribing you.'

He gave her his tortoise stare. 'No one buys ole Fred.'

'I'm sorry. I shouldn't have said that.'

He walked away, pushing through a gap in the hedge, letting the wet brambles fly back in her face.

She drove to the village shop. Mrs Dennshurst was

leaning on the counter, totting up a list of figures. She gave Ryder a cool, 'Good morning.'

'I've been rude to Fred.' Ryder smiled anxiously. 'Could you tell him I'm sorry?'

'Did you wish to buy something? I have to finish my accounts.'

Ryder flushed. 'I'll have a chocolate cake. One of your special ones. I know Violet likes them.'

Mrs Dennshurst wrapped the cake in paper and took her money. When Ryder reached the airfield the office was empty. One of the mechanics was manning the telephones. 'Where's Violet?' she asked him.

'Gone to tea with Mrs Dennshurst.'

She took the cake and threw it in the bin.

Never had she imagined that Bailing would censure her. But it did. The milkman stopped delivering to the airfield: he said it was too far. The postman pretended not to recognise her although she'd once employed his son. Silence fell when she entered Mrs Dennshurst's. Voices rose the minute she left. She would have shopped in King's Lynn, but she refused to give in.

'I know everyone thinks I'm in the wrong but I'm not going to be frozen out,' she told Violet as they went through the airfield accounts. 'Bailing's conveniently forgotten what my airfield did for business.'

'If you say so.' Violet buttoned up her pink cardy.

'Oh, now I've been rude again. I don't mean to be.' She sighed. 'Let's get on with the work.'

The airfield had slipped. The barbecues and air displays which attracted people had gradually ceased whilst she and Michael had been obsessed with Anglo Atlantic. Club membership had fallen. Members had moved elsewhere, taking their aircraft with them.

'I'll just have to build it up again,' Ryder told Violet, wondering how she would find the energy and the enthusiasm when she felt dead inside. 'Of course it'll be hard without Fred.' She cast a sideways glance at Violet.

'He won't come back.'

'What about you? I'd prefer to know the worst.'

Violet unbuttoned her pink cardy. 'I was planning to leave — but I'll stay a bit longer.'

Tears came to Ryder's eyes. She turned quickly to hide them. 'Thank you.'

Oliver arrived at Bailing on the day Laker's Skytrain collapsed. He looked annoyed and flustered. 'Ryder, I have to talk to you.'

They went to The Bailing Arms. It now had a small restaurant at the back. In a loud voice he asked for a secluded table. As they were led to it, Ryder caught sight of Fred in the bar. He pretended he hadn't seen her but she knew by the tilt of his head that he had.

'You've heard about Skytrain,' Oliver boomed at her.

'Yes. It's a shame.'

'Anglo Atlantic will go too if you're not careful. Ryder, you're the chairman of an airline of which I am a director. You can't just disappear to the country to grow roses because you have marital problems. What about the passengers for whom you promised to provide a service? Colossus are having a field day.'

'Did Michael tell you I was here?'

'Not till I demanded to know what was going on.'

She played with her glass. 'He wants to divorce me.'

'That's out of the question. You'll have to keep up a front for at least two years. You're Anglo Atlantic's figurehead. You must appear or the whole airline will lose credibility.'

'What . . . what does Michael say?'

'He agrees.'

'He does?' There was stark hope in her voice.

Offbach looked embarrassed and began to talk about Leo. 'Shall he come to us for halfterm? Would that help? Felicity and I are very sorry about you and Michael.' Before Ryder could reply, he switched to Anglo Atlantic's summer promotion plan. She tried to look enthusiastic but all she could think of was that Michael was prepared to see her.

For the first time in months Ryder slept well. She woke to brilliant sunshine and an intuition that Michael would come to Bailing. She washed her hair, painted her nails, and wore a figure-hugging white flying suit. The break in the bad weather brought pilots to inspect their aircraft in the hangars and a dozen enquiries to the flying school. Every time the phone rang Ryder jumped. Each time a car drove up, she was convinced it would be him.

'You're like a cat on a hot brick but I won't ask why,' said Violet, with the ghost of a smile.

'I just have a feeling about today.' Ryder bit her lower lip. 'I'm so miserable without him.'

Violet softened. 'I'm glad to hear you say that, dear.'

The afternoon began to drag. Ryder tried to concentrate on the safety measures for the Midsummer's Day Air Display but the words blurred. A car drew up outside. She didn't bother to look. He wouldn't come now.

Suddenly Violet picked up her bag and marched to the door. 'I'll be going. Your visitor is here.'

Ryder grabbed her scent from her desk drawer and squirted it down between her breasts, then quickly raked her fingers through her hair. She looked up smiling as the outer door opened. She was still smiling when Patrick walked in.

Her face fell. 'What are you doing here?'

'Darling, I'm your co-owner — or had you forgotten?'

'Don't call me darling!' she snapped, conscious that the windows were open and Violet was outside.

'What's the matter?'

She crumpled. 'Michael wants a divorce. That's why I came back to Bailing. But the whole village is on his side. I expect that's the last I'll see of Violet.'

He laughed his lazy, debonair laugh which she had

once loved so much. 'Who cares what a lot of backward villagers think? Put in a manager and come out to Palm Beach. A couple of months in the sun and you won't give a damn about anything or anyone.'

'Like you?'

He smiled. 'I did love you. But now I've seen you when I'm not the one you're trying to please, I don't think we'd have been happy. You're a steely, earthy person. That's why you care about Bailing.' He took out his car keys. 'Come out to dinner. I'm just up for the night. I'm selling the mill. Don't look so shocked. That's what I mean about us being different.'

She hesitated, but the evening stretched ahead, lonelier than ever because she had felt so sure to hear from Michael. 'All right. But not The Bailing Arms. I've had enough of being treated like the woman caught in adultery.'

Violet sent a note to say she was unwell and wouldn't be in till further notice. Simultaneously the clubhouse cook decided to retire and the cleaner announced she had found a better job. That left Ryder to run the airfield with two mechanics, the oddjob man, a typist, a clerk and the school instructors. She rose at dawn to stuff eggs, fill quiches, beat mackerel into paté, and scrub potatoes. When the postman arrived she raced to the office to answer the mail and book flying lessons. At noon, she was back in the clubhouse to serve salad lunches and make sandwiches. In the afternoon, she returned to the office. In the evening, she served drinks and snacks in the clubhouse. When the last pilot retold his last near-miss tale, and she could finally wave them goodnight, she could barely summon the energy to climb into bed.

Ryder hadn't spoken to Michael since she'd left but Judith sent her a progress bulletin every Friday and on Mondays she received Anglo Atlantic's weekly passenger and freight reports from the Gatwick office. They were initialled M.A. Not 'Love Michael' or even 'Michael'. She could have been a stranger. In the darkest hours of the night she wondered if he'd found another woman and tortured herself with images of him making love.

On their wedding anniversary she weakened. All day she waited to see if he would send her those daffodils he called a new beginning. In the evening she telephoned. She couldn't help it. As soon as she heard his voice, she started to cry.

'I don't think this is a good idea,' he said gently. 'I suppose you've been drinking.'

'I have not!' She slammed down the phone.

In spite of the continued recession and the price slashing by other airlines, Anglo Atlantic was slowly increasing its share of the market. Inflation was down to 10 per cent and the pound had strengthened to $2.38, making America an attractive holiday proposition and their loan repayments on the aircraft easier to handle.

She received a proposal from Michael for her views on his longterm programme concerning a new routing and the purchase of a second aircraft. He wanted Anglo Atlantic to operate seven days a week to New York and, in another year or so, to apply to the CAA for the Florida route. Flying twelve sectors a week was having its toll on the aircraft. They effected a rolling maintenance, whenever it was on the ground, but from time to time it needed repairs and they were forced to charter. On top of this, during the aircraft's annual A Check, when the whole plane was stripped down, they had to charter for the entire three weeks. From his report Ryder read that he had been to Seattle and she was stabbed by jealous anger at being excluded where she had once been a part.

Leo spent the Easter holidays with her father so she was able to continue a pretence but by the summer she knew she must tell him. She collected him at halfterm. He came sauntering out of the main building, his blond hair ruffled by the wind and her mother's beautiful smile on his lips. Ryder was stunned by how much he'd grown. He was suddenly not her little brother any more.

They stopped for lunch near Cambridge. 'Michael and I are living separately,' she said as calmly as she could.

'I know.'

'How?'

'He's in London and you're at Bailing. Have you both got someone else?'

'Of course not! I mean, I don't know.' She took a deep breath to drive away the image. 'There's nothing for you to worry about. Whatever happens, you have a home with me. You'll go to the same school and . . . spend part of your holidays with father. Only I'd rather you didn't tell him.'

'You're right. He'll only worry.' Leo ordered another portion of chips.

'Father doesn't fret about anyone — except himself.'

'He never stops talking about you. That's what drives Christina mad. Nothing she says is half as clever as what you say.'

'I'd no idea.' Ryder sat back in her chair.

She'd put off telling Debbie, although she knew Michael must have given some explanation to Susan. When Leo returned to school, she wrote each of them a long letter. It was a relief to confide.

Bruja died that summer, on the day Britain won back the Falkland Islands, which was the same day the new people moved into the mill. Ryder walked up the lane and leaned on the five bar gate. It seemed as if her last tie with Patrick had gone with the death of his polo pony born on the pampas.

In the late summer she was due at Gatwick to promote their first seven-day flight. Offbach briefed her on the telephone. Judith had added the details. Ryder had longed to ask, 'Will Michael be there?' but she stopped herself. She bought a wildly expensive emerald green dress in finest crêpe de chine which clung and whispered as she moved. For nights beforehand she could not sleep. All the way down to Gatwick she rehearsed her opening smile to him. But he was in New York on that day. She drove home after the reception. Just outside London she stopped and was sick in a layby.

The months rolled on. Business at Bailing picked up slowly. At the weekends the airfield buzzed with activity. During the week it was quiet. Ryder employed a couple of university students for the season. It wasn't the same as having Fred and Violet, but they were helpful. Sometimes at night she sat alone on the patio, in the scent of the pale pink rose which brought back memories of her mother and the arbour at Dingwall Court. Other times she joined in with the barbecues at the clubhouse. They were fun, but not the same as those evenings with Frankie and Susan and Immy — and Michael, who'd loved her but she hadn't loved him because she'd been chasing a moonbeam called Patrick Brendan.

In October, on the anniversary of her mother's death, Ryder drove up to Morston, to that desolate windswept place which meant so much to her. She walked across the mudflats to the rickety bridge and sat on its step, her face cupped in her hands, watching the marram grass ever pliant to the north east wind. She heard the cry of an oyster catcher and the distant voices of lugwormers collecting bait. In the little creeks the water oiled its way between the tufts of grass. Out at sea a few hardy sailors tacked their dinghies against the turning tide. Along the coastal path came a man and a woman. They stopped and kissed, their bodies pressing into each other. Then they moved on, passing close to Ryder but not seeing her, so wrapped in their exquisite isolation.

41

Ryder went to Scot's Farm for Christmas because she couldn't bear to be alone for a second year. As always Debbie met her in Minneapolis. They hadn't seen each other since the Anglo Atlantic New York launch, those last innocent days before Michael had closed the door.

Debbie had matured. It was the first thing Ryder noticed. She was no more a jolly girl, but a woman who looked after a sick old man and who worked the land through fierce winters and hot dry summers. Her long blonde hair, her prettiest asset, had been chopped to a practical bob. Never one to wear much make up, she now wore none. Nobody seeing her could imagine that she had once scandalised Prairieville by her affair with Carl. Surreptitiously, Ryder glanced at herself in the mirror. She too had small lines around her eyes, some of laughter, some not.

Her grandfather was sitting by the window in his bedroom, just as he had been on her previous visits. He neither moved nor spoke nor blinked when Ryder pulled up a chair beside him and took his hand in hers. He did not even call for Greta.

'I wish we could see him once more as he used to be and then he could die in dignity,' said Debbie as they went downstairs.

Ryder felt tears well up from the pit of her stomach at the thought of losing another link. 'You're a saint,' she said. 'I wouldn't have the patience to look after him.'

'You took on Leo when he was a spoiled brat.'

'Unwillingly and because there was no one else. It was years before I stopped resenting him. In fact, till Michael.' Ryder paused. 'But he's turning out okay. I used to think I'd drive him to misogyny.'

Apart from Rudy and Doctor Jeff, Debbie and Ryder hardly saw anyone during those ten days. She only visited her aunt and uncle once: their pursed-lipped reproval reminded her of old Fred. Each morning she and Debbie dug a channel through the snow to reach the garage. In the afternoon they left Rudy with their grandfather whilst they drove to Fox Lake and skated across to the island, Debbie cutting determinedly over the surface of the ice, pulling Ryder behind her on the end of a scarf as if she were a waterskier behind a motorboat. Every evening they battened down the shutters against the Alaskan wind, stoked up the fire, and stretched out on the squashy sofas which were well-sat-on like those at the Butterfly House.

'Are you sure Michael knows how you love him?' asked Debbie. 'You're awful good at concealing things.'

'I went to him pleading. We had one last, wonderful night. Beforehand he told me it would make no difference. I didn't believe him. But in the morning I read it in his eyes.'

They lay on their opposite sofas, listening to the dull thud of the snow sliding off the roof. Finally Ryder said, 'I guess I'm like Michael. I'm not a good forgiver. I seem to make a habit of falling out with people.'

'Oh, Frankie'll get over it once he accepts that Susan has the greater earning potential. But he's a man and a Milne — and Milne men think they ought to earn more than their wives.'

'What about you and Doctor Jeff?'

Debbie blushed. 'I like him but . . . he's just a friend.'

'Don't you get lonely?'

'I have Rudy.'

'You know what I mean!'

'I like being on my own. I like to go to bed when I want to and to get up when I want to. I never enjoyed sex that much.' With a flash of the old, carefree Debbie, she suddenly giggled. 'I just acted like I did for Carl's sake.'

'Maybe that was his fault.'

'Forget it, Ryder! I don't want the heartache. Look at you, breaking up inside for Michael.' Debbie added another log to the fire. 'Anyhow, Doctor Jeff was in love with your Mom for years and she was the prettiest girl Prairieville's ever seen.'

Ryder sat up straight. 'My mother was a vain, manipulative butterfly and she'd have made his life hell — and you've no idea how hard that was for me to admit.'

On the first day of March, Ryder was reorganising the mechanics' weekend rota when the Bailing florist delivered an enormous bouquet of spring flowers, all wrapped in cellophane and yellow ribbons. Ryder felt herself grow hot and cold. There were daffodils, narcissi, tulips and bluebells, but mainly trumpeting yellow daffodils, those heralds of spring which Michael loved. She carried the bouquet to the privacy of the control tower and closed the door. Carefully, she slid her hand up inside the cellophane to reach the envelope nestling amongst the blooms. She slit it open. Inside was a plain white card with '*Can we forget the past?*' typed in script.

She reached for the telephone, then withdrew her hand, wanting to relish this period when the initiative was hers, before she relinquished it and became vulnerable to his telephone calls, to his letters, to his decision. Pulling on a fisherman's heavy sweater and her Wellington boots, she drove up to Morston. It was drizzling but she didn't notice. She only knew that everything had become infinitely more beautiful.

Drenched but not cold, her cheeks glowing and her

eyes shining, she stopped at Mrs Dennshurst's. Silence fell as she stepped inside. 'One of your nice coffee cakes, please?' She smiled and raised her voice. 'The ones Michael likes!'

'Yes . . . dear.'

As Ryder drove away, she realised that Mrs Dennshurst had called her dear, as she used to. She laughed and turned on the radio. Everything was going to be all right, and this time she'd be so much more loving to Michael.

There were several unfamiliar cars at the airfield, including a sporty silver Mercedes, but that wasn't strange. Perhaps they were new clients. She pictured herself telling Michael that Bailing was booming. She could almost hear his late-night voice say that he was proud of her.

She parked outside the tower and dashed for the door, clutching the coffee cake to her chest, head bent against the weather.

'Hello, Ryder. I couldn't wait for your answer.'

Ryder looked at the flowers which she'd so lovingly arranged in their vase on the hall table. She tried to speak but couldn't. Dropping the cake, she swayed back against the wall and sank slowly to the ground. She buried her face in her bunched knees and began to shake. It was some time before she was able to say, 'Hello, Alix.'

'I shouldn't have come.' Alix picked up her exquisite and unscuffed handbag. 'You always were stubborn, Ryder, or you'd have seen that Adam only slept with me because he was jealous of your friendships and I only went with him because I was envious of you.'

'Fuck Adam! I thought the flowers were from Michael.'

'Your husband?'

'The man I love who wants to divorce me.' She thought of the walk across the mudflats when she'd been so confident of Michael's love, and she started to cry, covering her face with the sleeves of her damp sweater.

In the background Alix moved between the kettle and the coffee. 'Drink that!' She forced a mug into Ryder's hands. 'I've laced it with brandy. You need it.'

'Thanks.' She dragged herself to her feet and leaned against the wall, in her muddy boots and her mud-splattered jeans. Alix was immaculate in a white leather trenchcoat, her black hair drawn back like a ballerina to enhance her beautiful, sculpted face. Suddenly Ryder began to laugh, hysterically, tears rolling down her cheeks. 'In all the times I've imagined our meeting,' she said when she finally gained control, 'I've pictured myself, the epitome of success, dressed in my designer outfits, adored by a gorgeous man. But we have to meet when I've lost everything. Oh, damn you, Alix! How did you manage it?'

'I only came because of the award,' Alix said haughtily.

'What are you talking about?'

'You nominated me for the Business Woman of the Year Award.'

'I did not!'

'The publicity lady from Veuve Clicquot, the sponsors, told me so. She said that you particularly wanted me to know.' Alix lit a cigarette and began to smoke feverishly.

'I think this is Immy's way of getting us together again,' said Ryder. 'She must have written, pretending to be me.'

'Well, I've been shortlisted. I'm one of the six finalists. I came to ask you to the reception. If I win, I get a vine named after me and a bottle of champagne every year on my birthday and you, as my nominator, receive a dozen magnums!'

Ryder gave a half smile. 'I'll save them for when the three of us finally get together.'

Alix stayed till late that evening. They talked mainly of Immy. 'I'm partly to blame.' Alix concentrated on the chain of her handbag. 'I never thought I'd admit that, but it's true. She wanted to marry Tony. Jeremy and I put her off. He was a working-class married man over twice her age and she was so delicate, so ethereal, so talented. We felt it would ruin her career. We picked holes in him, till she began to have doubts. If it were you, you'd have married him just the same. But not Immy. She was so dependent. She wanted to please. Now I think we were wrong. Tony gave her stability. She's never had it since.'

'We've all been wrong about a lot of things.'

Alix stubbed out her cigarette. It was a gesture which took Ryder straight back to the flat in South Kensington. Alix looked up. She saw Ryder's expression. 'At least I didn't stub it out in the saucer as I used to,' she said.

On a blustery day in late March, Ryder attended the Business Woman of the Year Award. As she stepped from a taxi outside the Institute of Directors, she paused to smooth down her skirt and look for Alix. Around her, other guests were arriving. Smart women with transatlantic savvy. Cosmopolitan men. They headed up the staircase to the Nash room. Ryder followed.

A publicity lady hurried to greet her. 'Ryder Ashby of Anglo Atlantic? So glad you could come.'

'Thank you.' She felt a fraud. She shouldn't be Ashby because Michael didn't want her and she wasn't Anglo Atlantic. That was his too.

A waiter brought her champagne. She stood on the side, wishing she hadn't come. The room was full of wellknown faces from commerce and industry, journalists and previous winners. She knew most of them by sight. Once she would have walked up, hand outstretched, but months of solitude at Bailing had sapped her social confidence. She sidled towards the door. Then suddenly she remembered that day at Bailing when Michael had said, 'Picture them all stark naked,' and she turned back into the room. She was a Milne, and they squared up to life.

'There you are!' Alix wafted through the crowd. 'You're not running away?'

'Of course not!' Ryder smiled over-brightly.

'You were! I could see it in your face.' Alix lowered her voice. 'I haven't won. Debbie Moore has, with her Pineapple Dance Studios.'

'I am sorry.'

'Of course I wanted to win. But you have to shrug off disappointment and head for the next goal. That's one thing I have learned.' Alix paused. 'I'm afraid you won't get your twelve magnums.'

'Do you think that's the only reason I came?'

Alix's haughty, camellia face turned suddenly vulnerable. 'What a lot of years we've wasted.'

It was a hot summer. The airfield did well. Club membership was up, so was student intake. Oil fell by $5 a barrel and the bank rate dropped to less than 10 per cent. Ryder began to make money. But it did little to satisfy her. It was nearly two years since she and Michael had separated. Every morning she steeled herself for a letter from his solicitors.

Ryder didn't see much of Alix although they spoke on the telephone. They chose not to meet often. Their renewed friendship was so tenuous, neither of them wished to overload it. But Ryder thought a lot about her and what it meant to talk again. Some of her sense of failure, over her marriage and her inability to save Immy, disappeared in the renewal of her friendship with Alix.

At Christmas, she flew to Spain with Leo. She hadn't seen her father since the break up. On the telephone she'd successfully avoided the issue of Michael but now she had to tell him. He met them at Malaga, looking more and more the wealthy expatriate in his white flannels and his blazer. Driving along the coast road to Marbella, he talked of tennis and golf as if nothing else had ever touched his life. She felt like screaming.

'Christina's away,' he told her when Leo went to watch a video, leaving them to their lunchtime drinks on the terrace.

'She needn't have gone because of me.'

'She suggested it.' He reached across to take her hand, then thought better of it. 'I haven't been much of a father. I left you to pick up the pieces. You'll always resent that. It's not the only thing you resent about me. I know it irritates you to see me living well.'

She sat up. 'Because I can't forget about mother.'

'Do you think I have?'

'It looks like it.'

He leaned back in his chair. 'I shan't marry Christina. Carrie was my wife. As for living here, there's not much to do but enjoy yourself. I spent nearly six years in gaol. I've worn my sackcloth and ashes.' He paused. 'You're unhappy. I can hear it in your voice. Would it help to talk?'

She looked him straight in the eyes. 'Michael and I have separated.'

'I'm sorry. I liked him — as much as I am able to like the man who makes love to my daughter.'

'It's a mutual decision.'

'Don't talk balls!'

She was about to freeze him but suddenly she rocked forward and buried her face in her knees. 'I love Michael.'

'Then fight for him as I fought Dan Milne for your mother.'

413

42

Michael waited until Anglo Atlantic had completed three successful years before applying to the CAA for the Florida route. As usual Colossus objected. They were losing passengers in all directions, not only to Anglo Atlantic but also to the recently launched Virgin Atlantic.

It was Offbach who telephoned Ryder to say, 'We have a date for the public hearing: 15 November. I have to ask you to attend.'

'Because Michael can't bring himself to speak to me!' she said bitterly.

'I'm sorry, Ryder.'

'It isn't your war.' She sighed. 'You can tell him I'll be there, in my silent starring role. That is, unless he wishes to write my script!'

She arranged to stay with Alix at her flat overlooking Regent's Park, arriving late and exhausted from an afternoon's shopping to be met by Alix, immaculate in a white silk track suit, eating slivers of avocado and drinking Perrier water. For a moment Ryder wished she had stayed at Bailing and driven down from the safety of her own surroundings. Then she told herself not to be silly. She needed Alix's courage.

'Did you buy what you wanted for tomorrow?' Alix showed her into the spare room where she whisked back the door of an empty wardrobe full of padded satin hangers.

'This.' Ryder lifted a dark red silk jersey dress from a mountain of tissue paper. She slipped it on. The dress was tight and clinging and the drapes of the cowl neck fell open to reveal her cleavage. 'They'll expect me in a dark suit. Poor Ryder! Buried in Bailing! Chairman in name alone. Discarded by her husband. But I'm pleading no more. Damn him!'

'Bravo!' Alix clapped. 'Cinderella socks him one!'

'Your job,' said Ryder, unzipping the dress, 'is to make sure I don't lose my nerve in the morning.'

Ryder stepped from Alix's Mercedes outside the CAA building at the precise moment when Michael stepped from his Jaguar. It was perfect timing, because she and Alix had been parked around the corner waiting for him. She looked magnificent as she wafted across the pavement in her clinging red dress and Alix's long black mink which revealed her neat ankles encased in seamed stockings and the so dainty, so impractical red suede stilettos. 'Good morning.' She gave Michael a charming smile from her beautifully glossed lips and a small regal wave of one perfectly manicured hand.

He stared at her. The last time he'd seen her she'd been pleading for their marriage and wearing his duvet.

Offbach and Dagworthy were pacing the reception area like two funeral directors awaiting warring relatives. They glanced up as Ryder burst through the swing doors on a cloud of expensive scent. 'My dear Ryder!' gasped Oliver.

'Hello.' She offered a satiny cheek for him to kiss. Over his shoulder she saw Michael frown. His peculiarly straight thick eyebrows came down over his dark eyes. His sensuous mouth was fixed in a straight line. Ryder wondered what attracted her. He was tough. Ugly. Uncompromising. Then he flicked up his sooty eyelashes and looked straight at her, and she was reminded of the first time she'd met him, when he'd swung down from

415

the cockpit of his Curtiss Jennie like a marauding Cossak and she'd thought he was much taller than her. But he wasn't. It was his power.

She gave him a serene smile. He didn't smile back. As Alix had said that morning, whilst employing her techniques learned at Lucie Clayton to Ryder's nails and hair, nothing will irritate him more than the sight of you blooming with wealth and love. They went up in the lift. Ryder linked her hands to prevent herself from twisting them nervously. Out of the corner of her eye she saw Michael watching her. She lifted her chin.

The hearing was to be held in the same conference room. Anglo Atlantic took their seats opposite the panel. Offbach sat between Ryder and Michael. He looked most uncomfortable.

Colossus were objecting to Anglo Atlantic on their usual grounds of insufficient passengers to warrant further flights on the London—Miami route. They argued aggressively. Dagworthy, for Anglo Atlantic, was eloquent and contained. At one point Ryder saw Michael watching her. She pretended not to notice.

When the hearing broke for lunch, he turned to Dagworthy and Offbach. 'I've booked us a table at the Waldorf.' Then he nodded in Ryder's direction.

Had he invited her directly, she would have accepted. But she had no intention of tagging along. 'I have a prior engagement.' She draped the mink over one shoulder and sashayed out of the room. In the reflection of the door she saw he was watching her. She knew he'd be wondering for whom she wore silk stockings now.

When she returned, he rose and held her chair. 'Enjoy yourself?' he asked caustically.

'Yes, thank you.' She slid one leg over the other so that he could hear silk on silk.

A post prandial somnolence permeated the conference room. Colossus' barrister was talking. He droned on. Only Ryder and Michael were wide awake. She sensed

416

his anger and his agitation. She forced herself to sit absolutely still. As they rose in the late afternoon, the chairman of the panel announced he would give his verdict within a fortnight.

In the lift Michael and Ryder were silent. They stood next to each other but not touching. She tried not to think of the wonderful sex they had once shared. She crossed the reception ahead of him. He held the front door for her. She looked at him. She took a step forward. And suddenly he clamped his hand on her arm. 'Have you another prior engagement, Mrs Biggles?' he asked in his late night voice.

Her eyes took on their bruised look. Her mouth began to tremble. 'No.'

He beckoned to his driver. 'Take us to Wapping.' Then he turned to Ryder, drawing her closer, his mouth almost on hers. 'I want you in my bed.'

She froze. 'I can't. Not just like that, as if nothing had happened. It's been too long. I've been too hurt.'

'And I haven't been! You're damned lucky I'm giving you a second chance. I swore I'd never have you back, but I can't help it.' He seized her mink by its lapels and pushed it off her shoulders. 'Take this off! My wife doesn't flaunt herself in furs given by other men.'

'I shall wear what I please!' She pulled away. 'You've no rights over me and you've no proof I didn't buy it. You're a sanctimonious prig, Michael. You think I should be in sackcloth and ashes, doing penance because I was slow to realise how I loved you. And maybe still love you.'

'Then stop being a bloody fool!' he shouted, ignoring the startled passersby.

'Don't you yell at me! I pleaded. I begged. You returned my letter. I've eaten humble pie and I'm not doing it any more. I've had enough of your charade. I'm pulling out of Anglo Atlantic.' She raised a hand to hail

417

a passing taxi. 'If you want me, I'm at Bailing. Don't come unless you mean it.'

She stepped into the taxi but he grabbed the door before she could shut it. 'You're chairman of Anglo Atlantic whilst you accept your profit share, and you're my wife so long as you use my name.'

'I've changed it back to Harding,' she lied. 'I saw my solicitor at lunchtime. And I don't need your money. I'm starting my own airline!'

43

All the way to Bailing, Ryder had to force herself not to
turn round and drive back to Michael but once she saw
the runway lights reaching up into the frosty night and
she heard the sounds of her airfield, she felt stronger. If
she'd gone with him, what of tomorrow? If she returned
like a prodigal, how would he ever see her as anything
else?

Bailing Air had been merely a vague idea until she
voiced it to Michael. Now it became her objective. She
launched herself into collecting data for her CAA application, analysing financial information, obtaining quotes
for an extended runway, looking into types of aircraft,
and organising her market researchers. The quaint eigh-
teenth-century streets of King's Lynn, once the third
port in the country, attracted a number of tourists. But
they weren't Ryder's target. She was after businessmen
visiting the docks or new industrial estates, and to a
lesser degree Londoners with weekend cottages who
couldn't face the long haul up the A10. Bailing Air, as
she told people, would promote the area without despoil-
ing it.

Her chosen routes were Bailing to London on three
days a week, Bailing to Manchester twice a week, and —
eventually — Bailing to Rotterdam. Her market appeal
would be speed instead of traffic jams. Check-in time
would be ten minutes before take off. In London she
planned to use the City airport, soon to be opened.

Ryder heard nothing from Michael. She formally resigned from her chairmanship of Anglo Atlantic. For a couple of days she was besieged by journalists. Then it was quiet. Her only contact with Anglo Atlantic was when the name leaped at her from the newspaper. As far as she was aware, he never came to the Butterfly House. Once, she ventured down the lane which led to the lavender farm. In the gateway she stopped and peered up the drive. The windows were closed. The house looked sad. She drove on.

One Monday morning she walked into the office to find Violet sitting at her old desk, the sleeves of her favourite pink cardigan rolled up as she tidied the contents of the top drawer. 'I knew things wouldn't be in their right place.'

Ryder sat down on the chair beside the telex, shaking her head in disbelief. 'This is a surprise.'

'I thought you might need a hand with the airline, dear. Staff are that flighty nowadays.'

Ryder hid a smile. 'I certainly do need you. I have a mass of data to collate and analyse before I post my application and I need to go to Germany to look at an aircraft. On Friday I was so busy I nearly forgot to pay the wages.' She paused. 'Is Fred coming too?'

'No, dear.'

'I wish he would. I've missed you both.'

Ryder was so busy she had little time to brood. She rose at dawn and worked all day, her only break being when she paced the runway, hands deep in pockets, listing out loud the things which had to be accomplished before she could submit her application. She didn't even go to Morston. She wouldn't allow herself the time. Nevertheless there were moments when she would stop and remember how she and Michael had laughed and fought to set up Anglo Atlantic. Now she only had herself.

At Easter, Leo chose to stay at Bailing. He invited

Stefan. To keep them occupied, she bought Leo a small dinghy and booked the boys on an advanced sailing course. They camped on the dunes and only came home every couple of days to collect dry sweaters and to raid her freezer. From the smell of smoke on their clothes and the strong peppermints they were always chewing, she suspected they were drinking in pubs.

On the day their course ended, she had to fly to Dornier's factory in Germany to discuss a plane for Bailing Air. It was the first time she'd left Leo without an adult. 'You are responsible for the tower,' she told him. 'I don't mind you having a can of beer or a glass of wine but you're not to get drunk the minute my back's turned.'

He grinned. 'How can we, Sis? The Bailing Arms won't sell me a drink since you told them I'm not yet eighteen.' He picked up his tennis racket.

'Where are you playing?'

'The Butterfly House.' He swung his leg over his bicycle, shouting, 'Hurry up, Stefan!'

'Leo!' Ryder ran after him. 'Did Michael give his permission?'

'He suggested it, when we met him in the village this morning.'

Had Ryder been able to cancel her appointment in Germany, she'd have been tempted. Michael in London was almost bearable. Michael in Bailing was not. She craved to see him. But she couldn't postpone Germany: Bailing Air needed that aircraft, and if she'd learned anything from life it was that if a man wanted you, he'd find you, and if he didn't, you were better off without him.

Two days later she flew back to Gatwick from Munich. Loading from the nearest jetway was Anglo Atlantic's flight to New York. To see the black and red uniforms she'd so lovingly designed gave her an inner twist. It was dusk by the time she reached Bailing but the airfield was lit as though for a nocturnal air display. Two policemen with alsatians were standing beside a police van whilst two others were in the office talking to Violet.

Ryder's first thought was that there had been an accident. She jumped from her car. 'What's happened?'

'It's Imogen, dear,' said Violet gently.

Ryder turned pale. 'What about her?'

'She was arrested at Kennedy Airport for possession of controlled drugs,' said one of the policemen.

'Oh, God!' Ryder slumped against her car.

'She gave Bailing as her permanent address,' the policeman continued. 'When they searched her, they found a receipt for a parcel she posted to you recently. We believe it contains cocaine.'

'It hasn't arrived.'

'Are you sure?'

'Do you think I'd have drugs on my airfield when I'm trying to start an airline?' Ryder walked into the tower and dropped her bags on the hall floor. The television was on in the sitting room. She could see Leo's white anxious face. 'It's all right.' She gave him an encouraging smile, then she turned back to the policeman. 'I haven't heard from Immy in years. I wish I had. She was my closest friend. She opened this airfield. She bought me clothes when I had no money. But I couldn't help her. I tried!'

'She did, too.' Fred came shuffling out of the sitting room. He gave Ryder his tortoise stare. 'What a mess you get into when you ain't got ole Fred around.'

She was too choked to speak. From the television came the newscaster's voice: *The actress, Imogen Lydden, once voted the woman other women would most like to be, was arrested in New York for possession of cocaine.*

Ryder flew to New York on the day the CAA published Bailing Air's application. When Alix saw her off at Heathrow, she said, 'You're mad. You're jeopardising your airline.'

'You're putting up her bail — though you won't let

me tell her it's you.' Ryder walked down the jetway and on to the aircraft. She felt utterly defeated. She couldn't leave Immy to rot but she wanted to scream, 'Why me? Why now?'

Imogen was being held at the Women's House of Detention on Rikers Island. By the time Ryder arrived she'd appeared before a judge who'd set bail at ten thousand dollars, but no one had come forward to stand surety. So she'd been returned to custody.

Rikers Island was in the East River between the Bronx and Queens. It made Ryder think of Alcatraz. She was shown to a small stark room divided by a table with a chair either side. A door opened. Immy stepped inside. Ryder stared at her in disbelief. The ethereal girl with Renaissance curls and a dainty smattering of freckles had become an emaciated woman with dirty greying hair and a waxen face. When she saw Ryder, she began to cry. 'I knew you'd come. You're the only one who cares.'

Ryder was so shocked she couldn't speak.

'It's all a big mistake.' Imogen dropped on to her chair. 'They arrested the wrong person. The stuff was planted on me.' She glanced at the officer standing guard, and leaned forward. 'You will get me out of here?'

'I'll try.' Ryder took a deep breath. 'But if I put up bail you have to go straight into a clinic and stay there till you're cured.'

'I don't need a cure.'

'Immy, you're an addict.'

'I am not! I can stop any time I want to.'

Ryder stood up. 'Do you think I've come here for fun?' she shouted. 'Being linked to you may have cost me Bailing Air. If you want my help, you accept my terms. I'm not throwing ten thousand dollars down the drain. Don't forget, you've already stolen four hundred pounds from me and God knows how much from Alix!' She marched to the door. The officer let her out. Behind her, Imogen screamed abuse.

Outside the prison gates, Ryder felt so weak she thought she was going to faint. She sank to the ground with her head between her knees, oblivious of the passersby.

'Do you come to New York now without calling me?' said a familiar voice.

She glanced up. Susan was parked nearby, watching her from the open window of her car.

Ryder wanted to cry with relief. She dragged herself to her feet. 'I didn't like to ask for your help.' She reached for the passenger door, nearly adding, 'because of Frankie,' but instead she asked, 'How did you know I was here?'

'Michael.'

'He asked you to help me!'

'He telexed to say he'd pay Imogen's legal fees as you were putting up her bail.'

'But he couldn't pick up the phone and tell me!'

'He didn't know you'd left England till you were over the Atlantic.' Susan stopped to pay the Triborough Bridge toll. 'He had a call from someone named Bassingham.'

'Alix.' Ryder smiled. 'Tough, imperious, dear Alix.'

She left Imogen to reflect for two days before she returned to Rikers Island. Immy was led in, looking worse than ever. She had a bruise below her right eye. 'They hit me,' she hissed at Ryder, accusingly. 'The other women. They say I keep them awake with my crying. Then this big butch one tried to kiss me. And they all laughed.'

'Why didn't you call a warder?'

'Then they'd kill me. You shouldn't have left me here. It's all your fault.' Tears filled Immy's eyes. 'Please get me out. I'm scared. I'll never touch drink or drugs again. I promise.'

'It's the clinic or nothing.'

'I thought you were my friend.'

'That's why I'm doing this.' She walked to the door, forcing herself not to look back.

'All right!' screamed Imogen. 'You win. But I never want to see you again, you bitch!'

Bailing was dozing in the noonday sun when Ryder arrived home from New York. She paused in the gateway and looked across at the airfield. She was proud of what she'd accomplished at Bailing. The hangars were full of aircraft. The tower looked spruce. A class was in progress in the school. Lunch was being served in the clubhouse. She pictured how it would be with Bailing Air. The extended runway, the passenger lounge, the aircraft, the uniforms in that kicking yellow which had always brought her luck. She wasn't going to give up without a fight.

On the concrete track where Bruja's stable used to be, Fred was teaching Leo to drive in the old pickup. Ryder smiled and waved, and headed for the office. But she couldn't bear to be shut inside on such a beautiful day. With her shoulders hunched in thought, she paced the runway, bending from time to time to pull out the ragwort which returned so stubbornly each summer. Life was odd. She'd lost Michael and Immy and Frankie. But she'd regained Alix and Violet and ole Fred — and her father.

She turned for home as the pickup truck growled towards her. 'A letter for Bailing Air,' called Leo. 'Hand delivered.' He leaned out of the window to give her a typed envelope, then drove on, kangaroo-hopping across the tarmac with Fred shouting, 'Gently! Don't jerk her!'

For a moment Ryder was back in the air, riding her aluminium dragonfly, learning how to stall — and how to survive. She tore open the envelope. Inside was a telex: *'Please reserve one seat on Bailing Air's inaugural flight for Mr Biggles.'*

For those who have enjoyed this book, may we recommend the following coming shortly from **Rowan.**

THE FLIGHT OF FLAMINGO
Elizabeth Darrell

A strong family saga unfolds against the backdrop of marine aviation in its heady, pioneering days before the Second World War. When Leone Kirkland inherits her autocratic father's aviation business, she also inherits his murky past—and Kit Anson, his ace test pilot. Leone needs Kit and she could love him—but he has every reason to hate her.

THE QUIET EARTH
Margaret Sunley

For decades the Oak family have carved a living out of the tough and beautiful Yorkshire Dales, but now Jonadab Oak is facing rebellion from his children who want lives of their own. Margaret Sunley's tender and truthful pastoral saga celebrates mid-Victorian family life—its strengths, its tussles, its losses and gains—in a novel which rivals *The Shell Seekers.*

ELITE
Helen Liddell

Ruthless, politically ambitious, beautiful and clever, Deputy Prime Minister Ann Clarke is the modern Joan of Arc of the Scottish Labour Party. But has her dizzying rise to power been too swift? Helen Liddell's stunningly powerful drama of political and sexual intrigue keeps the reader guessing until the very last page.

A BOWL OF CHERRIES
Anna King

Frail and often in pain from a chronic disease, Marie Cowley grows up in London's East End surrounded by a large and lively family who feel that Marie is a novice when it comes to holding down a job—or choosing a husband. But Marie is determined to live a normal life, and she sets about it with typical courage and determination . . .

THE SINS OF EDEN
Iris Gower

Handsome, charismatic and iron-willed, Eden Lamb has an incalculable effect on the lives of three very different women in Swansea during the Second World War that is to introduce them to both passion and heartbreak. Once again, bestselling author Iris Gower has spun a tender and truthful story out of the background she knows and loves so well.